THE
HEARING

THE
HEARING

JOHN LESCROART

A DUTTON BOOK

DUTTON
Published by the Penguin Group
Penguin Putnam Inc., 375 Hudson Street, New York, New York 10014, U.S.A.
Penguin Books Ltd, 27 Wrights Lane, London W8 5TZ, England
Penguin Books Australia Ltd, Ringwood, Victoria, Australia
Penguin Books Canada Ltd, 10 Alcorn Avenue, Toronto, Ontario, Canada M4V 3B2
Penguin Books (N.Z.) Ltd, 182–190 Wairau Road, Auckland 10, New Zealand

Penguin Books Ltd, Registered Offices: Harmondsworth, Middlesex, England

First published by Dutton, a member of Penguin Putnam Inc.

First Printing, April, 2001
1   3   5   7   9   10   8   6   4   2

REGISTERED TRADEMARK—MARCA REGISTRADA

LIBRARY OF CONGRESS CATALOGING-IN-PUBLICATION DATA
Lescroart, John T.
The hearing / John Lescroart
p.   cm.
ISBN 0-525-94575-X (alk. paper)
1. Hardy, Dismas (Fictitious character)—Fiction.   2. San Francisco (Calif.)—Fiction.
I. Title.
PS3562.E78   H43   2001
813'.54—dc21   00-034119

Printed in the United States of America
Set in Sabon
Designed by Leonard Telesca

PUBLISHER'S NOTE

To Barney Karpfinger
and
To Lisa M. Sawyer, the love of my life

ACKNOWLEDGMENTS

First, I would like to thank my wonderful editor and publisher, Carole Baron, for her encouragement and support.

The legal world created in my books owes whatever verisimilitude it has to the rigorous oversight and unfailing intellect of my great friend and true collaborator Al Giannini, whose day job is to put on real murder trials in San Francisco. Without him the "legal stuff" which is the foundation for this (and my other) novels would often be inexact, stupid or just plain wrong. He the man—he really be the man.

Then there's Don Matheson, perennial "best man," who regularly consents to endure my artistic and various other angsts from four hundred miles away. Despite an unfortunate predilection for overcooking his food, he remains one of the planet's unsung wonders. Closer to home, all the Dietrichs—Pete and Sandy, Margaret, Chris and Jason— help keep the spirit alive. Pete, aka Peter S. Dietrich, M.D., M.P.H., also contributes mightily as medical guru and chief martini tester.

Others contributed in important ways: Fred Williams of the Davis Police Department saved one day; Mark Nicco told me all I needed to know about special masters; San Francisco homicide inspector Joe Toomey and Officer Charles Lyons were informative tour guides to the evidence room in the Hall of Justice. I'm indebted to Richard B. Seymour, M.A., managing editor of Haight-Ashbury Publications, and Dr. David E. Smith of the Haight-Ashbury Free Clinics for their insights into the terrible scourge of drug addiction.

I'm continually gratified by the generosity, expertise and support of many friends and associates: Anne Williams; Bill Wood; Richard Herman, Jr.; Max Byrd; Anita Boone; Nancy Berland; Frank Seidl; Gary F. Espinosa; Peter J. Diedrich; Mitch Hoffman; Kathryn and Mark J. Detzer, Ph.D.; Justine and Jack; and of course Taffy the wonder dog.

Where life is more terrible than death,
It is then the truest valor to want to live.
—THOMAS BROWNE

PART
ONE

1

Next to Lieutenant Abraham Glitsky's bed, the telephone rang with a muted insistence.

A widower, Glitsky lived in an upper duplex unit with his youngest son Orel and a housekeeper/nanny named Rita. During his wife's illness, he'd deadened the phone's ringer so that it wouldn't wake anyone else in the house when, as often occurred, it rang in the middle of the night.

He located the source of the noise in the dark and picked up the receiver, whispering hoarsely. "Glitsky. What?"

Surfacing slowly into consciousness, he didn't really have to ask. He was the head of San Francisco's homicide detail. When he got calls in the dead dark, they did not tend to be salespeople inquiring about his satisfaction with his long-distance service provider. It was nearly two hours past midnight on Monday, the first day of February, and the city had produced only two homicides thus far this year—a slow month. In spite of that, Glitsky spent no time, ever, wondering if his job was going to dry up.

The caller wasn't the police dispatcher but one of his inspectors, Ridley Banks, on his cell phone directly from the crime scene. It wasn't standard procedure to call the lieutenant from the street—so this homicide must have an unusual element. Though Ridley spoke concisely with little inflection, even in his groggy state Glitsky detected urgency.

A downtown patrol car had seen some suspicious movement in Maiden Lane, a walking street just off Union Square. When the officers had hit their spotlight, they flushed a man squatting over what looked like, and turned out to be, a body.

The suspect ran and the officers gave chase. Apparently drunk, the man staggered into a fire hydrant, fell in a heap and was apprehended. Cuffed now, in the backseat of the squad car, he had passed out awaiting his eventual trip to the jail.

"Guy appears to be one of our residentially challenged citizens," Ridley said drily. "John Doe as we speak."

"No ID of course." Glitsky was almost awake. The digital clock on the bed stand read 1:45.

"Not his own. But he did have the wallet."

"The victim had a wallet?" To this point, Glitsky had been imagining that this homicide was probably another incident in the continuing tragedy of San Francisco's homeless wars, where an increasingly violent population of bums had taken to beating and even killing each other over prime downtown begging turf. Certainly, the Union Square location fit that profile.

But if the current victim had a wallet worth stealing, it lowered the odds that the person was a destitute vagrant.

"Taken from her purse, yeah."

"It was a woman?"

"Yeah." A pause. "We know her. Elaine Wager."

"What about her?"

"She's the stiff."

Glitsky felt his head go light. Unaware of the action, he moved his free hand over his heart and clutched at his breast.

The voice in the telephone might have continued for a moment, but he didn't hear it. "Abe? You there?"

"Yeah. What?"

"I was just saying maybe you want to be down here. It's going to be crawling with media jackals by dawn or the first leak, whichever comes first."

"I'm there," Glitsky said. "Give me fifteen."

But after the connection was broken, he didn't move. His one hand dug absently into the flesh over his heart. The other gripped the telephone's receiver. He simply lay there, staring sightlessly into the darkness around him.

When the phone started beeping loudly in his hand, reminding him that it was still off the hook, it brought him to. Abruptly now, he hung up, threw the covers to one side and swung himself up to a sitting position.

And stopped again.

Elaine Wager.

"Oh God, please no." He didn't know he'd said it aloud, didn't hear his own voice break.

Elaine Wager was the only daughter of Loretta Wager, the charismatic African-American senator from California who'd died a few years before. Elaine—tonight's victim—had worked for a couple of years as an assistant district attorney in the Hall of Justice.

No one was supposed to know it, but she was also Glitsky's daughter.

Somehow he'd gotten dressed, made it to his car. He was driving, the streets dark, nearly deserted.

No one knew. As far as Glitsky was aware, not even Elaine herself. She believed that her biological father was her mother's much-older husband, Dana Wager—white, rich, crooked and connected. In fact, when Loretta had found out she was pregnant by Glitsky, she kept that fact to herself and pressed him to marry her. He didn't understand the sudden rush, and when he said he needed time to decide—he was still in college, after all, with no job and no money—Loretta dumped him without a backward glance and made her move with Wager, the other man courting her, with whom she'd not yet slept.

For nearly thirty years, the senator had kept her daughter's paternity secret, even and especially from the girl's true father. Until, finally, a time came when she thought she could use the fact as a bargaining chip to get Glitsky to agree that sometimes it was okay for a senator to commit murder.

That strategy hadn't worked. Abe and Loretta had once been lovers, true, but now he was a cop in his bones, and three years ago she'd killed someone in his jurisdiction. The knowledge that their past union had produced a daughter wasn't going to change what he had to do.

Which was bring her to justice.

So when Glitsky let her know he was going to expose her, she decided she wasn't going to endure an arrest, a high-profile trial and the loss of her national reputation. At the time she was, after all, one of the most prominent and respected African-American women in the country. She chose her own way out—an "accident" with a gun in her mansion.

After that, Glitsky had never been able to bring himself to reveal the secret to his daughter. Why would she need the baggage? he asked himself. What good could it possibly do her to know?

And now suddenly it was—forever—too late.

He'd followed her life, of course, the path her career had taken after she left the D.A.'s office. Plugged into her mother's political connections, she'd gone into private practice with Rand & Jackman, one of the city's premier law firms.

Through the grapevine, Glitsky heard that she'd gotten engaged to some doctor from Tiburon. She'd recently been short-listed for appointment to a judgeship. She also taught moot court at Hastings Law School and donated her honorarium back to the scholarship fund.

She was going to be fine. Her life was going to work out on its own, without any interference from him. He could take pride from a distance, privately savor her accomplishments.

She hadn't needed him as a father.

Now she was beyond needing anything.

Glitsky had himself tightly wound down. Hands in his pockets, he walked almost the length of Maiden Lane—maybe a hundred yards—from where he had parked his car on Stockton at the edge of Union Square. The body lay at the other end, twenty feet or so west of Grant Avenue. A small gathering of authorities and onlookers had already appeared and Glitsky used the walk to steel himself.

He saw a couple of black and white cruisers, what he supposed were some city-issued vehicles, and the coroner's van parked at angles, on the sidewalk and in the alley itself. He heard his steps echoing—the buildings were close on either side of him. Halfway down the lane, he suddenly stopped, took a deep breath and let it out. He was surprised to see the vapor come from his mouth—he wouldn't have said it was that cold. He wasn't feeling anything physical.

Casting his eyes up for a moment, over the buildings that rose all around him, he noticed the star-studded sky. Here between the buildings it was full night. The filigreed streetlights—four of them, two on each side—glowed. The street had that glassy, wet look favored by cinematographers, although the asphalt itself was dry.

A figure separated itself from the group and began walking toward him. It was Ridley Banks. After he'd closed to within fifteen feet, he stopped—perhaps catching the "keep away" vibe that his lieutenant projected—and waited until the two men were side by side. Glitsky's

usual style was all business in any event, and today it served him particularly well. "What've we got?" he asked tersely.

"About as clean as it gets, Abe. We got a body, a shooter, a weapon
and a motive."

"And what's that, the motive?"

They were still standing off a ways from the knot that had formed
around the body. Banks kept his voice low. "Robbery. He took her
purse, the watch, a gold chain . . ."

Glitsky was moving forward again. He'd made it down from his duplex to the scene in only a bit more time than it had taken the techs, and
now, just as he came up to the main knot surrounding the body, one of
the car's searchlights strafed the lane. Reflexively, Glitsky put a hand up
against the light, pressed himself forward, went down to a knee by the
fallen body.

It lay on its right side, stretched out along the pavement in an attitude of sleep. It struck Glitsky that whoever had shot her had laid her
down gently. He saw no blood at first glance. The face was unmarked,
eyes closed.

He'd come to love that face. There'd been a picture of her in the
Chronicle in the past year and he'd cut it out and stuck it in the bottom
of the junk drawer of his desk. Two or three times, he'd closed and
locked the door to his office, taken it out and just looked at her.

Seeing her mother in her face. Seeing himself.

In recent months, he'd told himself it was possible that if they came
to know about each other, it wouldn't be baggage after all, but a source
of something else—connection, maybe. He didn't know—he wasn't
good at that stuff. But the feeling had been building and he'd come close
to deciding that he would tell her, see where it took them.

The body was clad in an elegant overcoat, still buttoned to the neck.
Blue or black in color, it looked expensive with its fur-trimmed collar,
red satin lining. One black pump had come off her left foot and lay on
its side, pathetically, in the gutter.

She was wearing black hosiery—and again, there was no sign that it
had snarled or that the nylon had run when she'd gone down. Under
the overcoat, Glitsky saw a couple of inches of what appeared to be a
blue or black skirt with white pinstripes.

The lack of blood nagged. Glitsky stood, moved around to her back
side, studying the pavement. Ridley was a step behind him and antici-
pated his question. He handed the lieutenant a Ziploc bag which held

an almost impossibly small handgun. "One shot at the hairline in back, close contact, up into the brain. No exit wound."

Glitsky opened the bag and looked inside, put his nose against the opening and smelled the cordite. He recognized the weapon as a North American Arms five-shot revolver, perhaps the smallest commercially made weapon in America. It was most commonly worn as a belt buckle, out in the open, so small it did not seem possible that it could be a real gun. It weighed less than ten ounces and fit easily in the palm of his hand. Ridley was going on with his descriptions and theories and Glitsky ached to tell him to shut up.

But he wasn't going to give anything away and he didn't trust himself to utter a word. Instead, he left it to his body language. Zipping up the plastic that held the gun, he gave it to Banks without comment, and moved off, hands in his pockets. The message was clear—Glitsky was concentrating, thinking, memorizing the scene. Disturb him at your peril.

Ridley hung back with the body. After a minute, he started giving directions to the techs.

Twenty minutes later, they had triangulated the body in high beams and the alley had taken on an unnatural brilliance. The crime scene people had set up a cordon of yellow tape, uniformed officers, black and white police cars, all of them conspiring to block unauthorized access to Maiden Lane, although due to the hour that wasn't yet much of an issue. Still, half a dozen police radios crackled. The first news team had arrived—a van and its crew from a local television station—and the negotiations over access to the scene between the perky, aggressive newscaster and the supervising sergeant tempted Glitsky to take out his gun and shoot somebody.

Instead, he accompanied Ridley Banks to the squad car and the officers who had discovered the body and apprehended the suspect. Two uniformed men exited the vehicle from both front doors at the same time, introducing themselves as Medrano and Petrie.

"That the shooter?" Glitsky asked, pointing to the backseat where the suspect sat propped against the side door, slumped over. "I think I'll talk to him."

The two officers exchanged a glance and a shrug. The older officer, Medrano, replied. "You can try, sir. But he hasn't moved in an hour."

"Drunk?"

"At least that and plenty of it." The other uniform, Petrie, hesitated for an instant, then continued. "Also appears to be mainlining something. Tracks up his arms. He's gonna need some detox time."

Glitsky received this not entirely surprising news in silence. Then he nodded and walked around to the other side of the squad car, where the suspect leaned heavily against the door, and pulled it open quickly. With his hands cuffed behind him, the man fell sideways out onto the pavement. His feet stayed up in the car while his head hit the asphalt with a thick, hollow sound. The man moaned once and rolled over onto his back.

"Sounds like he's coming around," Glitsky said.

Ridley Banks pulled a toot sweet around the front of the car and got himself standing between his lieutenant and the lights at the head of the alley. There'd been so many accusations of police brutality lately that the media were watching for it at every opportunity. And now his lieutenant was giving them something. Ridley motioned with his head, a warning, then spoke in a whisper. "Cameras, Abe. Heads up."

Glitsky was all innocence. "What? The poor guy fell." The suspect lay unmoving at his feet. He hadn't moved after the first rollover. The lieutenant looked over the hood of the squad car to Medrano and Petrie. "Take this garbage to the detail until he wakes up."

Petrie looked at his partner again. Neither of them had ever met Glitsky before and he was making an impression—he wasn't one of your touchy-feely modern law enforcement community facilitators. The younger officer cleared his throat and Glitsky glared. "What?"

Petrie swallowed, finally got it out. "The detail, sir?"

"What about it?"

Medrano took over. "The guy looks good for medical eval, Lieutenant. We were thinking we'd show him to the paramedics."

Glitsky knew that this meant the suspect would probably wind up going to the hospital, where there were secure rooms for jail inmates who needed medical care. This prospect didn't much appeal to him. "What for?"

Medrano shrugged. It wasn't that he cared personally, but the lieutenant's suggestion ran counter to the protocol. He wanted to cover himself. "Get him cleared before we take him anywhere, maybe start detox before he goes into withdrawal."

Glitsky had a deep and ancient scar that ran across his mouth, and now with his lips pursed it burned as a whitish gash under the hawk nose, the jutting chin. Glitsky's mother had been African-American, his father Jewish—his visage was dark, intense, hooded. "How do we know he needs medical care?"

Medrano risked a glance to where the suspect slumped against the door in the backseat. He was at best semiconscious, filthy, still bleeding from where his head had hit the pavement. "We don't, sir. But the paramedics are here. To be safe—"

Glitsky cut Medrano off. "He's just drunk. I want him in homicide. You bring him up. That's the end of this discussion."

Petrie and Medrano looked at one another and said nothing. They were too intimidated to do anything but nod, get the man back into the car and start the drive down to the Hall of Justice.

Ridley Banks bit his tongue. Glitsky was putting out the word that he intended to let this suspect get all the way into withdrawal before he would acknowledge any problem. This would ensure that the man endured at least a little of what was purportedly the worst known hell on earth, and the orders struck Ridley as gratuitously cruel. More, they weren't smart. Neither was the earlier door-opening incident. He knew that if the suspect was in withdrawal from heroin, the paramedics and people at County could set him up in short order. Then the agony of withdrawal could be mitigated. They'd get a better statement from a set-up suspect at San Francisco General Hospital than they ever could from a sick, sweating junkie in withdrawal at the Hall of Justice. If he was merely drunk, he could be in a cell at the jail by midmorning. Either way, they would have a clean interrogation within a reasonable period of time. Glitsky's orders wouldn't accomplish anything good.

As he watched the squad car backing out of Maiden Lane, Ridley wondered what else might be going on. He and Abe had both known Elaine Wager, worked with her, when she'd been a high-profile rising young star with the district attorney's office. Ridley, himself, had found his guts more than ordinarily roiling at the scene when he realized the woman's identity. She was one of their own, part not only of the law enforcement but also of the African-American community. Even to Ridley, whose job was homicide, on some level it hurt.

Abe's reaction, though, seemed a long march beyond hurt. Ridley had come to know most of his lieutenant's moods, which generally ran the gamut from grumpy to glum, but he'd never before seen him as he was tonight—in a clear and quiet unreasonable rage, breaking his own sacred rules about prisoners and regulations.

Walking back to where the body lay, the knot of people bunched in the mouth of the alley, Ridley decided to risk a question. "You all right, Abe?"

The lieutenant abruptly stopped walking. His nostrils flared under piercing eyes—Ridley thought of a panicked horse. Abe let out a long breath, took in another one, looked down toward the body. "Yeah, sure," he said. "Why not?" A pause. "Fucking peachy."

Abe made it a point to avoid vulgarity. He'd even lectured his inspectors, decrying their casual use of profanity. His troops had been known to make fun of him for it behind his back. So Ridley was surprised, and his face must have shown it. The lieutenant's eyes narrowed. "You got a problem, Ridley?"

"No, sir," he replied. Whatever it was, it was serious. "No problem at all."

2

On that same day—Monday, February 1, at a little after five o'clock in the afternoon, Dismas Hardy placed a call to another San Francisco attorney.

He put his feet up on his desk and listened to the phone ring, was transferred to voice mail, heard the beep. "Mr. Logan," he began, "this is Dismas Hardy again. If you're keeping track, this is my fourth call. I'd really appreciate a callback. Same number I left the other three times."

Hanging up, Hardy stewed for thirty seconds, then stood and walked out of his office on the top floor of the Freeman Building on Sutter Street in downtown San Francisco. His was the only office on the top floor, and he had decided to take the stairs to the lobby a floor below him. Hardy leased his office directly from David Freeman and was the only attorney in the building who did not work for Freeman's firm.

His landlord was pushing seventy. He was short, almost fat, always slovenly dressed; his female admirers, and he had several, would concede that he had a prodigious, nearly mythic ugliness—unkempt hair, eyebrows of white steel wool, a turnip nose scarred by rosacea and alcohol, hanging jowls, liverish lips. But he had a great if unorthodox personal charm. And no one disputed that Freeman was a brilliant lawyer who lived for his work. With Mel Belli's passing, he had assumed the mantle of most famous attorney in the city.

The receptionist's station commanded the center of the lobby. At the phones, Phyllis, an attractive elderly witch with whom Hardy had an off-again, off-yet-again relationship, was handling what appeared to be several calls at once. Hardy sauntered casually past her station. He even nodded genially as he took a few extra steps toward the long hallway that housed the tiny airless cubicles of the firm's associates. It was all an elaborate ruse—his intention was to go and interrupt Freeman without having to explain himself to the Keeper of his Gate. And for an instant, even as he hung a hard left and strode toward the great man's door, he thought he would make it unmolested.

But no.

"He's busy, Mr. Hardy. He's not to be disturbed."

Hardy stopped. Phyllis was facing the other way. How could she have seen him? Further proof that she had a personal connection to the devil. She could spin her head around in a full circle like the girl in *The Exorcist*.

Now she fixed him with Favored Visage #1, Stern and Unyielding. He gave her back his winsome, disarming Irish smile, pulled a De Niro. "Are you talking to me?"

Phones forgotten, her body came around, up and out of her chair in one fluid motion. She was moving not toward Hardy but directly to Freeman's door, to all appearances ready to throw her body in front of it if need be to defend its inviolability. "He's trying to get a motion written. He was very specific."

Hardy kept his grin on, inclined his head in the direction of the hallway where the associates toiled. "That's just to keep the kids from bothering him. He'll welcome some adult companionship. Watch." Striking like a snake, Hardy reached around the receptionist and rapped quickly twice on the door.

"It's open!" Freeman bellowed from within. "Come on in."

Hardy stepped back, spread his palms in a gesture that said "See? What did I tell you."

"If he'd have said 'Go away,' I'd be gone. Promise." He turned the knob and pushed at the door. "Excuse me," he said politely, moving around her, closing the door behind him.

Pen in hand and a mangled cigar between his lips, Freeman squinted up over his yellow legal pad. A thick bluish haze hung in the air. Hardy recognized the wine bottle by the telephone as a Silver Oak Cabernet— at least fifty bucks retail if you could find it. The old man straightened up in his chair, put the pen down and drained the last inch from his wineglass, making appreciative smacking noises. "God drinks this stuff," he said.

"How does He afford it?" Hardy crossed the room to the window and threw it open. He enjoyed the occasional cigar himself, but the smoke in the room was nearly suffocating. "And while we're asking 'how' questions, how do you breathe in here?"

Freeman waved that off. "If you interrupted me on billable time to criticize my lifestyle, you can use the same door you came in at. Otherwise, get yourself a glass—you've got to have a sip of this."

Hanging by the window—the afternoon breeze had picked up, whipping down Sutter, pulling the smoke out—Hardy leaned against the sill. "As soon as enough of this clears to be able to taste it. Meanwhile, I've got a great idea for a good time."

"What's that?"

"We can fire Phyllis right now. It'll be fun. You realize that anybody wants to see you, they've got to mount a campaign."

"That's what I pay her for." He was pouring another glass for himself. "You got around her, I notice. Keeps you sharp." A slurping sip, another sigh of appreciation. "So? What else? You didn't come to talk about Phyllis."

"No. I came to talk about Dash Logan."

Freeman frowned deeply. "What about him?"

"Using the normal channels—say, the telephone—I can't reach him. I thought you might have an idea."

"Why do you want to?"

"One of my clients is getting sued by one of his clients. There are also some criminal charges. I thought I'd feel him out, see where he's coming from."

Freeman leaned back in his chair, drew in a breath. "You want my advice, forgo the conversation. He'll just lie to you. I'd file the response and prepare to fight dirty."

Still at the window, Hardy crossed his arms. "Not exactly a ringing character endorsement."

"Read between the lines and it gets worse." Freeman shook his head in disgust. "The man's a disgrace, Diz. Personally and professionally. If the bar had any teeth, they'd have yanked his card years ago."

"For what?"

"You name it. Malpractice, bribery, theft of client funds, extortion, perjury, drug and alcohol abuse. I can't believe you don't know him."

Hardy shrugged. "I've heard stories, sure. But people tell stories about you, too."

"Those are legends," Freeman corrected him. "Logan. Well, you know all the lawyer jokes?"

"Most of 'em."

"Well, they made them up about Dash Logan, especially the one about the difference between a catfish and a lawyer. One's a bottom-dwelling scum sucker and the other one's a fish. Here's a hint—Logan's not the fish."

"You don't like him."

Freeman chuckled, but he wasn't amused. "I really believe there's good in a lot of people, Diz, almost everybody. Almost." He came forward in his chair again, swirled his wineglass and took a mouthful. "Talking about him almost sours this wine, and that takes some doing."

Hardy had taken a glass from the sideboard and held it out. "Let a professional tell you how bad the sour is getting."

Freeman picked up the bottle and poured. "What do you smell?"

"Tobacco." He held up a hand—he was kidding—then took a sip and his eyes lit up. "Although I must admit there's a bit of wine in the aftertaste." He crossed the room, where he settled himself on the couch. "So if Logan calls back?"

"I'll tell you a story." Freeman pushed his chair away from his desk, faced Hardy and crossed one leg over the other. He drank some wine. "Fifteen years ago I got teamed with Logan on a two-defendant murder case. This was in the days before talking movies, remember, when we had a real D.A.—Chris Locke—who would put people in jail from time to time. Also, this is one of the few times in my illustrious career when I thought my client—Aaron Washburn, I still remember—was mostly innocent. Maybe he was driving the car, but that's all. He was too young and too chicken to agree to be the wheelman for a hit. In any case, his main flaw was loyalty to the shooter—Logan's client, a real loser named Latrone Molyneux.

"So anyway, Locke declares we're going to have joint disposition of our two defendants—either they both plead or they both go to trial. But he needs fifteen years from my guy. Well, I decide I'm going to trial, one because my boy, Aaron, didn't do it—he wasn't the shooter and didn't know it was going to go down and even if he did, they couldn't prove it. And two, because that's who I am. I'm not taking my client's money and lots of it to plead 'em to half a lifetime in the joint.

"And it's not as though I've got to sink Logan's client, remember. My guy just says he was in the car the whole time and has no idea what happened." Somewhere in this recitation, Freeman had gotten to his feet, reliving it again. He paced the office, door to window, a caged bear. "All right. Now I'm working on my kid's defense, keeping my no-good colleague Mr. Logan in the loop because, you know, that's what we do. But I notice he's not making too many of our joint motion hearings, he's got my witnesses spooked—I hear rumors that he's actually scoring dope off some of these people—the judge is getting pretty pissed off with delays and no-shows and really awful paperwork.

"But mostly old Dash is walking the walk, I'm giving him the benefit, you know, professional courtesy. We're taking this thing to trial and he's got to know what I know, right?

"Then, two weeks before we're scheduled for jury selection, guess what? No, don't. I'll tell you. Logan comes by here, says he's decided he's going to plead Latrone. He's got his fee. He doesn't have the time for a trial.

"So as you might imagine, things get a little hot between us. I remind him he can't plead if I'm going to trial, which I'm damn well going to do. So he threatens me—if I take it to trial, Latrone will rat out Aaron, say he was just standing around minding his own business when Aaron drove up and asked him to go for a ride. He—Latrone—didn't know there was going to be a shooting. It was Aaron's idea, Aaron was the shooter.

"Anyway, long story short, what could I do? They'd probably both get life. This way they both plead out—fifteen years. Now, you want to hear my favorite part?"

"That wasn't it?"

"No. Listen to this. Early on, I decided it might be worth a try to get bail for these kids. It was a shaky case, first adult offense for both of them. They weren't leaving the jurisdiction anyway. But Dash Logan won't go there. Gives me a line of shit about it's too risky, we'll alienate the judge, it'd be better to save any judicial favors for the trial—the trial! Hah! So he persuades me—if I make the motion for my client, he has to for his, and that won't happen. The judge will deny both, so what's the point?"

"I give up," Hardy said. "What was the point?"

"The point!" Freeman was nearly screaming now. "The point was he wanted to keep his boy Latrone in jail. You know why? 'Cause he was fucking Latrone's seventeen-year-old girlfriend, that's why."

"Well, see," Hardy said. "At least he had a good reason." But he was shaking his head and clucked in disapproval. "That's a pretty appalling story."

Freeman was breathing heavily. He went back to his desk and put himself on the outside of another inch of his wine, then poured some more. "He's an appalling—"

On the old man's desk, the telephone buzzed. He reached over and picked it up, listened, held it out to Hardy. "It's Phyllis, she says there's a woman out in the lobby asking to see you."

"She's lying. I don't have any appointments. She's just trying to figure out a way to get me out of here, return you to your blessed solitude. I wonder, does this guy Dash Logan need a receptionist?"

Freeman held up a finger, listened some more. "Dorothy Elliot? Jeff's wife?"

Leaving his superb wine in its glass on the coffee table, untouched except for that first sip, Hardy rocketed to his feet on his way to the door. Behind him, he heard Freeman telling Phyllis, "He's on his way out right now."

Dorothy greeted him with a nod, an apologetic smile, a few quiet words. It was immediately obvious that something was terribly wrong—her trademark cheerful spark was gone. It was equally clear that she didn't want to discuss any part of whatever it was in the lobby. The staircase was not wide and he let her lead the way.

Following her, he was struck by the stiffness of her carriage, her wide shoulders back, her arms hanging straight down at her sides. One step at a time, she was hiking a steep grade with a heavy pack at altitude. It occurred to him that her husband Jeff, one of his friends and a *Chronicle* columnist who suffered from multiple sclerosis, might suddenly have died.

At the landing, she stopped and he came up behind her, put an arm on her shoulder. She leaned into him for a second. Then he opened the door and they were in his office.

As he was closing the door, she found her voice. "I'm so sorry to come barging in on you like this, Dismas. I didn't know . . ." She lifted her hands, dropped them. Her lip quivered—sorrow? Or rage? She set her jaw, began again. "I don't know . . ."

"It's all right." He gave her a chance to continue, and when it didn't seem she could, he asked softly, "What don't you know? Is it Jeff?"

She shook her head. "No, Jeff's all right. Jeff's fine." She blew out heavily.

Hardy pulled a chair around and Dorothy stared at it for a minute as though she'd never seen one before. Finally, with an air of gratitude, she sat. "Thank you." She shook her head wearily. "I don't seem to know what to do. I started to go by Jeff's office but then I didn't want to interrupt him—he's on deadline. So I just found myself walking downtown and thought of you, that you worked here. Actually, I thought of you before."

"Before? When before?"

"When I was at the homicide detail."

Hardy found his desk and pushed himself back up onto it. With a bedside manner smile, he spoke quietly. "I don't think I've heard the homicide part yet, Dorothy. Maybe we want to start there. Why were you at the Hall?"

"My brother. Did you hear about Elaine Wager being killed?"

Hardy said he did. The news had depressed him. Not that he'd been that close to Elaine, but he had known her, had considered her one of the good guys.

"They have arrested my brother for it."

Hardy shook his head. "That can't be right, Dorothy. I heard they pulled in some bum."

Dorothy's lips were pressed tightly together. She nodded. "He's a heroin junkie. My brother Cole. Cole Burgess."

Not possible, Hardy thought. Flatly not possible. Dorothy Elliot, sitting in front of him, was the picture of corn-fed wholesomeness. He'd known her for over a decade, since she'd first begun dating Jeff. Now they had three daughters and she still looked like a farm girl—those big shoulders over a trim and strong body, clear eyes the shade of blue-bonnets, a wash of freckles cascading over her nose onto her cheeks.

Dorothy Elliot was pretty, smiling all the time, well-adjusted and happy. There was *no way*, Hardy thought, that this woman's brother could be the low-life animal that had shot Elaine Wager in the back of the head for some jewelry and the contents of her purse.

He sought some fitting response, said he was sorry, finally asked. "Did your brother know her? Were they going out or something? Working together?"

"No. Nothing like that. But the police are saying he was incoherent when they brought him in, they couldn't even confirm who he was until this morning. And when he finally could, he called my mother, which was of course no help."

"And where is your mother?"

"Jody." Dorothy's expression was distilled disapproval. "She lives here in town now. Out in the Haight. With Cole."

"With Cole? So he wasn't homeless after all."

"Well, that depends on your definition. He wasn't with Mom too often, but she was there if he needed to crash. He had a rent-free room. She moved out here from home—Ohio—to be near him." Another look of disgust. "To help him."

"And she wasn't much of a help?"

A snort. "But he called her from the Hall anyway. And then after she predictably flipped out and couldn't get anything done, she called me."

"What did she try to do?"

A calm had gradually settled over her. Hands had come to rest in her lap, shapely legs were crossed at the ankles. There was no sign of her usual cheerfulness, but her confidence was returning. The topic was awful, but she had facts to convey. "He's in heroin withdrawal, Diz. He needs to be medicated." She broke off and decided she'd said enough about that. "Anyway, Mom lost her credibility with the police in about ten seconds, accusing everybody of trying to kill her son, the poor lost little boy." She paused again, sighed heavily. "But he does need to get into a detox situation soon."

Hardy matched her tone—matter-of-fact. "They have programs in place for that. As soon as they book him . . ."

But she was shaking her head. "The police are saying Cole is only drunk and they're not through with him."

"So you're saying he wasn't drunk?"

"Probably that too." She impatiently brushed some flaxen hair from her forehead. "But if he was desperate enough to mug somebody, he was after cash for heroin. That means probably he was already into withdrawal, drinking to kill the pain with alcohol until he could score."

A silence settled. Finally, Hardy laced his fingers in his lap. He had heard enough to know he really didn't want to be involved in this. He liked Jeff, liked Dorothy, saw them socially three or four times a year. And now Dorothy wanted to hire him to defend the man who'd killed one of his colleagues. And though he'd been successful in his three previous murder trials, though he'd gotten himself a reputation, this time Hardy wasn't interested.

He'd known, liked and admired Elaine Wager. He had no desire to help her killer. There were other lawyers who could live with defending Dorothy's brother a lot more easily than he could. And they were welcome to do it. But the longer they talked, the more he would give her the impression of tacit acceptance. In spite of that, he couldn't resist the next question. "So what do you want me to do, Dorothy?"

"He needs to get into detox and I don't know the channels. I need somebody they'll listen to, who knows how to talk down there." Her eyes were telling him that she didn't like it any more than he did. But it was family duty. Her heartland values wouldn't let her shirk it.

Hardy told himself he wasn't agreeing to defend Elaine's killer. He'd see what he could do to get a suspect into detox. He was helping a friend, that was all, another heartland value that *he* couldn't shirk. It wasn't going to go beyond that.

Hardy figured he could get the fastest results by going directly to the head of homicide, who happened to be his best friend. On the fourth floor of the Hall of Justice, he exited the world's slowest elevator and was looking at Sarah Evans, a homicide inspector who was married to one of David Freeman's associates. He and Frannie would occasionally socialize with Sarah and Graham. He considered her a friend, and usually she greeted him warmly. But today her look was guarded.

"If you're here to see the lieutenant, maybe you want to come back another day."

"Less than his usual bubbly self, is he?"

She just shook her head, said "Good luck. I warned you," and pushed by him into the elevator.

So he was wondering as he walked the long hallway down to the homicide detail. This was a spacious, open area with grimy windows all along the back wall. The twelve inspectors in the unit had their desks here, most of them face to face with those of their partners. The usual bureaucratic detritus cluttered up the work space—green and gray metal files, a watercooler, a coffee machine that from the look of it might have been Joe DiMaggio's original Mr. Coffee. There was also the working stoplight, which added a certain tone.

To Hardy's right as he entered the detail were three doors. The two on either end led to interrogation rooms; the one in the middle to the audiovisual controls room. To his left, the lieutenant's office was a hundred-square-foot rectangle that some architectural wizard had carved out as an obvious afterthought.

Glitsky's door stopped him dead.

For many years, there had been no door to Glitsky's office. Finally, three years back, after months of trying to cajole the bureaucracy into buying a door, Glitsky had had enough. He came in himself on a weekend and hung one he'd bought with his own money.

Thereby admitting that he cared about it.

Big mistake.

Immediately Glitsky's prize door became an untapped bonanza for any psychologist who might want to study the effects of stress on otherwise normal people whose job it became to investigate murders. After the first impressive flurry of graffiti and property damage in the weekend after he'd hung it, Glitsky had made it a point of honor to refrain from comment or reaction no matter what his people did to it. And they did plenty.

Eventually the door had become a living testament to something profound and not particularly flattering about San Francisco's homicide detail. A large poster of Bozo the Clown with the international "NO" symbol commanded the center of it, but that was among the first, and the mildest, of desecrations. By the last time Hardy had come up here a few weeks before, there hadn't been a pristine inch left. Burn marks, spitballs, chewed gum, three bullet holes, assorted bumper stickers, picture ads for prostitutes, photos of murder suspects from ancient cases.

The homicide inspectors thought it was a funny, running gag. Glitsky didn't see it that way, but he wasn't going to whine about it. There were other approaches.

One night he had come down to the Hall on a late call and happened to arrive as one of his inspectors, Carl Griffin—now deceased—was adding some graphic flourishes to a wanted poster someone else had tacked to the door. Griffin had been engaged in his artwork and hadn't heard Glitsky come up behind him, didn't hear a thing even as Glitsky whacked him on the head with his sap, knocking him senseless for several minutes.

Glitsky thought *that* was funny.

Even funnier because Griffin could never say anything about it without appearing to be an idiot. But somehow the word had gotten out. And the stakes had been raised.

Now Hardy stared. The door was flat white. He could still smell the paint. And it was closed—a rarity during the working day. Struck by the stunning blankness, Hardy whistled softly and looked out over the open room. At least casually acquainted with most of the homicide inspectors, he recognized Marcel Lanier, who was seated at his desk, a pencil poised over some paper.

The inspector was looking back at him. He shook his head and spoke with a quiet authority. "I wouldn't."

"Somebody with him?"

"No."

"When did this happen?" The door.

A shrug. "He came in after lunch with a bucket and a roller. Took him ten minutes."

"Is he all right?"

A shrug. It wasn't for a sergeant to say.

Hardy thought about it. Two warnings from two solid professionals. The smart move would be perhaps to skip it for now, pick a better time.

But he'd just driven down from his office, paid to park, come all the way up for this personal visit with his best friend. It was the end of the day, anyway. Whatever it was, Abe would deal with it. Maybe Hardy could even help. Besides, he was tired of well-meaning gatekeepers trying to keep him from people he needed to see. First Phyllis with David Freeman. Now Sarah Evans and Marcel Lanier with Glitsky.

"I think I'll just see how he's doing," he said. "No guts, no glory."

He knocked on the post next to the shocking white door and heard the familiar growl of a response. "It's open."

Inside, Hardy's first reaction was to reach for the light switch, but Glitsky spoke again. "Leave it." The room wasn't exactly dark, but with the overheads off and the shades drawn on both windows, it wasn't exactly light either. "You want to get the door."

Hardy did as instructed. "I couldn't read a damn thing in this light. I don't know how you do it. It's got to be tough on the eyes."

"What do you want, Diz?"

Hardy found the wooden chair opposite the desk and lowered himself into it. "Nice door. I love the color."

No answer.

"What's going on, Abe?"

"Nothing."

"You all right?" After a lengthy silence, Hardy said, "You want to talk about it?"

"There's nothing to talk about." Glitsky's chair scraped. He pushed himself back from his desk and leaned into the wall behind him on the chair's back legs.

Hardy's eyes were adjusting. He gave it another try. "It's after five o'clock. You feel like a drink?"

"I don't drink."

"Really? Since when?" Hardy had only been Glitsky's pal for twenty-five years. "Sometimes it's not the worst idea in the world."

Glitsky came forward in his chair, clasped his hands on the desk before him. When he spoke, his voice had softened. "I'm trying to work something out, all right. Meanwhile, what can I help you with?"

There was nothing to be gained from pushing Glitsky's issue, whatever it was, so Hardy drew a breath and started. "You've got a guy across the way there, Cole Burgess—"

"Yeah. Elaine Wager's killer."

"Alleged killer, as we say in the defense biz."

"Are you defending him?"

"No."

"I hope not."

"And I'm not here to spring her killer."

"Okay. Then what's this about?"

Hardy calmly and briefly stated the reason for his visit, his connection to Cole's sister Dorothy, the rest of it. "His sister's worried that he slipped through the cracks when they brought him in and the paramedics never got around to diagnosing him as a heroin user. Anyway, the point is he's got to get into detox pronto or he's going to have a bad week."

"Really? That would be sad."

"Well, anyway . . ."

"He was drunk, Diz. We've had him up here since last night, mostly puking his guts. We're still talking to him."

"Yeah, but now it's been what? Eighteen hours? He might still be hungover, but he's dry. All I'm saying is we *know* he's a junkie. He's got to get in a program."

But Glitsky was shaking his head. "No. I'm not buying into that scam."

"What scam?"

"Couple of days on the county in a nice soft hospital bed. That's not happening. He was drunk, that's all."

This was not the response Hardy expected. Abe was a due process freak—he played by the rules. Maybe, Hardy thought, it was the other thing, the dark room, whatever else was eating him. He started to debate. "C'mon, Abe, how can you know . . . ?"

Glitsky slammed his palm flat on his desk, raised his voice. "He was drunk! That's all he was, all right? We Mirandized him, he's talking, we'll book him when we're through. You hear me? Just leave this one."

Stupefied, Hardy sat back in his chair. "What's going on, Abe?" he asked quietly. "I can't just leave it. You know that."

"He killed Elaine."

"Okay. And we hope he burns in hell for it. But his sister told me he was probably already in withdrawal this morning. He's got to get some treatment."

Glitsky remained unmoved. "When they process him in, they'll give him the standard tests. If it's heroin, they'll know soon enough."

"When will that happen?"

A shrug. "When we're done here."

Hardy took that in. "You mind if I ask what he's doing here right now?"

"Answering questions." Glitsky came forward in his chair. "And FYI, he waived an attorney. Though maybe if he'd known it was you . . ."

"He doesn't know me." Hardy sat back, shifted angrily in his chair. "You're sweating him, aren't you?" He glanced toward the door, came back to the lieutenant. "If you were sitting where I am, Abe, you'd tell me something was wrong here. That I wasn't doing my job right. This isn't how it's supposed to happen."

Glitsky's face was a slab. He said nothing.

Hardy sighed. "Have you videotaped a confession?"

A crisp nod. "I believe we're in the process of doing that very thing."

Hardy's blood was running now. He spoke carefully. "So if I'm moving ahead and getting him processed into a program, you're telling me I've got to go around you, is that it? Maybe a judge? Get a writ?"

Glitsky stared over his desk. "You do what you've got to do."

"I intend to." Hardy paused. "I hope you know what you're doing."

"It's possible." The lieutenant looked through him. "Talk to you."

The visit was over.

• • •

Glitsky's conscience was a mangy dog gnawing at his insides.

After Hardy left, he remained sitting behind the desk in the dim confines of his office for over an hour, until the quality of the light shifted. Outside, it had come to dusk.

He rose, went to his door, opened it and looked out into the homicide detail. The workday had ended, but the door to the interrogation room was still closed. He heard voices behind it. Ridley still had Elaine's killer in there.

He surveyed the detail. The old school clock over the watercooler said it was six-fifteen. Wearing headphones, head down over his desk, Marcel Lanier moved his lips and jabbed corrections with his pencil as he ran his interview tape and proofed it against what the transcriber had typed. Paul Thieu, who already knew everything anyway, had his nose in a book with what looked like Cyrillic script on the jacket—he was working a Russian mafia-related homicide and Glitsky thought he probably wanted to conquer the language before the case got too far along.

Neither of the inspectors looked up.

Nobody had messed yet with his door, either.

He closed it behind him and pushed in the lock. Flicking on the light, he got in his chair and pulled out his junk drawer, lifted out Elaine's picture. He couldn't look at it for long. He realized that his daughter wouldn't exactly be proud of how he'd handled things so far. But he'd told himself, when he'd given Ridley his marching orders, that this was an instance of bad things happening to bad people. Karma.

Now he was trying to sell himself on the idea that it wasn't as though he'd been actively complicit in torture, but it wasn't easy. Though it truly had been Glitsky's intention to "sweat" the young man in the interrogation room, this might be cruel but it wasn't unusual—homicide inspectors did it frequently. Under the stressful conditions in that closed-up space, a suspect occasionally would waive his rights to an attorney, or tell a story that he'd later wished he hadn't. Once in a while, as in Burgess's case, he would even confess under conditions that might not qualify as legally coercive.

But now he realized that it had gone on long enough. He'd better go and tell Ridley to end the interrogation, get the suspect in the system. Burgess had killed Elaine. There was no doubt about that, and it was important that no screwup create a hole he could slither through.

He stood, grabbed his leather jacket, opened his door again. If Ridley had gotten the impression because of Abe's obvious hostility to Burgess that the suspect should be sweated beyond human endurance, Glitsky would have to try and correct that. There was an important difference, he knew, between wishing pain and suffering on someone and making him experience it.

It was called civilization.

3

Sharron Pratt, the district attorney of the city and county of San Francisco, sipped a preprandial new-fangled cocktail concocted from gin and chocolate liqueur and served in a tall blue martini glass. Perched on a high stool at one of the financial district's power restaurants, Sharron cut an elegant figure in her tailored blue suit. She wore her hair shoulder length and made no effort to hide the gray that had once lightly peppered and now dominated it. Lightly made up—a touch of mascara and a subtle shade of lip gloss—she was very easy to look at. Rimless bifocal eyeglasses added a few years to her true age of forty-four, but behind them, green-flecked eyes sparkled youthfully. Her wide mouth animated her face, the plane of her cheeks was well defined, her skin smooth. Even with the added gray and the no-nonsense glasses, she was a woman who'd come into herself as she'd aged, and was now far more handsome than she'd been a decade before.

But internally, she suffered from a great discontent. Since the upset victory resulting in her election three years before, Sharron Pratt had suffered a steady decline in popularity. Now, with her chance for reelection coming up in November, she had eight months to recoup the eleven points which the latest poll told her she had lost.

"I don't understand how this has happened, Gabe. I really don't."

Gabriel Torrey, her chief assistant D.A. and political mentor, was methodically breaking apart the pistachios from the bowl on the bar, gathering the nuts onto his napkin. When he'd accumulated somewhere between eight and a dozen, he would pop them into his mouth, washing them down with nonalcoholic beer.

Torrey had no trouble understanding what had happened to Sharron Pratt's fans. Conveying it to her was the difficult part.

He shrugged, cracked a nut, keeping a casual tone. "Crime's up, Sharron. Convictions are down. That's the short answer. People are tired of it."

"I'm tired of it, too, Gabe." Pratt leaned forward on her stool, moved a hand onto his sleeve. "But the damn police are so hostile and we can't seem to get any coverage . . . what?"

Torrey was shaking his head. "People are impatient with the excuses, too, Sharron. It's been three years. People are thinking that if you haven't been able to fix things in that time, you're not going to." He'd only cracked two shells, but he threw the nuts into his mouth early. "I'm sorry to be the bearer of bad news here, but the agenda you got elected on last time just hasn't played in the real world."

"It would, though. If everyone would just get behind it."

Torrey knew he had to answer with a great deal of care. This woman might be his bedmate at widely spaced intervals when the stars were aligned just right, but every day she was, after all, his boss. Traditionally she did not warm to philosophical argument.

She'd worked the legal trenches in San Francisco for years—social worker, public defender, lawyer for various civil rights coalitions—and she knew what played in this town. Her election had confirmed that the people were behind her. They were ready for a change. No more white guys prosecuting minorities. It was going to be a new age.

She had won by, among other things, promising to do all she could to stop police brutality. Stop prosecuting victimless crimes. Don't charge petty drug users or prostitutes. Institute counseling and rehab programs for people whose emotional and substance problems caused them to break the law.

Her administration was going to be known not for enforcing outmoded laws but for doing what was right. And Sharron Pratt always knew, without doubt, what that was—no matter what, she was on the side of the angels.

But if Torrey wanted to get Sharron elected again, he was going to have to get her to bend, except Torrey knew—to borrow from an old song—that Pratt was an oak, not a willow. She did not bend.

Maybe, though, he could get her to acknowledge that a private moral position did not have to be reflected absolutely in the political arena. Maybe there could be a gray area, although gray areas, too, God knew (or at least Torrey did), were not Pratt's long suit. "I don't know," Torrey began again. "Maybe people didn't realize how the results of your—our—programs would affect them."

Pratt's nostrils flared and her vibrant eyes flashed. "What do you mean by that, Gabe?"

"Well, let's take the homeless, for example. Now, being homeless is not a crime in itself."

"Not a crime at all." Pratt employed a crisp schoolmarmish correction almost as a verbal tic.

But Torrey was used to her, and her response didn't slow him down. "And no one's saying it is. But you'll recall one of your campaign issues was that we treat the homeless with respect, and that seemed to strike a positive chord with the voters."

"Absolutely, as well it should."

Also, Torrey was thinking, remove the word "should" from her conversation and his boss would become functionally mute. "Yes, well, in practice you have to admit the policy caused some problems."

This, Torrey knew, was a whopper of an understatement. After Pratt had been swept to power on a tide of benevolent humanity, she formed a coalition with the mayor and several supervisors and, to a great deal of positive press, announced to the country that under this administration, San Francisco would be a haven for the homeless. No longer would the police hassle the poor and downtrodden. There would be no more rousting. There would be city-funded programs for free meals. Armies of volunteers would move out from the soup kitchen base and take sandwiches to the hungry where they lived.

In short order, this utopian policy resulted in a mass migration of many of the nation's chronically unemployed to the City by the Bay. Within months, camps of vagrants, drunks, the psychologically impaired and drug addicts had essentially taken over Golden Gate Park, Dolores Park, any number of neighborhood green areas. The downtown streets became gauntlets of panhandlers, drunks in doorways, public urinators. And then, as the worst became bolder, polite requests for spare change became belligerent demands and gave way to intimidations, purse snatchings, shakedowns and muggings.

"But those weren't the homeless we were trying to help," Sharron said. "They were the criminal element, that's all. People needed to see that. We just need to educate them."

Torrey was shaking his head. "No, Sharron. They'll never see it. They think you let the bums in. You ruined the tourist industry."

Pratt straightened her back and lifted her martini glass to her lips. She sipped contemplatively. "Is it too late?"

"Let me ask you one, Sharron. Are you sure you want to keep doing this? That you want to run again?"

"That's two." She smiled halfheartedly, lightly touched Torrey's arm again. "Do I want to keep doing this?" she repeated. "We've done a lot of good, Gabe, haven't we?"

Again, Torrey crafted a careful response. "I think we've changed the agenda in a positive way, Sharron. People are thinking about the office—the district attorney—in a way they never had before, now more as a force for social, maybe even moral, leadership. And all that's to the good."

"But . . ."

Torrey popped a couple of nuts. "But the fact remains that most of the electorate seems to have returned to the theory that the main role of the district attorney is to prosecute people who break the laws. And that's never been your forte. You want to help people. That's always been what's driven you. Which is why I ask if you want to keep doing this."

She sighed, considering. "It's a bully pulpit, Gabe. We're way ahead of the curve in our thinking. We knew that going in. We can't just keep building more prisons and throwing more people into them. We've got to—"

Torrey put his hand on Pratt's arm, stopping her. They had to educate the masses, and the criminals, and the victims, and do counseling, and rehab, and yada, yada, yada. At some point, before he'd come to work full-time in the Hall of Justice and become immersed in the stupidly hopeless march of crime through the system, he'd even believed a good portion of it. But that day was in the past.

"Let's keep this discussion on point," he said a little more firmly than he'd planned. But before his boss could react negatively, he pressed on. "We've tried to raise the moral bar, Sharron. We've done the right thing time and time again. But the polls are telling us that the people aren't getting the message, or it's not the one they want. Now the question is, do you want to go ahead? And if you do, I really think the wise move would be to consider"—he paused—"refining your position slightly."

Her mouth twisted in distaste. "No."

He almost said, "Well, that was a delightful exchange of ideas." But the words that came out were, "No what? You don't want to go ahead?"

"No. I don't want to quit. I've worked hard for this position, for the people's trust. I am the absolutely best person for district attorney. And let's not forget that I'm running the office the way it should be run."

Torrey brought a hand to his mouth to hide the grimace. That old "should" again. Pratt's vision was at least entirely, self-righteously consistent, he thought: never mind the way things actually were. Pratt had a vision of a better world, and the people who didn't share it were stupid, damned, ignorant, venal, criminal, clueless or all of the above. Therefore, they didn't count. But her adviser had to try to get Pratt at least to realize that their votes did. "Okay," he said. "Then maybe it's just a question of perception."

Pratt's bright eyes sparked. She liked this direction. "Of what?"

"That you're soft on crime."

The spark turned dark. "That's rubbish. I *hate* crime. Why do you think I ran for the job in the first place? It's criminals—the people—that I don't hate. I try to understand them, see what happened, how they got—"

He brought some more pressure to her forearm. "Sharron. Perception, okay?"

A show of reluctance, then she nodded. "Go on."

"The killing of Elaine Wager by this vagrant."

"That is so horrible. I loved Elaine, Gabe."

"Everybody loved Elaine, Sharron. That's my point. Here's a much-loved, well-known community figure, daughter of a popular ex-senator, and African-American to boot. She is brutally murdered by a homeless white man for a few coins in her purse. Are you seeing where I'm going with this?"

To his satisfied surprise, he saw that his idea had clicked with Sharron.

"And one other thing," he said.

"What's that?"

"If you don't mind, I'd like to try the case myself."

This did bring a clearly visible reaction, almost a start. "But I need . . ." She slowed herself down. "Why would you want to do that, Gabe?"

Torrey had stopped chewing his nuts. He put down his glass, met Sharron's eyes. "When she first came up . . ."

"This is Elaine?"

He nodded. "When Chris Locke was D.A."

Her mouth tightened. In private, Sharron referred to Locke's administration as "the Neanderthal years." Since her own election, she had purged the office of all but a very few of Locke's old prosecutors, and it was no secret that this was part of the reason that now her office couldn't seem to convict anyone. She'd had to let them go for their political incorrectness, to say nothing of the general culture of incorrigibility. Locke had been black but he'd hired, in Pratt's view, far too many white males who'd adopted a macho "win at all costs" mentality that had infected the office—getting convictions, sure, but at what cost?

Sharron's own motto was: "There's more to being a prosecutor than getting convictions." To which the Locke crowd tended to respond, "Oh yeah? Like what?"

So any mention of Chris Locke and his administration put Sharron Pratt on the defensive, and it was immediately apparent that she was on it now, the fingers of her right hand thrumming uneasily on the bar.

Torrey carefully reached over and covered her hand with his. "Elaine was having an affair with Locke."

"With the D.A.? While she worked for him? How much younger was she than he was? God, that man!"

Torrey suppressed his desire to point out to his boss that the two of them—he and Sharron—were in precisely the same relationship that Elaine and Locke had enjoyed. There would be no point—Sharron would be hard pressed to see any similarity, in spite of the fact that in both cases the D.A. was sleeping with an assistant D.A. But Locke had been a predator of gullible young women; she was nothing like that. She and Torrey had a mature relationship between equals, and that could not have been true with Locke and Elaine.

Instead, he waited her out in silence. Then: "In any event, after Locke was killed, she needed a shoulder to cry on, and we—"

Pratt pulled her hand out from under his. "Don't tell me. I don't want to know."

"It wasn't that, Sharron." He took her hand again, patted it soothingly. "It wasn't that. Okay?"

She finally nodded. "Okay."

"There wasn't anybody she could talk to here. The office was changing. She felt there were spies everywhere." He shrugged, making light of it. "I was doing some neighborhood work in the African-American community, outreach stuff, you know, just like you were. Anyway, Elaine and I, we got to be close for a while. Platonically. Really."

He squeezed her hand. "She'd lost her mother and her lover within a week. She wanted to talk ideas. What was the place of a strong, smart black woman in a white man's world? What was the price of her mother's fame? Was any of it worth it? Was it wise to have affairs with married men? Where was she going? What had she done? That kind of thing."

He paused. "Eventually, she got it together. I put her in touch with Aaron Rand and you know the rest. But she was just very special somehow. And now . . ." A sigh. "I cared about her, and now I feel I owe her something."

"What? You couldn't have prevented what happened with her. It wasn't anything to do with you."

"No, I know that." He considered his phrasing. "Let's just call it a payback. This bum who killed her, if somebody's going to take him down, I'd like it to be me."

Two hours after he'd left Glitsky, after a visit to Frank Batiste, the chief of inspectors, Hardy was coming out of his shock but still wasn't sure how to proceed. He had, at least, gotten Cole Burgess booked into the jail, and now he wanted to talk to him, get some take of the damage. He took the outside corridor from the back door of the Hall. It was bitter with a wet wind, and when he got inside the door to the jail, he stood a minute getting the warmth.

The admitting sergeant at the counter was a short, skinny Caucasian with the name tag "Reilly" and a buzz cut of orange hair. Glitsky was six foot two, half black and all buffed. After his first three minutes with Reilly, Hardy thought it was amazing that they could look so much alike.

Because whether he knew it or not, the desk sergeant was giving Hardy his Glitsky imitation and doing a hell of a good job at it. Yeah, he was pretty sure Cole Burgess had been processed in. No, he hadn't heard about any heroin. Sorry, he hadn't made it into the computer yet.

He couldn't say for sure where he was, even if he'd been taken to the sixth floor or to the hospital.

Hardy took that runaround until it became obvious, then demanded to speak to Reilly's superior. Reilly told Hardy that, well, darn, he really wasn't sure whether anybody was in this time of evening. Deliberately pitching his voice so low that Reilly had to lean closer to hear it at all, Hardy whispered, "All right, Sergeant, then get me the watch commander, and if he's not in, I'll call Dan Boles"—the sheriff—"at home. Oh, and I almost forgot, your inmate Mr. Burgess is the brother-in-law of Jeff Elliot, who writes the 'CityTalk' column for the *Chronicle*."

Within two minutes, Reilly had located somebody who might know something. Big, black and beefy, the man appeared from a door behind the reception desk, made a show of spotting the man in the lawyer suit, pointed at Hardy and closed the space between them. "I'm Lieutenant Wayne Davies, Mr. . . . ?"

Hardy said who he was, laid out the problem. Then: "This man needs detox. His medical evaluation hasn't moved forward, not as far as I can tell. Your admitting sergeant tells me he's not even in the computer yet."

"Then he's probably not been processed. That's when they do the med eval." Davies had his arms crossed, his brow furrowed. Hardy was to understand that he was thinking hard about all this, trying to remember one in what must have been dozens of people brought to the jail today for processing. "And you're his attorney?" he asked.

The veneer of patience now transparently thin, Hardy nodded. "His sister retained me on his behalf. And he's been in custody now for almost a full day."

"Hmm . . . and you say Lieutenant Glitsky brought him down?"

"Look, Lieutenant, I'm talking about Cole Burgess, the suspect in the Elaine Wager murder. He's here. He's in withdrawal and you're responsible for him. What are you going to do?"

Davies decided, although he dressed it up for Hardy's benefit, pretending it had all just come back to him. "Elaine Wager. That guy? Yeah, he's here, but I don't know how far he's gotten."

"What do you mean?"

"I mean processing him in. It was busy today, thirty admits. There might still be some delay." Another elaborate shrug. "I don't know."

Hardy had heard more than enough. "Okay, Lieutenant, let's cut the bullshit. I demand to see my client now. If he's not in detox immediately, you personally can probably look forward to being named in about a billion-dollar lawsuit against the city . . ."

Davies held up an authoritative hand. "Keep your shorts on, Mr. Hardy. I'm sure he's here. We'll find him and get him checked out. He'll be upstairs in jail or on his way to County Hospital. You can see him either place when we're through, Mr. Hardy. But not before."

Cole Burgess wanted to be dead.

There was nothing but the pain and no way he could make it stop. Not here. Not without the god.

When he was a boy—still active, still doing sports—he'd get cramps in his legs that woke him, screaming, from sound sleep in the middle of the night. The calf on his right leg, or a muscle somewhere under the tendons of one of his feet.

Knotted muscle curled on itself, squeezing every nerve around it in a concentrated orb of agony.

But localized, at least. One place. One muscle per spasm. His mom would come in and rub it, knead it out, talk to him. It would pass, though the memory—the ache—would linger for days.

But it wasn't like this, now, when it was everywhere all at once. Never ending. Unbearable.

Somebody, please, come and kill me.

Did he say it? He didn't know. It was his only thought, but there really wasn't any thought as such, any words. There wasn't even consciousness outside of the pain. It consumed his entire being. Only the pain. He hadn't had any god in three days.

His body was draped in the jail's orange jumpsuit. It twitched, making small noises, on the floor of the cell used for the psychologically impaired.

The guard opened the cell door and held it while two other guards lifted the body onto a gurney and began pushing it down the hallway to the elevator that led to the jail's rear entrance.

Cole Burgess was sure he was getting his wish now. Dying. Any second it would end. It would have to.

Lights were exploding in his brain, every flash accompanied by another blinding stab, more intolerable agony beyond where he would have said—if any communication were possible, which it wasn't—that no more could be borne. No one could take this much torture and survive.

Kill me! Kill me!
god god god god god

Davies returned without any sign of Cole Burgess. "Mr. Hardy."

"Where's my goddamned client?"

The lieutenant remained tolerant. "Your client is fine. We had a computer problem and lost him for a few minutes, that's all."

"Where is he? I want to see him."

The smile didn't change. "You can see him, but he's not here to see. He's at County. I can't guarantee he's conscious right now, but you're sure welcome as all hell to go and find out for yourself. You want, I could call over and tell them to expect you."

4

Frannie Hardy had pulled her long red hair back into a ponytail and it hung halfway down her back. Barefoot, she wore a pair of old jeans and an oversized green pullover sweater. She was standing in the front doorway, waving good-bye to her children as they ran out to their car pool. Hardy came up behind her, put a hand on her shoulder, called out. "Have a good day, guys. See you tonight."

They turned together and walked through the family room back to the kitchen, where Hardy took his seat in front of his coffee. Frannie silently moved some dishes to the sink, wiped a surface or two with a dishcloth. Finally, some psychic energy shifted and Frannie came over and sat down with him. She smiled wearily, reached a hand over and put it on her husband's. "Hi."

A reflexive sigh, Hardy's own weariness breaking through. "Wow."

His wife nodded. "I know. She is trying, you know."

"Yep."

"It's not some scam to get our attention. She really does worry."

He nodded, never doubting it for a moment. This morning, once again, his daughter had been afraid to go to school, and they'd done their parental tag team, trying to calm her myriad fears, for nearly an hour while their son Vincent grabbed his English muffin and disappeared into his bedroom so he wouldn't have to deal with it.

The Beck's fears.

The constant flow of news and information, even her school curriculum, kept the Beck hyperkinetically aware of and sensitive to every disaster that happened on the planet—a plane crash in Calcutta, a hostage crisis in the Balkans, famine and genocide in Rwanda, church burnings in the South. All the world's problems brought home to her own little plate every day.

This was the backdrop of everyday life, the white noise of her daily existence.

Hardy had trouble believing that the nature of human beings had changed so completely in one generation. Surely there had always been criminals and perverts, ugliness and evil; it just hadn't felt as if it was everywhere. Perhaps life now for his children was not really much more precarious than when Hardy had been a boy. But now it seemed that nearly every detail of every crime everywhere got into the societal fabric via the front page, television, the Internet—a racial killing in Detroit happened *here;* an abusive father killing his wife and kids in Miami was *here;* a massacre at a school in North Dakota might happen *here,* today.

The Beck seemed to feel that if she let her guard down for an instant, she would *die.* Kidnappers lurked in every public bathroom, you got cancer if you caught a whiff of secondhand tobacco smoke, bombs and handguns proliferated in high schools everywhere, you caught AIDS if you even kissed your boyfriend. God forbid you got a sunburn, or forgot to fasten your seat belt.

Government warning: Everyone who breathes, dies! Watch out!

She was trying to sort it all out, one fear at a time. Three out of seven days a week for at least the past year. At bedtime. On school mornings. Whenever something struck her. It was wearing her parents down.

"She worries," Frannie repeated.

"I worry, too," Hardy replied. "But I'm old, that's my job. The Beck's a healthy kid whose parents love each other and have enough money. She ought to spend a couple of seconds thinking about that every week or two. The good stuff in the world. There is some left, I hear—sunsets, food, the occasional tasteless joke."

"She tries, Dismas. She's doing the best she can."

"I know." Hardy sipped at his cold coffee, let out another lungful of air. "I really do know. It just breaks my heart."

The phrase hung in the room. After a long minute, Frannie squeezed his hand. "What else?" she asked.

Hardy paused, then feigned ignorance. "What else what?"

"Good try," she said. "But not flying. Something else—not the Beck—has been bothering you since you got home last night."

Hardy glanced across at his wife. She brushed a stray stand of gleaming red hair from her lovely forehead, offered him a sympathetic look.

"You're good," he said.

She shrugged. "Part of the job description. So what is it?"

He sighed a last time and gave in. "Abe."

"That doesn't sound like him at all," Frannie said after she'd heard the story. "Do you think it's possible he had a crush on Elaine?"

The question was unexpected and Hardy considered it carefully, then shook his head no. "She was engaged. Besides, Abe isn't what I'd call the crush type."

"He had a crush on Flo for almost twenty years."

"That wasn't a crush, Frannie. They were married."

She gave him a pretty pout. "And the two are mutually exclusive?"

He took her hand, kissed it, shook his head. "What I mean is I can't see him carrying some kind of torch. He'd come out with it . . ."

Frannie broke a half smile. "Abe? We're talking the effervescent and loquacious Lieutenant Glitsky? You want my opinion?"

"At every turn."

"I think if he was attracted to somebody who was somehow off limits—like engaged—wild horses couldn't drag it out of him."

Hardy sat up straight. "You don't think he would even mention it to the involved party?"

"No. Especially not her. Not unless she gave him some signal that she might be interested. Why do you think Abe hasn't had a date in three years?"

"Women hate and fear him?"

"Dismas."

"He's a hideous gargoyle?"

It was no secret that Frannie considered Abe one of the more attractive men on the planet. "I don't think that's it either."

"How about if he hasn't liked anybody enough?"

"Maybe, but not mostly, I don't think." She came forward on the couch. "He hasn't asked anybody out—I'd bet you anything—because he doesn't want to reveal anything going on inside him. It's his protection since Flo."

Hardy knew that his wife was mostly right on this. Since Flo had died, he'd spent hours with Glitsky, both socially and professionally, and knew that his friend wasn't exactly the poster boy for celebrating the inner child. The walls were high and thick. But Frannie hadn't gotten it all, and Hardy's expression grew serious. "I think he's scared, all right, but not about having somebody see who he is. I think he's afraid that if he starts with somebody he might get to care about her. That might turn into caring a lot. And then he might lose it all again."

Frannie put her hand back over his. "That was your demon, Dismas," she said softly, "maybe it's not Abe's."

Hardy's first son, Michael, had died in infancy. The event had plunged him into divorce with his first wife, Jane, and then a decade of lethargy in a haze induced by Guinness stout, during which he eked out an empty existence on his bartender wages at the Little Shamrock. His passion for his work and for justice—for sunsets and food and sexual love, too—had dried up. And then, somehow—the precise mechanism of it was still a mystery to him—Frannie had gotten through to him, and he'd begun to feel again, to be able to handle feeling.

Now he tightened down his mouth, looked over at her. "Maybe that's why I recognize it, though. With Abe. How did we get on this anyway?" he asked.

"Abe dating. His possible crush on Elaine."

Hardy gave it another minute. "Whatever it was, it was serious. He wanted the kid to suffer. It was personal."

"So what are you going to do now?"

"About Abe?"

"I don't suppose you'll have to do anything about Abe. He's got a way of taking care of himself. I was thinking about the boy. What's left for you to do? Are you in this?"

After a minute of consideration Hardy said, "Let's say I'm not comfortable with the idea of defending the person who killed Elaine. I liked her. If Cole did it, I'll turn Dorothy onto somebody else, tell her I've got a conflict of interest."

"You just said 'if Cole did it.' "

"He did, Frannie. He's confessed. That's usually a tip-off."

"But you're going to want to find out a little more, aren't you? Make sure."

Hardy's reluctance showed like a fresh bruise. His expression changed two or three times until it rested on a grimace. "Probably, knowing me," he admitted, "although there's no such thing as sure. It just feels a little pat up to now, that's all. I'd want to talk to him at least, get his side of it. But if it seems like he did do it—strung out and screwed up or not—I'll let David or somebody else take him. I wouldn't want to be involved in defending him."

"But what if . . . ?"

Hardy held up a hand. "Let's not go there. Not yet, okay."

"Abe would be pretty unhappy, though, wouldn't he, if you did?"

He nodded somberly. "You know, my love, sometimes you show a remarkable talent for understatement."

It surprised Hardy, but neither Jeff nor Dorothy Elliot had any real problem with his decision not to represent Cole. They even said they thought it was a smart one. As they talked, it came out that the boy had done a pretty good job of alienating everybody in the family.

When he'd first begun having "problems," Jeff and Dorothy had tried to be understanding and supportive in his struggle. Cole told them that he'd come out to San Francisco because there wasn't any real empathy regarding his situation in the Midwest. He *was* trying but people just didn't understand.

So the Elliots invited him to stay with them and their children until he got settled in. In the next month, Jeff "lost" a watch and they had a daytime break-in where the burglar got away with most of Dorothy's jewelry. Dinners became upsetting for the children when Uncle Cole's place would be set and he wouldn't show up. On top of that, Cole had two minor traffic accidents while he was driving Dorothy's car, both of them the other driver's fault—except that in both cases the other car had fled. Finally, when one of the girls' piggy banks that had held four hundred dollars turned up missing, they'd told Cole he had to go and not come back.

So they understood Hardy's decision. He was a friend to have gone to the jail in an emergency and make sure he got into the detox. They didn't expect him to do anything else.

But for his own peace of mind, Hardy did want to eyeball the man and get to the bottom of this confession. What had Cole said? Glitsky's behavior had stuck in his craw as well. It wasn't that he thought Cole might be innocent, but the fact that everyone was treating him as though it had already been proven bothered the lawyer in Hardy.

He didn't need certainty beyond a reasonable doubt. He was ready to cast Cole off in a heartbeat, but he couldn't let go completely until he'd at least totally satisfied himself that the man had actually killed Elaine.

Then let him be damned. Hardy wouldn't care.

5

In the women's room at Rand & Jackman Law Associates on Montgomery Street, Treya Ghent tried to fix her eyes, but she knew it was a losing fight. Between the horrible, senseless murder of her dear friend and boss Elaine Wager and the unrelenting demands of her wonderful but high-maintenance fourteen-year-old daughter Raney, she had averaged less than three hours of sleep for the past four nights.

She was at work this morning because she didn't want to use up any more sick days frivolously. She needed to keep a bank so that she would be available if her daughter absolutely needed to have her stay home to care for a real illness, or to counsel her during a real crisis. And Treya didn't kid herself. Raney was a teenager—she was desperately going to need her mother from time to time in the next couple of years, just as Treya had needed her own mom. And thank God Raney—like Treya had been—was the kind of child who would ask.

Certainly she wasn't going to waste any of those precious sick days on *herself*—she hadn't missed a day of work for anything related to herself in six years. They paid her to be here and contribute and she wasn't going to let her employers down. They counted on her.

But the eyes were going to betray the fact that this morning at least she was a functional zombie, and she hated to have anyone, much less Clarence Jackman, the firm's managing partner, see that. When she'd gotten the summons that Jackman wanted to see her in his office, she'd been sobbing quietly in her little cubicle.

And why not? How could somebody have killed Elaine? It had

wrenched her heart when she'd first learned of it, and the pain hadn't let up much since. Elaine had been a friend and confidante; they often joked that they were sisters separated at birth. She and her boss had been the same age—thirty-three. Both were smart, neither of them entirely black or white. Intuitively, they both understood that the sometimes vast differences between their social standing, their jobs and their prospects were merely the products of background, education and—that greatest of all variables—luck.

She threw a last splash of cold water over her eyes, blinked hard and patted them dry with a paper towel. She'd kept Mr. Jackman waiting long enough, too long really. Staring at herself in the mirror for one last second, she willed a tiny spark of life into her tired eyes, squared her shoulders, lifted her chin. "Okay, girl," she whispered firmly to herself. "No whining."

Sixty-three-year-old Clarence Jackman was a power player. The company he'd founded with Aaron Rand thirty years ago was the most successful majority-black law firm west of Chicago. Though Rand & Jackman represented perhaps fifteen percent of the Bay Area's minority-owned businesses, the rest of their receivables came from a mix of premier entities without any reference to ethnicity. The firm's client roster included banks, hotels, construction firms, HMOs, several Silicon Valley companies, dozens of sports and entertainment celebrities, and hundreds of other lower-profile but high-income individuals and corporations.

Imposing nearly to the point of intimidation, Jackman had been a star fullback at USC in the sixties. He carried nearly 250 pounds of muscle on his six-foot-three-inch frame. He favored Italian suits, double-breasted in browns and greens, white shirts, conservative ties. Intensely black-hued, with an oversized head capped now in tightly trimmed gray knots, just two months ago he'd had a middle-aged applicant for the firm's CFO position walk out of the job interview before a word had been spoken while Jackman looked him over to see if he could take it.

Understandably, Jackman had not risen to his current eminence by having a soft heart. The law business was competitive enough if you weren't black. If you were, it could be startlingly brutal. Rand & Jackman had known this at the start. They'd felt that they had had to build their firm on the assumption that if things ever went wrong with a client or a case, they would *never* under any circumstances get the benefit of the doubt. They could afford no mistakes. They had to be the best. Not just the best black—the best, period.

And so, perhaps ironically, the firm was much more a meritocracy than most of its competitors. The younger associates worked endless hours like—well—slaves, so that they could become partners and keep working even harder. Mental or physical weakness, excuses, moral lapses, failure—all were grounds for termination.

Jackman, unhampered by any laws mandating sensitivity to race issues, ran what he thought was a good, old-fashioned firm. When he and Aaron had first started out, they'd set the tone immediately, getting rid of deadwood on sight. And soon enough the word got out and the stars came calling from the good law schools and from other firms—the diligent, the brilliant, the ambitious. Workers all. Here his attorneys could accomplish great things, could kick some real ass and make real money without anyone wondering whether they'd been hired to meet some quota or kept on because they couldn't be fired.

Now, saddened on many levels by the murder of one of his true stars, Elaine Wager, Clarence Jackman was going to have to deliver one of the tough messages to one of the good people. He had seated himself behind his desk—always an effective tool for reinforcing emotional distance—and was shuffling papers as the door opened. He kept at it for a few more seconds, then looked up. "Ah, Ms. Ghent. Thanks for coming up."

"You're welcome." She was standing in a classic military at-ease position by the Empire chair that he'd placed in front of his desk.

"Please. Have a seat."

Nodding briskly, all business, she thanked him and took the chair, sitting ramrod straight and managing to do it without appearing stiff or nervous. She looked at him expectantly, then surprised him by speaking up first. "What can I do for you, sir?"

In spite of the message he was about to deliver, Jackman found himself almost enjoying the moment. This was a woman with presence. A slight puffiness around her eyes in no way detracted from her appearance. If she was wearing any makeup, it was very subtle—she sat about ten feet from Jackman and he saw no sign of any, not even lipstick. Her face was handsome—Jackman decided that if she made it up it would be close to beautiful, which was probably why she didn't bother. It had an angular, almost exotic cast—some hint of an Asian bloodline in the racial mix. Conservatively dressed in a honey-colored silk blouse and knee-length skirt, she still managed to project a powerful physicality. There was no sign of any extra weight on her, but she wasn't petite. She came across, more than anything, as strong.

These impressions coalesced in the seconds it took Jackman to frame his response. His own expression was grave, his body language sympathetic as he came forward, his arms on his desk. "Well, first," he began in his deep, soothing voice, "I wanted to see how you're holding up in the wake of . . . Elaine."

"I've tried to do most of my crying at home." He admired the self-deprecating way she phrased it, meeting his eye. "I haven't always been successful."

"It's a tragedy," Jackman declared. "A terrible tragedy."

"Yes, sir, it is." She inhaled deeply and waited. Jackman might be both sympathetic and sincere, but he hadn't called her up here to share condolences.

It didn't take any time at all for the managing partner to get to it. Jackman pulled himself up straight in his chair and cleared his throat. "On another note, a bit unpleasant I'm afraid, I wanted to make sure that your situation over the next few weeks isn't any cause for awkwardness." He paused. "I understand that you worked for Elaine pretty much exclusively."

Treya nodded in acknowledgment. Jackman, of course, wasn't guessing. He knew that Treya and Elaine had evolved a working relationship that was unique in the firm. All of the other paralegals "floated" between loosely defined teams of three to five attorneys, taking assignments from any of them. Treya, on the other hand, got all of her hours assisting Elaine. Though it was an unusual arrangement, Jackman had allowed it to continue because it had worked. Elaine had been a workhorse with a case and business load of incredible diversity, and Treya was organized and efficient enough to keep up with her.

But now, the arrangement loomed as a liability. Jackman drove home the point. "I assume that over the next six weeks you'll be helping out with the distribution of Elaine's caseload and that should keep your utilization high."

"I was thinking the same thing."

"Good. Beyond that, I'd like to recommend, if I may, that during that transition you also begin taking assignments from some of the other attorneys if they are offered to you."

"Yes, sir. I was hoping to do just that, too."

"Splendid." Jackman didn't have to issue the warning any more clearly. Left unspoken was the hard truth that if Treya could not find enough work with one of the teams to keep her fully utilized, Jackman wouldn't be able to justify keeping her on. "You've been with the firm quite a while now, haven't you?"

"Almost seven years. I came with Elaine when she moved over from the city."

Jackman had his fingers intertwined on the desk. He was rolling his thumbs ponderously. Something was going on in his brain, though his face didn't show it. "Well," he said with resignation, "your good work hasn't gone unnoticed." He paused again, offered an avuncular smile. "Let's call it a soft six weeks, shall we? If you need a little extra time, please come up and see me."

"I will," she said.

The discussion was over, though they both sat unmoving for a long moment. Then, as though on cue, they both nodded, and Treya stood. She said "Thank you" without inflection and headed for the door.

As she walked down the hallway back to her cubicle, the knife kept turning in her stomach. Whatever sympathetic spin Jackman might put on it, she knew the reality behind his words—she had just been politely, regretfully, fired if she couldn't find another attorney in the firm who'd want to use her.

Six soft weeks.

She knew that Jackman meant he might give her seven weeks, maybe as many as nine if he let her continue to work through her two weeks' notice.

My God, she was thinking, what am I going to do?

Six weeks!

She knew there was little chance she would get anywhere near full utilization in that amount of time. First, her fellow paralegals were under the same pressure as she was to keep working. Nonattorney staff at Rand & Jackman would "bank" their overtime so that they could apply the hours to their utilization during slack periods—though technically illegal in California, the firm winked at the common practice. Too many weeks of low utilization—the exact number was unknown but low—you were gone. And everyone at the firm knew it.

Beyond that Treya was aware that her special relationship with Elaine had been a source of jealousy among her peers. She had done nothing purposeful to make this happen. She was unfailingly polite and friendly. She bent over backwards, to tell the truth. But there was no denying that she enjoyed a slightly exalted status that some of the other paralegals resented. A few lawyers might have harbored even more negative thoughts—Treya was a mere paralegal who on some level must have thought she was equal to someone who'd passed the bar. A ridiculous notion if ever there was one.

No one was going to throw her a bone, and several people she could mention might even be glad to see her laid low.

So unless a miracle occurred, and she had long since stopped counting on them, she was going to be unemployed before springtime. She couldn't let that happen, not to herself and not to Raney. She had to whip her résumé into shape, get out there at lunchtime and start interviewing.

If only Elaine . . . oh, poor Elaine . . .

Blinking back the unexpected new flash flood of tears, Treya hurried the last few steps to her cubicle. She would be damned if she'd let anyone see her crying. If she could just make it back to the safety of her workstation, she could get herself back under control.

These sudden attacks of crying had to stop. Before the beginning of this week, Treya couldn't remember the last time she had cried. It must have been just after Tom's death, when Raney was two. Twelve years, so long ago.

Tom.

She couldn't let herself think about him, not now, about what they could have had if . . . It would all be so different now if it hadn't been for the stupid red light, the stupid truck . . .

Her awful, awful luck . . .

The floodgates threatened to open. Nearly bursting with the effort to hold back tears, she finally turned the corner into her cubicle.

A hard-looking man was leaning against her desk, his arms crossed, impatience etched on his face. He had a hatchet nose and a scar through his lips. "Treya Ghent?" he said brusquely, straightening up and holding out a badge. "I'm Lieutenant Glitsky, homicide. I'd like to talk to you about Elaine Wager."

She collapsed into tears.

"I thought you'd already arrested somebody."

Nearly ten minutes had passed, during which time Glitsky waited at the workstation, allowing Treya to go to the bathroom to regain her composure. Now she was back with him, her emotions clamped down. If anything, she exuded a kind of cold fury he'd seen before, which he interpreted as self-loathing and anger that she'd lost control.

She sat at her desk and he'd pulled a chair around from someplace and straddled it backwards. So they were at about eye level in the small cubicle. "We do have someone in custody, yes."

"So what does that have to do with me? Or with anything else that might have happened here?"

More hostility. This woman, spooked by the police visit, shattered by a recent murder, didn't want to talk about it. It should just all go away.

"You're right. It may have nothing to do with anybody or anything here," he replied in his professional tone.

"What could there be? It was some bum, wasn't it? She didn't know him."

Glitsky's lips tightened. "We're trying to make sure of that."

"Didn't I read that he confessed?"

"You may have." The leak on that development hadn't made Glitsky's day, and his face showed it.

"Well? That ought to settle that, don't you think?"

Glitsky crossed his arms on the back of the chair and purposefully looked away. Bringing his eyes back to her, he waited yet another moment. Finally, when he thought she was about to begin squirming, he spoke quietly. "It's my understanding that you and Elaine were close."

The question deflected some of the anger. Treya bit at her lower lip, then nodded. "Yes."

"Then it would seem to me that you'd want to cooperate in any way you could with the investigation into her death."

"I do, but—"

Glitsky cut her off. "Sometimes people confess to things they didn't do."

"Did that happen here?"

"No." The lieutenant drew in a deep breath and let it out slowly. "But even with a righteous confession, we still need to collect all the evidence we can."

"Why?"

"Because when the killer gets a lawyer, which he will, he'll change his mind and plead not guilty."

"After he's confessed?"

"It happens. In fact, it always happens. What has he got to lose?"

Treya sat back in her chair, digesting this. "Then what about the confession?"

A grim smile. "Oh, the argument will be that it was invalid. It was coerced somehow. Or the police beat it out of him. Or his memory was impaired. Maybe it was a dream, or he just mixed up what had happened."

"Mixed up that he *killed* somebody?"

"Yeah. You'd think you'd remember something like that, but you'd be surprised how many people don't after saying they did."

Abe and Treya's eyes locked in some kind of shared understanding across the small space between them. Not for long, though. Both of them, realizing it, looked away. "So," Treya said, "you need evidence. Of what?"

This was difficult for Glitsky to explain, for the truth was that he was grasping at straws. It was bad enough that Elaine was dead, but to admit that she'd died in such a *senseless* attack was almost too much for Abe to bear. She couldn't have lived her interesting and committed life, done all she'd done, touched so many people, only to have it all wiped away in a completely random moment as though she were no more important than a bug.

Although, of course, that's exactly what did happen.

But with his own daughter?

He couldn't fit it anywhere, couldn't live with it. At least until he knew more—about Elaine, about her killer, the intersection where some meaning could be attached to it.

It was important. It was stupid and made no sense. He had to do it.

Again, he met the woman's eyes. "If, for example, Elaine worked at all with the Free Clinic or Legal Aid, if she had any professional contact with junkies . . ."

"Then she might have met with the man?"

Glitsky made a face. "The point is, if Elaine volunteered with any of these people . . ."

Treya was shaking her head. "She did volunteer, do some pro bono work, but not on the streets. She considered those people lost for the most part. If they were going to get back, it was going to have to be on their own. They weren't her issue."

"So what was?"

"Students. People who were trying to do something with their lives. So she taught moot court at Hastings, for example. She didn't have much patience for professional victims—she always wanted to yell at people to not let themselves get in that habit." Treya's eyes briefly flickered bright with a rogue memory. "One of her great expressions was that there were only two kinds of people—victims and warriors."

"I like that," Abe said. "But maybe Cole Burgess hung out with some students."

"Law students? I don't think so." Another shake of the head. "I don't remember ever hearing the name."

"All right."

Treya bit at her lower lip again and Glitsky found himself watching her. The swollen, nearly pouting mouth.

"When was the last time you saw her?"

The question startled her. "Why do you want to know that? You can't think I was . . ." She was staring, doe-eyed, in disbelief.

"I don't think anything." Glitsky hadn't meant to spook her. He softened his voice. "I'm trying to start somewhere, get a timeline of her last hours. It's really routine."

"Isn't that what the police always say when they suspect somebody? That it's routine?"

Glitsky's mouth turned up a fraction of an inch, another humanizing touch. "Actually, they do, you're right. But I'm not doing that now."

She sighed heavily. "Sunday afternoon. Here." At Glitsky's expression, she felt the need to explain and pressed on. "I'm often in on weekends, and she was doing some special master work."

Glitsky nodded in understanding. This wasn't unusual. A special master was an attorney appointed by the court to help serve a search warrant on material that might be privileged—doctor's records, lawyer's files, psychiatrist's tapes—and deliver whatever was not privileged in the requested records to the court. If the person who had the records was uncooperative, the master would do the actual searching and separate out what could lawfully be seized from the private records of other clients and patients, whose right to privacy was therefore protected from the police.

"And Elaine came back here when she was done with that?"

"Yes."

"What time was that?"

Treya's face showed her concentration. "I'm not sure, exactly. It was just turning dark, so maybe five-thirty. I was finishing up."

"And what did she come back here for?"

"Just to leave me some files. Then she was going out for a meeting and then home."

Glitsky was leaning forward now. This was an unexpected bonus. Treya had talked to Elaine on the last day of her life, within hours in fact of her death. "Did she say who she was meeting, or where?"

"No. I've tried to remember for myself. But she never said. I'm sure. She just said she had a meeting and she'd see me tomorrow. She was always going to meetings."

"And she didn't seem upset? Did she act as if anything was bothering her?"

Treya hesitated, met Glitsky's eyes again. "It's so hard to say now, knowing what happened. Everything has a different feel. You wonder if you saw something or not."

"But you think you did?"

She shook her head. "I'm not sure. If she'd come in on Monday, smiling and happy, I never would have given it a thought. I know I didn't think about it when I got home Sunday night. I just thought she was overbooked, like she gets. Got." The tense shift bothered her, and she stopped.

"It's okay." Glitsky had to fight the urge to reach over and touch her, offer her some comfort. Instead, he sat back, no threat and no push, and let her find the thread again. "It's okay," he repeated.

"I know, I know." Her look was grateful, and she held it on him for an instant. Then she nodded and sighed. "Now I'd say that, yes, something might have been bothering her. She seemed a little . . . detached." Treya hastened to protect her boss. "But she'd get that way sometimes. She always had a lot on her mind, on her plate."

Suddenly Treya's expressive face took on a different look—a sudden impatience with all this, an almost angry frustration.

"What are you thinking?" Glitsky asked.

"I'm thinking she didn't know her killer. This is stupid. Her murder wasn't connected to anything. Nobody she knew could have wanted to kill her." She raised her eyes, a challenge with some barb in it that he didn't quite understand. "You had to know her."

"I did," Glitsky replied. "I thought she was fantastic."

"She never mentioned you as a friend." Suddenly the barb in her voice was pronounced, unmistakable—all of her protective instincts on display from out of nowhere.

"Well, no, not exactly a friend. I knew her when she worked at the Hall."

"I knew that. I knew who you were. I was there then, too, as a clerk."

Glitsky had no response to this, although Treya seemed in some way to hold it against him. He attempted to get beyond it. "In any event, that's another reason why I'd like to know what she might have been working on. I've got kind of a personal interest as well."

But if he thought this admission would ally him with Treya, he was mistaken. "So you've kept up on her career since she'd left the Hall?"

He answered guardedly. "A little bit, yes."

"In a kind of a hands-off way."

Glitsky raised his shoulders awkwardly. "I guess you'd say I admired her from a distance." He wondered how suddenly everything had gone so wrong with this interview. "I'm sorry if I've offended you."

"Not at all," she said. "You're only doing your job. But Elaine is very personal to me. I know who her friends were and it's a little insulting to pretend you were close to her, too, so maybe I'd tell you more."

"That wasn't what I was doing."

"Really?" she asked with ill-concealed disbelief. "Then I'm sorry I got that impression. Perhaps I overreacted." All business now, Treya cut off further inquiry as she stood, signaling—although it was not her place to do so—that the interview was over. "I'm sure the firm wouldn't object if you got a warrant for her files or to go over her client list. You might find something there that you're looking for."

Glitsky rarely felt either inept or out of his depth, but now he felt both, and acutely. Perhaps it was a sense of foolishness because he found her so physically attractive and at such an inappropriate time. Whatever it was, he was standing along with her, not willing to risk falling any further in her esteem.

He hadn't gotten anywhere here, and in fact he'd had little confidence that any real evidence was going to come from this quarter. But it had been the only place he could think of to begin, to connect with someone who had known her.

"Ms. Ghent, please." His shoulders were sagging. He was a pathetic figure—he knew it. Regal, she stopped at the entrance to the cubicle, turned back to face him, challenging, her arms crossed, her color now high in her cheeks.

"I want you to understand that I'm not looking for specific evidence.

I'm trying to get a sense of her work, her life, if maybe there was some reason . . ." Too close to revealing the nonprofessional truth about why he'd come here, he stood mute and helpless.

Treya Ghent gave every appearance of considering his words, but when she finally spoke, there was no sign of cooperation. "I really don't think so, but if anything occurs to me, Lieutenant, I'll let you know."

This time, it was a dismissal.

6

At high noon, Hardy walked into the small lobby for the segregated jailing rooms at the hospital. It was a depressing and cold room, dimly lit, with high barred windows and a strong smell of antiseptic, sweaty yellowing walls and a couple of battered wooden benches, although no one was using them at the moment. To his left, a uniformed female officer sat at a pitted green desk equipped with a computer terminal and a telephone. She looked up at Hardy's arrival with a kind of relief. He went across to her and stated his business.

"You know he's already got a visitor. His mother."

It didn't take phenomenal cosmic powers to realize that Jody Burgess had made a poor impression on this woman. Hardy gave her a sympathetic smile. "Her poor baby isn't a criminal, he's sick. There's been some terrible mistake. You can't keep him here and it's all your fault and she's going to sue."

The officer smiled back at him. "You've been reading my mail."

"Maybe I can calm her down."

"Maybe." She pushed a button on her desk and an instant later another uniformed officer—this one a large white male—pushed open the door at the other end of the room. Hardy thanked her and she gave him a shrug. "Have fun," she said.

When the guard unlocked the door to Cole's room, Hardy understood why seasoned jailbirds might try to pull some kind of scam to get a few days here. It wasn't the Ritz, but it was far better than a shared cell at the jail behind the Hall of Justice—a private room with a window and a television set, now blessedly dark and silent, suspended from the ceiling.

Cole was propped halfway up in a hospital bed, a clean sheet covering him to the waist. Wearing a standard hospital gown, he might have been any badly beaten-up patient except for the handcuffs which shackled him to the bed's railing. An older, slightly more corn-fed but not unattractive version of Dorothy Elliot sat holding his free hand on the window side of the bed.

"Knock if you have any trouble," the guard said, and closed the door. Hardy took a step forward and introduced himself—Dorothy's friend.

"Thank God," Jody Burgess exclaimed, standing up, coming around the bed with a kind of buoyantly expectant expression and both arms outstretched. "Mr. Hardy," she enthused, "Dorothy told me what you did and I don't know how we'll ever be able to thank you."

She wore an expensive-looking, baggy, dark green jogging outfit with an unfamiliar logo over the left breast. As she came closer, Hardy noted the carefully applied makeup, dyed blond hair and a lot of baubles, costume jewelry—earrings and bracelets, rings with large colored stones on both hands. He pegged her at sixty-two or -three, going for forty without great success.

"I didn't really do much." Hardy felt that he had, in fact, done nothing. From what he'd been told, Cole had been here in the hospital by the time Hardy had arrived at the Hall of Justice yesterday afternoon. He assayed a polite smile. "They would have gotten to testing your son, Mrs. Burgess, but . . ."

"Don't be so humble. If you hadn't stepped in, Cole would still be over at the jail. They wouldn't be taking care of him like this." The woman's effusiveness was slightly overwhelming. She grabbed Hardy's hand in both of hers and held it tightly.

Eventually freeing his hand, he cast his eyes beyond her, to the suspect. He had to work to keep his tone neutral. "And you're Cole. How are you doing?"

Jody popped right in, answering for her son. "He's going to be fine, just fine, aren't you, Cole?" Protectively, she was moving back toward the bed.

"I don't know, Mom. I don't know if 'fine' really covers it." The young man's voice was deep with a raspy quality and a slight but recognizable defect in enunciation. Hardy knew the latter could be simple fatigue, but more likely it was the telltale slur of long-term drug use. "Another day in that cell," he said, shaking his head. "I don't know."

"They were going to let him die," Mrs. Burgess offered. "They just wanted him to suffer."

Hardy shook his head, told her a white lie. "I don't think so," he said. "Not intentionally anyway. They don't do that."

"Then why . . . ?"

"They process a lot of people every day at the jail. This was just one of the times somebody fell through the cracks. The good news is we found out soon enough." Hardy saw that he was going to have to talk through Jody and didn't know how long he was going to have the patience for it. He addressed himself directly to Cole. "So they've got you on methadone?"

"It's kicked in, yeah."

Again, the mother. "It's to help with the withdrawal pains. The idea is to lessen the dose so his body gradually—"

"Mom!"

She stopped, clamping her mouth tight with a pained expression. "I'm sorry. I just want Mr. Hardy to understand . . ." Her voice trailed off.

"He's probably got the idea." To Hardy. "Right?"

"Some." He softened his inflection, gave her another reassuring smile. "Mrs. Burgess." A pause. "Jody. I'd like a few minutes alone with Cole if you don't mind."

It hurt her anew, but there was no avoiding that. Her worried gaze fell on her son, came back to Hardy. "Of course, sure, I understand."

But she didn't move until he prompted her. "Just knock at the door and the guard will come and let you out. We won't be too long."

"She's all right, really," Cole said when the door had closed behind his mother. "She's trying to help."

But now, suddenly, with the innocent mother out of the room, Hardy abruptly abandoned chitchat mode. He might have wanted to spare some of her feelings, but he felt no similar compunction toward her son. Moving down to the foot of the bed, he rested his hands on the railing, looked Cole hard in the face, spoke with a flat deliberateness. "Tell me what happened the other night."

The change in tone met its mark. The young man inhaled sharply, shifted his eyes from side to side, finally focused on the sheet in front of him. "It was bad."

Hardy gave it a second, then reached over and slapped the bed next to Cole's foot.

Startled, Cole looked up. Hardy's expression made him take another deep breath, which he let out slowly through puffed cheeks. "I mean, I was in bad shape. It was cold as hell, man. I remember that. I hadn't scored all day."

"Why not?"

"I had to get some money. I thought I might go and hit up Mom, but then"—he sighed again—"then the cramps started to come on, so I didn't want to go all the way out where she lives."

"Where's that?"

"Like Judah, out in the Sunset. I score at Sixteenth and Mission. It was too far."

"So you decided to mug somebody instead?"

"No! It wasn't like that." Hardy gave him no reaction so he felt pressed to explain further. "Look, my last score must've been heavily cut, okay? I mean, I was shaking already, cramping up, you know? It was like midnight. I'd scored a couple of pills but they weren't doing it. I had to do something."

Hardy waited.

"So I lucked out. One of the bums was crashed with his cart . . ."

"His cart?"

"Shopping cart. In this spot, I don't know exactly where, south of Mission I think. Anyway, he was passed out and had most of a whole bottle of bourbon by his head, just lying there. So I lifted it. I needed *something*, you know?"

"He let you take his whiskey?"

"No, he was out already. I lifted it."

"You didn't hit him and take it?"

"Come on." Cole actually appeared offended at the question. "Nothing like that."

"How about the gun? Did you threaten him with that?"

"I didn't have any gun." His brow darkened for a minute. "Not then."

"Did you get it from him, too?"

"No." Then: "I don't think so."

"You don't think so," Hardy repeated. But he had no choice but to accept it for now. "All right, then what?"

"Then I guess I drank most of it. The bottle."

"Where were you then?"

A shrug. "Just around. I don't know. I was hurtin'. I mean, *hurtin'*, you hear me?"

"For the record, Cole, you're not breaking my heart. How'd you get up to Maiden Lane?"

But the lack of sympathy had its price. "I don't know, man. Maybe I levitated, huh? Maybe I took the Monorail."

Hardy straightened up. "You think this is funny, huh? You're looking at the rest of your life behind bars and you're getting wise with me?"

"Hey." Cole went to hold up his hands in a gesture of innocence. The handcuff on his left wrist brought him up short. "I'm just saying I don't remember getting uptown. I drank the booze. I got loaded. I walked around, tried to keep warm. Maybe I'd run into somebody I knew, I don't know. Maybe score some 'g.' "

" 'G'?"

"God. Smack. You know, heroin."

"And pay for it with what?"

Cole shook his head miserably. "I don't know. It didn't happen anyway."

"So what did happen? Did you see Elaine come out of some building? Or just walking alone? What?"

"Elaine?"

Hardy's temper flared. "Elaine Wager," he snapped, but then checked himself, got his voice under control. "The woman you've confessed to killing. Elaine Wager."

"What about her?"

"I asked when you first saw her."

"I don't really remember, you know? I told the cops this."

"Why don't you just tell me, too? What's the first thing you *do* remember?"

"The gun. In my hand." Cole made eye contact. "Like, there it was."

"Where?"

"Well, I mean it was there on the street and I picked it up. Anybody'll give you money for a gun, right?"

"So you remember picking up the gun? And then what?"

He closed his eyes, shook his head. "I've been through this already. Then I guess leaning over her."

"You guess? What do you mean, you guess? Did you see her walking? Did you come up behind her? Or was she already on the ground?"

Cole's face was taut with the effort at recall. "I must have blanked it."

"What does that mean, you must have blanked it? Are you saying you blanked on pulling the trigger?"

As though trapped in a cage, the young man looked from side to side for an exit. "Well, I mean I had the gun, then I was leaning over her and saw all the gold, the necklace, then her purse and the other stuff."

Hardy's hands were white on the bed's railing. "You don't remember firing the gun?"

"No."

"Ever?"

Cole gave it some thought, then shook his head no. "But the cop said it was common, blanking the moment. Like people in car wrecks don't remember the last minute before."

"What cop?"

"The guy who questioned me. Black dude. Banks, I think his name was."

Hardy tore his eyes from the pathetic young man and looked through the barred window to the gray afternoon outside. Traffic was stopped in both directions on the freeway. Rows of boxlike apartment buildings clung to a dun-colored hill. He wasn't going to find any solace in the view, and after Cole's last words, he needed some. "But Cole," he began quietly, "listen to me. You confessed to killing her."

He nodded. "Yeah."

"But you don't remember stalking her? Firing the gun?"

"No, none of that. But I must have."

"Why do you say that?"

Cole stared down at the sheet covering him. "I shot the gun. They tested my hands. I shot the gun." He brought his eyes up to Hardy. "So I must have done it. And by then I couldn't hold out anymore anyway."

"Hold out on what?"

This got an exasperated rise out of him. "Hey, come on, what are we talking about?"

"Elaine Wager's death, Cole. How about that?"

But he was shaking his head. "No, man. We're talking 'g.' They got me in that room and I'm coming down hard. *I'm dying!* You understand? Then Banks tells me he'll see he gets me something as soon as I say I did it. So I told him."

"That you killed her?"

"Yeah." He shrugged. "But hell, I would have told him I'd shot Kennedy if that's what he wanted to hear."

The chief assistant district attorney of the city and county of San Francisco did not have a big office. In fact, Gabriel Torrey's office was the same size as the other third-floor offices which were shared two to a room by the rank and file assistant D.A.'s. The big difference was in the furnishings—a sofa and matching armchairs of exquisitely soft leather, built-in floor-to-ceiling bookshelves, plantation shutters, twin original Tiffany lamps, a Persian rug over the hardwood floor Torrey had installed. And, of course, there was also the Desk—a large, custom-crafted, beautifully finished cross section of redwood burl from an old-growth stand of trees that had been clear cut in the late 1970s.

The desk had been a gift to Torrey from the CEO of Pac-Ore Timber. In those days, Torrey was a young attorney working as a lobbyist in Washington, D.C., representing whatever clients were willing to pay him back then, regardless of their political agenda. The provenance of the Desk was old news by now—it was simply the stunning centerpiece of an intimidating work space. The old-time D.A.'s, a handful of old white guys who remained from past administrations, remembered the office from the days when Art Drysdale had been the chief A.D.A. Back then it had been just like their own—a mess. Battered green files, sagging metal bookshelves that held binders full of active cases, a cork bulletin board, one wall-mounted six-foot length of two-by-four that held Art's baseball memorabilia.

But Gabriel Torrey believed in the trappings of power. The prosecutors who reported to him would never have cause to doubt that he was hugely important, more so than they would ever be. Victims of crimes and their families would be reassured that their cases were being handled at the highest level. Other visitors to the office—personal guests as well as opposing attorneys and political acquaintances—were greeted not by a faceless bureaucrat but by an affable, self-assured gentleman in total control of his world. The subtext, Torrey thought, was clear—this man didn't get here, in these surroundings, by mistake. He was a winner. You crossed him at your peril.

Now, a half hour after he'd finished a wonderful lunch at La Felce, he sat behind the Desk, the jacket of his Armani suit draped over the wooden valet behind him. He wore a silk tie in deep maroon with gold threads over a starched shirt with a subtle purple hue. On the sofa opposite him was a mid-thirties attorney named Gina Roake. Next to her on the cherry end table, a cup of freshly brewed Blue Mountain coffee, untouched, was turning tepid—Ms. Roake was so angry that she couldn't have swallowed a drop to save her life. She was representing another woman named Abby Oberlin in a will contest between Abby and her brother Jim, and things had gotten beyond ugly.

"But my client *loved* her mother, Mr. Torrey," she managed to say. "She's the one who has taken care of her for the past seven years. Jim hasn't so much as visited in, I don't know, forever. Five years, maybe more."

"Which is why your mother left Abby the lion's share of her estate?"

"Yes. Of course."

"And it's valued at around eight million dollars?"

"That's right."

"A lot of money." Torrey let the words sink in. "And all of it to your client. Less your fee of course."

This got Gina's back up. She chose not to respond to the latter comment, but she was going to stick up for her client. "She took care of her mother and loved her. Jim is just a selfish . . ." She bit at her lip. "He is lying, that's all there is to it. There was no abuse. Abby didn't . . ." The words stopped.

Torrey leaned forward. He was in prosecutor mode and Gina's client stood accused of a serious crime. Gina could protest about her innocence all day. Torrey would listen patiently, conveying that he'd heard all this before from other attorneys in other, similar cases, and in his vast experience most of them had done what the other family members had accused them of. He spoke quietly, but with a firm edge. "Nevertheless, your client's brother contends that the will is invalid. That his mother signed it under coercion. Additionally, he has reported this criminal conduct of his sister and this office is going to have no option but to pursue a vigorous prosecution."

"But it makes no sense. There's no evidence of—"

Torrey's expression became even more stern as he interrupted. He tapped a file folder on the desk in front of him. "Don't play games with me, Ms. Roake. There is a real case here—"

"Her mother fell. She broke her hip. Then she tried to get up too soon and fell again. It happens."

"Yes, it does. And after the second fall, she contracted pneumonia and died."

Gina could not entirely keep the panic out of her voice. "You're not implying Abby killed her, are you? Or caused her death somehow? Even Jim's not saying that, and he'd stoop to anything to get some of the money."

Torrey shook his head. "I'm not accusing your client of anything. What I am saying is that we've got significant resources that we can and will bring to bear in this type of investigation. Prosecuting instances of abuse of the elderly is one of Sharron Pratt's highest priorities. We can and will subpoena your client's mother's medical records. Jim Oberlin contends that he believes his mother was oversedated." He sat back, lawyer to lawyer. "Look, Ms. Roake, you know how it works. Investigators will talk to Abby's friends. If she's ever complained about all the work her mother required—"

"Well of course she did! She's not a saint. I'm sure there were days . . ." Gina Roake shook her head.

"Even so." Torrey spread his hands wide as if to tell her that's what he meant—it could look very bad for Abby Oberlin. He let a silence gather and then sighed heavily, a brief wash of compassion coming to his face. "Ms. Roake. Gina. Did I not ask you to come and see me as a courtesy?"

She nodded.

"Why do you think that is?" He patted the folder again. "When, based on the accusations your client's brother has brought against her, I would have been justified sending out some officers to place her under arrest?"

"Under arrest?"

"That's right. Her name in the paper with the whole story, everything Jim has accused her of."

"No, you can't do that. It's not . . ." Visibly, she brought herself under control. When she spoke after half a minute, her voice was calm, reasonable. "Jim just wants money, Mr. Torrey. He has no career. He'll never hold a job. That's just who he is. He's desperate. Abby didn't do anything he says."

Torrey crossed his hands on the Desk, reapplied the stern visage. "You didn't answer my question."

She wrung her hands. "I'm sorry. What was it again?"

"Why do you think I asked you down here today?"

"I don't know."

"Well, I'll tell you." The tone softened again. "I've prosecuted more cases like this than I'd care to tell you about, and I've developed a good sense, a very good sense if I may say so, of how these things play out. In this case, there was verifiable physical trauma to Abby's mother. A finder of fact will conclude that there are grounds for a hearing, and after that in all likelihood a full-fledged trial. You know this. Your client probably will be arrested"—he held up a hand, stopping her protest—"although bail will be reasonable. She'll spend, if she's lucky, about half a million dollars in attorney's fees, experts, investigation, which is good news for you, except that she won't be able to take any of it out of the estate while it's being contested. The process will take a minimum of two or three years out of your client's life and after all that, even if we don't prove she did anything she's charged with, some civil jury might give her brother all the money on the theory that definitely he did no harm and your client might have."

Gina had all but collapsed back into the soft leather of the couch. "So what do you suggest?" she asked helplessly, talking all but to herself.

He leaned forward, suddenly friend and perhaps savior. "The truth is that I believe you. Jim doesn't care what happened to his mother, beyond that she is dead."

"That's what I've been—"

"But that's not saying he won't let all of this . . . unpleasantness . . . proceed. From where I sit, it's a no-lose situation for him, and it's no-win for your client."

She came forward on the sofa. "She's not going to give him any of the money, Mr. Torrey. He doesn't deserve it. He's an evil man, and this is wrong."

The chief assistant nodded in agreement. "Nevertheless, if this prosecution moves forward, the next time I see you, we won't be talking like this." He leveled his gaze at her. "Tell your client that although it's a repugnant solution, if you throw a bone to her brother, I believe you could settle his civil claim. And if he's satisfied, I don't think we'd see any need to file a criminal case. If I were her, from a purely self-protective, even selfish motive, I'd think about that."

"But it's so wrong . . ."

Torrey couldn't argue the point and didn't try. "Be that as it may, that's my advice while I'm still free to give it. After today, we're on opposite sides."

Gina Roake stood and thanked Torrey. He told her he appreciated her coming by, and hoped that she would come to the right decision, and she told him she'd discuss it with her client, but they would both consider his advice very seriously. Then she left. He could still hear her footsteps in the hallway outside as he picked up the telephone.

7

Sharron Pratt chose the moment with some care.

She had been invited to give a talk at the Commonwealth Club on her tenure to date as district attorney, the office's most notable successes and failures, the evolution of her philosophy on criminal justice, and her plans for the future. Quite a few members of the media were on hand, as well as many of the city's business and political elite. It was an ideal setting—quite a bit more high-toned than an impromptu Hall of Justice press conference, a slam dunk of a photo op, a chance to explain her absolutely unexpected position shift in word units longer than sound bites.

Because it had been playing so well in the business community and the newspapers for over two years, she began with a recap of her office's continuing, high-moral-tone campaign against Gironde Industries, the French company whose winning low-ball bid for the $25 million airport baggage carousels had rocked the Board of Supervisors and infuriated many of the largest and most well-connected construction firms who did business in the city.

A foreign company like Gironde wasn't about to be able to fulfill their contract without working with armies of local subcontractors—sheet metal workers, tile layers, painters, electricians, brick masons and so on. These companies, named by Gironde in their proposal, had in turn all guaranteed that they were in compliance with the city's minority subcontracting quota.

Gabe Torrey understood business far better than Pratt did, and he had alerted her to the likelihood of fraud in the negotiations. Gironde simply couldn't do the job for the amount that they had bid otherwise. Torrey's opinion was that Gironde hired subcontractors for the proposal period, then laid them off immediately thereafter; that none of the subs had anywhere near the mandated number of women or minorities; he'd bet that many had women or minorities as titular owners who were paid minimum wage. Gironde would put people on the payroll, then give them a handful of cash to stay home and lie about working on the project.

Pratt had taken it from there.

And the district attorney's office had gone to work with a vengeance, convening a grand jury, subpoenaing witnesses, obtaining search warrants on the offending subcontractors, seizing their records without warning, bringing the frauds to light time and again.

It developed into a major story—reporters soon discovered that Gironde had human rights violations reported on jobs they had worked on in Senegal, in the Caribbean, in the Philippines. The owner of the company, Pierre Coteau, owned another company that sold animal furs. How, Pratt demanded, could a benevolent and liberal San Francisco award a contract to such a despicable company?

At the request of the Board of Supervisors, Gironde was now preparing a revised second bid with a new list of subcontractors. But the feeling on the board and in the city at large was so strong against them, and in favor of Pratt on this issue, that no one believed they would keep the job. "And," Pratt concluded, "this is the kind of law I will continue to practice in my second term. These are the kinds of people I will prosecute—those who would unfairly take jobs from the honest citizens and hardworking businesspeople of this city."

The applause washed over her. She loved Gironde. It was the perfect San Francisco prosecution. Not only was the issue one of high moral tone, it had opened the coffers of local contractors who before Gironde would not have given her the time of day.

And now, having reminded everyone of that, she moved on to the usual pablum that her staff had spun from the statistical flotsam garnered from any number of often-conflicting sources, taking whatever numbers made her look best.

They'd had setbacks early on, she admitted, but the numbers on violent crime were down in "the last several months"—actually only in January, but this number had been down enough that Sharron could bring in November and December, when crime had actually been up, and the average would still be less than it had been in the late summer and early autumn.

They were sending more criminals to jail. This was true because the D.A.'s prosecutors were accepting pleas in exchange for shorter jail terms rather than taking criminals to trial. This speeded up the process and let felons out of jail sooner, but Pratt could say they were sending more bad folks to the slammer.

She followed up by stating that she was accomplishing all of her good works in spite of the continuing lack of cooperation from the police department. During her last election campaign, she'd fashioned some minor, unproven and isolated allegations of police brutality into a major plank of her platform. She was going to seek out and prosecute bad cops. She was going to create a task force. She was going to bust the "good old boy" network of redneck cops, never mind that the San Francisco police department was fully integrated as to gender and race at all levels of command, and also had fewer police brutality incidents or complaints than any other city of comparable size in the United States.

The district attorney's office, Pratt concluded, was functioning "with an efficiency that is the envy of every other bureaucracy in the city and county of San Francisco."

She looked out over the crowd, deciding that she had them, that the time was ripe. Lifting some pages from the podium, she dropped them onto the table next to her. "All that said," she continued, "it must be admitted now that, with hindsight, I can see that some of the outreach programs, initiated by my office in the early days of this administration, and with the best of intentions, may not have achieved the success that I hoped for."

A palpable sense of expectation swept the room. Suddenly people were sitting up straighter, paying attention. She paused significantly, lifted her chin, steeled her gaze. "In preparation for coming to talk to all of you today, late last week I had written the usual political speech to tell you how well we're doing. And in fact, as I've indicated, there are areas of success to which we can point with pride. Now, though, I'm going to leave my prepared remarks. Please bear with me as I speak from my heart.

"Last weekend, the city suffered a terrible loss. I'm speaking, of course, of Elaine Wager, not only the daughter of our late beloved sena-

tor but in her own right one of the great lights in the city's firmament."
Pratt paused for a sip of water, gathered herself and went on. "One of
the most difficult lessons I've had to learn on the prosecution side of the
bar is that there is real evil cast among us. My training and background
has led me to try and understand the causes of antisocial behavior and
to seek solutions through incarceration, yes, but also through counseling and education. I remain proud of the programs we've adopted that
seek to temper justice with mercy, that have tried to inject compassion
and understanding into the judicial process.

"But the events of the past few days have brought home some hard
truths and today I am here to deliver a message that may have become
blurred in my administration's zeal for fairness, tolerance and empathy
for desperate people who are driven to desperate acts. And that message is this: People who break the law in San Francisco are going to be
punished."

Pratt let the substantial round of applause wash over her, took another sip of water, then waited for silence. When it came, she spoke in a
voice thick with conviction—it was time to go into campaign mode.
"There are those who say that I am soft on crime, that I am too com-
passionate to fulfill the duties of district attorney. To those people, let
me announce what may be correctly interpreted as a sea change in the
policy of this administration.

"The police have arrested a man—a homeless man, a drug addict—
who has confessed to the murder of Elaine Wager, a murder in the
course of which he took her purse, jewelry and other possessions. California law defines murder in the commission of a robbery as a special
circumstances crime and prescribes only two possible penalties—life in
prison without the possibility of parole, and death."

Pratt was aware of the drama of the moment. The silence in the room
was perfect—even the waiters were still, hanging on her conclusion.

"I want there to be no mistake. It is the intention of the district attorney to seek the death penalty in this case. This is the word I'm
putting out to the criminal element in this city, the line that today I
draw in the sand—street violence, all violent crime, stops here. The law
will be enforced. For as long as I remain district attorney, here is the
policy of my office: If you are unfortunate or dispossessed, mercy will
still have its place"—her hands gripped either side of the podium as she
looked out over the multitude—"but if you break the law, justice will

trump mercy every"—she brought down her fist—"single"—again, the fist—"time."

After a short stunned silence, a man at one of the front tables began to applaud and it was as though a dam had broken. The ensuing ovation brought the entire dining room to its feet.

8

Sick of conjuring with imponderables, Hardy called a fifteen-minute recess for himself. He stood up, stretched and walked to the window. Late afternoon, a listless gray day downtown. He and Frannie had their traditional Wednesday Date Night scheduled to begin in a couple of hours, and Hardy was tempted to call it a day and go wait for his wife at the Shamrock, discuss some philosophical conundrums with his brother-in-law Moses, who would be working behind the bar. He could have an early cocktail on the theory that it was always five o'clock somewhere.

He wasn't getting anything done here, that was for sure.

His reaction to Monday's problems with Glitsky and the jail had settled uneasily enough, but after his visit with Cole Burgess yesterday, the whole business lay curdling in his stomach. Something was very wrong, but he really didn't want to get involved any further. He was too close to it, one way or the other. Also, he didn't want to risk a serious rupture in his friendship with Abe over a lowlife such as Cole Burgess—to say nothing of the logistical problems he'd doubtlessly have with his friends Jeff and Dorothy, and her difficult mother.

When the dust cleared, he was all but certain that Cole would cut some kind of deal and get low double digits in the state prison. Every homicide was a manslaughter to Pratt's trial-shy prosecutors. Even the public defender called the city's system a "plea bargain mill." Best case, Cole might even get out of San Quentin with his habit broken. In any event, it wasn't Hardy's problem.

What *was* his problem right now, though, was Dash Logan. The damned guy was proving harder to contact than the Pope, and Hardy's client Rich McNeil was understandably losing some patience.

In the mid-eighties, McNeil had just turned fifty and decided to invest his 401K money in San Francisco real estate. He could have done better with Microsoft, but back then the stock market made him nervous. In any event, he wasn't complaining. The sixteen-unit apartment building on Russian Hill had cost a hefty million five when he purchased it for a quarter million down; its most recent appraisal pegged its value at six million plus. Rich was now sixty-four years old, primed to sell the thing and retire.

So here he was, this nice guy and good citizen who'd worked and saved the way good Americans were supposed to, and instead of some carefree years of leisure, he was suddenly looking at some very serious trouble.

A year and a half ago, he'd finally succeeded in evicting Manny Galt, who'd been a tenant in the building for nearly ten years. The tenant from hell, as it turned out.

The first sign of trouble was when he painted his entire unit, including the windows, black. When McNeil had demurred, politely requesting Galt at least to leave the outer windows clear, Galt had not so politely declined. It was his fuckin' place, he said, McNeil could go piss up a rope.

To say that San Francisco's rent control laws favor tenants over landlords is to say that Custer favored Southern belles over the Ogalala Sioux. So when Hardy's client explored the possibility of evicting Mr. Galt over the paint job, he found that this would be legally impossible. Galt had his five rooms, he paid his four hundred dollars every month, and as far as the law was concerned, that apartment was *his,* and at that price, until he gave it up on his own.

Which he wasn't inclined to do.

Over the years, Galt's one unit became a constant source of dissatisfaction to the other tenants as well, and a regular feature of McNeil's life became dealing with complaints about loud noises, awful odors, unsavory people.

Galt's apartment was just inside the front door to the building on the ground floor, and he decided it was a safer place to keep his Harley than the garage. Though he ostensibly, and sporadically, worked as a bouncer, he once boasted to McNeil that he really got his money for gas, rent and beer (his only necessities) selling or brokering crank and dope deals to other bikers.

The man himself was a giant—a vulgar, terrifying Neanderthal with an enormous gut, a voluminous, unkempt beard and a shaved head. He dressed perennially in black—T-shirts and leathers, boots and chains. If he bathed at all . . . but no, he couldn't have and smelled the way he did.

The only problem McNeil had with turnover in his building were the units adjacent to Galt's—over the years, the average tenancy in these units—despite the great location, the cooperative landlord, the reasonable rents—was ten months.

Finally, one happy day eighteen months ago, Galt had suddenly disappeared. McNeil didn't receive his rent check by the tenth of the month, which was the statutory grace period. He immediately served written notice and filed to evict. Under normal conditions, in San Francisco McNeil would have had to wait six months or more before any action would be taken on the filing, but the unprecedented support of every other tenant in the building—all of whom personally showed up for the hearing—convinced the judge that this was an extraordinary situation, and he ruled in McNeil's favor.

When he opened the door to the apartment, even McNeil—who'd expected the worst—wasn't prepared for the damage. The place was totaled. Eventually, it took a crew of four men forty-six days to restore the apartment to habitability. The removal of debris alone was a weeklong process. After that, it had to be cleaned, deodorized, cleaned again. McNeil had had to install new hardwood floors and drywall, new lights and fixtures, all new kitchen appliances. Finally, after the new paint was dry, when the work was all done at a cost to McNeil of thirty-one thousand dollars and change, he put it on the market for twenty-four hundred dollars a month, and had eleven qualified renters the first day.

Then Galt returned.

He hassled McNeil for a few months, came to his house a few times, once with some biker friends, scared everybody, made a big stink, eventually went away. And Rich had thought the nightmare was over at last.

But three weeks ago, after all this time, Galt had resurfaced, and in a guise beyond McNeil's worst imaginings. According to the complaints, both civil and criminal, filed in the courts, Galt came home to shock and dismay that he had been put out of his castle.

Contrary to his landlord's sworn statements, he had not abandoned the property. As Mr. McNeil well knew, he'd had to leave with his Harley on an emergency road trip to Kentucky to care for his dying mother. Before he left town, he had paid McNeil twelve hundred dollars in cash for three months' rent in case he had to be gone that long. Upset, worried about his mother's health, in a hurry to be back at her side, he had not concerned himself about a receipt for the transaction—he was a man of his word, and assumed McNeil was as well. They'd had a relationship for years. It never occurred to him that either one of them would cheat the other.

He was stunned upon his return to find that Rich McNeil had stolen his money, taken away his home, disposed of all his treasures. After all, Galt had been a solid, rent-paying tenant—he had never, *not once,* missed a rent payment! And now he was ruined, with no place he could afford to live in the city he loved.

McNeil had obviously been driven to this inhuman fraud by simple greed—after all, he stood to make, he was currently making, two thousand dollars more *every month* on Galt's apartment alone. It was a horrible travesty.

So Galt, through his attorney Dash Logan, was appealing the eviction ruling. He was also suing McNeil to get his apartment back at the old rent, to restore his lost property, to compensate him for mental anguish, the pain and suffering he'd endured, for his attorney's fees and for punitive damages—to the tune of a million dollars.

What made it worse for Hardy's client, though—far worse—were the criminal charges.

Like everything else in San Francisco, rent control was a political issue. And in her election campaign three years before, Sharron Pratt had made it clear that she hated slum landlords nearly as much as she loved the homeless. Her administration had pledged itself to protecting the rights of the poor, the unempowered, the disenfranchised masses. Besides which, renters in the city constituted a huge voting bloc.

And here was a Russian Hill nabob pitted against an unsympathetic biker—it was the perfect opportunity to illustrate just how venal these landlords could be in their immoral pursuit of the almighty buck.

Hardy knew McNeil well and considered his client pretty much a working stiff who'd put in thirty-five hard years behind desks in various management positions, eventually reaching the eminence of executive vice president of Terranew Industries, a biotech firm specializing in the ever-glamorous field of fertilizer products.

But in Sharron Pratt's opinion, Rich McNeil, by the very fact that he'd been successful and invested wisely, was of the landed class, the privileged class. Never mind that he'd earned it—that was irrelevant. And Manny Galt was low class. In fact, in the eyes of many, he was barely a citizen at all. This conflict boiled down to a class struggle. It was as simple as that.

Traditionally, as Pratt knew (and if she forgot, Gabe Torrey reminded her), the Rich McNeils of the world got their way by being in the men's club, by having the money to afford better lawyers, by buying elected officials to do their bidding and dirty work. Well, as Torrey had counseled her, she couldn't let that happen on her watch, no siree. It wasn't going to be business as usual in San Francisco, not while she was district attorney. That's why she'd been elected, to shake up the status quo, to ring in a new age.

She had to make the message crystal clear that her office saw through Rich McNeil's transparent grab for more income, more money that he didn't even need. Pratt had to be the people's protector here, and this was her chance to show the traditional power structure that the old way wasn't going to work. More than a landlord-tenant dispute, this had to be, by her lights, true white-collar crime, the kind that was too often tolerated in our society—and she had committed herself to punish it.

So the city and county of San Francisco brought criminal charges against Rich McNeil—grand theft, perjury, conspiracy to commit fraud. If it went to jury trial, and if he was convicted on all counts, Rich McNeil could be facing four years in state prison.

It was not the retirement he'd dreamed of.

Hardy was just turning from the window, intending to throw a couple of rounds of darts, when the telephone rang on his desk. "Dismas Hardy."

"Dismas?" the voice said. "What the hell kind of name is Dismas?"

"It's the name my parents gave me, the good thief on Calvary. Who is this?"

"The good thief. That's great. Dismas. Dash Logan here. Sorry it's taken so long to get back at you. I've been busy as a one-legged man in an ass-kicking contest."

Hardy bit back a sarcastic reply. "I won't take much of your time, then. As I mentioned in my messages, I'm representing Rich McNeil and I thought we could—"

A short, barking laugh interrupted him. From the falsely hale sound on the phone, Hardy formed the impression that Logan might already have downed a cocktail or two. "Oh, sorry," the voice said, "somebody said something." There were unmistakable bar noises in the background, Ricky Martin and La Vida Loca. "So you're with McNeil?"

"And his fifteen witnesses," Hardy replied.

"To what?" Another disconnected laugh. Clearly Logan was following another conversation—or something—going on in front of him. "On me, on me. Jerry, you let him pay I'll break your arm—"

"Look," Hardy interrupted, "if this isn't a good time . . ."

"No. It's fine, fine. I'm just down here at Jupiter. You know the place?"

Hardy did and said so. A few blocks south of the Hall of Justice, the bar was kind of the up-tempo version of Lou the Greek's. Great fast food, loud music, bartenders with personality—a major hangout of the law crowd, serious drinker division.

"You free? 'Cause I'm here awhile. Meeting a client." The voice shifted, another focus. "Yeah, you're talking to the duck. I heard it." Back to the phone. "So? Hardy? What do you say? Come on down, I'll buy you a drink."

"I've got clients, too, Mr. Logan. Some other time, maybe. But I'd really like to talk with you."

"Anytime, anytime. You thinking you want to settle?"

"Actually, we're talking more about a cross complaint."

This really seemed to strike Logan as funny. "*Get out!* For what?"

"That's one of the things I thought we'd discuss."

"That'll be a short talk."

"Maybe. Maybe not."

Hardy heard ice tinkling in his ear. He felt a pulse in his temple. This kind of posturing could go on forever, and he wasn't up to it today. "Mr. Logan," he began, but again the voice cut him off.

"Dash, please. Everybody calls me Dash."

David Freeman appeared at his door, and Hardy held up a finger, he'd be right with him. Back to the phone. "So is there a time that might work better for you?"

"I'm here almost every day, this time. Beyond that, it's pretty wide open. But if you're not talking settlement . . ." He let that hang.

"I think that's premature."

"Yeah, but they crank up the criminal charges, it's going to be much more expensive."

"First they have to prove them, which they can't do."

"Yeah, well, that's what everyone thinks. Then they do. Just a friendly reminder."

"I'll keep it in mind."

"I'll be here." The line went dead.

Hardy clutched at the phone, realizing that he'd finally managed to connect with Dash Logan only to fail to discuss anything substantive about his client's case or even to make an appointment to meet with him. He looked down at the receiver. "Thanks a lot," he said. "*Dash.*"

"Dash. Hmm." Freeman moved forward into the office. "That would have been the inimitable Mr. Logan, I presume?"

"Either him or his impersonator," Hardy said, "and about as cooperative as you'd led me to expect." Suddenly Freeman's appearance in his office struck him as the unusual occurrence it was. "So what brings you up here to the nosebleed seats? Don't tell me—Phyllis quit and you wanted me to be the first to know. No, that couldn't be it. You'd have brought champagne."

"Not that," Freeman said. "Dear Phyllis is still with us."

Hardy shrugged. "Okay, then, I give up."

Freeman didn't answer right away, and that in itself was instructive. Hands in his pockets, he slouched his way across to the window, where he stared down for a moment, then turned and leaned back against the sill. "You may recall this morning we spoke about your involvement with Cole Burgess?"

"Noninvolvement," Hardy corrected him. "I was just going down to talk to him at the hospital, get his side of what happened. I did. End of story."

"So you're not representing him?"

Hardy began to shake his head no, then narrowed his eyes at the old man. "What happened?" he asked, and the questions continued to tumble out. "He tried to kill himself, didn't he? He *did* kill himself? No. Somebody else killed him, didn't they? Tell me it wasn't Glitsky."

Freeman had to chortle. "Easy, Diz, easy. He's alive as far as I know. But my trained legal mind can't help but notice that you seem to harbor a little concern for him."

"Not really that." A defensive shrug, then he gave it up. "I came away not exactly convinced that the confession is righteous."

"In what way?"

"He was in withdrawal and they promised him relief. He would have confessed to killing his mother. Hell, he might have actually killed his mother if they asked him to. In any event, it ought to be on the tape."

Freeman shook his head knowingly. "No, it won't. No cop is that dumb. They make the promise off camera, then sweat him on it." He straightened up and sighed heavily. "Either way, though, whether he did it or not, the boy's got worse problems than he had this morning."

"That'd take some doing."

"Well, listen up. Evidently some doing got done." Freeman filled him in on Sharron Pratt's speech at the Commonwealth Club.

By the end of the recital, Hardy had lowered himself down into a chair opposite the couch. His expression was one of shock and disbelief. He finally managed a word. "Death?"

Freeman nodded. "Unequivocally. And the arraignment is tomorrow morning."

"But Pratt's never even asked for specials before."

"She is now. She called it a sea change in her policy. Get tough, get votes."

Hardy still couldn't imagine it. "But he has no priors. They'd never ask for death on a guy with no record." Freeman had no reply, but Hardy kept arguing. "Death isn't possible for any number—"

"It is if she can prove first degree with specials."

"But she can never hope to get a jury to do that. Even if he did kill Elaine, he was drunk or stoned or both at the time. Everybody admits that, even the cops. So you got a guy with no priors and serious psychiatric and substance issues. They don't get death. It's just not doable."

"Maybe not, assuming he's got a good attorney." It was getting dark outside and the room wasn't bright, but Freeman's eyes shone in the dimness.

"Don't give me that look, David."

All innocence, Freeman spread his hands. "No look," he said.

"I didn't say he didn't do it." Hardy filled his lungs and let out the air in a whoosh. "I said I thought his confession might have been coerced. That's not saying he didn't do it. There's a lot of other evidence."

"I'm sure there is." Freeman waited, his basset eyes unmoving. "But the death penalty?"

"She can't go there," Hardy said calmly. "That's just flat wrong."

"I thought you might feel that way." The old man's poker face gave nothing away—even his eyes had gone flat. "You don't want the case, I'm on it. But you're already there, he thinks he's your client. You've successfully defended death penalty cases before. You hate Pratt and everything she stands for, especially this decision."

Hardy stood up abruptly, walked over to his desk, tapped it a few times with his knuckles, then turned back to face the old man. "So what am I going to do?"

Freeman nodded. "I guess that's what I came up here to find out."

2

Glitsky left the office early, carrying the videotape that contained the Burgess confession tucked into the inside pocket of his heavy shepherd's jacket. Back home, at a few minutes after five, he walked purposefully through the kitchen and down the hallway to the room on the left that had until recently been Orel and Jacob's bedroom. Now Jacob was nineteen and living in Milan, the half-black cop's son actually getting small parts as an operatic baritone. Isaac, Abe's eldest boy, had left the home, too. He was now a senior at UCLA, majoring in economics, pulling down a four-point. Orel had moved down the hall to Isaac's old room.

He walked the few steps over to the VCR, punched the power button, pulled the videotape from his pocket. Suddenly some sense of the place stopped him. His shoulders settled imperceptibly. He laid the tape on top of the television, raised his eyes to glance around the room.

He closed his eyes, feeling it the way it was only yesterday, though that was four years ago. The two boys had their bunk beds against that wall where the couch was now. And here, at the oak entertainment center, had been the pair of back-to-back desks where they did homework and piled their stuff. There had been junk everywhere—hockey sticks and football pads, every type of ball in the known world, sports and music posters all over the walls. The ineradicable smell, the incessant noise. Isaac still at home, his room down the hall. The growing boys filling every speck of the place with life, with potential.

And Flo. Flo singing in the kitchen or humming quietly at the living room table where she did the bills. She was always singing or humming. She'd had a beautiful voice, a deep and rich contralto. Glitsky was sure that was where Jacob got his. His wife hadn't really been much of a softie, but she had loved melodic ballads, show tunes—"Over the Rainbow," "Till There Was You," "The Rose." Her favorite song from the day he'd met her was "Unchained Melody." It was as though the song were part of her very being. She'd be combing her hair, unaware that she was singing, and Abe would stop whatever he was doing, caught in it.

He made it a point to keep his guard up, but now, somehow, it had fallen. Standing there in his boys' old bedroom, inside a memory he never consciously decided to dredge up, he started to allow himself to hear her singing it once again.

Oh, my love, my darling . . .

The room came up at him. He put a hand to his eyes. "Lord," he whispered.

Blindsided, he found himself over on the couch, wondering what had hit him. At the same time knowing what it was. Finally amazed in some way that these bouts occurred as infrequently as they did.

It was Elaine's death, he decided. Stirring up all the other gunk.

That, and the Treya Ghent interview this morning. That still nagged at him, too—not only the lack of any tangible result about the Burgess case but the reaction he'd had to her.

The door to his office.

The foolish, immature way he'd handled the visit from Hardy, who deserved better than that.

He wasn't under constant attack here at home. He couldn't be seen, didn't have to work so hard to hide whatever might be troubling him. So all of it—Flo and the older kids being gone, Elaine, everything—all of it had bubbled over for a minute. Here, where it was safe. That was all it had been.

Okay, now he had himself back under control. He was in his TV room. It wasn't some loaded mnemonic weapon. It was four walls, a window, door and closet, some inexpensive, durable new furniture. In three steps, he was back at the VCR, where he inserted the tape and turned on the television.

•   •   •

Frannie reached Hardy before he'd left the office. She'd heard of a great new restaurant that they needed to try and she'd been able to get last-minute reservations. So instead of the Shamrock, for their date could he meet her at the Redwood Room in the Clift Hotel?

Since this was less than a dozen blocks from where he worked, he told her he thought it might be possible. "No promises, but a pretty good chance."

"Well, I shall arrive in ribbons and curls at seven sharp," she said in her most cultured high-British tones. "If you're not there to meet me, someone else will ask for my company and I expect I'll have to go off with another escort."

"I expect you would," he replied drily.

"It's the great curse of a certain superficial charm, the swarms of men."

"I can only imagine."

"Though one's heart is set on one's husband."

"Of course. He shall then redouble his efforts to be prompt."

"In that event, sir, I shall reward those efforts."

"One's heart soars at the possibilities. Until then, then?"

"Until then. Ciao."

Smiling, he put the receiver in its cradle.

He hadn't moved a muscle when the phone rang again. He snatched it back up—"Dismas Hardy"—and Glitsky was on the line, speaking without preamble. "What are you doing?"

"Just a moment, let me check. I seem to be talking on the telephone."

"Are you going to be there for a while?"

"I'm meeting Frannie in an hour and a half."

"That's enough time."

"For what?"

"To see the Burgess tape."

Hardy sat forward, his hands suddenly tight around the receiver. "What about it?"

"I brought it home. Just watched it through for the first time. Compared it to the initial incident reports. I thought you'd like to take a look at what I've got."

This was highly unusual. Hardy and Glitsky might be friends, but the police did not make evidence available to defense attorneys. That role—called discovery—was the exclusive providence of the District Attorney. But Hardy wasn't about to look a gift horse in the mouth.

"The video of the confession?" he said. "You could probably talk me into it."

There was an emptiness in the line, then Glitsky cleared his throat. "I also wanted to apologize."

"All right. If that was it, it's accepted. You should know that I've got a few questions of my own."

Glitsky responded with a long silence. Then: "I can be there in a half hour."

The confession was near the end of the sixth hour of tape. Cole was speaking in a voice thick with fatigue. The camera was on him the whole time—one continuous shot of an exhausted man sitting at a table in a small room, patiently reciting his part without any animation.

It took seven minutes to watch it once. They immediately rewound and were midway through the second viewing when Hardy stopped the picture. "Here," he said, "right here." He pressed play again.

On the screen, Cole was answering an interrogator's question about the actual moment of the shooting. "I don't know, I'm maybe ten feet behind her. She's just turned into the alley."

The interrogator asked what he did next.

"She just got in the shadow, so it was real dark."

"Go on."

"What do you want me to say?"

"Just what happened. Tell us in your own words what happened."

"Okay." A long hesitation. "I shot her?"

"Is that a question? I don't know if you shot her. You tell me. Did you shoot her?"

Cole's confused eyes flicked somewhere out of the camera's line of vision, then came back. "Yeah, I did. I shot her then. When she got in the shadow."

"And what did you do then?"

"Well . . . she fell and I, I remember I walked over to her. She was this shape on the pavement, so I crossed over to her. And then the purse and the necklace and so on."

"What about the gun?"

"The gun? Oh yeah. I put it down on the street for a minute. The necklace . . . I needed two hands. Then the cop car hit me with the light and I remembered I had to get the gun."

"And then?"

"Then I started running."

The two men were watching, maintaining an uneasy silence on either end of the couch. Hardy hit the remote and the screen went black. He spoke into the air in front of them. "Close contact wound. The gun was right up against her head, right. And she didn't fall hard. She was wearing hosiery that would have ripped or run or something. Somebody did her right next to her, then caught her and laid her down."

"Not somebody." Glitsky answered. "Burgess."

Hardy threw him a skeptical look. "Maybe. Maybe not. But Cole was ten feet behind her, and as drunk as we know he was, how did he put one shot perfectly into the exact base of her skull in the dark with a gun just three inches long?" Hardy thought he'd serve his client better by being straight with Glitsky than by keeping the letter of the attorney-client privilege. "He told me he didn't remember shooting the gun, but thought he must have."

"Thought he must have." Glitsky dipped into his own well of skepticism. "There's a phrase. Did he mention why?"

"They ran GSR"—gunshot residue analysis—"and he had it on his hands."

"I'm not surprised," Glitsky said drily. "He fired the gun, that's why." A pause. "Probably twice, in fact."

"Probably twice. Talk about a phrase." Hardy looked him a question.

Abe gave it up. "You'll find out anyway. One of the arresting officers, Medrano, says in his report that the gun went off when they were chasing him."

"Went off?"

"Yeah."

"Well, Abe, while we're talking fascinating turns of phrase. The gun 'went off'? That's a funny way to put it, don't you think?"

No response.

Hardy continued. "You're a street cop in a dark alley with one body already down. You're on foot after a fleeing suspect, the adrenaline's off the charts and you're on full alert, right? You're telling me you hear a gunshot but you're sure the gun *just went off*? It wasn't a shot at your own self. But you're *positive*? Enough that you don't shoot back. I don't think so."

"It's a stretch," Glitsky said.

"It's more than that, Abe." Hardy was fiddling with the remote again. "Now on top of that, we've got this—this is the part I really don't like."

Cole was back up on the screen: "I, I remember I walked over to her. She was this shape on the pavement, so I crossed over to her."

Hardy stopped the tape, gave Glitsky his full face. "Notice he says 'I remember.' What I think is that right here suddenly Cole came back to what he *really* remembered. Not what Ridley Banks wanted him to say. Did you hear? He says he *crossed over* to her. Does that sound like something you'd say if you'd just shot somebody point-blank from behind? And while we're on that, how does a drunk junkie get close enough to Elaine Wager in a dark alley to press a gun to the back of her head? If it was a street mugging, he grabs her purse and runs."

The lieutenant nodded ambiguously. Hardy could hear Glitsky's heavy, nearly labored breathing and suddenly he needed to stand up. Walking over to his dartboard, he pulled the three customs from it, walked to the tape line on the floor and threw them back where they'd been. Sliding a haunch back onto his desk, he looked across at his friend. "Somebody hit her."

Abe's eyes met Hardy's. "Cole Burgess."

"Really?"

Glitsky raised his eyes, let out a long breath. "The confession's bad, that's all. Ridley got a little too enthusiastic sweating him. It was my fault. I gave him the message."

Hardy's mind raced over the variables in the situation. It was ugly from any angle. If Pratt hadn't already formally charged Cole with special circumstances murder—and it wouldn't surprise him to learn that she'd rushed the paperwork through—she'd at least gone public with her position. More, she's made it the centerpiece of her new campaign. In the city's reality, there was no chance that she would be flexible.

This meant that the progress of Cole's prosecution was no longer in Abe's jurisdiction. The police had done their job, arresting a guilty suspect. If now the department hesitated even slightly *after Cole had already confessed,* there would be no end to the political ramifications.

Hardy wanted to offer some solace, but the pickings were slim. As the head of homicide, Glitsky had overreacted, leading his troops into unsafe and even forbidden territory. As a result, a man was looking at the death penalty and some of the evidence might be tainted. And nobody could afford to question it in public.

Glitsky got up. He walked over to the window and stood looking down into the darkened street.

"You all right, Abe?"

"The confession can't be part of it."

"It might be more than that."

Glitsky knew what Hardy was implying, but he shook his head no. "Don't kid yourself, Diz. It's Burgess all right. And now I've jeopardized taking him down." When he spoke again, it was all but to himself. "I'm too close. I can't be in this."

"What do you mean?" Hardy asked.

Glitsky turned to him. "I mean why Elaine? That's what I keep thinking about? Why Elaine?" Hardy couldn't remember ever seeing Abe so distraught, so downright human. Even while his wife was dying, he had kept his public facade in place. And now he was in visible pain.

His wife's theory on the nature of Glitsky's true involvement with Elaine Wager teased at Hardy. "I didn't realize you two were that close."

Glitsky's head went down. He parted the blinds with his fingers, let them go. When he raised his head again, he was biting at his lip. He stared ahead into nothing. "All right," he said at last.

And told him.

Frannie wore a basic black cocktail dress. Pearls. Spaghetti straps over her lovely shoulders, which were often lightly freckled during the summer, but now—midwinter—the color of cream. Her bright red hair was severely pulled back, held with a thick gold ribbon. She was waiting at the bar, one knee crossed over the other, a lot of fine leg showing.

The enormous, high-ceilinged Redwood Room, paneled with an entire tree's worth of wood—hence its name—is one of the more elegant and festive locations in a city that is packed with them. Standing in the room's doorway, catching sight of his beautiful wife, listening to the first-rate piano music, Hardy could almost for a moment forget the case that, now that he'd seen the "confession," promised to dominate his life for at least the near future.

He fancied that this was the way San Francisco used to be. Or, if not that, surely how it liked to remember itself. Hardy wore jeans and corduroys with his sweatshirts around the house, but he gloried in the fact that he lived among people who sometimes dressed for dinner, who lived a bit on the large side of life, celebrating the good things in it. Thank God.

But it wasn't just the physical confidence on display wherever he looked. This room was an oasis in the vast desert of cultural vulgarity. It fairly buzzed with energy and optimism, sure, but that was because there wasn't one television set to assault your peace and insult your intelligence. No advertising posters desecrated the walls. He loved the place. He loved his wife for thinking to meet here, for the reservations she'd made to wherever the great new place might turn out to be.

Unconsciously, he straightened his tie, checked himself in the mirror, thinking that it was just plain neat to be a part of this, San Francisco at the turn of the new millennium. He crossed to his wife, kissed her and got kissed back, pulled a seat at the bar, gave a last expansive glance around at the glorious room. "This is the way the world should be, you know that?"

The new place was called Charles Nob Hill.

Hardy gave it a ten.

They sat at a table for two in an alcove of their own. The waiter won their hearts by having the same name, Vincent, as their son. Young, knowledgeable, not too funny, he had mastered the art of appearing when needed, and otherwise being invisible. The restaurant's walls were soft to the touch, upholstered. With the candlelight and muted golden color scheme, a burnished glow filled the room. Hardy had eaten foie gras on port-poached figs, then slices of rare duck breast over some ambrosial vegetables, Frannie her raw oysters and salmon. Now they were holding hands over the table, splitting a decadent chocolate torte while they savored the last sips of their excellent Pinot Noir.

"I still can't get over it," Frannie said. "Or why he didn't tell us."

"He never even told her, Frannie."

She was shaking her head. "But I really don't understand that. How could he not tell his own daughter?"

"Maybe he thought it wouldn't help her to know." Hardy sipped his wine. "He didn't know himself until a few years ago. He didn't want to intrude."

But his wife had no doubt. "She would have wanted to know. She would have dealt with it somehow. And Abe and Loretta Wager? The senator?"

"There's that, too. The political side. Not exactly Abe's long suit, I think you'd agree."

"Although he now seems to be in it up to his neck."

Hardy nodded. "At least that far. Maybe even over his head."

"Where he can't breathe."

"I hope not."

They fiddled with the dessert crumbs. Frannie sighed. "So what is he going to do now?"

"Follow up. Try to get Pratt not to use the confession. And that isn't going to happen."

"Then what?"

"I don't know. Resign, maybe."

"Abe won't resign. The job's his life."

"He talked about it. It would be a stand against Pratt."

"I don't see that. What I see is that she'd love the brutal cops man-handling the poor but guilty suspect. She'd play it both ways." Suddenly, she put down her fork and stared across the table at her husband. "Dismas, she might even prosecute him."

"He'll be okay, Fran. He's a survivor."

But she was shaking her head again. "I'm not worried about him surviving. It's how he's going to live. He's not exactly Mr. Cheerful on his best day. Now, without a job, without something to do . . ." Her voice faded away. "And I suppose if Pratt goes ahead, you will too."

He nodded. "I already called Dorothy and Jeff. At least I've got to do the arraignment."

"And when is that?"

"That would be tomorrow morning." He made a face. "I can't let Pratt hang this kid on bad evidence."

"And of course that means your claim will have to be that somebody else killed Elaine?"

"Looks like."

"So you and Abe . . ." She gathered herself, drank off the last drops in her wineglass. "Well, maybe you both can try taking care of each other."

But he shook his head, making light of her worries. "It won't come to that. Abe and I—"

"Don't!" She pointed a finger at him. "Please don't say you're bulletproof."

"I never would," he replied. "That's David Freeman, not me. I am merely methodical and fabulously competent."

"Those are useful traits. Now why don't you use them to make Vincent materialize so we can go home and get to bed."

10

CityTalk
By Jeffrey Elliot

In a highly publicized talk before the Commonwealth Club yesterday afternoon, District Attorney Sharron Pratt put on a new hat and, like the others she's tried on in her bedeviled administration, this one doesn't fit her too well either.

Yesterday's reincarnation of our most chameleon-like elected official featured herself as the tough-talkin', straight-shootin', crime-stoppin' Avenger of Evil in our fair city. And about time, too. With a new election coming up this fall and her poll numbers at an all-time low, Ms. Pratt needed something to perk up her fuzzy-headed liberal image and lackluster conviction rate.

Although she has gone to bat big-time for the interests of her political cronies and contributors, especially in the ongoing Gironde matter—at this rate we may never have a finished airport—this district attorney has declined to prosecute any number of lower-profile offenses, including prostitution, recreational drug use, vagrancy, trespassing, vandalism (especially graffiti-tagging, which she terms a "creative expression of underprivileged youth") and many others, up to and including murder if it appears the death might have been motivated by the proper political position. If it's not Ms. Pratt's kind of law, she's not going to prosecute anyone for breaking it.

Nevertheless, yesterday's talk marked a breakthrough, as it seemed to acknowledge for the first time that at least part of her job as the city's chief prosecutor is to put criminals behind bars. Actually, in a flurry of hyperbole, she took things rather farther than that, actually going so far as ask for the death penalty for the young man who is accused—though note, not yet convicted—of killing former assistant district attorney Elaine Wager.

The man's name is Cole Burgess. He is my brother-in-law. He is twenty-seven years old, a college graduate, a homeless person and a heroin addict. Though he has confessed to the crime, he does not remember committing it. He expects to plead not guilty, and a jury will have to convict him, then sentence him to death. To do so, it will have to ignore the man's blood-alcohol level as well as the fact that he was suffering from heroin withdrawal. The jury will need to overlook that, except for drugs, Cole Burgess has little criminal history, much less a history of violence. He is no worse than two dozen other murderers where Ms. Pratt has declined to ask for special circumstances, much less death.

And yet she has already passed her verdict on Mr. Burgess, and has rendered her judgment. Politics dictate that she must call for the death penalty.

The district attorney has chosen well the first victim of her war on crime. Cole Burgess isn't going to have many defenders. A straight white male, he is politically unconnected in our Balkanized burg. As a homeless man, he is already hated by the majority of San Francisco's citizens, who have grown weary of panhandlers and bums. As a heroin addict, he is confused, outcast and without hope.

One is hard-pressed to believe that Ms. Pratt does not know all this, and has not considered it cynically. But it will get her votes, and she's going to need every last one.

She should be ashamed of herself.

Although it wasn't ten blocks from his own duplex, Glitsky had never before been to the home of the chief of the Inspectors' Bureau, Captain Frank Batiste.

Now, still before eight o'clock this miserable morning, he found himself shrouded in fog, ringing the doorbell on the front porch of a charming Victorian house on Cherry Street. He'd passed from the sidewalk up through a trimmed yard. A couple of matching white wicker chairs claimed some proprietary spots on the porch, thriving plants sprouted out of pots all over the place. For a fleeting moment, he felt a stab of envy. Batiste had been Glitsky's immediate predecessor as head of homicide. Other cops whose careers had followed pretty much the same trajectory as his own, how could they live in such serenity? How did they get there? Not that his place was a dump, he didn't think so, anyway. It was clean, but . . .

The thought, unwelcome in any case, got interrupted by the door opening, Batiste's honest face, his hand outstretched. "Hey, Abe. You're the first one here, come on in."

"Sorry to bother you at home, Frank."

A "get real" look. "Please. You want some coffee? No, I remember." Batiste snapped his fingers. "Tea. Earl Grey okay?"

"Better than that."

"Good."

They walked the long hallway to the back, Glitsky vaguely aware of the family pictures all along the wall, the dozens of sports trophies on a long, thin table. He'd known Frank for twenty years and was hardly aware that he was married, much less the father of what looked to be at least four kids.

In the kitchen, a huge black Lab lay sprawled by the back door. "That's Arlene," Batiste said, crossing over to her, petting her head. "She won't bite. In fact, she probably won't move. She might be dead, I'm not sure." He grabbed a handful of pelt and pulled it back and forth. "Arlene, you dead yet?"

The giant old dog opened one eye and Batiste lit right up. "Whoa! Arlene. Putting on a show for our guest, now, aren't you?" He turned to Abe. "She must like you." Then, an afterthought. "Not dead."

After he'd left Hardy's office the previous night, Abe had paid a call on his old, wise father, Nat. They'd shot things around awhile, and when they'd finished, Abe had called the captain. He and Batiste had served together in the homicide detail. They had a long professional history and understood each other, especially in their shared belief that politics sucked.

In the past couple of years, Glitsky had realized with certainty that in spite of his exalted rank, Frank was at odds with the movers in the department. The chief, Dan Rigby, inhabited a different landscape, seldom venturing from the rarefied air of policy—money, budgets, numbers, arrest rates, diversity issues. Rigby "interfaced" with the other city departments—the mayor's office, the D.A., all the crap for which Glitsky had no use.

And in this, he was sure that Batiste was still a cop's cop, and hence his ally.

Which was why he'd finally called him and laid out his role in this situation, clearly and without any excuses. He admitted that things had gone wrong in the Burgess case from the very beginning, and it had largely been because of him, his influence, his attitude.

Abe didn't feel he could do much in the way of correcting things until he'd first cleared the slate with his coworkers, with Batiste, Medrano and Petrie, with Ridley Banks. That matter of honor was his priority. After that, he could take his fight anywhere else he needed, but not without telling his men first. He also wanted the coroner, John Strout, to hear what he had to say. So Batiste had suggested the early morning meet.

It was a modern kitchen and Batiste moved about it easily. He produced a genuine whistling teakettle, then a separate teapot. He spooned leaves from a porcelain canister into a silver ball and closed it up, dropping it into the pot. "Be a minute," he said, then added, without missing a beat, "So. This thing's going to heat up?" He wasn't talking about the teakettle.

Arms crossed and face set, Batiste stood leaning against his kitchen counter. The rest of them had taken seats around a battered wooden plank kitchen table that had seen a zillion meals—the remnants of some recent ones still remained.

Glitsky finished his spiel and scratched at a petrified lump of ketchup, waiting for the reactions. Judging from the body language and the palpable air of tension in the room, they were not going to be positive.

Arlene, still not dead, groaned in the agonies of some dog dream.

Inspector Ridley Banks scraped his chair forward, straightening up at the table. His face was a dark mask, the voice strained. "The man confessed, Abe. On tape, he admits he shot her."

"That's right. And that's why we're here, Rid." Glitsky didn't blame Ridley for his fury. He had given his lieutenant what he had wanted. Now, because of it, he was screwed. "The message here today is that the buck stops with me on this one. I'm taking the heat."

"If we dump the confession," Ridley said.

This, of course, wasn't the job of the police, but Glitsky knew what he meant. "If we go to the D.A., yeah . . ."

"And you want to run by me again why we want to do that?" Ridley's insubordinate tone would ordinarily have drawn a rebuke, but not today.

"Because of what I just told you," Glitsky replied. "There are problems matching what Burgess said with what apparently happened."

"So what? There's always problems. The guy confessed. He had the GSR . . ."

As Batiste had noted, things were heating up. "It's not about guilt, Rid. Nobody's talking about guilt. But there's going to be a hearing on the confession, and I'm going to tell the truth."

Ridley glared. "You're saying I'm not?"

"No. I'm not saying that."

"You weren't in the room, Abe. I was."

"I saw the tape, Rid. I know what I told you to do."

"And I did it. By the book. It's my ass on—"

"Guys, guys. Easy." This was Batiste, stepping in. I think the point is we're trying to get clear here on the confession. Isn't that right, Abe?"

Glitsky nodded.

"Excuse me, sir." Ridley hadn't cooled off much. He was talking to Batiste, not Abe. "I must be missing something. I got a confession from this dirtball. Anybody see on the tape where I'm telling him he gets some smack if he talks? No? No, I don't think so. What? I'm an idiot?"

"Nobody's saying that, Rid." Glitsky again.

"No? That's funny. 'Cause it sounds like you're saying I made him lie, then tried to hide it off tape."

"No. Only that he should have been cleared by the paramedics and I ordered otherwise."

"Uh-uh, no." Banks wasn't having it. "You didn't sweat him. I did. It's me on the tape. And it's a righteous confession."

"I don't think so," Glitsky said. "A good chunk of what he said is just wrong. He said he *crossed over to her*. After she was shot. *He remembered* she was this lump on the ground."

The lanky coroner figured it was time he got on the boards. Meeting the eyes of the men around the table, he stretched out his arms and cracked his knuckles, inserting his laconic drawl into the silence. "She was shot with the gun right up against her hair. There wasn't no abrasions on her knees, legs, anywheres. She was laid down gentle as you please."

Glitsky, the voice of reason. "Burgess was drunk as a lord, Ridley. If he'd tried to hold her up and let her down easy, he'd have fallen with her."

"Maybe he did," the inspector replied. "He fell under her, broke her fall." He turned to Strout. "No abrasions then, am I right, John?"

Strout cast a glance at Glitsky. "It could have happened."

Banks continued. "I really don't see the problem, Abe. I didn't put a gun to this kid's head and make him talk."

"He wasn't in withdrawal? He wasn't just agreeing to what you said?"

"Maybe. I don't remember exactly, it was a long day. But either way, nobody's gonna prove it. And even if he was, what of it? He could tell the truth and get the interrogation over with. So for once in his life the scumbag made a good decision."

"The details are all wrong."

"So his brain's fried. He gets things wrong. Big surprise. Let a jury work it out. We got plenty, more than enough to charge him. Isn't that what we do?"

Glitsky was unwilling to give it up. "We can't get him this way. That's all I'm saying."

Banks shook his head. "Burgess was there, Abe. He took her stuff, he had the gun, he *fired* the gun, *he fucking said he did it,* all right? Jesus. So he changes his story when he starts feeling better? Who wouldn't?"

Batiste cleared his throat. "Abe?"

The lieutenant raised his eyes.

"It's admirable that you wanted to protect your men when you thought you'd pushed them to excesses, but I don't see evidence that anything went too far here. I'm coming down with Ridley. Going back to Pratt at this point would be pointless. We're going to stand behind the confession. *We're* going to stand together on it . . ." He let that hang, the message clear.

Glitsky, defeated, scanned the faces around the table. "Well," he said, "I want to thank you all for coming."

11

Hardy checked his watch—8:35. Cole was already supposed to have been delivered. After his experience at the jail three days ago, he was finding himself challenged in the patience arena regarding the jail's employees. But here in the hallway behind the courtrooms on the second floor of the Hall of Justice, he knew that five minutes was a unit of time that had no real meaning. Until somebody was at least fifteen minutes late, they were on time, so he cooled his heels outside the holding cell behind Department 11 and tried to ignore the show, which—given the traffic—was not all that easy.

The hallway, which ran most of the length of the building behind the courtrooms, hummed with life or, more precisely in Hardy's view, with lowlife. Defendants in their orange jumpsuits went shuffling and clanking along—in handcuffs and sometimes chains—escorted by their bailiffs. This was the morning delivery from the jail next-door to the courtrooms here, a steady and depressing parade.

It reminded him of nothing so much as a zoo, the inmates chained and moved from one cage to another by their handlers, who only forgot the dangerous nature of their charges at their own peril. Hardy had been here a hundred times and it never failed to depress him, because in fact he knew that every one of these defendants was a human being who'd been born with rights, dignity, hope. Even, in most cases, a mother and perhaps a father who had loved them, at least for a while. Now, here, they were reduced to little more than animals—to be caged and controlled.

Sadly, he realized that this was pretty much the way it had to be if the system was to handle them. Because he didn't fool himself—nearly all the inmates passing him had lost their hope, abandoned their dignity, forfeited all but their most basic rights.

He wished they'd hurry up and deliver Cole. He'd be ready for Prozac himself by the time his client arrived. So he leaned against the cell door, then went inside and sat. He put his briefcase on the concrete bench, intending to take the opportunity to get some paperwork out of the way, keep his attitude up.

But it wasn't to be.

He saw the whole thing, since he was just checking the holding cell for Cole's arrival one last time when it began. He heard the bell of the elevator and, as the doors cracked open, the sharp command. "Move it! Move it! Now!" From the tone, something was already going very wrong.

Looking over, he was watching as something huge filled the elevator door opening. Two bailiffs stood slightly behind and to either side of a gigantic Samoan. The man probably weighed three hundred pounds. The bailiffs had no room to move.

The man was handcuffed but not shackled. He wore a hair net. The jumpsuit he'd been issued didn't even come close to covering the enormous flesh of his tattooed torso; the sleeves ended midway between the elbow and the wrist. Hardy didn't know what had been going on in the elevator, but by the time the doors opened, the inmate's face was a mask of rage.

One of the bailiffs prodded him—it didn't seem to Hardy as though it was the first time—and suddenly, with a true primal scream, the man slammed himself backwards into the bailiff. Then, with surprising agility, he shifted and body-slammed the other guard into the elevator's walls.

The two guards were both on the floor.

"Jesus Christ!" Hardy leaped back toward the holding cell, putting distance between himself and the Samoan, who was exploding out of the elevator in his direction.

But everyone on the floor had heard the scream, and now doors were opening all over the place, alarms going off, bailiffs appearing from courtrooms, judges from their chambers, other inmates—already under escort—starting to get into it.

A Klaxon sounded and voices were yelling "Lock it down! Lock it down!"

The Samoan had obviously been in the hallway before and knew just where he wanted to go. He broke left in a shambling run, taking out another bailiff who was, stupidly, trying to pull his radio and perhaps try to fight it out in a hallway jammed with humanity.

Stopping the man was going to be a problem.

The Samoan had reached the end of the hall, bailiffs and other inmates hugging the walls lest they be crushed in the rush. But there was no real way out. The same alarm that sounded the Klaxon effectively closed off the corridor, automatically locking the double doors at the end of it. By the time the Samoan realized he couldn't open them and turned again for another run at the hallway, three bailiffs stood in his way, as well as three uniformed officers with their guns drawn.

Hardy heard another scream, an anguished and rage-driven cry. Other bailiffs and cops were backfilling behind the original six until, in under another minute, a phalanx had formed, effectively sealing off any possibility of escape.

The Samoan turned back to the locked doors. Turned around again, held his cuffed hands out in front of him. "Shoot me," he screamed. "Please, shoot me."

Because of the incident, Cole was even later. He told Hardy that they'd picked him up at the hospital during the night, and this had obviously disturbed his beauty rest. In his orange jumpsuit, with his slack posture and unkempt hair, the boy appeared malnourished and pathetic. But Hardy thought his eyes were clearer than they had been the day before. That wasn't saying much, but it was something, and this morning Hardy would take whatever he could get.

He was still shaken by what he'd witnessed. A little more critical mass of inmates and it would have been a riot. Another rush by the Samoan and he would have been shot dead. Instead, he had finally gone terrifyingly quiet. He sat on the floor and let them come and shackle him and take him away, belted down to a gurney.

Cole sat on the concrete bench. Hardy had already done enough time on the damn thing this morning—he was standing now, leaning back against the door.

Because the morning's routine had been so violently interrupted, they weren't going to get much time to work out any kind of strategy—but Hardy wanted to get at least a few things straight if he was going to defend this boy. The plea. Bail. Money. Timing issues.

But again, it wasn't going to be that simple.

"What's waiving time mean?" Cole asked after Hardy had told him he was going to have to do just that.

To Hardy, this was merely a logistical detail. Cole had an absolute right to a speedy trial. In practice, though, defendants very rarely wanted one. The conventional wisdom was that it was always to the defendant's advantage to delay. Delay put off an eventual verdict, and until a verdict was rendered, you were presumed innocent, a small detail but a critical one. Delay also provided the opportunity for key witnesses to get run over by a bus or disappear or forget what they had once clearly remembered, thereby strengthening your case. The victim or the family of the victim might lose emotional fire, the need for revenge or, if the delay was long enough, sometimes even closure. The cop who arrested you might get another job. D.A. priorities could change and you could get offered a better deal to cop a plea.

The possibilities varied, but the general rule held true: A continuance is half a dismissal. Delay was a good thing.

Hardy tried to explain this to Cole. "The courts are so backed up that no judge wants to assign a preliminary hearing in ten days, so we just say we're okay with putting it off for a few months . . ."

"A few months?"

"Maybe. Longer if we can."

Cole was shaking his head. "And I stay in here? No way. I can't do that."

"I hate to break it to you, Cole, but you have to do that. You've got a D.A. who's talking death penalty to help her get elected, so at the very least we want to put off the trial until after the election, which is next November, nine months. At least."

But Cole was still shaking his head, frowning, struggling with it. "I can't stay in here for nine months," he said. "I'd die."

"You've got a lot better chance of dying shooting smack for nine months out on the street."

But this fell on deaf ears. "No."

"Cole, listen . . ."

"I can't be here for nine months! Do you hear me?"

It was a violent outburst, and after the morning's earlier events, it got people's attention up and down the hall. A bailiff was outside the cell before Hardy had any time to react on his own. "Everything all right here?"

After assuring him that it was, Hardy watched the man move uneasily off, then turned back to Cole. "If you go to trial now, Cole, with the city still pretty inflamed over Elaine's death, some of the jurors will undoubtedly—"

"I can't," Cole interrupted. "I just can't. My mom says you can get me off."

"I haven't even talked to your mother yet, Cole. And I can't get you off in ten days. If nothing else, I'll need more time just to decide how I'm going to approach the damn thing."

"Just say I didn't do it."

"Did you do it?"

He shrugged.

Hardy got a little short. "Because you've already said you did on tape, in case you don't remember. That's going to take some undoing."

"You can undo it as well now as you can in nine months, don't you think?"

"No, I don't."

The back door to the holding cell gave into the courtroom, and now that door opened and a bailiff appeared. They had called Cole's case first. "Let's roll it out, boys. Showtime."

Hardy gave his client a last look. "We'll continue this later." He stepped back and let Cole pass in front of him, out into the courtroom.

At Cole's appearance through the door, there was an audible rise from the gallery. Hardy, frustrated nearly beyond endurance, nevertheless gave his client a friendly upper-arm squeeze and urged him forward.

As they passed the prosecution table, Gabe Torrey motioned for Hardy to stop, and he let Cole go on over to the other side with the bailiff. He looked again out into the courtroom. More than a decent crowd was on hand, and it seemed restless.

Hardy knew Torrey from half a dozen other dealings, and he didn't like him. He considered the chief assistant D.A. pompous, petty and political, to say nothing of underprepared and officious. Now he would be talking death penalty and other similar nonsense, and Hardy knew it was going to get ugly, probably sooner rather than later.

Still, they'd never before crossed the line into hostility, and he saw no reason to go there now.

Torrey put out his hand in greeting and Hardy took it. "I just wanted to give you a little heads up, Diz. You probably heard we want to move this one along due to Elaine's standing in the community. There's a lot of outrage . . ."

Hardy listened with half an ear. He noticed the gallery again. It really was humming. Cole was turned around at the defense table. His mother was leaning over the rail, trying to talk to him, but he, too, kept his eyes mostly on the prosecution's side of the gallery, which projected a true sense of menace. This was unique in Hardy's experience—there were people in this room who hated Cole already, and he felt it.

Torrey had finished the self-serving part and was getting down to his point. ". . . with the confession on tape and all, you know I could get a grand jury indictment in five minutes, so if you're inclined to ask for a long delay, you should know I've scheduled the grand jury for next Tuesday. Unless, of course, you decide not to waive time. Then we'll do the hearing in two weeks as the law provides."

With a sick feeling, Hardy realized that Torrey was right. There were two ways by which a case got scheduled for trial. There could be a preliminary hearing to determine if the evidence was sufficient to bring to trial. Or the grand jury could come to the same conclusion and issue an indictment.

Hardy wanted to delay, but his client didn't, wouldn't. Torrey was telling him that he would seek an indictment and potentially an even earlier trial date if Hardy tried to stall on the preliminary hearing. Actually, he realized, Torrey might not understand it completely—his strategic grasp of things lawyerly had always seemed weak—but he was doing him a favor by letting him go for a preliminary hearing at all. He could indict at will. If Hardy didn't waive time, he would get at least another ten days to prepare for the hearing, maybe even get his discovery—the evidence in the case—a little earlier.

But ten days! It was an impossible joke. Still, better than a grand jury indictment.

And maybe in that time, he could at least convince Cole that it would be in his best interests to agree to a delay before they went to trial.

But either way, this thing had just jumped to the fast track, where any number of disasters were more likely to occur, and where the damage from high-speed impact was likely to be that much greater.

Hardy forced a casual smile. "It never crossed my mind to waive time."

• • •

"Cole Burgess." From his bench, Judge Timothy Hill gave it the dramatic reading. The judge was an ancient patrician. Wispy white hair, combed back over his ears, clung close to a bony skull. His skin was parchment stretched over long bones and his robe hung off him like a shroud. The physical look, combined with an utter lack of personality, had earned him the nickname of the Cadaver. But today with the full house, he possessed, if not a youthful exuberance, at least a detectable pulse. "You are charged by a complaint filed herein with a felony, to wit, a violation of Section 187 of the Penal Code in that you did, in the city and county of San Francisco, state of California, on or about the first day of February, willfully, unlawfully and with malice aforethought murder Elaine Wager, a human being."

Hardy was standing in the center of the courtroom next to Cole.

At the prosecution table, in a highly unusual appearance in an actual courtroom, Sharron Pratt had entered at the last second and taken a seat next to Gabriel Torrey. Judge Hill nodded to his clerk, who began to read out the special circumstances that could make this a death penalty case.

Driving downtown, Hardy had tried to predict what Pratt would produce on this score, but she proved more creative than he was, and he only got one out of two, a killing in the commission of a robbery. The one Hardy hadn't guessed—because it was so grossly incorrect—was a hate crime, in that Elaine Wager was black and Cole was white. And when he heard it, he had to speak up. "Your honor!"

The word seemed to strike the Cadaver with a physical force. Clearly, he did not expect any objection during the reading of the complaint. Straightening to his full height in his chair, he frowned down into the bull pen. "To what, Mr. . . ." Shuffling some paper. "Mr. . . ."

"Hardy, your honor." He was willing to risk the judge's displeasure. This idiocy could not go unquestioned, and Hill might as well get used to it early. "With respect to the second special circumstance, your honor. Regardless of who committed it, there is no race or bigotry issue associated with this crime."

The chief assistant D.A. was already on his feet. "I'm shocked to hear Mr. Hardy's characterization of the murder of a black woman by a white man . . ."

"Your honor, that's absurd. Just because someone of one race kills a person of a different race, we can't assume race is the motive."

But Torrey knew his constituency. "Any time a black person is killed in a white neighborhood, race is an issue."

Hardy came back at him. "Union Square is not a white neighborhood, your honor. It's downtown."

The Cadaver scowled down from the bench. "Enough! I know where Union Square is, Mr. Hardy. Have you got a problem with the complaint? File the appropriate motions. Meanwhile—" he looked at the prosecution table—"is this a capital case, Mr. Torrey?"

"Yes, your honor. The People seek the death penalty."

Hill nodded, keeping it moving, snapped, "Mr. Hardy, how does your client plead?"

He and Cole hadn't really formally gotten around to this, but he nudged his client and the young man looked up, very much aware. He didn't hesitate at all. "Not guilty, your honor."

An immediate and angry buzz filled the room. Hill seemed to have been expecting it. Certainly, he made no attempt to gavel things to silence. But the electricity created an opportunity, and Hardy took it to turn around and check out the gallery again.

Jeff Elliot, whose column in the *Chronicle* had already significantly raised the level of dialogue around this case, had gotten his wheelchair up to the front, and sat at the end of the first row, next to Dorothy. Significantly, Hardy thought, Jody Burgess was a couple of seats away, not right next to her daughter, the intervening spots filled with reporters.

To Hardy's left, the prosecution side of the courtroom, particularly, continued its foment. Three fourths of the gallery on that side were people of color. Hardy was again struck by the thick, nearly palpable sense of outrage he felt from Elaine's friends and colleagues. And beyond that contingent, at least a dozen young people—Hardy thought they must be students from Elaine's classes—were turning and squirming in their seats, reacting with an obvious disgust and fury.

In the front row, Hardy recognized a couple of assistant D.A.'s and the homicide inspector Ridley Banks. There was Clarence Jackman, famous lawyer from Elaine's firm, sitting next to a striking dark woman who was staring at Hardy with a smoldering malevolence. Next to her, a very handsome, early middle-age white man sat back in his seat, a statue, hands folded in his lap. Who was he? Hardy wondered.

Glitsky hadn't made it down from the fourth floor.

Finally, suddenly, Judge Hill had let it go on long enough. Perfunctorily, he tapped his gavel several times and waited for the noise to subside, then spoke to Torrey. "The People seek to deny bail?"

"Of course, your honor. This is a capital case. There can be no bail."

Hardy spoke up again. "Your honor, if it please the court . . ."

The Cadaver was losing patience with these interruptions. This was supposed to be, after all, a simple administrative procedure. He snapped out a response. "There is no bail in a capital case, Mr. Hardy."

"Yes, your honor, I'm aware of that. But again, there is no way this should be a capital case, or even a special circumstances case." Hardy took a deep breath, then forged ahead. "This charge is a clear case of politics with Mr. Burgess as the pawn. Women get raped and murdered and this D.A. doesn't allege specials; policemen get killed, no specials. Now, in an election year, all of a sudden we get not just specials but a request for death. They want my client to die, your honor, so Ms. Pratt can make a last shoddy attempt to hold on to her office. And it stinks."

"Your honor, please!" Torrey was out of his chair, his voice at full volume, and it served as a prod to the gallery, which responded with another outburst, the anger welling all around.

But this time, perhaps sensing a rising tide, Hill decided he'd better take control, and slapped his gavel hard three times in rapid succession. "There will be order in this court or I'll have the gallery cleared." He barely paused, brought his gaze back to Hardy, spoke sternly. "Now, counselor, if you want to object to the specials, write your motion, but for the moment, there they are. And bail is denied."

But Hardy's blood was up now, and he found himself unable to let it go. "In that case, your honor, before we go any further in this game of political football, I'll also be making a motion about the so-called confession that the prosecution unethically keeps putting in the newspapers."

This really set off the crowd, with several identifiable explosions— "Hey, he confessed!" "The guy did it!"—punctuating the general uproar.

The gavel banged away. But Hill's real ire had become directed at Hardy. "I'm warning you, counselor. This is not the appropriate time or place. Take it up at the prelim."

But it was as though Hardy didn't hear him. He'd had enough for today already, and his patience was at an end. He raised his own voice over the hubbub. "Your honor, Mr. Burgess was held for hours before he was charged, he also was not adequately apprised of his right to counsel—"

"That's a black lie!" Ridley Banks was up in the first row. "We Mirandized him as soon as—"

"He was drunk and barely coherent, your honor! The tape of his interrogation shows it clearly. There's no way this tape will ever be played for a jury. The prosecution has no right to try and prejudice prospective jurors by even calling it a confession."

Now, in the gallery, things were truly getting out of hand. Everyone seemed to be talking, yelling, swearing. Hardy caught a strong whiff of sweat, and couldn't say if it was Cole and his fear or the collective scent of the mob coalescing behind him.

"Sit down, everybody!" The Cadaver had finally come to life, bellowing. "Down in the gallery." He slammed his gavel again and again. "Bailiffs!" The three men in uniform appeared from their various posts around the wall and began moving up to the bar rail.

Ten minutes later, the arraignment was over. Hill called a stop to the bailiff's slow charge as they reached the bar rail. He really didn't want to have to try to remove nearly a hundred people by force. Not only would that be a bad precedent for his fellow judges, he sure as hell didn't want the word to get out that Judge Hill couldn't control his courtroom by force of will alone.

The spectators in the room settled back down. Hill denied bail again and this time nobody argued with him. When Hardy didn't waive time for the preliminary hearing, the judge asked him a second time to make sure he'd heard it correctly. Then he set the hearing for ten o'clock, Wednesday, February 17, in this same courtroom.

He ordered Cole back to the jail and called a recess. He stood without so much as a glance at anyone in the courtroom or gallery, and left the bench in a swirl of black robe.

Hardy realized that he had been lucky to escape without a contempt citation. And he really hadn't accomplished anything substantive for his client, though he'd certainly succeeded in getting the judge and half the courtroom mad at him. So as the disgruntled masses filed out behind him, he stalled for time, gathering his papers at the defense table. He knew he had a gauntlet to run on the other side of the bar rail and out in the hallway, but he felt oddly satisfied. He'd served notice—no one was railroading his client without a fight.

He felt a light touch on the back of his shoulder and turned to face the D.A. "Mr. Hardy."

He straightened up and nodded, set his jaw. "Ms. Pratt."

Hardy and Pratt had a history. A year before, he had gotten her a public reprimand from the bench for her office's cavalier abuse of the grand jury. She, in turn, had nearly filed criminal charges against Hardy for insurance fraud, and had directed her own investigators to explore Hardy's possible criminal involvement in the murder case he was defending. There was no love lost between them.

And now she had another crack at him. "That was a fairly unprofessional and tawdry display."

"Maybe it was." Hardy's lips turned upward, but no one would have called it a smile. "But I prefer that to self-righteous hypocrisy. Are you really such a political hack that you'd kill somebody for a few votes?"

Pratt turned red at the frontal assault. "Making false accusations about my motives will get you in trouble with the bar, Mr. Hardy."

Hardy nodded again. "I couldn't agree more, which is why I don't make them falsely. And while we're enjoying such a full and frank exchange of ideas, I'd be interested to hear about your decision to ask for special circumstances, much less death."

"She doesn't have to explain anything to you, Hardy." This was Torrey. Hardy had been "Diz" before the arraignment had begun, but now the gloves had come off. "You go play your cheap defense tricks, and when we get to it, we'll see what a jury thinks of them."

"What a neat idea," Hardy said. "That was kind of my plan, anyway. See what a jury thinks. If it ever gets to that, which I doubt."

"Oh, it'll get there. That's what happens when you get a confession. The presumption of guilt goes way up."

"It does? That's funny," Hardy said. "I'd always heard it was presumption of innocence."

"Your man isn't innocent."

"Well, there you go. I guess we're back to that jury thing again, aren't we?"

Torrey wore an expression of great disdain. "You knew Elaine, didn't you?"

"Yes, I did." Hardy answered without irony. "I thought she was great. And the idea that you'd want to kill somebody in her name, that makes me gag."

Torrey shook his head in disgust. "I just don't see how you can live with yourself."

"It's easy," Hardy replied. "I've got a really good personality."

"Let's go, Gabe." Sharron Pratt all but pulled him by the arm. "Oh, and Mr. Hardy? If I were you, I'd go easy on accusing me of playing politics with a man's life."

"So what would you like me to call it?"

She ignored that. "If you keep it up," she said, "I'm not going to be disposed to drop it when this is over. And you're going to be very sorry."

Hardy took that in, then nodded thoughtfully. "You know, that sounds an awful lot like a threat. Are you threatening me?"

She glared at him levelly. "You take it any way you want."

"All right," he said. "I'll take it as a threat. And as such I'll be passing it along to the Bar Ethics Committee. Since we started here talking about ethics, that'll bring us around full circle."

Torrey couldn't resist a parting remark. "You wouldn't know an ethic if it bit you on the ass."

For a long moment, Hardy gave him a flat stare. "Whoa. Clever. I've got to remember that one." He turned to gather the rest of his papers.

Hardy decided he'd just as soon forgo the excitement in the hallway outside. He was all too familiar with the back way out—it was the way he'd come in—but his client Cole had just had bail denied. Even when this was expected, and it had been, it was never an easy moment.

He caught Cole just outside the holding cell behind the courtroom. The bailiffs were busy transporting other defendants up and down from the jail, and there was another defendant and his attorney waiting in the cell itself, so they'd handcuffed Cole to the elevator bars until they could get to him, which would be when it was.

Hardy stood next to him. "We'll keep trying on the bail," he said. "It still could happen."

"So what do I do between now and the preliminary hearing?"

"We'll have to talk a lot. Maybe see if you can remember something."

But Cole didn't seem to hear him. "No," he said, as though to himself.

"No what?" Hardy asked. "You're not going to remember anything new?"

"Not that. I mean . . ." He rolled his eyes back and forth. "I mean remembering something . . . that's not what I'm thinking about."

Hardy knew what Cole was thinking about—his next hit. "That's what you ought to be thinking about, Cole. Maybe you can use the time to clean up."

A shake of the head. "No. I don't think . . ." He stopped.

This was foreign soil to Hardy. He'd of course been around for much of the beginning of the drug culture in the late sixties, early seventies, but as a marine in Vietnam, and then a cop before law school, he had grown increasingly uncomfortable with the idea of illegal substances. He'd found his excitement without resort to chemicals, and then, later—when he felt the need to escape from the pain of his failed marriage and the death of his son—he gravitated to what the Irish called the good man's weakness, drink.

But even that had never controlled him. He chose to drink, sometimes copiously, then chose when to stop.

This boy, he knew, was in a completely different world.

"Do you want to get out of it?" he asked.

He shrugged. "If I do, there's a program for it." A mirthless laugh. "There's a program for everything, isn't there?"

"It does seem like it." It surprised Hardy—this first moment of connection he'd felt with his client—but he felt the same way. Here in San Francisco, tolerance and understanding for every human frailty or aberration had been politicized, funded, institutionalized. Someone was being paid to help you with whatever ailed you in San Francisco, and if nothing ailed you, someone was being paid to find something that did. "Is there anything I can do?" Hardy asked.

Cole turned his head. "What do you mean?"

"I mean, if you decide, to move the process along, get you counseling, like that."

"Probably not." Cole let out a breath. "If it's going to happen, it falls to me." He tapped his heart. "In here."

Hardy knew that this was true, but it was still good to hear Cole say it, to acknowledge that his fate was to some extent his own responsibility. Maybe he wasn't completely lost after all.

"So what happens next," he asked, "in the law world?"

"Next I file a few motions. The stuff I was talking about in there." He pointed at the courtroom door. "The procedural problems, these special circumstances . . ."

"Will that really work?"

"In what sense?"

"I mean, if they didn't read me my rights—"

Hardy narrowed his eyes. "At the hospital the other day, you told me you didn't remember if they did. You thought not. Now you're saying 'if' . . ."

He corrected himself. "No. They told me I wasn't arrested for the murder so I didn't need a lawyer yet. They were just questioning me because I was in the alley and I ran."

"So you do remember that?"

"That was after they'd kept me for hours. I kind of woke up halfway through things. "

Hardy wasn't thrilled with the constant shifts Cole's story took, but he saw no advantage in fighting about that now. "Well, if that's really what they said, then you might have pulled yourself a break. We could get it tossed."

"I'll tell you one other thing, though. About those special circumstances." He shuddered involuntarily. "I sure as hell didn't kill that girl because she was black."

The world was suddenly still. Hardy sharpened his tone. "Then why *did* you kill her?"

"What?"

He snapped it out harshly, under his breath. "Why did you kill her, if it wasn't because she was black?"

After he'd seen Glitsky's videotape and reasoned things out for himself, Hardy had come to accept at least the possibility that Cole hadn't been the agent of Elaine's death. So he'd decided to stay with the case. But now here—apparently—was a second confession. Unsolicited, uncoerced.

Cole's face registered confusion at the rapid change in Hardy's demeanor. From protector to inquisitor in the blink of an eye. He twitched. "Hey, come on, what? All I said was it wouldn't have been because she was black."

"Wouldn't have been? Or wasn't?"

If there was a difference, Cole didn't seem to understand what it was. He strained to come up with something. "I'm saying black, white, brown. Who cares? It wouldn't have been a race thing is what I mean. I don't even think like that."

Hardy leaned in close, and this time the sweat was his client's. "You just admitted again that you killed her. Don't you understand that?"

A deer in headlights, Cole was shaking his head. "I don't know. I didn't. I said that?"

"You don't know if you killed her?"

Finally, a rise. "I don't *remember* killing her. I told you that. I don't think I killed her, but I might have . . . if I shot the gun."

"You *might have*? Cole, listen to me. You just said you didn't shoot the girl because she was black. Those were your exact words."

But he was shaking his head from side to side, side to side. "See? No. That's not what I meant."

"Okay, tell me."

He sighed deeply, did something with his hands that caused the cuffs to rattle against the bars. Hunching his head down into his shoulders, he cleared his throat, spoke in a voice barely above a whisper. "Look. If I was ever going to kill somebody, which I wouldn't, it wouldn't be because they were black, okay? So if I killed this girl . . ."

"Elaine."

"Yeah, Elaine. If I killed her—which I don't remember, so it's possible maybe I didn't, too—that wouldn't have been the reason."

"But if you don't remember killing her, why did you admit that you had?"

Cole rolled his eyes. "Didn't we already go through this? I told you. I was coming down so hard—"

Hardy reached over, put a hand on his shoulder briefly. "Stop, just stop."

But he couldn't do that. "You know, man—"

"Cole, call me Dismas, would you? Or Diz."

"Okay. But I also don't remember *not* killing her, I just don't. I don't remember the gun, how I got the gun . . ." The voice trailed off.

"Did you find it by the body? On the street, maybe?"

"It seems like."

"Before or after you saw her?"

He closed his eyes, trying to bring it back. "I don't know. It seems like before, because after . . . I mean, there was no time after, right? I'm leaning over her and the cops came."

"And you remember that?"

Cole grimaced, the effort at recall out of his reach. He shook his head hopelessly. "Not really."

Hardy leaned back again. He had lived much of his adult life as a bartender and had great respect for the effects of alcohol, but the kind of total blackout that Cole seemed to be describing was far beyond that. "Cole," he asked gently, "what do you remember after you picked up your bottle of whiskey?"

The young man raised his eyes. They had become glassy. "I don't know, man. I just don't know."

12

Taking the back steps, Hardy made it unmolested up to the fourth floor, down the long hallway, into the homicide detail. Four inspectors looked up from their paperwork, but none of them ventured any kind of greeting. Glitsky's still-pristine white door was closed again, but this time there was light behind the shade. "Somebody in with the lieutenant?" Hardy asked the room.

A mute chorus of shrugs, so he knocked.

"It's open."

He turned the knob and stuck his head in. "Actually," he said, "it was closed."

Glitsky had his feet on his desk, his fingers tented over his mouth. "Why don't you make it that way again?"

"I could do that." Hardy did, then reached across the desk, opened one of the drawers and withdrew a handful of peanuts. "I must say, though, that the old open-door policy you used to take such pride in seems to be in jeopardy, and this, in turn, might precipitate a drop in your tremendous popularity with your troops, which I'd hate to see."

It might have been in spite of himself, but Glitsky's face softened—all the way, say, from diamond to granite. "I wish I was Irish and liked to hear myself talk as much as you do."

"Were," Hardy replied.

"Were what?"

"You said 'was.' I wish I was Irish. But it's 'were.' Present conditional contrary to fact takes the subjunctive. I wish I *were* Irish. People don't seem to know that anymore."

Glitsky shook his head, pulled his feet off the desk. "That's exactly what I mean. Twenty words when five will do."

"Five can be good," Hardy replied. "Brevity and all that. But it's not all it's cracked up to be. Twenty words, if they're the right ones—and that, my friend, is the key—can be downright sublime. And, of course, though few acknowledge it anymore in our jaded age, proper use of the subjunctive is the hallmark of a civilized man."

Worn down, Glitsky finally came all the way to a smile. "Were I to care, I would make a note of it." He popped a peanut of his own. "So how'd it go downstairs?"

Hardy sat back. "I somehow escaped contempt of court, but I don't think by much." He briefly outlined the highlights of the arraignment, concluding with his surprise that Glitsky had not been in attendance. He indicated the empty desktop. "But then, seeing the piles of work you're wading through . . ."

A silence settled.

Hardy continued. "Afterwards I had another nice chat with my client. It didn't exactly perk me up. He doesn't remember anything. The night's a complete blank, which is more drunk than I've ever been."

"And you've pushed the envelope a few times if I remember, which you don't."

"From time to time in my youth. For research purposes only. Anyway, I like to consider myself an aficionado on the subject, and I've never had the kind of blackout Cole is describing, which makes me have doubts."

But Glitsky was shaking his head. "There's all kinds of new pills nowadays, Diz. The date rape drug. Also, more easily available, Halcion could do it."

"Halcion?"

"The sleeping pill. When you were doing your drink research, didn't you ever take Halcion before tying one on?"

"I don't remember, really. It's all a blank." But he broke a smile. "Just kidding. Is that what happens?"

"That's the word. Complete blackout." Glitsky glanced at the closed door. He lowered his voice anyway. "I had a meeting of my own this morning. Batiste, Ridley Banks, Strout, the guys at the scene. I wanted to talk about the problems in the tape."

"Banks was downstairs in court."

"Yeah, I figured he would be. I told him we ought to back off from the confession."

"You suggested that?" This was further than Hardy thought Abe would have taken it. "Out loud?"

"Yeah, but Ridley was a little sensitive to the idea that the confession was bogus. Seemed to think it would reflect on the way he conducted it."

"And he wouldn't be all wrong."

"And he knows that, too." The lieutenant blew out wearily. "It's tricky, Diz. These are my guys. They gave me what I asked for. I don't blame them for being ticked off."

"I don't either, but ticked off is one thing, letting a guy go down on bad evidence is another."

"Well, there you go. Anyway, my colleagues and superiors were of a like mind. There was plenty to arrest Burgess, still is. He gave us more when we talked to him. Now he goes to trial. It's not our job anymore. End of story."

It was Hardy's turn to sigh. "But it's not, Abe. You know it's not."

"Don't give me that, Diz. It might be. And don't confuse bad evidence with not guilty. Your boy killed Elaine all right. It's all about how we prove it. I want a clean case, that's all."

"I think you want more than that."

Glitsky cracked a peanut shell. "I'm trying to figure out how to conduct an investigation and get more evidence when we've got a suspect already in jail and presumably going to trial."

"Carefully." Pointing a finger, Hardy stopped his friend's response. "See? I can be brief. Pithy, even."

Glitsky was about to reply again, and again was interrupted, this time by a knock at the door. "It's open."

Hardy clucked disapprovingly. "You keep saying that."

But in an instant it was true. Standing in the doorway was Chief of Police Dan Rigby himself, accompanied by Sharron Pratt and Gabriel Torrey. An uncomfortable Frank Batiste. Behind them was an amorphous assemblage of humanity—workers from the D.A.'s office, uniformed cops, a couple of reporters, perhaps the random passerby. Hardy could see the homicide inspectors from the detail gathered around at the outer fringes.

"Well, well, well," Torrey said over Rigby's shoulders. "Isn't this cozy?"

• • •

There wasn't room for a private party in Glitsky's office, so at Rigby's command the players trooped across the homicide main room and poured themselves into one of the interrogation areas—in fact, the very one in which Cole Burgess had spent his sweat time.

Airless and without windows, with a small table now pushed against one wall and three chairs, the interrogation room probably wasn't a brilliant choice for a meeting either, but the mood was somehow, suddenly, *urgent*.

Torrey, in a kind of triumphant rage, kept repeating "I knew this. I knew it" to whomever would listen. Rigby, torn between the urge to protect one of his men and the need to contain any possible scandal on the force, wanted a door he could close with all the principals behind it, and he wanted it *now*.

"We don't need Mr. Hardy sitting in on this, Chief," said Pratt.

Rigby ignored her. He wasted no time on preamble, but turned to his homicide lieutenant and let fly. "Mr. Torrey tells me that this morning, Mr. Hardy here referred to a videotape at the arraignment on Burgess. How'd he get to see it?"

"We're nowhere near releasing discovery yet," Pratt butted in pointlessly. "He didn't get it from our office."

Everyone already knew that. Rigby kept his eyes on Glitsky. "Abe?"

But Hardy, whose slip in the courtroom had put Glitsky on this hot seat, wasn't going to let his friend burn. "I never said I saw a tape," he said. "Cole told me they'd videotaped him."

"How did he know?" Banks interjected.

"Come on. He assumed," Hardy shot back. "It's not like this is some secret procedure. Everybody gets taped."

But Torrey was ready for this denial. He pulled a piece of paper from his pocket, directed his gaze to Rigby. "Here's what Mr. Hardy said exactly. I took the liberty of having the court reporter type it up for me." He read. " 'He was drunk and barely coherent, your honor! The tape of his interrogation shows it clearly.' Sounds to me like he saw it."

Hardy wasn't backing down. "Doesn't prove a damn—"

But Glitsky put a hand on his arm. "It's okay, Diz." He turned to Rigby. "I played it for him."

After a shocked moment of silence, Banks blew out heavily. "Jesus."

Torrey pumped a fist. "Fuckin' A," he whispered.

Pratt cleared her throat. "Well, Chief, in light of this admission, you can't—"

"Sharron! Please." Rigby stopped her with his palm, turned to his chief of homicide. "Lieutenant Glitsky, are you telling me you gave evidence in a murder trial to a defense attorney. Am I hearing this right?"

Glitsky inclined his head an inch. "Yes, sir."

The chief sighed heavily. "All right." His mouth worked. He might have been grinding his teeth. "All right," he repeated. "We've got to look into this. Meanwhile . . ."

Torrey: "What's to look into? He's admitted—"

"MEANWHILE . . ." Rigby bellowed to shut him up. He turned to Batiste. "Meanwhile, Frank, I'd like you and Abe to meet me up in my office in"—he checked his watch—"thirty minutes. Lieutenant, if you'd like to bring a grievance officer along with you, that might be prudent. Everybody else"—his voice hardened—"I'd appreciate it if anything mentioned behind these doors stays here until I can prepare a statement after we get to the bottom of what went on." He glared at Pratt and Torrey. "And if there is a statement to make, we'll make it together. Is that clear?"

"We can agree to that," Pratt stated.

"Though it should be sooner rather than later," Torrey added.

"As soon as the facts are in," Rigby replied crisply. He cast a last slow look around the room, finally rested on Glitsky, shook his head. "Jesus Christ, Abe," he said under his breath, "what were you thinking?"

Then he turned the knob and was out the door, leaving it open behind him.

Gene Visser's law enforcement career began in a promising fashion. He spent three years working the streets in a squad car, then got moved up and earned a stripe and an inspector's job in burglary. After three years in that department, he put two more in vice, took the sergeant's exam, and applied for the next opening as inspector of homicide, which was pretty much the top rung in the ladder for working cops. When he got that promotion at thirty, he was one of the youngest inspectors ever to attain that rank and position.

But Visser had a couple of character flaws that were going to negatively impact his aspirations on the force. The first one was a tendency to theorize before all the evidence was in. He'd get a feeling about who among the various suspects in a case was the most likely culprit, and he'd focus his energies trying to prove his point. The first couple of cases he'd handled, this approach had even worked—quite often, the guy who looks like he did it actually did.

But not always.

And the law of averages—along with the complexity of motives and situations in real-life homicides—finally caught up with him in a high-profile case.

This was where his second major failing—a lack of focus regarding loyalty—came into play. Visser thought it only made sense to have friends in the press and the D.A.'s office as well as with the police. It couldn't hurt to give a reporter a little advance heads up on what might be coming down the pipeline, sometimes before it was supposed to be public. These people—the D.A.'s and reporters—after all, were the end users of his product. They ought to be entitled to an early look.

And in their zeal for convictions (pre-Pratt), the occasional prosecutor would sometimes use Visser to funnel something to the press that they couldn't say themselves. If you were nice to reporters, they were nice to you in print. It was you scratch my back, I'll scratch yours. Visser may even have thought that everybody did it, although in this belief he was mistaken.

Until one day, stunned, he found himself transferred out of homicide. Soon he found it prudent to resign and get another job as investigator for the district attorney's office, where he was pretty much like a police inspector, but not really.

That new position lasted only eighteen months. He could have stayed on, of course—he hadn't really done anything wrong—but he felt frozen out. He became the prosecutor's last choice if they needed a real investigator. Finally, deeply embittered by the system that had rejected him, he quit and, encouraged by several defense attorneys with whom he'd become friendly and who promised him steady work, he hung up a shingle as a private investigator.

Visser had once been handsome, with a full head of sandy-colored hair, chiseled cheekbones, a well-trimmed goatee. In the decade since he'd had his own business, though, he'd gained forty pounds and two inches of forehead. He'd also lost the facial hair that had hid his chins. Now the skin of his face stretched tightly over too much flesh through which smallish eyes perpetually seemed to squint.

Right now he was on his way to see Dismas Hardy's client Rich McNeil at Terranew Industries. He didn't have an appointment; that wasn't his style. McNeil's office was on one of the upper floors of the company's headquarters on California Street halfway up to Nob Hill. The room was of reasonable size, with modern furnishings, built-in bookshelves, windows on two of the walls looking out over downtown. When his secretary buzzed him and said a private investigator with the Manny Galt case was outside, he let himself hope that maybe Hardy had hired a PI, and maybe he had come up with some good news about something and couldn't wait to tell McNeil directly.

But as soon as he saw Visser, he realized that this was wishful thinking. This beefy hunk of trailer trash couldn't be Hardy's man. Still, McNeil had let him into his office, so he'd be polite. He rose out of his seat, came around his desk, extended his hand. "Mr. Visser. Rich McNeil. What can I do for you?"

The big man's grip crushed his hand. Intimidation with a smile. "Thanks for seeing me on such short notice. You mind if I sit down a minute?"

McNeil opened and closed his hand, relieved that it still seemed to be working. "Not at all. I'm afraid I don't have a lot of time, but . . ."

"I won't take much, then." Visser pulled his pants at his thighs, settled back into one of McNeil's leather armchairs, looked around the office. "Nice place," he said. "I got an office in an old warehouse on Pier 42. Great view, right on the water. Treasure Island, the bridge. But no chairs like this."

"Well . . ." McNeil didn't have a chitchat answer prepared. He pulled a chair up, put on an expectant expression. "So . . ." He waited.

Visser took another moment appreciating his comfort level, the buildings out the windows. He shifted his shoulders, leaned into the leather, came back to McNeil. "Just so you know," he began, "so we're clear, I'm working for Dash Logan, Mr. Galt's attorney. He thought it might be . . . helpful if you and me had a discussion about what we're looking at here, kind of off the record."

But McNeil was shaking his head. "I don't know if that's a good idea. My lawyer told me . . ."

"No, c'mon, hey. Lawyers, I know. I work for one. Dash talked to your lawyer yesterday, which is why I'm here today, call it a courtesy. Your guy—Hardy, is it?—he seems to think settling this case out of court isn't a good idea, says we've got no criminal case. But I gotta tell you . . ." The squinting eyes shifted around the office.

"What?" McNeil prompted.

With some effort, Visser brought his bulk forward on the chair. "Here's the thing," he began, all sincerity. His voice dropped a few decibels. "This stuff happens in these cases, the lawyers, they start pissing at each other, pretty soon everybody loses. Mr. Logan, he hates to see that . . ."

"Well." McNeil wanted no more of this. He started to stand up. "Be that as it may, I really can't—"

"The thing is, Rich," Visser interrupted, almost coming out of his own chair, intimidating McNeil again back into his. "I used to be a cop a lot of years. I know the kind of things they're looking for and they're going to get it. I mean, everybody's got a skeleton in their closet—tax stuff, couple of times you maybe took cash for rent without receipts. This is stuff your guy Hardy wouldn't know about."

"I'd be surprised at that," McNeil said levelly. "He used to be a cop himself."

"Hardy did?"

McNeil pressed his advantage. "That's right. So I get the feeling he's pretty much on top of what's going on, and he's telling me there's no case. Which is also what I believe, since I know Manny Galt is a liar, especially about giving me cash for rent. That didn't happen. None of it happened. So if that's all"—McNeil started to get up again—"thanks for coming by, but I'm afraid we don't have anything else to discuss." He braved a smile. "We're just going to have to let the lawyers duke it out."

But Visser didn't take the hint. Instead, he leaned back again, rubbed a palm against the smooth leather armrest. "Well, okay. It's just a case like this goes forward, it can get ugly. And Mr. Logan doesn't want that."

"Neither does Mr. Hardy. We'll just have to let the facts decide." He gestured with his palms out, forced another smile. "Well, if that's all, I do have a pretty busy morning . . ."

At last, Visser got himself out of the chair. "Okay, but just for an example."

"What's that?"

"You used to have a secretary named Linda Cook, didn't you?"

McNeil felt his stomach go hollow. "What about her? That was a mistake. A long time ago. My wife knows all about it."

"Yeah, sure. But the kids, you know, the grandkids. That whole thing comes up, it'd be kind of sad for them, the whole way they think about you."

A shaky breath, steel now in the voice. "Get the hell out of here."

The fury and fear had no effect on Visser. He spread his own palms in a reflection of McNeil's earlier dismissal. "All I'm saying is this kind of thing gets around in the public, it doesn't do you any good. You hear what I'm saying? Nobody needs that kind of aggravation, huh? Aren't I right?"

They were in the front window of a tiny little lunch place on Union, and Jody Burgess had given up even picking at her salad. Instead, she glared across the table at her daughter, who had just told her after a meal full of preamble that she and Jeff were not going to contribute to the payment for Cole's defense. "I don't see how you can be so unfeeling," she said. "This is your own brother."

Dorothy hadn't even touched her sandwich, and it was her favorite—focaccia, goat cheese, sun-dried tomatoes. She had no problem understanding how she could be so unfeeling—she'd had lots of practice, that was how. Every time she'd been tempted to feel something like compassion or sorrow or simple pity for her brother over the past half dozen years, she'd regretted it, and now the temptation wasn't all that great any longer. In fact, it was no longer a temptation at all.

But she told herself that this was her mother, and although they'd had similar discussions hundreds of times before, she felt she still owed her somehow. Damn it.

So she answered with her trademark enforced calm. "My own brother," she said, "desperately needed a place to stay and because I *felt* something for him, I let him live in my house with my rather seriously handicapped husband and *my own children*. And Mom, you may remember this, you know what his thanks was? He stole from us. Repeatedly. From the kids' own piggy banks even. Can you believe that one? That was my reward for being nice to him, that the kids now will always remember Uncle Cole as a thief, if not a murderer. And isn't that a special thing for them to carry around for the rest of their lives?"

Jody nodded, swallowed. She'd heard of all this before. And, because it was her nature, she was ready with a response. "He's not a murderer."

"Well, he damn well is a thief."

"He can't help himself, Dorothy. He's in the grip of something bigger than he is."

"Oh, please."

"It's true. You know it's true."

"It may be, Mom, but *I just don't care anymore*. I don't care. Do you hear me?"

Jody stared into the face across the table, reached out her hand, touched her daughter's. "Honey . . ."

"No!" Dorothy pulled her hand away. "No. Not this time."

"So what are we going to do?"

"I'm not going to do anything."

"You'll just let him go?"

Dorothy nodded, her jaw set. "Yep."

"They're asking for the death penalty, Dorothy. You can't want him to die?"

A sigh. "This is San Francisco, Mom. No jury is going to give him the death penalty. He's not going to die."

"Well, the district attorney sure doesn't agree with you."

"The district attorney . . ." Dorothy's gaze was flat. "He's gone anyway, Mom. He's not coming back."

"I don't believe that."

"I know, but you should. Because it's true."

Another silence.

Jody often thought that she was beyond tears. Certainly, only a few years ago if she'd heard Dorothy say that her only son Cole wasn't ever coming back, wasn't ever going to be her wonderful boy again, she would have welled up. But now there was nothing like that—only a deep weariness, but one that somehow didn't threaten her resolve. "Look, how about if we just talk to Mr. Hardy and . . ."

Dorothy was shaking her head. "Mom, we've got three children to send to college if we can. Jeff's medical expenses are sure not going to go down. We just can't help here, even if we wanted to, which we don't. And frankly, Mom—I've got to say this—I don't know why you do."

"He's my only son, Dorothy. That's why."

"That's not a good answer, Mom. Cole's ruined your life. Don't you see that?"

"He hasn't."

"Oh no, that's right. He's enriched it, I suppose?" Dorothy picked up her napkin, wiped her mouth nervously, took a deep breath. "He's ruined your life."

"You keep saying that."

"Because it keeps being true, that's why. Come on, Mom, look what he's done. He's forced you to move out here—"

Jody held up her hand, stopping her. "No! There! That's a good example. He didn't force me."

"You sold the house we both grew up in, where you'd planned to live the rest of your life—you told me this, remember?—because after we threw him out, you wanted a place near Cole in case he couldn't make it on his own. Tell me that isn't true!"

Dorothy couldn't say that, since it was.

"So now you're living in some dreary little apartment, uprooted from all your friends, everybody you've known your whole life, all alone . . ."

"I get to see my grandchildren."

"Which wasn't an issue until Cole moved out here. That's not why you're here, Mom. You know that. It's Cole. It's always Cole, all the sacrifices, and you know what? He doesn't care. They haven't done any good."

Jody cast her eyes around the restaurant, to the street outside, back to her daughter. "He has stayed with me. He needs a place."

"So let him get one, Mom. Christ, he's twenty-seven years old."

"I can't let him die."

"You can't save him. Don't you see that? He'll never grow up if you don't let him. You're letting him go on the way he does."

"I don't have any option, hon. He just needs—"

"Stop talking about his needs!" Dorothy, suddenly, had heard enough and her string snapped. Her voice had a hoarse quality, but everyone in the restaurant heard it. "He needs to get a life. He needs to beat this thing, okay, but you can't help him. Nobody can. He needs to fail and figure it out or else he needs to die." She brought the napkin back to her lips, shocked at her own outburst.

But she wasn't really through, not yet. She leaned forward, her voice more modulated. "And now you're going to pay Mr. Hardy by yourself, aren't you? Do you know how much that's going to be? It's going to wipe you out, your savings, and then what? Then what's it all been for?"

"But he didn't kill this woman. He needs a good lawyer."

"He *confessed*, Mom."

Which meant nothing to Jody. "Not really, and if Mr. Hardy can get him off, then he can get in some program . . ."

"Oh, Jesus, when will it end? Give me a break."

"Can I get you ladies some more water?" It was the waiter, solicitous in his white shirt and black vest. "Some dessert? Coffee?"

Embarrassed, getting the message, Dorothy shook her head. "Just a check, please, thanks." After he'd nodded—relieved—and gone off, she leaned across the table and whispered, "You know, Mom, I shouldn't even have gone to see Dismas. That was my last mistake for Cole. I should have just let him die then in jail if he was going to. Get the whole thing over with."

"Don't say that," her mom implored. "You don't mean that."

Shaking her head in disgust, Dorothy threw her napkin down on her plate. It was hopeless.

13

Clarence Jackman was seated at the head of the mammoth mahogany table that filled the center of the conference room at his firm's offices. Assuming correctly that the arraignment of Cole Burgess would attract a number of Elaine's friends and colleagues, Jackman had arranged a catered lunch and had passed the word outside the courtroom that those whose hearts were in the right place were welcome.

This turned out to be a sizable group, nearly two dozen people, although by now—getting on to one-thirty—many had returned to their jobs or classes. The general buzz had subsided and most of the food was gone. Jackman shook hands good-bye with a young law intern who wanted to send in a résumé, then grabbed a bottled water from the sideboard and pulled up a chair near the knot of people—most of them, Jackman gathered, from law school—who remained at the far end of the room, deep in a conversation that had progressively picked up some heat.

"There wasn't any reason, that's the whole point! You admit a reason, you give Hardy his ammunition to get the scumbag off." This outburst came from Elaine Wager's fiancé, Jonas Walsh. In his mid-thirties, big hair, extraordinarily handsome face, expensive clothes, Walsh was a surgeon who looked like he hadn't slept in a week, and maybe he hadn't. He was clearly not in the habit of hearing his opinions questioned, and the wringer he'd been through since Elaine's death probably made him sound testier than he intended.

The current object of his wrath was Peter Nesbitt, associate dean of

Hastings Law School. He was a reedy-voiced logician in bow tie and corduroy sports coat. "All I'm saying," Nesbitt persisted, "is that if Burgess in fact didn't voluntarily confess—"

"But he did, for Christ's sake." For corroboration, Walsh turned to the others gathered around. "Am I wrong here? Is this really in dispute?"

"Not really, Jonas." Treya Ghent sat next to him. It was obvious to Jackman that the two knew each other, perhaps well. Treya didn't really smile, but there was something almost like humor in her attitude and body language as she attempted to pour oil on the waters. She patted Walsh's hand reassuringly. "They're only talking about lawyer strategy."

"The ever fascinating . . ." One of the female students, to general appreciation.

Jackman again noticed the sense of quiet strength that the Ghent woman exuded. Today, as always, she wore the simplest of outfits—black slacks, a fashionably baggy gray sweater, a thin gold chain necklace, little or no makeup. He had to force himself to take his eyes off her.

Billable hours or not, he resolved, I've got to think hard before I let this one go.

"So what are you saying, Jonas?" Jackman asked, eager to be in on it. "What's the argument?"

"I'm saying that all this shoptalk about maybe somebody having a reason to kill Elaine, it plays right into his lawyer's hands. Hell, you're a lawyer. Don't you think that's right?"

Jackman appeared to ponder, looked over at Peter Nesbitt. "I suppose. But what I hear from Peter is don't let your rage over the act blind you to the facts. If this man Burgess didn't do it, you'd want to know who did, right?"

"Of course. But he did do it."

Nesbitt spoke up again, shrugging. "What I'm saying is that this Hardy fellow is just doing his job, trying to create doubt from the outset. It's a good technique."

"Well, excuse me all to hell if I can't get behind it. What I know is that Elaine's gone. It doesn't leave me much in the mood for all this hypothetical bullshit."

Treya touched his hand again. "Jonas. They don't mean . . ."

He hung his head. "Okay, I know, I know." Abruptly he stood up, rubbed a palm down the side of his face. "Sorry," he blurted. "This just isn't some mind game for me." He looked around the table. "Down in the courtroom, all of you seemed as disgusted as I was. And now here . . ."

"We're only saying it raises some interesting points," Nesbitt said.

"I'm not interested in them. It seems to me they caught the guy, now they're figuring out how they're going to let him go."

"Well," the woman who'd made the earlier comment said, "if she did have enemies, and we all know she did . . ."

Walsh wasn't having it. "If she did, it wasn't one of them. It was this kid."

Jackman felt he ought to intervene. The young doctor was in the grip of his emotions. He wasn't used to the endless debate which was the cornerstone of nearly every gathering of law students and which could, Jackman silently agreed, in fact get wearisome. "We all agree with you, Jonas."

"That's funny. It doesn't sound like that."

"We were all outraged by the events in court today. I think you heard that during the arraignment. We all walked in there having heard about the confession, wanting blood, believing that Mr. Burgess was guilty. I think we all believe it still."

Nods from around the table.

Walsh had remained standing, now nodding in acknowledgment. Suddenly a shadow seemed to cross his face. He bit down on his lip, brought a hand up to his mouth. "I'm sorry," he said, his voice cracking. "I can't . . ." He shook his head again, got some composure, managed to speak. "Excuse me." Then he was out the door.

Treya Ghent excused herself as well, pushed back her chair, got up, followed him.

As her steps receded down the hallway, the room grew silent. Several of the students exchanged glances—an awkward moment. The woman spoke up again. "The grieving man and his comforter." But this time there was no appreciative chortle from the group.

"If it were me," Nesbitt began. His voice told it all. He was in debate mode. He addressed the seated students. "I think I'd go along with Mr. Jackman's comments. It's important to nail the case down against every possible doubt. Eliminate every other possible suspect. Disprove every alternative. Do any among you not feel that way?"

There weren't any takers.

The thin voice pressed the point. "And yet Dr. Walsh, apparently, has no interest in that pursuit. Which could mean . . . what?"

Jackman wasn't in the mood to listen to any more theorizing. Nesbitt's hypothetical point was the bloodless logic of the academic. Walsh's genuine emotion was much more real—he was simply too upset to deal rationally with the case. In any event, the table would be cleared soon, and the last of his guests dispersed.

Time was money. He had to go back to work.

Treya saw him turn into Elaine's old office, across from her cubicle. He'd closed the door and she knocked, waited, knocked again—no answer. She turned the knob.

"Jonas?" Whispering.

The shades were drawn and the room was dim, but she had no trouble making him out, slumped in Elaine's chair, feet up on her desk, hands over his eyes. Treya quickly checked the hall in both directions, saw no one and slipped inside. She closed the door again behind her.

"Are you all right?"

"Yeah, sure. Great." He drew a deep, audible breath. "I don't want to hear about her enemies."

"I know."

She waited, standing by the door. When her eyes had adjusted more to the light, she crossed the small room, removed some of Elaine's files from where they sat on her usual chair, stacked them on the file cabinet next to the desk. Sitting, she waited some more.

He barely lifted his head. "Pretty mature display, huh?"

"Could have been way worse. I wouldn't lose any sleep over it."

"I think I'd have to get some to lose it."

"Well, when you do."

She'd known Jonas for a little over three years, since he and Elaine had first become an item, and although over time he had ceased to be among her favorite people, early on they had bonded as coconspirators. This was because in the first few months of dating between her black activist boss and her white doctor boyfriend, the relationship had been extremely clandestine—secret meetings in hotel rooms, daytime trysts where Treya would loan them her apartment, lunch in this room at the firm.

All this was before Elaine had been ready to commit, and Treya hadn't been able to blame her, though at first, before she'd seen his ego and tantrums and selfishness, she did feel for the pressure it put on Jonas.

As the daughter of a prominent African-American U.S. senator, Elaine had been informally claimed by the Bay Area black community as one of its new generation of leaders. The political side of her—she did, after all, have her mother's blood—loved it. In the first couple of years after she left the D.A.'s office, she had been squired around to her fund-raising appearances and campaign dinners by a succession of high-visibility black men. Over the years, the *Chronicle*'s society column had linked her romantically with not a few of her clients, with a city supervisor, with a running back for the 49ers, with a coanchor on one of the nightly news programs.

Elaine had liked each of them for various reasons, though none of these or several other boyfriends had lasted more than a couple of months. This wasn't a matter of much concern to her—she'd been in love once when she was younger and she knew what it felt like, and it wasn't this. She assumed it would only be a matter of time before she met the right man again, and then she would marry him and settle down.

Working at Rand & Jackman, speaking at neighborhood organizations, black business seminars, inner-city development projects, she was leading a full, busy life that only rarely intersected with the white community.

Treya knew that Elaine didn't think much about this segregation. It was simply a fact of her life. She had no strong prejudice against white people—the man who'd raised her, Dana Wager, had been white—but except for formal gatherings, there was little opportunity to meet anyone, socially or otherwise, who wasn't black.

Then she came down with a stomachache that sharpened and deepened—right side, localized—over a two-day period. On the third morning, she was at her desk trying to work when Treya came in with some papers and gently brushed against her. Elaine screamed, nearly blacking out from the pain as her appendix burst. The fever peaked at 104.

Jonas was the emergency room surgeon, and he saved her life.

But in the first months, Elaine didn't trust the feeling. It wasn't at all like the earlier, star-crossed love she'd experienced with Chris Locke, the older, married district attorney. No, Jonas was young, brilliant, sexy. And the feeling, she'd confided to Treya, was like nothing else—it was much better. In fact, she thought, it was too good to last.

And since it would have to end, Elaine was at first afraid to threaten her standing in the community over a few moments of passion. Terrified of losing clients, clout and credibility, she wanted to keep the affair hidden until it blew over, as it surely would.

But it didn't.

They went public, and despite Elaine's concerns, the whole race thing turned out to be pretty much a nonissue. About the only fallout she'd experienced was that she'd lost a jihad-oriented Islamic student she'd been mentoring, and that Elaine had come to view as a blessing. Finally, a year ago, she and Jonas had announced their engagement.

Treya, for her part, certainly understood the original attraction. Jonas had movie-star looks and projected a superconfident *maleness* that was undeniable. She hadn't been completely immune to it herself on some level. But after she got to know him, she wasn't completely thrilled that this man had been Elaine's life choice.

His world, she discovered, revolved entirely around himself and his work. During the courtship rush, he'd made time for Elaine whenever he could, but when that ended—once he'd won her love and commitment—he reverted to his old schedule and his main passion, which from Treya's perspective was himself.

She told herself that maybe she was being unfair. And to be truthful, Elaine really didn't seem to mind. They both worked long hours under great pressure. Obviously, they had reached some accommodation where stolen late-night hours or a rare weekend when Jonas could get away was enough for both of them. Each was, in their own way, a trophy, a catch—Treya understood that this was no small part of it for either of them. Maybe they were a true match—two narcissists locked in a centrifugal dance around the image each admired. But that really wasn't the Elaine that Treya knew.

Treya couldn't imagine standing for it herself. When Jonas missed a dinner or a movie or a show because he was in surgery, when he never made it home because of some hospital emergency, Elaine seemed to deal with it. But if it was her, if she got hung up at work and had to cancel out on one of his events . . .

Treya remembered the first time she'd seen it. She had left a message for Jonas that Elaine was in a deposition that was running very late. She and Jonas had been due to go to L.A. for some medical convention and Elaine was going to have to catch a later flight. She would miss the introductions, the cocktail party. She'd try to make it down by the next morning at the latest. Jonas had shown up in front of Treya's desk in a fury. It was as though he'd never met her before, as if they'd never plotted together to find a quiet place he and Elaine could meet. Treya had called and left a message for Jonas. If the deposition had been taking place in one of the offices at Rand & Jackman, she had no doubt he would have broken into the room, interrupting the proceedings. But she'd told him, untruthfully, she really didn't know where Elaine was working. "Well, find her," he'd snapped at her.

After that, Treya had never felt the same about Jonas Walsh.

Afterwards, of course, he'd apologized, told Treya he'd been under a lot of stress, yack yack yack. But she saw it from him, heard about it from Elaine, too many other times. Even today, at the lunch they'd just left—Jonas unwilling even to listen. He knew the truth. It was obvious. Everybody should just stop wasting his precious time.

But for some reason, Elaine had put up with it, even apologized for him. "He's under a ton of pressure every day, Trey. Life-and-death stuff. You watch, after we start a family, he'll get his priorities straight. He's got a great heart."

Now Treya looked across at the dejected figure and, in spite of their differences, she felt for him, as she felt for herself. The world as they both knew it had ended, and neither felt ready to move on. A gust of wind slapped at the window, and they heard the beginning of rain.

His hand was still resting over his eyes, his face half hidden. The voice came out guttural, low enough—almost—to be distant thunder. "She was talking about leaving me," he said.

Though she'd heard him clearly, the truth of it didn't seem to register right away. She would not have believed it possible that Elaine had come close to making that decision and kept it from her. "I'm sorry, what?"

"You didn't know?" Now he did look over. "She really didn't tell you?"

"Are you joking?"

"Am I joking?" He shook his head. "She told me she hadn't told anybody yet. I didn't believe her."

Treya sat back, stunned by the news. "She didn't tell me," she said simply. Then added, "She never even said she was unhappy."

Another half laugh. "Well, there you go." He brought his feet down off the desk, swiveled in the chair to face her. "I wasn't going to let her go. I told her I'd change."

"From what?" But, of course, she knew.

He made a face. "All the hours. But hell, it wasn't like she didn't work around the clock, either. Still, I told her I could take on less work. I would."

"Was that it, then, the hours?"

"That's what she said—if we weren't ever going to see each other anyway, what was the point . . . ?" He left it hanging.

"But?"

Another awkward shrug. He began to say something, stopped, blew out some air. After a minute, he raised his eyes again, met Treya's. "Hell, you know me, Trey. I'm not the best person in the world. I know I've been shitty to you and there's no excuse for that. I guess Elaine, too, taking her for granted. But my work . . ." He paused, realizing that this wasn't going to fly. "No, not my work. It was me. I know it was me." His eyes implored her to believe him.

"So what happened?"

"Nothing, really. At least no one event. That's what she said. But I think it was." The rain suddenly picked up, loudly tattooing the window. Both of them turned their heads, then Walsh brought his attention back to her, continued. "A couple of weeks ago, you might remember, we had a weekend planned, go up to Mendocino, leave the pagers home . . ."

"But you had some intern problems and it didn't happen." Treya suppressed a smile. "She did mention something about that."

"I bet she did."

"Well, okay, she wasn't happy, Jonas, but she didn't talk about moving out." Treya paused. "She said she just thought you two needed to find some time to talk, get some things worked out again."

"She told you that?" A show of great relief. He leaned into the chair, stretching out. With both his surgeon's hands, he combed the flowing black hair straight back off his forehead. "That helps."

The words—the self-absorption they betrayed—struck Treya like a blow. "How does that help, Jonas? How can it possibly make any difference now?"

"No. I don't mean . . ." With an apologetic gesture, he started over. "Of course it doesn't. What I meant was I thought she'd made up her mind—she *told* me she'd made up her mind. But she might have listened." Again, his eyes implored her to believe him. "I could have changed. I could have convinced her to stay, don't you think?"

Treya shook her head sadly. "I don't know, Jonas. I really don't know."

"I wasn't going to let her go," he repeated, now almost to himself. "I would have done anything."

She was pretty sure she knew what Jonas Walsh thought he was try-ing to say. But what she heard sent a chill up the back of her spine.

There was a message from Jackman on her desk, another summons to his office.

His secretary flashed some attitude this time. It was subtle enough to allow denial if it ever came up, but Treya read the message clearly—uppity girl wasn't making any friends putting the moves on another partner. Same as she had with Elaine. Too good to work with the rest of us. And admitted inside right away, too, yes ma'am. Certainly, Mr. Jackman. No waiting for this paralegal, and isn't that a fine how-do-you-do when Mr. Jackman had been known to keep *the mayor* wait-ing? Girl must think she is *something*.

But there was nothing Treya could do about the jealousy. It was an office, after all, filled mostly with women working for powerful men. The claws were out, protecting territory, at all times.

So Treya entered the sanctuary, and Jackman told her to take the seat set up in front of his desk. She took it, then thanked him for the lunch. "It was a nice idea. I think people really appreciated the opportu-nity to talk."

The senior partner shrugged. "I'm afraid it may have upset Dr. Walsh, and that wasn't my intention."

"No." She paused, wondering how much more to say. "He was up-set to begin with, sir. He and Elaine . . ." This time, she stopped dead. He and Elaine what?

"Of course, of course. Naturally." Jackman hadn't gone behind his desk. Instead, he moved an out basket from the corner of it and threw a leg across, settling into a casual pose. "When was the wedding going to be?"

"June." She cleared her throat. "June."

He nodded for a moment. "It's awful," he said. "Just awful."

"Yes, sir."

He nodded again, got up, walked a few steps back to his own win-dow and looked at the rain. It almost seemed to her that he was steeling himself. To fire her early? She held her breath.

"Well, Treya," he began, then caught himself. "Do you mind if I call you Treya? What kind of name is that, by the way?"

A feeling of relief washed over her. It felt like the first time she'd smiled in a week. "Treya's fine, and I don't know what kind of name it is. I think my dad was just weird, sir. He liked the sound of it. I've got an older brother named Sixto, if that's any help, and he's the first child."

"Sixto?"

"We call him Six."

"And who wouldn't?" Smiling, Jackman walked the few steps back from the window, put his haunch on the desk again, leveled his gaze at her. His expression grew serious. "So, how is it going on the job front?"

She drew a quick breath, put on her brave face. "Not too bad, sir, though it's only been a couple of days. I've still got a few weeks on Elaine's files."

"But you do have some other work lined up?"

"Not quite yet. But I've put the word out. I'm sure it'll begin to trickle in before long. These things don't happen overnight."

"No, I know that." But Jackman easily read between the lines. There wasn't much, if any, firm work for her on the horizon.

"My first choice *is* to stay here." Her expression revealed that she hadn't premeditated the remark, was somewhat embarrassed by it.

"Well, that's good news. It's refreshing to see loyalty in a person nowadays." He threw a quick glance over her shoulder, but he wasn't looking at anything. His mind was working. "Well," he said matter-of-factly, "I didn't want to step on the toes of any of my colleagues if they'd already claimed you to work, but since it appears they haven't, it happens that I might have a small project of my own if you could find some time. It's mostly grunt work, I'm afraid, an old civil case that's been on continuance for four years and now suddenly Judge Branard has decided he's ready to review data, all of which needs to be updated. It's probably five hundred deadly dull hours, but it would give you some billable hours until you can fill your book."

Five hundred hours! He was giving her five hundred hours of work. Twelve weeks' reprieve! She struggled to keep her face impassive, and wasn't entirely successful. "I'd be very interested in that, sir. I could start—"

He nodded genially, interrupting her. "Next Monday will be fine. The files are still in storage and I've got to get them moved up here. And I wouldn't want you to give it all your time—say twenty hours a week—I know you've got Elaine's work to finish. But I must warn you again, this is a tedious job. You might want to look it over before signing on."

She heard herself say that that was a good idea, although she knew she would dance barefoot on hot coals if it meant keeping her salary and benefits.

"Let's say nine o'clock Monday morning, then?"

"Yes, sir. And thank you."

He smiled at her. "You might not thank me when you see what it is." He turned to look at the rain hammering the window. Told her it was good to see the rain. They needed rain.

She didn't get up.

Perhaps she would like some coffee. He always had some in midafternoon—he tended to go all logy after lunch. He had his own espresso machine. She could bill the quarter hour or so to administrative.

When he'd made and poured it, he set the cups on the coffee table and gestured her over to the couch, where they sat on opposite ends, four feet apart.

It was excellent coffee.

Jackman took a sip, nodded with satisfaction, placed the cup back on its saucer. He stole a glance at her, waited while she tasted the brew, put her own cup down. Apparently reaching some decision, he turned slightly toward her. "I want to ask your opinion about something if you don't mind." He took another moment, choosing his words with care. "About Elaine."

Treya came forward on the couch, put her elbows on her knees, leveled her eyes at him. "You have concerns about the case."

"I don't know if I'd go so far as to call them concerns. If it wasn't a politically charged death penalty, I don't know that I'd have given it another thought. But since it is . . ." A shrug. "I don't know. I ask myself what I would have thought if the police hadn't so conveniently found Mr. Burgess leaning over the body, if the D.A. hadn't already crawled so far out on her public limb. What would you have thought, Treya? You knew her better than anybody else here."

"If what, specifically?"

"If she'd been found shot with no suspects close at hand."

She let out a long breath, remembered her coffee and picked up the cup to get herself a little more time, held it in front of her mouth. "But that wasn't what happened."

"How do we know what happened?"

She had not asked herself why the hypothetical question had been so difficult for her. Maybe it was just easier having a ready answer to a painful question—she didn't have to keep coming back to it. Now, however, it looked as though it wasn't going to go away. "When he talked to me, Lieutenant Glitsky wanted to know the same thing—if I knew anybody who might have wanted to kill her. I told him that no one who knew her could have . . ."

"Is that what you really think?" Jackman leaned toward her, onto something. "This Lieutenant Glitsky," he pressed, "he's not a cop playing lawyer games, is he?"

"No."

"Yet he had a confession and still wondered about if he had the man who'd actually killed her? That sounds like doubt to me."

Treya shrugged. "He said he'd need evidence even if it proved to be Cole Burgess. He told me he'd plead not guilty and they'd have to convict him at trial anyway. They could expect years of appeals. So if they could put Elaine with him at a clinic or a school or something, maybe they'd have a motive, and that would help."

"But he was really asking about other people?" Jackman suddenly got up, paced a few steps with his hands in his pockets, turned back to her. "What I'm getting at is what that woman said at lunch in the conference room, that everybody knew Elaine had enemies. And nobody really seemed to dispute it. I knew of a few problems, so I'm guessing you must have as well."

Treya sat back into the deep cushions. "I suppose I must be a little like Jonas. It was hard enough getting it settled in my mind, just putting the bare fact of it someplace . . ." She shook her head as if to clear it. "I don't know why you brought this up exactly, sir. What do you think I should do?"

Jackman came back to the couch, sat again at the far end of it. "I'm not completely sure myself. It's just that no one knew Elaine better than you did, so you of all people might want to keep an open mind about who killed her. Or why."

Suddenly Treya cocked her head. "So you're really not certain it was Cole Burgess?"

"I'm not saying it wasn't. Just . . ."

She was facing him on the couch now, her eyes burning into his. "Just that maybe it wasn't."

He shrugged. He didn't know.

And now, suddenly, neither did she.

• • •

As a result of his meeting in Chief Rigby's office, for the first time in nearly thirty years, Abe Glitsky wasn't working as a cop. The powers had decided to place him on administrative leave for an undisclosed period of time. So he was relieved of his command of the homicide detail. They had not asked for his badge or his gun, but he had no trouble seeing that moment in his future. They gave him an escorted half hour to clear the personal items out of his desk and file cabinet. It only took him fourteen minutes. He'd packed all his stuff into a battered black briefcase. None of his inspectors were around to say good-bye. He had the feeling that this was not a completely random event. Someone had passed the word to his troops that it would be better if they were gone while their ex-lieutenant cleared out.

Rigby said he would be getting in touch in the next week or so, after the preliminary investigation. Until then, Abe might want to prepare some defense; and if not that, lie low.

It was nearly six o'clock. Glitsky had it on the highest authority that, contrary to conventional wisdom, the darkest hour was not just before dawn.

It was right now.

Perversely, the halogen lights over the parking lot behind the Hall of Justice had not switched themselves on. Further proof, although Glitsky didn't need it, that even the inanimate world had entered into the conspiracy against him.

Rain pelted the asphalt, the heaviest downpour he'd seen in the past couple of years.

He'd set the briefcase down next to him. Hands in his jacket pockets, he stood under the awning that covered the otherwise open and usually windswept corridor that led out the back door of the Hall, past the coroner's office and the entrance to the jail. His leather flight jacket was buttoned to his neck, the fur-lined collar turned up nearly to his ears. A gust of wind threw a spray of mist into his face and he backed up a step.

The effort to take his hands from his pockets and wipe his eyes seemed impossibly great.

Three or four people passed him going to their own rides—moans at the weather, shoptalk, a snatch of laughter. At what? he wondered.

Unable to bring himself to move forward, he eventually turned around, picked up the briefcase and retraced his steps halfway back to the door of the Hall. There he turned left, ran a few steps on wet concrete and pulled at the glass door that proclaimed the offices of John Strout, coroner for the city and county of San Francisco.

It was after hours, though, and the door was locked. The night bell was marked out of order. Glitsky almost laughed, might have even thought he was laughing, except that the sound in no way resembled laughter. The rain fell on his uncovered head, trickled down the back of his neck. He knocked hard, the doors shaking beneath his fist. Then, saving his knuckles, he turned his hand to the side and pounded hard. He was certain Strout was inside. This was the middle of the day for him. He pounded again.

Some helpful soul passing in the corridor yelled over that he thought they were closed.

"Thanks," Glitsky replied. He waited a reasonable period of time, then pounded again at the door.

A uniformed patrolman suddenly appeared behind him, tapping him on the shoulder. "Let's go, pal," he said. Glitsky noticed the rain dripping from the bill of his cap. He had one hand on his nightstick and looked like it wouldn't take much in the way of temptation to induce him to use it. "No loitering here. Building's closed up for the night. Let's move it along."

Scowling, which didn't make him prettier, the lieutenant turned, brushed the hand away. "Easy, cowboy," he said. "I'm with homicide, upstairs. Glitsky."

The cop did a double take and must have recognized him. He all but fell backwards, sheepish. "Oh, excuse me. Sorry, sir. I thought you were a bum."

Glitsky nodded. "Join the club."

PART
TWO

14

He'd be the perfect bartender."

Not that Glitsky had applied for the job, or ever would, but Hardy thought his friend might profit from a spell working behind the bar at the Little Shamrock—give him something to do while he waited out his suspension, keep him from going stir-crazy, polish up those people skills that cops kept getting lectured about.

He was in the driver's seat, stopped at a red light, trying to sell the notion to his brother-in-law, Moses McGuire, who not incidentally was the majority partner in the bar—three fourths to Hardy's quarter.

McGuire looked across the seat at Hardy as though he were a Martian. In fact, the two men had been in each other's lives for nearly thirty years, since they'd platooned together in Vietnam, where Hardy had saved Moses' life. Later, when Hardy's first marriage and life had fallen apart after the death of his son Michael, McGuire had returned the favor by giving Hardy sanctuary—a bartending job at the Shamrock that he'd kept for nearly a decade. So the two guys were connected, but Hardy's suggestion—even in jest—that Abe Glitsky work behind their bar was still too much to abide. "Perfect? In what way perfect?"

"Honest . . ."

"Hey, there's an idea. We could call him Honest Abe. I bet he'd love that."

"I'm serious. He'd work hard, show up on time, take no abuse from customers . . ."

"Because he'd have driven away all the customers?"

"Why would he drive away customers?"

"Gee, I don't know. Could it be because he's scary, intimidating, unfriendly . . ."

"Abe?"

"We are talking about Abe Glitsky, aren't we? The guy we're on the way to pick up? Black, mean-looking, scar through his lips, never drinks, never smiles? Him?"

Moses, atypically, was dressed in a somber brown suit with a black shirt and black tie. Not so atypically, he was having a morning tipple—one of the airplane-issued one-shot bottles of Lagavulin that he was carrying around with him in the pocket of his suit coat. He was drinking early because he'd declared it more or less a holiday—he wasn't opening the bar today. He'd assigned the shift to one of the regular night guys because of the memorial service.

Not that he had known Elaine Wager. But his wife Susan, a cellist with the symphony, had been hired with several other musicians to play at the service and he wanted to hear her. The acoustics of the cavernous Grace Cathedral were legendary—Art Garfunkel had once sung his vocals for an album there, just him and a microphone and the vibrations off the old stones. Terrific stuff. When he'd heard that his brother-in-law was going to the service, too, it cinched it for him. They could make it a road trip, a very short one, true—only thirty blocks or so—but McGuire made it a point to take his fun when he could get it.

The car moved through the intersection. "He's a good guy, Mose."

McGuire was clean-shaven this month. He hadn't been in a fight since before Christmas. The last broken nose had somehow set straight, and with his salt-and-pepper hair combed back, he looked almost dashing, albeit twenty years older than his chronological age. "I know he's a good guy," he said. "Often I'll say to myself, 'That Abe Glitsky, what a good guy.' But that doesn't mean he'd be a good bartender. You know why?"

"Tell me."

"Because bartenders, in theory, should have personalities."

Hardy threw a glare across the seat. "Abe's got a personality."

"Okay, let me rephrase it. Bartenders should have *good* personalities. Warm, inviting, even charming, much like myself." He savored a mouthful of Scotch. "Even you, on a good day in your youth, from time to time would achieve the lower rung of charming. But Glitsky? I don't think so. No."

Hardy turned the car onto Lake, pulled to a stop at a once-in-a-decade curbside opening almost directly in front of Glitsky's duplex. It was nine-thirty on a bright, cold and sunny Monday morning, one week after Elaine's murder. Hardy let himself out of the car, then leaned back in, an afterthought. "I don't think we need to bring it up, okay?"

"I'll be my usual sensitive self," McGuire assured him, and tipped up the tiny bottle.

In spite of his promise to be sensitive, McGuire started providing hot job tips almost as soon as Glitsky got into the car. He'd already opined that maybe Abe could find work selling real estate, setting up web pages on the Internet; he could open a chop house—with all the great gourmet restaurants in the city, the place was crying out for a good old-fashioned chop house.

Glitsky, in the backseat, dangerously calm, started rattling them off. "Alfred's, John's, Jack's, Little Joe's . . ."

"Okay, then, okay, forget the chop house. How about maybe private investigator for Diz." It went on and on. Maybe it wasn't too late for Abe to go back to school, become a doctor or lawyer or something. An accountant? Was Abe good with numbers?

Like McGuire, Glitsky was in a business suit—although he rarely saw the need for it, the lieutenant could dress when he wanted to. Adjusting the knot on his electric blue tie, he squinted out the back window, then reached into an inside pocket, removed some sunglasses, put them on.

McGuire happened to catch the move. "I like it," he said. "Very Samuel Jackson." He was twisting the cap on his third little bottle. A thought struck him and he stopped, snapping his fingers. "Hey, maybe acting . . ."

Hardy glanced sideways, wishing his brother-in-law would shut up, but he was shooting more Scotch, oblivious. Until suddenly—Hardy didn't even see it—Glitsky was leaning over the front seat, his gun in his hand, up against McGuire's head. His voice rasped, but the tone was one of exquisite calm. "I'm going to blow your fuckin' head off," he said.

McGuire swore violently, pulled himself away, banging his head against the passenger window, dropping his Scotch. His face was a mask of terror. Hardy was startled, too, slamming on the brakes, tires squealing. He swerved right. "Jesus, Abe . . . !"

But, quick as he'd come forward, Glitsky was leaning back into his seat, getting comfortable, replacing the gun in his shoulder holster. In the rearview, Hardy saw the scar burning white in his lips. Glitsky was actually smiling enough to show a few teeth, which was almost unheard of. "Acting," he said, nodding. "I think I could do that. I had you guys for a minute there, didn't I?"

The rest of the way downtown, McGuire didn't say a word.

Parking on a normal day was bad enough, but Elaine's memorial service drew a substantial crowd. Hardy couldn't find anyplace within five blocks. Since Grace Cathedral is at the summit of Nob Hill, they had a long walk, all of it steeply up. When they rounded the last corner and came in sight of the church's steps, they stopped, and McGuire took the opportunity to tell them he wanted to go inside early, make sure he got a spot where he could see his wife.

Glitsky and Hardy hung back. Hardy didn't think it was because they needed to catch their breaths. "That was a nice little moment back there. Subtle. Though I did almost crash the car."

"I knew you wouldn't. I wasn't worried about it." Glitsky's mouth lifted a quarter inch.

"Well," Hardy said, "that made one of us." Hardy felt as though he wanted to say a little more about it, but realized that the subject had been thoroughly covered. All issues resolved, messages delivered.

They stood together awhile in silence. Glitsky got out his sunglasses again. Put them on, perhaps against the glare of all the people he recognized from his work. Police brass were showing up in significant numbers.

"You sure you want to do this?" Hardy asked.

There was no trace of a smile now. "I've *got* to do this."

This was what he'd told Hardy over the weekend. He hadn't been there for his daughter's birth, or in her life. He was damn well going to be here for this. And this was the only reason Hardy had decided to come—moral support for his pal, who in the wake of recent events could certainly use some. Now, though, catching some sense of the mood of the place, Hardy wondered if it would turn out to be a good idea after all. "Yeah, but you don't have to be seen here with me."

Glitsky shrugged.

"I mean, you and me together . . ."

"I know what you mean," he said. "I'll try to keep my hands off you, I promise."

There was no impetus to move inside. In the open area by the cathedral's main entrance, people continued arriving on foot, got let out of cars and taxis. Singles, couples, small groups. It was twenty minutes until the service was scheduled to begin and already the forecourt was packed.

A snatch of narration carried from somewhere. ". . . expecting close to five hundred mourners from every walk of the city's public life, this charismatic young woman's tragic death has fired the imaginations of . . ."

It being San Francisco, of course there were already several groups of demonstrators hanging around—any excuse for a party. They were just starting to get organized. On the periphery of the crowd, Hardy could see placards for and against the death penalty. In the park across the street, he could make out where earnest groups had set up tables giving out literature on drug abuse awareness programs, the Nation of Islam, homeless advocates, gun control lobbyists and their opponents.

A mime, dressed as a World War I doughboy, had sprayed himself head to toe in bronze paint and gotten himself up on the pillar by the cathedral's door. He didn't move a muscle, a living statue with his rifle trained down on the crowd.

Three of the local news vans had scored some primo reserved parking nearby, and teams with their reporters and cameras were unloading and shooting, getting some B-roll local color.

A limo slowly pulled up through the congestion and stopped behind several others. As the mayor emerged from behind the tinted windows, one of the news crews recognized him and yelled something about it. Around Hardy and Glitsky, the crowd seemed to become more dense, pressing into itself. It no longer seemed cold.

"Lieutenant?"

Glitsky turned around, nodding matter-of-factly. "How you doing, Ridley?"

The young cop shifted uncomfortably. "Not too good, I guess." Tongue-tied.

It wasn't much Glitsky's nature to give anything away, but he'd considered himself in some ways the boy's mentor in the years since he'd come up to homicide, so he cut him some slack, making conversation, indicating Hardy. "You know my friend?"

Banks said sure, nodded again, didn't offer a handshake, though. He kept his attention on Abe. "I thought you'd be here," he said awkwardly.

"Looks like you were right." Glitsky could throw him a bone, but he wasn't about to spoon-feed him. If Ridley wanted to say something, he'd have to figure out how.

It took him a minute. "The thing is," he began, "okay, I'm not blaming anybody else. It was completely my fault, but you should know that Torrey sandbagged me."

No response. None.

The sergeant continued. "When the arraignment got over, we were standing around outside in the hallway afterward, you know, talking about it, all of us pretty pissed off, mostly at . . . uh . . ." He made a gesture.

"Let me guess," Hardy put in. "That would have been me."

Banks seemed grateful for the help. "Yeah. So anyway . . . I knew you had problems with the tape, I knew you and Hardy here, you went back. So Torrey is all bitching and moaning about how'd Hardy know so much about everything so soon? And I just blurted out that I wouldn't be surprised if you showed him the tape."

"Sometimes blurting out is a strategic error."

Banks looked directly at Hardy. "Yeah, but in court you made it pretty clear you'd seen it." Back to Glitsky. "Torrey didn't seem to remember that, but I did. So I figured it had to be you, Abe."

Glitsky finally was moved to speak. "Deduction's a great tool." It didn't come out as a compliment.

Ridley kept on. "But I didn't think he'd . . . I mean, I didn't know it was going to go this way. That wasn't why I brought up the tape, to get at you. I know we disagreed about it, you and me, and I didn't want you to think . . . What it was, was we were just all talking, wondering out loud, and I guess I got caught up in it . . ." The rambling narrative wound down. Ridley looked as though he'd been having a miserable few days worrying about all this.

Glitsky couldn't say that the boy's malaise bothered him too much— maybe Ridley would pick up a useful lesson about politics that would serve him well in his dotage. But in the here and now, the sergeant had messed up his lieutenant's life pretty good. Now he was saying he hadn't meant to do it. Which helped exactly zero. Glitsky removed his sunglasses and folded his arms over his chest. His voice, when he spoke, had a resigned quality to it, the anger all leached out. "Well, I guess we both got caught up in it then, didn't we, Rid?"

After a moment, Banks realized that this was about all he was going to get from Glitsky in the way of absolution. He took in a breath, let it out heavily. "So what are you going to do now?"

"I'm waiting until somebody in Rigby's office decides something." A shrug, a glance at Hardy. "Meanwhile, I'm exploring some other career opportunities."

"He's thinking of opening a chop house." Hardy, poker-faced.

"Not really?" Banks asked.

"It could happen," Glitsky replied, equally deadpan. "You never know."

The church bells began to peal, cutting off the riff. It was a quarter to ten, still fifteen minutes until the service, but at the signal, the crowd shifted, began to move.

Ridley wasn't ready for that, yet. He still wanted some more resolution. "Anyway, Abe, listen, if there's anything I can do . . ."

Glitsky raised a hand, a farewell. He was going inside now. "Rid, listen, it's done. Don't worry about it." He turned for the cathedral, leaving Banks out where he'd found them.

Hardy hustled a step or two and fell in beside him. "You know what I can't believe?" he asked.

"What's that?"

"My brother-in-law doesn't think you have a sense of humor."

Glitsky threw him a sideways glance. "He's not paying close enough attention."

It was the day that Treya was supposed to begin on the *Grayson* project for Mr. Jackman, but he and Mr. Rand had closed down the firm for the morning so that all of Elaine's coworkers could attend the memorial. Treya had arrived early to pay her own private respects.

She found Grace to be an odd sort of cathedral. With its classic lines, stained glass and cavernous open space, in some ways it almost seemed to fit the medieval mold—an imposing edifice calculated to reflect the majesty and glory of God. But this church, for the past twenty years or so, had also been the locus of compassion, support and empathy for the victims of AIDS. And now the heartbreaking quilts hanging over her seemed to fill all the open space, humanizing the cold stone. In a tragic way, yes, but Treya found it strangely comforting.

She felt it strongly—this was no longer the home of some harsh and angry deity, but a true community center, with an almost palpable sense of forgiveness, acceptance, serenity. Outside the large crowd might be milling uneasily, but in here there was only peace.

She'd wandered about inside for a while and finally seated herself in the sixth row on the right—she had no need to claim any pride of place.

People had begun filing in, talking quietly among themselves. It was no surprise to see a lot of her colleagues, if she wanted to use that word, from the firm. It was even less of one that they held mostly to their cliques. None of them sat in her row.

Clarence Jackman tapped her on the shoulder, said hello, introduced her to his wife Moira, a regal matron in black. Treya recognized some of the students from Hastings who had been to Rand & Jackman for the postarraignment gathering last week. The mayor, arm in arm with the district attorney. Then her chief assistant, Torrey, the prosecutor at the arraignment, someone who was actually trying to do the right thing, to bring Elaine's killer to justice.

The volume steadily increased, echoing in the open space, and Treya turned in her pew to catch a glimpse of the incoming flow. She had to catch her breath as, almost directly behind her, she recognized Abe Glitsky and—she had a hard time even believing the gall of it—the lawyer, Hardy, who'd been in the courtroom representing Elaine's killer.

The lieutenant seemed as disconcerted to see her as she was to see him. He put out a hand, stopping Hardy, then nodded. Now abreast of her, he halted. "Is this pew reserved?"

In somber and measured strides, Gabriel Torrey walked up the center aisle and slowly mounted the lectern to the left of the altar at the front of the cathedral. The dying strains of the string quartet's powerful arrangement of "Amazing Grace" still seemed to hang in the air. The chief assistant district attorney wore a charcoal Armani suit, a white shirt with a black silk tie. His left lapel sported a little red AIDS ribbon, his right a tiny red rose.

For a short while, he gathered himself. When he was ready, he raised his head and looked out over the enormous congregation—more than five hundred souls were seated in the pews and standing behind them and to both sides, filling in all the space to the far walls.

After adjusting the microphone, he spoke with a quiet, even intimate familiarity, his voice firm and evenly pitched. "This is a remembrance," he began.

• • •

Midway through the service, she couldn't take it anymore. Suddenly, she stood, walked the length of the pew away from Glitsky and strode toward the back door of the cathedral. Outside, the cold sunlight glare stopped her, and she stood on the steps, blinking, drawing gulps of air.

"Are you all right?"

She turned, knowing who it was. He'd followed her out. Her hand went to her neck, her hair. She started down the steps before her eyes had adjusted, stumbled. He was right with her and caught her by the arm, preventing her from falling. As soon as she recovered and realized he was still holding her, she all but shook off his hand. Immediately, he let go and stepped back. "Are you all right?" he repeated.

"I'm fine. Fine." She straightened up. "I don't need your help."

"No. It's just that you . . . I thought you might faint."

"I don't faint. I've never fainted in my life." Shaking her head, she spun for a moment back toward the cathedral's doors, then took another step away from them, toward the park. Getting away. Finally, her breath hitched, and she focused on him. "I can't believe you came here. I think it's appalling."

He backed away a step.

But she wasn't through yet. "And your friend, that's a great touch. Elaine's killer's lawyer. What's that all about, him being here? This is supposed to be for her friends, for the people who miss her, not for . . . not for somebody like him. And you." Having said her piece, she was done. "Good-bye, Lieutenant." She started down the steps again.

Glitsky didn't know what he was doing. Not exactly. He certainly hadn't planned to move into her row in the church, to sit next to her.

To follow her out.

Now she was telling him good-bye again, dismissing him, and he was following after her. "Ms. Ghent. Please."

After a few steps, she slowed and came to a stop. Her shoulders heaved in a deep sigh, and when she turned to face him, he noticed that her nostrils had flared in anger or frustration or both. Hipshot, she crossed her arms. "What?"

"I'm going to need to look at Elaine's files."

He *really* didn't know what he was doing now. There was no way on earth he could look through Elaine's files. He was on administrative leave. He couldn't get a warrant. It was ridiculous even to suggest. But suddenly he knew what he had to do. The police—his own police department—weren't going to look. It was going to come to him to lock down this case. And Elaine's files were the best place to begin.

"Haven't we been through this? Didn't I just see Cole Burgess arraigned the other day for her murder." She took a breath. "Look, I know those files and he's not in them, okay? She didn't know him."

"I'm not saying she did."

"So what *are* you saying?"

He realized that he'd been seeing her face since the last time he'd been with her. Now he raised his eyes, looking out behind her. He had to take off the gloves and he didn't want to see the effect it would have on her features. "The first thing is I'm wondering why you're so hostile."

Now he did meet her eyes. A cold, empty stare came back at him.

He ignored it. "Normally, somebody's so hostile to the police, we wonder why that might be."

Her reaction, if she had one at all, seemed to be a greater depth of loathing. If Glitsky thought intimidation would affect her, he was dead wrong. She set her jaw, narrowed her eyes in disparagement. "What's the second thing?"

"The second thing . . ." He wrestled with it internally. "The second thing is I'm not absolutely, positively beyond any doubt sure that we have the bastard that killed Elaine. And I've got to be sure of that."

"And get, what do you call it, the collar? Another feather in your cap."

Surprised at this direction, he shook his head. "I don't care about that." Another short pause. "I cared about Elaine."

This time she snapped back at him. "And that's why you're here at this memorial, aren't you? Because you care. Because you were her friend." She was in a high fury, her eyes threatening to spill over. "And that's why you brought your friend with you I suppose. Because you both *care* so much. Well, let me tell you something. It's pretty damn transparent and it makes me sick."

"What is? What are you talking about?"

"I'm talking about your pretending to be close to Elaine so maybe witnesses will talk to you."

Glitsky was rocked by her vehemence. He held his hands out, supplicating. "I don't even have any witnesses. And even if I did, why would I do that? I couldn't care less if witnesses like me. You never get a witness who likes you. And who cares? They talk if you can make them." He didn't realize it consciously, but the habits of twenty years were kicking in. He was a cop. This was turning into an interrogation. "What I want to know," he said, "is why *you* don't want to talk to me. You were Elaine's friend, coworker, maybe confidante. And yet you don't want to help me make sure about who killed her. I wonder about that."

She challenged him with her expression, spoke into his face. "I don't believe you. How about that? I don't believe anything you say. You didn't care about her then, and you don't now." She moved forward, almost close enough to kiss him. "She knew," she whispered hoarsely. "About you. Don't you understand? Her own father, her real father. And you never acknowledged her, never even tried."

Glitsky's mouth opened to defend himself. But there was no defense and no words came.

Treya kept at him. "And she didn't dare approach you. Big, tough, hard-ass homicide lieutenant with the big sign saying 'Keep away. Everybody keep away.' And you're trying to tell me you cared? Well, excuse me, but I was there, I saw how much you cared. How much it hurt her. How you broke her heart."

Glitsky was a stone embedded in the pavement. Behind them, the doors opened and the strains of the string quartet floated out. A lone trumpet played a mournful solo, piercing the morning air. Finally, Glitsky turned as the first mourners appeared.

There was a tingling sensation in his face and then, on its heels, a great, almost unendurable pressure in his chest. He turned back to Treya Ghent, the beautiful outrage, the righteous indignation.

He opened his mouth again, and again no words came. His own heart felt as though it was exploding. Pain shot out through his limbs and he felt himself falling, crumbling.

He felt the cold of the day come up at him. He had a vision of an almost purple sky, of a noise like a rushing wind, of Treya Ghent somehow reaching for him just as he'd caught her minutes earlier.

And then it was dark.

15

It was dark.

Hardy rubbed his hand over his eyes and realized that night had fallen outside while he'd been sitting at his desk. He looked at his watch—9:15. Had he called Frannie to tell her he was missing dinner? Said good night to the kids? He didn't even remember.

Oh yes, he did now. Frannie knew what he was going through and he could stay down and catch up as long as he needed. Things at home were under control—the kids had already finished homework and were on their way to bed. Tomorrow would arrive bright and early. Maybe it wouldn't kill him if he wanted to put something off, come home? But it was his call. No pressure.

He stood up and put his hands on the small of his back, did a half turn in each direction trying to get the crick out. Coming around his desk, he flicked on the room lights by the door to his office. He'd been reading in the pool of light created by the green banker's lamp on his desk, studying the first of the discovery documents in the Cole Burgess case—pictures of the crime scene, the arresting officers' reports, autopsy, interrogation transcript with Ridley Banks.

Outside in the hallway, he stood a minute listening for other signs of life in the building.

Nothing.

He walked down the half-dark stairs until he could get a view of David Freeman's office. The door was closed and no hint of light came from under it, so apparently even the old man had gone home for the night.

The laggard, he thought. Imagine Freeman going home before ten o'clock. Whatever for? He had no life outside the law. But Hardy wished he had been there, wished he could talk to him. He stayed for a long moment on the stair, then walked the rest of the way down, into Freeman's unlocked office. If Phyllis could only see him now, he thought. But it gave him no real solace.

He went to the wet bar and poured himself three inches of Scotch, then went back to the door with his glass and took a last look at the room. "Lazy slug," he muttered aloud.

Back upstairs in his office, his drink on his desk, he pulled three darts from the board and paced off the distance to the tape line he'd put down at the eight-foot mark. Throwing easily, willing his mind to go empty, he hit the "20," "19" and "18" on the first round. He noticed, but just barely, and went to the board to retrieve the round, then went back around his desk, swallowed a mouthful of his drink and picked up the telephone again, punched in the hospital's number. "Intensive care nurses' station," he said.

Glitsky was still incommunicado. As of now, it wasn't certain he would ever again be otherwise. He was under heavy sedation.

The call got bounced to the nurse's station, where they filled him in on more of the nothing that had changed in the two hours since he'd called last time. There was no one else at the hospital that Hardy could talk to. Glitsky's father and son had gone home. His condition was listed as guarded.

Hardy hung up, looked at the darts, still in his hand, wondered where they had come from. He drank some Scotch. Halfheartedly, he opened one of the folders in front of him.

And there it was again, staring him in the face—the damning, nearly incontrovertible evidence against Cole Burgess.

Who, Hardy reminded himself not to forget, had never, not once, denied that he had killed Elaine Wager after all. At best, he'd said he couldn't remember.

And Hardy didn't kid himself. He thought that there was an excellent chance that Cole had in fact killed Elaine. He might be able to fashion an argument to convince a jury that his client was legally innocent. He absolutely believed that this was not a special circumstances death penalty murder no matter what. But nothing could hide the terrible *fact* of what had happened.

And if Cole had been prowling the alleys looking for prey—and that appeared to have been the case—and then killed Elaine because he was strung out and just didn't quite understand what exactly was happening—then Hardy didn't like where he was.

And the more he looked, the more he saw.

Both of the two arresting officers told essentially the same story, even if their reports had slightly different details—most notably, one of them said he heard a shot and its ricochet during the chase. But the rest of the facts were undisputed and, from Hardy's perspective, depressing and damning.

One of the most difficult problems Hardy was going to face when this thing came to trial was the whole question of the character of the defendant. Now, the good news regarding character is that neither side could mention character in any relevant context *unless the defense brought it up first*. After that, though, it was open season.

So Hardy sensed that he was going to be faced with a dilemma. If he brought it up that Cole was really an okay person who just had a disease—addiction—and could supply witnesses such as high school teachers, old friends, his mother and so on to prove it, then Torrey could bring up the years of theft, petty crimes and minor assaults that were part and parcel of Cole's history. And even if Hardy didn't raise Cole's character in the guilt phase of the trial, the jury would hear about the facts of this crime.

And they were particularly ugly.

The police had come upon Cole after he had picked the body clean of its jewelry. They discovered all of it on his person, in his pockets. He had ripped a heavy gold necklace from around Elaine's throat, slicing the skin of her neck in the process. He'd pulled a half-carat diamond engagement ring off her finger, breaking the finger at the knuckle as he did so. He had ripped the earrings from her pierced earlobes. He had inflicted all of these injuries postmortem, according to the autopsy. They were the only bruises and marks, except the bullet entry wound, on Elaine's body.

And Cole had—quite definitely—inflicted them.

He didn't remember that, either.

He'd gone through her purse, taking the money from her wallet, leaving the credit cards, apparently realizing, even in his stupor, that no one would mistake him for an Elaine.

Which led Hardy to the whole question of Cole's sobriety or lack of it during the commission of the crime. Everyone—the arresting officers, Banks, Glitsky—agreed that he seemed to be either drunk or stoned, but as he read over the documents, Hardy realized that there was no proof of that either. No one had given him a breath or blood test, and they'd sweated him long enough that by the time he'd been admitted to the hospital, his blood-alcohol level was about at zero. The prosecution could easily argue that Cole's apparent unconsciousness after his arrest in the police car was an act, and Hardy would be hard put to refute it.

Especially in light of Cole's flight when the arresting officers flushed him. His eventual crash into the hydrant notwithstanding, Cole had run swiftly and with determination away from the pursuing officer, so much so that he had been pulling away during the chase and, if not for the hydrant, nearly invisible on the dark night at street level, would quite possibly have escaped. He was not staggering, not speaking with any slur more noticeable than his usual drug-addict drawl.

After they put him in the squad car, he apparently passed out. Hardy could argue that the adrenaline had kicked in, then worn off. But it was not going to be an easy sell.

He closed the folder again, looked at his drink, which had evaporated, checked his watch. It was ten-thirty. He considered calling the hospital again, but realized he couldn't bear to hear it tonight.

If Glitsky were dead, he'd still be dead in the morning.

The alcohol hadn't touched him. It was time to go home.

Wearing his paper slippers and orange jail jumpsuit, a sullen inmate named Cullen Leon Alsop sloped into the visitors' room in the homicide detail. He got himself arranged in his wooden chair—leaning back as comfortably as he could with his hands cuffed, a slack-jawed smirk in place. It was the middle of the night, after lockdown, and he was alone here except for the cop who'd escorted him over from the jail, a black guy he incorrectly figured to be about his age. Cullen knew he was a cop but he couldn't have told from what he wore—a blue nylon windbreaker, black shirt with the top button loose, royal blue tie.

Across the table in the airless room, the cop adopted pretty much the same posture as Cullen, and the inmate found this disturbing. He was the one turning over important evidence in a murder case. They ought to be treating him with more respect, give him some doughnuts and coffee or something, at least get his cuffs off, and instead here's this spear-chucker yo-yo giving him 'tude. He had half a mind to call the whole thing off, but he had to get out of here and this was the only way, so he settled deeper into the unyielding wood and waited.

The cop finally came forward with a weary exhalation of breath. He withdrew a small portable tape recorder from a pocket and put it on the table. "Sergeant Ridley Banks, Badge Fourteen-oh-two. It's ten-thirty on Monday, Feb 8, and I'm in an interrogation room on the fourth floor of the Hall of Justice, San Fran, talking to . . ." Consummately bored, he consulted the folder in front of him. ". . . Cullen Leon Alsop, white male, twenty-five years old. Case number . . ." He rattled off a bunch of numbers.

Alsop had had enough. He'd been through this type of thing more than once, and this wasn't feeling right to him. He interrupted. "Hey."

Banks looked up, eyes dead. "Quiet please."

Cullen shook his head, made some "I don't believe this" gesture, straightened up in his chair. "Hey," he repeated, "I got a deal going here with the D.A. and you—"

Banks reached for the recorder and snapped it off. "Did I just tell you to shut up? When I ask you a question, you answer me. Otherwise, I don't want to hear you. Do you hear me?"

Cullen shrugged.

And Banks came forward like an attacking animal, up out of his chair, slamming a flat palm with a noise like a gunshot on the table. "THAT WAS A QUESTION! I asked if you could hear me? So if you're smart you say 'Yes, sir.' Do you hear *that*?"

Cullen decided to be smart. "Okay, yeah. Yes, sir."

"Good." Banks picked up the recorder, pushed the button again, resumed in his monotone, "Now, Mr. Alsop, for the record, you're in jail for selling crack cocaine, your fourth offense, is that correct?"

"Yeah."

"But you were out on the street again. On probation."

This seemed vaguely amusing to Cullen. "Three probations, man. I mean, I don't know why you guys don't all talk to each other or something."

"Who?"

"All you guys. Cops, D.A.'s, the judges. Decide between you whether it's against the law or not to deal in this town."

"Okay, next time you're worried about it, here's the answer. It is."

Cullen barked out a laugh. "So tell it to some judge. I got three convictions in the last seventeen months—I'm talking *convictions,* man, not arrests. The judge says, 'Hey, cut it out, really.' I tell him okay, I promise, and he puts me out on the street that day, and tomorrow I'm back in business. Next time, it's 'Hey, you promised.' So I say I'm sorry and promise again. Then the third time, same thing."

"Well, this time it isn't the same thing."

A shrug. "Maybe. We'll see. Anyway, it's why we're talking right now."

"About the gun."

"Yeah, that. The one I lended to Cole."

"Lended?"

"Yeah. Lended. Something wrong with that?"

"He paid you money for it?"

"He was gonna. That was the plan."

"When. After he got a day job?"

Cullen Leon Alsop conveyed his disbelief at Banks' stupidity, but saw something in the inspector's eyes and cut it off. "Here's the deal," he said. "We hang a lot together. Sometimes I get him stuff, you know, put him in touch. But Saturday he's got no money and he needs to score. I mean, bad, you know. And I'm out, too, or he woulda done me I'm sure, friends or no friends. But I got a hold of this little popgun."

"How'd that happen?"

An evasive shrug, eyes all around the room. "Somebody traded me one a few weeks ago."

"Who?"

"I don't know. Some guy."

"For what? What did you trade it for?"

"I don't remember. Something I had. You know, you got a big barter community out there." Banks made an impatient face, and Cullen got back onto the point. "Anyway, so I showed it to Cole."

"And why did he want it, the gun? To rob somebody?"

Cullen flashed an empty smile. "Hey, good, maybe you oughta be a cop. You got it all figured out." Something in Banks' face backed him away, though, changed his tone. "So he was gonna go score, bring me back the piece and fifty bucks on top for my trouble. But I didn't know he was going to kill anybody with it. He wasn't planning anything like that. That's not who he was normally."

"So who was he?"

A shrug. "A guy to hang with. Party. You know."

"I don't know, actually. I understood he lived on the street. Most of those guys don't go to a lot of parties."

"Yeah, but he lived with his mom. He could get his hands on some wheels when he wanted them. He just liked to party, that's all. Score, get high for a few days. Then maybe he wouldn't get home and crash somewhere else."

Banks was digesting this, but not comfortably. "Okay, but you got arrested last time. When was that?"

"Maybe Tuesday morning. I don't know. You could look it up easier than me."

Half an hour later, Ridley Banks was at his desk. His elbows were planted on the blotter in front of him, his hands steepled at his lips. A couple of times a minute he blew into them heavily. His eyes burned with fatigue. It had been a long day in the field and then, returning to the office after nine o'clock, he'd picked up his messages and heard about Glitsky's heart attack and also Cullen Leon Alsop, the purported source of the gun that Cole Burgess had used to kill Elaine Wager.

He hadn't felt right since he'd gone up against his lieutenant on the Burgess confession. Then came the startlingly swift decision to put Glitsky on administrative leave, now the cardiac arrest. Ridley couldn't shake the feeling that it was all related and part of it was his fault.

Abe had been his most ardent supporter, helping to get him promoted into homicide from robbery. Then, once he was aboard, he'd acted as Ridley's mentor—getting him up to speed, keeping him from at least a dozen egregious errors in his first year or two. And, he asked himself, was this his payback to Abe for all of that loyalty and concern?

He hated it, hated himself.

This was why he'd seen this lowlife Cullen immediately. If at least some new evidence came to light that could make the case stronger against Cole Burgess, Ridley would be able to console himself with the fact that he was even more right than he'd been before. It wasn't all going to come down to the confession.

He'd played that over, both on the physical tape and in his mind, almost continually since they'd busted Abe. In his career, Ridley had sweated maybe half a dozen other suspects into confessions. He kept asking himself whether he'd treated Burgess any differently than any of

those. He couldn't really say he had, except maybe for the heroin connection, the supposed withdrawal. But he'd done the same kind of thing
before by simple persistence, by using whatever leverage worked. The
pressure applied by a trained, relentless interrogator could be great.
This didn't make for false confessions.

In his experience, while people sometimes would confess to something they didn't do, usually this was when they weren't even suspects
in the first place. Some lunatic would walk in or call the station and say
that they'd committed some crime. Banks had once seen a man come in
and confess to a murder because he'd become enamored of the published pictures of the woman who was actually on trial for the murder
and he thought she'd be grateful to him for taking the heat off her,
putting it all on himself. Greater love than this. And perhaps later when
the guy got out of jail or acquitted at trial (because after all he hadn't
really done it), he and the woman could date or get married or something, raise little murder suspects of their own.

But Ridley believed that the Burgess confession—which he'd carefully wrung out of him—did not fall in this category. He believed that if
you had a suspect at the scene of the crime when the crime was committed, with the weapon nearby and physical evidence that gave him a reasonable motive, and that person finally got persuaded to admit he'd
done it, it was a virtual certainty that he had. People wanted to confess,
to tell what they'd done. This was human nature, although sometimes
you had to use a mental cattle prod to get down to basics.

It was far more a cerebral endeavor than a physical one. And even
on the physical plane, it hadn't gone nearly so far as to be cruel and unusual. There was discomfort perhaps—Cole hadn't been on a picnic up
here—but Ridley's interview, in his mind and memory, had been a true
interrogation, a far cry from the pain-induced confessions of the world's
myriad torture chambers.

Even given all that, though, another link in the chain of culpability
was always a nice thing, and Cullen Leon Alsop might have been just
that. This was why, late as it was, tired as he was, Ridley had wanted to
bring him up here and interview him right away. If he was convincing, if
he had something truly substantive to add about the provenance of the
gun, maybe *tonight* Ridley wouldn't toss in bed until the fitful dawn
broke.

Big ifs, and neither had panned out to Ridley's satisfaction.

Which was not to say that Cullen's evidence wouldn't get a lot of attention. Apparently it did eliminate one of the unanswered questions in the prosecution's case—where Cole Burgess had acquired the gun.

It also strengthened the argument for murder.

If he believed it.

He did believe in the truth of the rest of the facts in this case. That was the irony. He'd been there, sitting four feet across the table from Cole Burgess, when he'd said he'd done it after all. He was sorry. He didn't know why. He didn't really remember. But he did do it. He was sure of it. And Ridley had believed him, believed they'd finally come to the truth.

But now Cullen's vague, unsubstantiated testimony, which seemed to fill a hole, but which was really unprovable testimony of the "he said, but then he said" variety. And the timing of it bothered him, the snitch appearing at such an opportune moment. It didn't make him doubt that Cole had killed Elaine, but it did make him wonder.

A yawn overtook him and he stretched like a cat, his whole body. All right, he had to get some sleep. Enough was enough.

But the interview with Cullen hadn't gone on for too long—maybe fifteen minutes. He should listen to the tape once through and make better notes before copying it for the D.A. They wouldn't get the transcript back to him for at least a week, and he wanted a clear memory of what had been said.

So he rewound the tape, pushed the button and began listening. After his intro and Cullen's first interruption, the next words he heard were: "I got a deal going here with the D.A., and . . ."

He played it again.

Ridley himself hadn't made any deal with Cullen. The D.A. hadn't mentioned a deal to him. The message from that office had been that an inmate at the jail had information on the Cole Burgess case and Ridley might want to interview him. But no one had said they had made a deal, although it seemed as though Cullen was under that impression.

One thing was for sure—Ridley was going to look into it and find out.

"Mom?"

Treya was in her tiny breakfast nook—six elongated windows in a semicircle off her slightly larger kitchen. There was one light in the nook, off now, a fan under it, spinning gently, although the night outside was cold and the house cool. She was sitting on the first four inches of her chair, ramrod straight, both palms flat on the table. She might have been trying to make it levitate.

"Mom?" Raney stood silhouetted in the dim light from somewhere in the back of the duplex. She was already taller than Treya's five feet seven, skinny with no hips and just-budding breasts. She wore her hair shoulder length and had it tied off to one side in a kind of pigtail. Tonight she'd worn jogging shorts and a Giants sweatshirt to bed. "Is everything okay?"

Treya had tucked her in nearly an hour before and come out here, turning out lights as she went. She poured herself a glass of tap water, sat down at the table, hadn't moved.

"Oh, I'm fine." Treya often thought that it was her fate to exist in a limited world with a single acceptable public posture, crisp and, when possible, cheerful efficiency. All the rest of her feelings, emotions, aspirations and opinions had best remain unspoken, unexpressed. It was safest that way, where nobody could fault you for a bad attitude, an unguarded remark. She had always most keenly felt this need for control in the presence of her daughter. In this complicated world, Raney didn't need a role model who complained, who couldn't cope, who might die like her dad had. Raney needed strength, all of Treya's strength. She didn't need to see anything else.

Treya put a false brightness in her tone. "But what is my girl still doing on this side of dreamland on a school night? You're going to be dragging come morning." She started to force herself up, ready to tuck her in again.

"I've been standing here in the kitchen for ten minutes, Mom. You haven't moved a muscle. What are you thinking?"

Another smile. "I guess I just don't know, hon, to tell you the truth. I don't suppose I'm much for thinking this time of night. Maybe I was sleeping sitting up."

"Your eyes were open. You were just staring straight ahead."

"Well . . ." An embarrassed shrug. She sat back down, tried to smile, although it came out a little crooked.

Raney moved up next to her and put her arm around her shoulders. Keeping it there, she pulled a chair up close and sat in it, then laid her head against her mother's. "Are you sad about Elaine?"

Treya didn't know if she trusted herself to talk. She cleared her throat, forced a matter-of-fact tone. "People die, girl. The living have to carry on."

For an answer, she felt her daughter's arm tighten around her shoulders. She felt her lips kiss her temple. "I love you, you know."

She let out a deep and labored breath. "There was a policeman at the service this morning," she said. "Lieutenant Glitsky."

"About Elaine?"

She nodded, waited, whispered. "He was her father."

Raney straightened up. "I thought her father was dead."

"No," she replied. Another sigh. "It's a long story, but her mother—the senator, Loretta Wager? Well, she and Lieutenant Glitsky were lovers when she was young, before she got married." She paused. "Just before. Anyway, Loretta was pregnant when she got married, and she made her husband believe that Elaine was his."

"Did she tell Lieutenant Glitsky?"

"No. Not 'til much later, just before she died."

"You mean all that time he didn't know his own daughter?"

"Right."

"That's horrible. I'd be so mad if that happened to me."

Treya wasn't much in the mood, but she had to smile. "Well, that's yet another great thing about being female, girl. You generally know it when you have a baby."

"But Elaine didn't know it, either? Didn't know her own dad?"

"No, not until after her mother died. She'd left her a letter."

"A letter? About something like that?" There was a lengthy silence. "So then what did she do? Elaine. Did she go and see him?"

"No. She didn't think it was her place. She thought he should come to her. Which he never did."

"Never?"

She shook her head. "It never happened. He's just a cold man. He didn't care."

"Was that why?"

"Why what?"

"Why he didn't tell her? Didn't he care?"

"I would think so." Treya reached for her water glass and took a drink. "Why else wouldn't he?"

She shrugged. "Maybe the same reason she didn't tell him. He might have thought it wasn't his place. He didn't want to butt in."

The simple truth of it rocked Treya and she shook her head. "No. You'd have to meet him. He's just hard as nails."

"Maybe he just doesn't show things. I know somebody like that."

The arm tightened again, and Treya leaned into it. "So he was there this morning? What happened?"

She was back to the thought that wouldn't go away. "I think I might have killed him."

At Jupiter, things were hopping.

At earsplitting volume with the bass boosted to rattle the bones, Shania Twain was telling her honey she was home and wanted a cold one, and the way the bartender was hopping behind the bar, she wasn't the only one.

It was a rectangular room, sixteen feet wide and a good bit more than twice that long. The stools at the bar itself were all taken—fifteen men and six women, all of them between twenty-nine and thirty-five, none of them destined to go home alone tonight. Another three or four dozen people stood behind them on the thin stretch of floor between the bar and the booths or in the bull pen opening just behind them. Shoulder to shoulder and hip to crotch, the young professionals drinking here were mostly in law enforcement—police and attorneys, law students and clerks. A smattering of excitement groupies who loved the scene.

Jupiter was their place. They could let it out here among friends and colleagues. Most of the people here felt that outside, they lived in a constricted powder keg of frustration, tension, even danger. Some of the married ones existed in a constant state of schizophrenia—their daily life in the cop world and their home in suburbia. Jupiter was the decompression chamber that allowed them to survive the passage from the soul-eating, mind-numbing pressure of the one to the soul-eating, mind-numbing boredom of the other.

Tiny windows, high up in the bare yellow walls, dripped with condensation and gave a subterranean feel to the place. Even in the daytime, with its long and narrow shape, the bar felt like the inside of a submarine, but by night this feeling was especially pronounced. It is illegal to smoke cigarettes in eating or drinking establishments in San Francisco, yet the air was blue and acrid, thick with tobacco smoke. A few complaints had actually been filed from random walk-in do-gooders, but somehow they'd all mysteriously gotten lost.

Whatever it was that rose from the vats of french fry oil and the hamburger grills back in the kitchen added its own weight and odor to the air. Tonight at 11:51, the temperature outside was forty-four degrees.

It was eighty-six degrees—hot—in the furthest of the six booths from the front door.

In that booth, Dash Logan had removed his coat and draped it over the Naugahyde behind him. The top two buttons on his dress shirt were undone, his tie was loose. Clean-shaven, with a boyish face and perennial smile, he passed in the dim light for mid-thirties. The gold post in his left ear didn't hurt, either. He fancied that the neat, short ponytail and the subtle dye job drew attention away from the fact that the reddish hair was thinning, and he might not have been all wrong.

Certainly, tonight he was doing all right with Connie, and she couldn't have been thirty yet. He'd had his eye on her since she came in with some secretaries he knew from the federal courthouse. She was a first timer here. At least he hadn't seen her before, and he would have noticed. And in this showroom, you didn't waste time if some quality merchandise moved itself out onto the floor. He knew one of the girls with whom Connie—he loved that name even—had come in, and before they knew what had hit them, he got himself introduced and bought a round for the bunch of them.

Connie had undone some of the top buttons on her purple silk blouse, too. She was turned on the seat toward him, and the light material fell tantalizingly away from her breasts. He could just make out the black lace at the top of her bra. She'd had four whiskey sours since she'd come in.

Just across the table at the same booth, one of Connie's friends had hooked up with another guy—Dash knew him, a young lawyer with the public defender's office, married. They had been talking, yelling over the music, about some *case* for most of the past hour, and it looked to him as though that's where they would stay—she pretending to be interested in his work, him trying to find the guts either to finish what he'd started or to call it a night. Dash thought he probably wasn't up to either.

The problem with youth these days, he thought. In spite of ads exhorting Just Do It! everywhere you turned, they couldn't seem to just *fuckin' do anything*!

This waffling right across the table with one of Connie's own friends could ruin the whole vibe. He'd seen it happen—the girlfriend hits her boredom quotient, looks at her watch and goes, "Oh, Connie, look what time it is. And we've got work tomorrow." And then they both split.

But Dash was going pretty good here, telling funny stories, keeping Connie laughing, keeping her drink filled. He had a good feeling about tonight, but he had to act before this dweeb across the table ruined everything. He wanted to yell at the kid: "Get a clue. She's half in your lap with four drinks in her and her tits falling out of her blouse. What do you *think* she wants?"

It was time to make some magic. "Connie." He had to lean in closer to be heard. He kissed the side of her cheek, pulled back. "Sorry," he said, "I couldn't stand it anymore."

"It's okay." She was smiling at him. Perfect teeth. Great skin. One of those terrific northern Italian noses. "That was cute."

Cute was good, he thought. He'd take cute. "So are you a little warm? You want to go outside and cool off?"

She nodded. "That does sound good, actually."

"Here, I'll get your coat."

Her girlfriend noticed. "Where are you going?"

Dash leaned across the table. "Back in five. Promise. Save our places, will you?"

With a light hand on her back, he guided Connie through the crowd, then outside. When the doors to the bar closed behind them, Dash came up beside her. "Loud in there."

Connie was hugging her arms. "But cold out here."

He had carried both their jackets out, and helped put hers on. "Better?"

"Some." But clearly not enough.

With no hesitation, he took his own coat and draped it over her. Jupiter was in an industrial neighborhood and the street was wide, with a railroad track down the center of it. Streetlights illuminated the entire block. It was a cop bar—city services tended to work. The street, though deserted, actually looked inviting.

He held out his hand, she took it and they began to walk.

He'd parked two thirds down the street and they stopped to admire his BMW Z3. "Would you like to sit in it?" He opened the door, let her in, went around to his side. It was a convertible, but the top was up, and inside he turned on the motor and the heat. "Okay." He put on an accent. "You want to kick it up a notch?"

She nearly squealed with delight. "Oh, you watch Emeril. I love him."

Dash was shaking his head. "Nobody loves him as much as I do. I even love it that there's nobody on the Food Channel anymore except him. Except one other, what is it, the Iron Chef?"

"Something like that." Connie was into it. "But Emeril . . . let's kick it up a notch. Bam. I love that."

He reached over and touched her knee. The skirt had ridden up to her mid-thigh. He popped the glove compartment and took out a small vial of white powder. "Kick it up a real notch." In half a minute, he had poured it out onto the mirror from the glove box and arranged it into four short lines. "Just good old-fashioned nose candy. I don't want to force you to do anything." One of the lines disappeared up his nose. "See? Harmless." Then he made a face, and blew out comically.

She watched him. He finished the second line. "You know, some nights I'll get home all wired and turn on the tube and watch like three Emerils in a row. Now that is loving the man. What I don't understand is how come *he* doesn't get tired. I do three shows in a row at two a.m. and I'm gonna be dragging, I promise."

"Not with that in you."

In ten minutes, they were talking about going back to his apartment, which wasn't more than three miles up across Market. "But what about your friend?"

"Oh, she drove. We talked about it. If I'm not there, she'll just go home."

16

At seven-fifteen on this Tuesday morning, Rich McNeil, bundled in a heavy overcoat, was looking over a guano-stained railing into the green waters of the bay. Further along the railing, a lone Asian fisherman smoked and walked back and forth, pausing every few steps to tug at one of his lines. In the fifteen minutes McNeil had been waiting, he'd pulled up two small fish and put them in a burlap sack he had suspended into the water.

A light but steady glissando of traffic noise emanated along the Embarcadero, wheels hissing on the dew-slicked cobbles. The water vanished into a moderate fog at fifty yards and somewhere far off seals were barking. Their cries carried over the trackless distance in a symphony of desolation.

Hands deep in his pockets, McNeil shuddered against the chill.

At the sound of footsteps approaching behind him, he turned. "Hey, Diz."

Hardy wore a raincoat over his business suit. He extended his hand and the two men shook. "This is a cheerful spot."

McNeil turned his head as though seeing where he stood for the first time. "It is a little bleak, I guess. I've got some deliverables coming in by boat at Pier 18 and I want to be there to meet it. But I wanted to see you first, before work." He hesitated. "Before I had any more time to change my mind."

"About what?" Although Hardy had a pretty good idea.

"Well ..." He took a breath, steeling himself. "I appreciate all you've done for me on this problem with Galt, but I've talked to Sally and we've pretty much decided to just say the hell with it, sell the damn building, take our money and pay off that bastard just so he'll go away. Maybe the insurance company will cover the civil settlement."

Hardy had his hands in the pockets of his raincoat. He cocked his head to one side. "Are you sure you want to do that, Rich? Your insurance won't cover it—they'll say the theft charge isn't covered by your policy. It's going to cost you close to what you originally paid for the whole building."

"Well." He sighed. "I know, I know. Sally and I were just thinking about what the trial was going to put us through, cost us, all of that. And for what?"

"To keep Manny Galt from shaking you down, Rich. How about that? You didn't do anything he's accusing you of."

McNeil shook his head wearily. "If we lose, though, I could go to jail, Diz."

"We won't lose. There's no case."

A brittle smile. "But you can't guarantee that, can you? You've told me a hundred times, you just can't predict what a jury's going to do. And if they find me guilty, I go down."

"That's a big 'if,' though."

"But it's my life. Why do I want to risk it?"

It was an unassailable point, and Hardy couldn't answer it. Still, it galled and upset him. He jammed his hands further into his pockets, walked over to the railing and peered down into the waters of the bay, then turned back to his client. "You're just going to let him steal a quarter million dollars from you because he's an asshole?"

A desultory shrug. McNeil was embarrassed by the decision, although that didn't mean he was going to change it back. "The building's going to go for five and a half or six million. That's plenty to live on. I'll put it on the market like everybody's been advising for the last decade. Give the cretin his goddamn blackmail money, well worth it to get him out of my life at last."

But Hardy just couldn't let it go. "I thought we were going to press our own countercharges against him. Punish him because he, not you, was the one doing something wrong. If I remember, you were pretty pissed off. You wanted to fight him. So did I. So do I."

"I know."

Hardy waited.

His client tried another tack. "It'll cost almost the same as a trial, anyway."

"No it won't. A quarter mil is about twice as much as a criminal trial would cost you, Rich. At least. Hell, I'll knock my own court appearance fees down to my hourly rate." Hardy charged private clients three thousand dollars for every trial day in court, far in excess of his hourly rate of two hundred dollars. "If the trial goes a week, that alone will save you a ton."

McNeil shook his head. "It's not about money, Diz."

"That's kind of my point, too. Galt is the criminal here. Not you. So why are you the one being punished? After all he's put you through, don't you want to get this guy?"

No answer. McNeil pulled his own overcoat more tightly up around his neck. "So look," he said, "what do we have to do to get the charges dropped?"

This morning, like most mornings, a good-sized crowd waited in a cold and sullen line that extended out the door of the jail and along the outside corridor behind the Hall of Justice.

Jody Burgess wore jeans and a down parka, hiking boots and gloves. She'd been living here now for over a year and still couldn't get used to the California weather. This morning, for example, it felt really cold, arctic cold. Which was funny, because back in Ohio when it was in the mid-forties in February, it felt almost like springtime. People would go out in shirtsleeves, crunching through the snow, commenting about how nice it was, how warm. Here, though, in the damp fog, the cold ate right through to her bones. Even bundled up, she shivered.

Finally, she got inside the lobby to the jail, where it was a little warmer anyway. She gave her name to the guard and waited some more. She tried not to spend these interminable minutes worrying, or thinking about how all this would turn out. She would just concentrate on trying to be there for Cole, who was a good boy in his heart. He might have made some mistakes, might have some serious problems he'd have to overcome, but he would never intentionally hurt anyone. He was a good boy.

The time came and the guard escorted her down yet another hallway, to yet another dark doorway. She thought there must be at least a couple of visiting rooms—this one felt different from the last one she'd come to yesterday. The high windows let in a different light, although otherwise they were pretty much identical. Fifteen gray metal chairs on this side of the glass, each one at its own station. All the chairs taken now, except the one to which they were directing her.

She got to the seat and sat down. Cole wasn't across from her yet. She reached out and touched the little mouthpiece embedded in the glass.

Her son.

A guard let Cole through the door on the other side and pointed to the chair opposite her. The boy nodded, shrugged, doing what he was told. He didn't even look to see her—just the chair, where he was supposed to go and sit.

Slack hair, shuffling gait, flat expression. The orange jumpsuit again. Always.

She tried to conjure an image of when he'd been younger—she still had his high school graduation picture on the dresser next to her bed at home. His hair was shorter then, neatly combed. Freckles and a wide-open smile.

Where had that boy gone? Although she knew. She knew.

"Hey, Mom."

"Hey, Cole." She waited to see if he had something to say, but evidently not. She leaned forward, her mouth close to the speaker. "Are you all right?"

His first answer was a humorless chuckle, but he didn't want his mom getting upset, so softened it. "Better," he said. "Yeah. Fine."

"Really?"

"Well, the massage girl didn't show up last night, but other than that . . ."

"But they're taking care of you? You're eating?"

He leaned back and patted his stomach. "They're fattening me up for the kill."

Jody frowned. "That's not funny. Don't say that."

He came forward again, serious. "It's really not so bad. You just stay out of people's way."

"But you're getting your . . . medicine."

"So far." His flat gaze challenged. "And it's not medicine, Mom. It's methadone."

"I know that," she answered quickly. "I know what it is. And you're doing okay with it?"

"It's all right." He brought his own mouth closer to the glass. "I'm thinking . . ." Nervously, he ran his hand along his jawline.

"What?"

He considered it for another long moment. "Well, I don't know. You know my lawyer?"

"Yes, Cole, I know your lawyer. Mr. Hardy."

"Yeah, well, he suggested maybe I ought to think about asking them to cut back on the dose. If I wind up being in here awhile, it might . . . I don't know."

Jody did not dare succumb to hope, but it was the first time she'd been tempted in years. She was careful to try to phrase the reply in neutral terms. Too much enthusiasm from Mom might kill the impulse. "It might be worth a try, Cole, but you've got a lot of other issues you're dealing with through this."

He leaned back, folded his arms across his chest. A deep sigh escaped. "I'm thinking it might be the only issue."

She nodded carefully.

"I really do," he said after a minute. "I mean, it'd be easy enough to try here. If it didn't work, I could just go back to where I am now."

"Well." Jody's voice was resigned, low-key. "It's worth thinking about."

"They've got a program." Then he added quickly, "I'm not sure."

She was happy to leave it there. "If you think you could handle it."

"I don't know," he said. "Maybe." He came forward again. "You don't have to come here every day, you know."

"I know that. But I want to. I like seeing you, after all." This admission seemed to make him uncomfortable, though, and she changed the subject. "You should know that I'm meeting with Mr. Hardy today to talk about money and things. You don't have to worry. That's all under control." She glossed over it and kept on talking. "Has he mentioned anything to you yet about what he plans to do? In terms of your defense?"

"Not really. We haven't really talked."

Jody frowned. "Well, I'll get something on that today, too. But did you see . . . do you get the paper in here?"

He shook his head. "No mints on the pillows before bedtime either. In fact, no pillows. But why?"

She scratched at the counter. "Because there was an article this morning about Cullen."

"What about him?"

"Well, evidently he's saying he gave you the gun."

Cole came forward, sat up straight. "What gun?"

"The gun that was used to kill Elaine Wager. The murder weapon."

"Cullen?"

She nodded.

"He never gave me any gun."

"Well, in the paper today, there's a story about Cullen giving you the gun."

"When did he do that? Did it say?"

"Friday or Saturday."

"Friday or Saturday?" He was trying to dredge it up. "That didn't happen."

Jody leaned up to the glass, her mouth all but flush up against the talk box. She whispered, "Are you telling me the truth here, Cole? I want to be able to tell Mr. Hardy . . ."

Cole was glaring, his mind engaged. "I'll tell him myself, Mom. Cullen didn't give me any gun on Friday or Saturday or any other time. I picked that gun up out of the street. It was such a little thing, at first I didn't even know what it was, just sitting in the gutter down next to her and . . ." He stopped. His mouth was open, his eyes searching somewhere within himself.

"What?" For a terrifying moment, Jody thought that her son might have had something like a stroke. "Cole? What's wrong?"

The recovery was as abrupt as its onset. His eyes snapped back into focus, and if his mother wanted to see a greater clarity in them, perhaps she wasn't entirely mistaken. "I didn't kill her," he whispered in something like awe. "She was already dead."

17

After his dawn meeting with Rich McNeil on the Embarcadero, Hardy had turned around and driven back out to St. Mary's Hospital, which was halfway back to his home from downtown. Now he was next to Glitsky's bed in the ICU. On the other side of the bed, a green heart monitor beeped steadily and repeatedly drew a jagged line across a small video screen.

"So," he was saying, "there's these two guys and the one goes, 'That's how I want to die, just like my grandfather, where he's just sitting there talking, enjoying life, and suddenly his jaw drops down on his chest and his eyes close and he's gone. Yep, that's the way I want to go—' " Hardy paused. " 'Not kicking and screaming like the other guys in the car.' "

"Dying jokes?" Glitsky shifted under the sheets. "You're telling me dying jokes?" The patient blew out a long and slow breath and closed his eyes.

Hardy thought he looked like hell. His pallor was pronounced. An oxygen tube wrapped around his face and settled under his nose. Some IVs were set up and apparently dripping into him. He opened his eyes again. "I've got one."

Hardy took it as a good sign. "Hit me."

"This rich guy is near death, fretting that he can't take his money with him when he goes." Glitsky took another deep breath, adjusted the oxygen tube into his nose. "So he asks God if he can. 'Please, I've been good.' And God finally gives in and says okay, he can take one suitcase full of anything he wants to heaven. So he decides that gold is always good and fills his suitcase with bricks of the stuff."

"How'd he do that if he was near death?" Hardy asked. "Gold weighs a ton. He'd have to get out of bed, go to the bank, if they even keep gold in a bank. How sick was he, anyway? What did he have?"

Glitsky glared at him. "A heart attack. I don't know. Suspend your disbelief for a minute."

"Yeah, but a detail like that—"

"Anyway, sure enough, the guy dies . . ."

"And about time, too."

Glitsky collapsed back into his pillows. "Never mind."

"What?"

"You want to hear this or not?"

Hardy acquiesced. "Okay, the guy is dead . . ."

"Right. He gets to the pearly gates. St. Peter says, 'Hold it, no luggage allowed,' and the guy tells Peter that in his case God made an exception. Peter should check with the boss."

"This is a long joke," Hardy said.

Glitsky ignored him, forging ahead. "So God says our guy isn't lying. He's allowed to bring one suitcase. And Peter says, 'You know, I've been here a long time and nobody's ever brought anything with them before. I'd be curious to know what it is.' So the guy proudly opens his suitcase. And Peter looks at him and goes, 'Pavement? You brought pavement?' "

Hardy crossed a leg and sat back. A smile played at the corners of his mouth. "That's not really a dying joke."

Glitsky pushed the button to raise his bed, his eyes now with some life in them. "What are you talking about? A guy dies in it, so it's a dying joke, okay? It's not like there's a formal definition."

A partition sheet hung from the ceiling and set off Abe's bed from the others in the room. Someone was pulling it back and Hardy turned to see Abe's spry and spunky seventy-something father, a yarmulke over his white hair, plaid pants, baggy polo shirt. "Definition of what?" he asked.

"A dying joke," Hardy said. "Hi, Nat."

"I got a good one of those," Nat replied. "How you feeling today, Abe?"

"Abused."

Hardy smiled, translating. "Normal."

Nat went around to the monitor side, leaned over the bed and kissed his son on the face. "They have toothbrushes here? Maybe you want to use one."

Glitsky had been extraordinarily lucky, although that did not mean he was out of trouble yet. At the peak of Nob Hill, Grace Cathedral had seen more than its share of heart attacks, more even than the famous and appropriately named Cardiac Hill, the steep and lengthy grade upon which some genius architect had erected the main walkway into 3Com Park. Almost anyone walking any distance to Grace from any direction had to climb, and history had shown that many elderly hearts—and some not so elderly—weren't up to it.

Accordingly, a well-attended event such as Elaine Wager's memorial service usually featured an ambulance staffed with paramedics parked nearby. There had been one there on Monday morning when Glitsky's heart had gone into ventricular fibrillation. They'd had the electrodes on him and shocked the muscle out of its spasm in—everyone agreed—a miraculously short time.

"So what are they saying now?" Hardy wanted the facts, but they were maddeningly inexact. "What's the prognosis?"

"They're saying it was moderate," Glitsky told him.

"Which means what?" Nat put in.

Glitsky cast an eye over to his dad. "More or less it means they don't have a clue what happens next."

"Swell," Hardy said. "That's really swell."

"I like it," Abe said, agreeing with him. "It could be a dying joke, after all."

"What are the options?" Nat asked. The boys liked to run with tough-guy irony, but Nat didn't find any part of it funny. "What are they actually telling you?"

"Anything I ask. Although like everything else, if you know nothing about something, it's hard to pick the right questions." Glitsky drank from his water glass. He lifted his shoulders. "The only way they can figure actual damage to the heart muscle for now is the enzyme count, which, they say, is in the moderate increased range. Also, they're doing an angiogram before they let me out of here to see if I've got blocked arteries, which looks like a good guess. Then they'll either do a bypass or decide I don't need one."

"So what does moderate heart muscle damage mean?" Hardy asked.

"It means maybe not as much muscle died as could have, so I've got a chance to keep living."

Nat needed to clarify. "You mean some of your heart could be dead right now—the muscle—and you wouldn't know it?"

Glitsky nodded. "The part that didn't get any oxygen for long enough, that's my understanding. But they don't think that was too much."

"But if it was?" Nat persisted.

A shrug. "Then it ought to show up in a couple of days. And that would be a problem."

"How big a problem?"

"A problem," Glitsky repeated. His father's hand was on the bed and he covered it with his own. "But I'm lucky so far, Dad. They're saying these enzyme levels are okay. Let's go with that. If nothing gets complicated, I'm out of here by the weekend. Dancing."

Nat looked across at Hardy. "This I would like to see."

Dr. Campion—mid-fifties, exuding competence—had come and gone. He'd shooed both Hardy and Nat out for the morning exam. When he came out, he told them he'd ordered the nurse to give Glitsky a light sedative. They could go back in to say good-bye—that was enough visiting for this morning. He cautioned both of them to refrain from talking about anything that might be upsetting. The feeling was that they were just going to give him another day to rest, then they'd evaluate the situation and make some decisions.

Hardy stood by the bed and waited while Nat talked domestic details. Abe's youngest son, Orel, was in school today but would be back by visiting hours tonight. Nat hadn't heard back from Isaac, the eldest, until late last night. He was driving up today from L.A. and he'd be by tonight as well. Nat hadn't been able to reach Jacob in Milan, but he was still trying.

"Don't do that." Abe was appalled at the idea. "There's no reason to bother him about this."

"You don't think he'd want to know his father had a heart attack? Wouldn't you want to know if, God forbid, I ever have a heart attack?"

"You don't have those genes. This," he said, pointing to his chest, "was Mom."

"Or forty years of junk food and no exercise." Hardy smiled helpfully.

Glitsky glared at him and spoke back to his father. "Besides, what's Jacob going to do about it over there?"

"How about fly home, make sure you're okay?"

Abe was shaking his head. "He doesn't have the money for that."

"I'll pay for it, Abraham."

Glitsky raised his voice. "I'm not trying to get out of paying, Dad. I'm saying he doesn't need to come. By the time he gets here, I'll be home. I'm fine."

Nat took his case to Hardy. "He's fine. His heart muscle might be already dead inside his chest and he's fine."

Hardy decided he ought to step in. "Abe. Shut up. Your sons need to be here. All of 'em. End of story."

"Thank you." Nat touched his forehead in a gracious gesture. "Listen to your friend here, Abraham. He knows what's good for you."

Glitsky took in the two of them. "God help me," he said.

Nat went away, muttering. Glitsky had motioned Hardy to stay back a minute.

Now he sat down again. "Dr. Campion said keep it short. And we're not supposed to upset you."

"Really?" Glitsky deadpanned. "Good going."

"He also said the nurse gave you a sedative. I'm thinking you palmed it or something."

"It must not have kicked in yet." But to Hardy, it seemed that it was starting to. Glitsky laid his head back against his pillow and closed his eyes for a moment, then visibly seemed to gather his strength so that he could talk. "So what did I miss on Elaine's case?"

Hardy shook his head. "That would go under the general topic of things that might upset you."

"Not telling me will be worse. Was there something?"

Hardy sighed. He didn't know about Treya Ghent's verbal attack on Glitsky the day before, and therefore didn't know that it had been a good bet as the proximate cause of the heart attack. He did know, however, that his friend had lost his daughter and his job in the same week—that could do it, too. And the doctor had warned about creating more stress.

Still, Glitsky was probably right. If he didn't tell him, it might be worse. "Some snitch is saying he gave Cole the gun on Saturday."

"What is Cole saying about that?"

"I wish I knew." Hardy gestured. Frustration. "The story broke in the paper this morning. I haven't had time to see him, what with you and all."

Glitsky chewed on it for a long moment. "It was in the paper this morning?"

"Yep. Front page. The last unanswered question in the case, if memory serves. And it does." Hardy ran down the details on Cullen Leon Alsop.

When he finished, Glitsky said, "So Pratt leaked it."

"How do you come to that?"

"Because a snitch would have drawn Ridley Banks. He's the inspector of record and he doesn't leak. It would be interesting to see the timing on the leak. If maybe it got to the paper before Ridley even found out about it."

Hardy was intrigued. "Which would mean what?"

Again, though, Glitsky leaned back into his pillow and closed his eyes. Opening them, he lifted the corners of his mouth a fraction of an inch. "See, I'm not upset. I'm relaxed."

"Good. But we were on—"

A restraining hand. "I know where we were. A couple of months ago, there was another little stink about a snitch—maybe you remember? Pratt denied it, but hey, that's what she does."

"What was it?"

"Same kind of leverage. This was a third-strike case, one of those drive-bys where nobody died, not even the usual three innocent bystanders, so it didn't go high-profile. Still, it was a screwup." Hardy waited through another hiatus, another recovery. "They couldn't put a weapon together with the shooter, so there was this story in the paper that this snitch—"

"Okay, I do remember that now." Suddenly, it came back to Hardy. "He knew where the gun was, in the shooter's girl's garage or someplace, but then after he talked to the police, he changed his mind."

"Right. Decided three strikes and life in prison beat being dead, which would happen if he snitched. But he told us the D.A. had offered him a deal if he'd plant the gun with the guy they knew was the shooter.

Of course Pratt denies this. But the story ran before he talked to any inspectors. And the snitch sure didn't leak it on his own. No access to the press, right? So it was the D.A."

"But why in the world would they do that?"

"What? Leak? Or create bogus evidence?"

"Either."

"Second nature. They get something, they gotta tell some reporter. It makes it real—the headline is good PR and later, when it goes to hell, it's old news and nobody pays attention." Glitsky had closed his eyes again. "If it got to the paper before Ridley talked to this bozo . . ."

"Jeff Elliot might be able to find that out." Hardy hung his head, hands clasped and elbows on his knees, thinking about it for a minute. When he looked up, Glitsky hadn't moved a muscle. "Abe?" he asked quietly. A long pause, then again. "Abe?"

He put a finger to his friend's neck, waited until he felt a pulse, let out a sigh of relief and stood up.

18

Hardy had no memory of his last meal.

He was leaving the hospital when a stab of light-head hit him so hard he had to stop and sit quickly on a convenient low wall just outside the main doors. For an instant, it crossed his mind that he might be having his own heart attack, until he realized that there was no pain or pressure. Just a gaping hollowness somewhere in his center.

He tried to remember the last time he'd eaten—he thought it must have been breakfast yesterday morning, but he couldn't recall if he'd even been home. He just didn't remember anything except that he drank some Scotch last night. Then, this morning, McNeil had woken him up with his urgent business, and Hardy had run out before coffee.

It was now nearly ten o'clock in the morning. The day loomed full before him. He knew he had to go see Cole at some point, though his inclination was to wait until after he'd had his business meeting with his mother. There was also McNeil's proposed settlement, and that meant another six or eight calls before Dash Logan, probably drunk at Jupiter, found it in his best interest to return one of them—the thought of it curdled his stomach.

It was growling at him now.

Which brought him back full circle. He had to get some food.

Frannie Hardy had majored in urban planning at USF, but work in her field was scarce. After she graduated, she had rent to pay, so her first jobs had been a couple of entry-level clerical positions. These did not bring her any great sense of personal fulfillment. Within two years, she was married and pregnant with Rebecca.

The direction her life had taken had determined her "career" for the past decade or so. The kids were growing, and so was a void within her. But the concept of urban planning had lost whatever thrill it once had held for her. She saw things on a smaller scale now, a more personal one—individual relationships, marriages, parents and children. She wanted to work doing some kind of counseling. She was filling out applications for graduate school at the dining room table when she heard the front door opening. "Hello?" She came up out of her chair.

"Yo." Her husband's voice. "It's only me, Maynard." He came into view, shrugging out of his raincoat.

"Maynard?"

"Maynard G. Krebs. Surely you remember Maynard G. Krebs?"

"With all that junk in your brain, how do you ever remember anything important? But why are you home?" Then, remembering, her breath caught. "Oh, God, Abe...?"

"He's doing okay so far, they think."

"So far? They think?"

"I know. Real strong." He shrugged. "More tests today and tomorrow. He's cranky as ever. I'm taking that as a good sign. His dad was there, the boys are coming in today." Hardy was moving toward the kitchen. "As for me, my wife hasn't been feeding me. I've been driven to forage on my own."

Following him in, she clucked understandingly. "She must be awful."

He nodded. "Pretty bad."

He pulled his cast-iron pan off the marlin hook from which it hung on the wall behind the stove. He sprinkled salt into it, a grind of pepper.

In the refrigerator, he discovered vegetables—peppers, potatoes, green beans, an onion—and laid them on the cutting board along with three eggs. Cutting now, he asked her how the application process was going, and she said it wasn't too bad. She was doing one of her admission essays on Abe and Elaine.

Hardy stopped chopping. "What?"

"Not using names, of course."

"No, okay, but what about them?"

"Abe knowing he was her father, but not telling her for all this time. Why he'd want to do that?"

"I don't think he wanted to, Fran. Knowing Abe, he probably felt duty-bound not to tell her."

"And look at the toll it took."

"It didn't make his heart stop, Fran."

"Maybe not, but on top of everything else. I thought it was pretty interesting, just the idea." She paused. "That he never even told us, and we're his best friends."

Hardy was back to cutting. "People have secrets. Elaine had her own life. She didn't need him."

"Don't kid yourself. Kids need their fathers." Frannie folded her arms and leaned back against the counter. "I find it sad that he didn't ever get to know her, that he chose that. For whatever reason."

Hardy dumped vegetables into the pan. "I think he'd agree with you. I think that's half the reason he keeps looking for more evidence. So he'll have an excuse to get to know her."

"In spite of the confession?"

Hardy cracked the eggs directly into the pan and stirred with a slotted spoon. "The confession was bad, that's all. They've got enough evidence to convict Cole without it. Abe just needs to keep looking."

She waited, then asked. "So what do you need?"

"What do you mean?"

"I mean why are you defending him? If he killed Elaine . . ."

He stirred his omelette and considered for a moment. "I guess because no matter what, this shouldn't be a death penalty case. I'm trying to keep that from happening, that's all."

"Even if he did it?"

"Even if he did it. It won't make it harder to get him off. It won't make it easier. It doesn't matter."

"It doesn't matter? God, I hate it when you sound so much like a lawyer."

"I do, too," Hardy admitted ruefully. "But the sad truth is, that's what I am."

And now the lawyer was trying to get around to doing something else he detested—talking about fees. Jody Burgess was sitting with him on his office couch. He didn't like to put his clients across his desk from him. It put a psychic distance between them that felt awkward.

But Jody was filled with optimism, fueled by good news. She wasn't ready to discuss the cost of the trial and Hardy's representation. Like

Frannie, like so much of the rest of the lay world, Jody seemed obsessed with the fact of Cole's guilt or innocence. According to her, he'd recovered a repressed memory that morning, one that contained the absolute and final new version of the truth of the events of early Monday morning.

To Hardy, this simply meant that Cole was changing his story again. First he did it, then he didn't remember doing it, now he didn't do it at all. Who knows? he thought. Next he might remember that he'd actually been by her side trying to save Elaine's life.

Hardy thought he preferred Door #2, where Cole didn't remember either way whether or not he'd done it. That answer comported most closely with the facts of some kind of unconsciousness defense, which in turn seemed the most likely to succeed. Thinking this, he realized with something between pride and a pang that he must have been hanging around David Freeman too much. He was really beginning to think like a lawyer.

It was a cold afternoon outside, the fog having lifted to a low cloud cover, but his office was warm. Jody, though, still wore her heavy coat. She was drinking hot coffee. Hardy almost started sweating just looking at her.

Finally, he broached the fee issue, since he had an idea that really was reasonable, given what they had to work with. And it was certainly the least expensive way to proceed, since it would end things fairly quickly. "Where I thought we'd go"—he was speaking carefully because, low cost notwithstanding, this was not going to bear even a slight resemblance to good news—"was get the charge lessened in exchange for a guilty plea." He pressed ahead quickly. "That way the D.A. gets to count it as a conviction, we get out of the death penalty arena before we even have to argue the special circumstances." He spread his palms. "Everybody wins."

For a second, he thought she might not have understood. "A plea bargain?" she said. "But he didn't kill her at all."

"Well, he's really not too sure about that."

"But this morning . . . he really remembered. I saw it in his eyes, this great relief."

"I'm sure you did."

She put down her coffee cup with a clatter. "You don't believe me."

Hardy told her he believed her completely. "But I don't know whether a jury would, and that's the problem."

Jody sat with it for a while. Eventually she went back to her coffee. "Let's just say we don't make a deal, just for discussion's sake. What then?"

"Then we have a hearing next week, during which Mr. Torrey will show the tape of the confession, and that should be enough to convince the judge that there's sufficient evidence to go forward with the trial."

"But won't you argue that the confession—"

"Was coerced? Of course. Beyond that, I'll argue that Cole's words contradict the facts as we know them. But in the real world out there, in the courtroom, neither of those things will make any difference."

"Why not?"

Jody didn't like to hear this, but if anything, Hardy was sugarcoating. He had to get her to understand the gravity of Cole's situation. "Because a preliminary hearing isn't about whether Cole is guilty or not guilty. It's only to determine whether or not there's a case. Then it goes to trial."

She was still having trouble accepting it. "This is so unreal," she said. After another minute, she shook her head in frustration and finally sat back on the couch with almost an air of collapse.

Hardy waited until her reaction had run its course, then decided it might be useful to agree with her. "It does feel like that, I know." He couldn't leave it at that, though. He had to instruct her. "But it is real, believe me, and the decisions we make right now are going to matter later, so we ought to make sure they're the right ones."

She rose up, challenging, her voice shaking. "And you think the right one is saying he did it when he didn't?"

"You know for sure that he didn't? You are a hundred percent certain?"

She didn't even have to think about it. "Absolutely. He's not a murderer."

Hardy nodded, not at the validity of the point but in acknowledgment of what had to come next if he was going to continue with his representation of her son. If he was going to get anywhere here with her today, he would have to break through her resistance, her blindness. It was time for hardball. "Mrs. Burgess, has Cole ever lied to you?"

The question surprised her. "This is nothing like—"

He held up a finger, stopping her. "It's a simple question. Has he ever told you a lie?"

She found herself unable to answer.

"Many lies? More lies than you can remember? Has he ever stolen anything from you? I know he lied to Jeff and Dorothy when they put him up. He stole from them. He stole from *their children,* Mrs. Burgess. Did they tell you anything about this?"

She'd come forward to the edge of the couch. She crossed her arms low over her stomach. As though the questions were hitting her there. "Well, okay, but—"

"Do you know anyone that your son hasn't lied to in the past several years? Or stolen from? Do you think he's trying to get off heroin right now?"

"Yes, yes, at least that." He could see she thought he was throwing her a rope. "He said he thought he might get in a program—"

"Has he done that? Has he done anything in that direction other than talk about it? Do you think he was trying to kick the habit before all this happened?"

"I do. He'd been back to the halfway house, I know that was pretty recently. He was really trying. It's really hard, you know. It's not that easy." She was leaning over into her arms now, as though her stomach was cramping.

"I appreciate that," he said. "It's hard enough when you're really, really trying, when you're in a program and working with counseling. Was Cole in one of those, I mean outside?"

"No, but he couldn't find the right mix somehow. You know, some of those counselors don't—"

"It's the counselors' fault he couldn't quit? Is that right? And when he came and stayed with you, and then stole your car, for example. You punished him for that, didn't you? You let him know he'd done something really wrong."

"Yes. Yes, I did." She was almost pleading with him now, her eyes becoming glassy with unshed tears. "I did tell him how disappointed I was, Mr. Hardy. That I loved him and how much it hurt me. It did hurt me."

Hardy hated to continue, but his only hope to work with her demanded that she recognize the reality they were facing. "And he said he was sorry—"

She fired it back at him. "He *was* sorry. He just . . . he was . . ."

"And so, because he was sorry, you let him come back and stay with you again, right?"

"What was I supposed to do, Mr. Hardy? I'm his mother. Let him sleep on the streets?"

"Other parents have," he said simply. "It's been known to happen."

"Well, I couldn't. He was trying." She took a deep breath. "He was trying." The staggered breaths kept coming as though she'd been running.

He wanted to ask if she thought Cole had been trying Monday morning when he stole the other bum's whiskey and went off wandering downtown, trying to find his "g." But that would just be more talking, more arguing. He had a different idea, one that he suddenly knew would be far more effective.

His discovery documents were on the desk at his elbow, and he lifted a labeled manila folder, extracting from it what he needed—one of the coroner's close-ups of Elaine Wager's ear. He crossed back to Jody and laid the perfectly focused, full-color eight-by-ten on the table in front of her. "Look at her ear, Mrs. Burgess," he ordered harshly. "Where Cole ripped her earring out. He also broke her finger getting her ring off, Mrs. Burgess. Was he trying then? Was that trying? Was that your good boy?"

"You're horrible!" she screamed. "He didn't—"

"Yes he did, Mrs. Burgess!" he snapped back, his own voice raised. "He sure as hell did." Hardy turned abruptly, calming himself, and when he felt he could speak, he did. "It's horrible, all right," he said softly, "but it's not me."

He was breathing hard himself now, half expecting that the next sound he heard would be the door opening and closing behind him. Instead, he heard nothing, and eventually he turned.

She was doubled over, her whole body shaking. He came around the table and sat closely next to her. He put an arm around her shoulder.

It didn't seem to help.

Afterwards, the office seemed a little constricted, and they went downstairs to the building's unique conference room. The residents had nicknamed it the Solarium because when there was afternoon sun, which happened frequently, though not today, this room miraculously caught some of it. Enormous potted plants thrived under its greenhouse windows and glass roof. It opened onto a small enclosed garden that in the summer bloomed with impatiens and pansies, vinca and lobelia, and that today featured dirt, a bench and a hundred square feet of brown lawn.

Hardy brought his discovery documents down with them. Jody had recovered somewhat after first breaking down completely. She'd wanted to see all of the photos, then to scan the police reports, so Hardy put his folders in front of her and sat on her right.

In the garden area outside, he watched some sparrows flit about, picking at the lawn.

After about ten minutes, she closed the last folder. Hardy waited another moment or two, then spoke conversationally. "That's the person Torrey wants the jury to see. If he succeeds, Cole is in trouble. I need you to understand that."

"These pictures, what these policemen wrote. It looks like . . ." She swallowed her own words, couldn't continue.

"Yes, it does. And even if we argue that he just came upon her after she was dead, the theft of the jewelry doesn't exactly cast him in the most sympathetic light."

"And you're pretty sure he took the jewelry? That he did that?"

He was loath to punish Jody any more, but this he couldn't deny. "All of it was on his person when they brought him in. The best you could say is that he knew she was already dead while he was robbing her. He wasn't hurting her."

She dabbed at her eyes. "That's not much of a best."

"No, it's not." Whether he'd been excessively cruel or not, Hardy now at least had her where she might be receptive to what he had to say. "This is why I'm talking about a guilty plea. Once we get to trial, if we do, this case will be hard to win on its merits in front of a jury. Do you understand what I'm saying?"

She nodded miserably.

"That's why I thought it would be worthwhile to explore some legal solutions short of trial."

"Where you admit he did it?"

"Where he pleads guilty, yes, which is not exactly the same thing."

"In return for what?"

"I would hope for no death penalty, to begin with. Then a possible parole someday."

"Oh God, prison." She looked at him sharply. "What do you mean, you hope?"

"I mean it wouldn't stun me to have Torrey turn us down." He explained that the D.A.'s office was already taking a lot of flak for pleading out important cases. Sharron Pratt had already handpicked this one, hitching her political fortunes to it. Getting her to agree to a plea wasn't going to be a slam dunk by any means. And the bad news wasn't over yet. "Even if we go to trial and convince a jury that the murder was a lesser offense, which is about the best we can expect, we're going to wind up about where we are today—in jail, going to prison for a very long time."

Jody's face told Hardy that this was the first day of her season in hell. Her eyes were shot with red, heavy lidded and swollen. Her skin had taken on a mottled look. She barely dared phrase the question. "But what if they do find him not guilty? What if you convince them?"

"Then he goes free." He reached over and touched her hand. "But Jody, so we have no misunderstanding, I have to tell you I'm not inclined to try to do that."

Earlier in the afternoon, she might have regarded that announcement with horror. Now she closed her eyes for a moment, took in a deep breath, gathering her strength. "Why not?"

"Because here's that story: Cole, a heroin addict, is walking around drunk and maybe stoned early on a Monday morning. He's carrying a gun . . ."

"But he isn't. He said that wasn't true."

Hardy acknowledged that, but so what? "The jury will have heard he was carrying the gun. He's looking for someone to rob so that he'll have money for his drug habit, and he happens upon Elaine Wager. When the police arrive like two minutes later, Elaine is dead and Cole is stripping her body of jewelry. He runs. He's fired the gun. A few hours later, he confesses to killing her."

Hardy softened his voice nearly to a whisper. "The jury is going to hear all that, Jody. There is physical evidence to back it all up. I'm not even saying here that I think he did it. This isn't me. This is the jury. If I go in front of them and just say 'No, all of that's true except it wasn't Cole who killed her,' you know what's going to happen? They'll convict him of everything. And then when we argue that they should spare his life, our credibility will be shot."

She looked at him, knowing he was right.

He had to go on. "I can do that if that's what we all decide. We can try to get Cole straight and put him on the stand all dressed and cleaned up and he can deny it, deny Cullen gave him the gun, tell the whole truth. But if I let him do that, I'm not giving him his best defense."

"Even if it's true? That he didn't kill her?"

"Yes, even if he didn't kill her. Even if he was just the unluckiest man alive on Monday morning. He has no alibi. There's precious little, if any, evidence in his favor." Hardy knew it sounded hopeless. What was worse, the more he talked about it, the more he was coming to believe that it was hopeless. He tried to explain it a last time. "Jody, I want to tell the truth to the jury, and I believe the truth is that whether or not Cole killed Elaine, he wasn't in his right mind as the law defines the term. He was unconscious. He shouldn't be executed."

"And that's what I should be praying for? That my son won't be executed?"

Hardy nodded somberly. He looked out at the sparrows again, still pecking for crumbs on the dead winter lawn. "It might be a good place to start."

19

Gene Visser was whistling the children's song "It's a Small World" through a toothpick as he exited the elevator into the basement of the Hall of Justice. He was accompanied by his friend and employer Dash Logan and a sergeant of narcotics named Bills Keene, whose father had been a fanatic follower of football from Buffalo. As a child, Bills had been a tough enough kid to grow into the name. He still rooted for Buffalo's team, which last night had killed the 49ers on Monday Night Football.

"I'm telling you, Dash, it was the best night of my life. Here I am, giving ten points, and I had half the department lining up to give me their money."

Visser stopped whistling. "You were giving ten on the Bills? Next time, call me."

Keene looked over happily. "I'll put you on the list, or you can direct-deposit into my account, either way."

"So how'd you make out?" Dash asked.

They were moving into the reception area just off the records room/evidence locker. The time was a little after three o'clock in the afternoon, and they were the only people downstairs except for the officers assigned to evidence security.

"Eight hundred forty dollars."

Logan whistled, impressed. "I hope you're declaring it."

"Every penny." Keene was grinning broadly, having a fine old time on an otherwise slow workday. The cop behind the window came up and greeted them. "Including the twenty of Officer McDougal here. Hey, Gary. How 'bout them Bills, huh?"

McDougal had his wallet out and handed Keene a twenty over the sign-in counter. "Want to go double or nothing next week?"

"We're talking my own Buffalo Bills, right?"

McDougal was appalled. "Get real. We're talking the Niners. Who cares about the Bills?"

Logan was enjoying the exchange as well. He appeared to have a bit of a runny nose and from time to time would sniff delicately. "Am I mistaken," Logan asked, "or is gambling still frowned upon in this state?"

"Absolutely," McDougal replied with a smile.

"It's a scourge," Keene added. "But you know, the mafia."

Everybody enjoyed the moment of the manly camaraderie. "So what brings you gentlemen down here today?"

Down to business, Logan gave a small sigh and put his briefcase up on the counter. "I'm going to trial on *People v. Lawson* next Monday." He gave McDougal the case number. "It's Inspector Keene's case here. I thought I ought to look at what the D.A. had actually collected before I tried to save my client's poor ass."

McDougal shook his head in mock disbelief. "I don't know how you do it."

Logan looked at him questioningly. "What?"

"Keep your clients if you don't even look at the evidence until a week before trial. Don't they get a little pissed off?"

A blustery laugh, followed by a sniffle. "What? I tell them? Come on, get a life." But then he backpedaled a bit. "I generally know what's supposed to be there. It usually is. If it isn't, I make a motion to dismiss." He shrugged. "It's worked out."

Visser added his two cents. "His real talent is making it look like he's not working. The man works all the time."

Logan made a gracious gesture toward his private eye. "An unsolicited testimonial from an unbiased source. Thank you, Eugene." Sniff.

He turned to Keene. "So, Sergeant, shall we go?"

McDougal buzzed the door for them, and Logan and Keene went inside to sign the book. Visser, at the reception window, leaned in and asked how long they would be.

Logan shrugged, looked a question at Keene, who did the same. "I don't know. Fifteen, twenty? Hey, Gary, you mind letting Gene in, sit his ample posterior on a chair? We might be a minute."

McDougal frowned at the request. He wasn't supposed to let in anyone who wasn't accompanied by a police officer, and they had to sign in to a specific case. But he wasn't supposed to gamble either, especially here on police premises. And these were pretty good guys—he knew them all. Visser had even been a homicide cop when McDougal had first come up. There was a chair he could sit in right next to his own—it wasn't as though Visser was here in the evidence lockup to rip something off. He'd never be out of McDougal's sight. He spoke up to Keene. "You want to sign him in on your ticket?"

From out at the window, Visser said it wasn't any big deal, he could stand.

But Keene said sure, buzz him on in.

"So what'd you guys do to pull this assignment?"

Visser was seated next to Gary McDougal in the sign-in area, making conversation with him and another young cop—the name tag read "Bellew"—from the gun room next door. He knew that being stuck down here in the basement as records and evidence room custodian was not exactly a sought-after position among the uniforms. It wasn't quite an official, on-the-books reprimand, but neither did anybody ever mistake it for a reward.

McDougal made a face, shook his head in disgust. "We ate a couple of doughnuts we didn't pay for." The men all exchanged glances. "I know," McDougal continued. "You don't have to say it."

But Bellew felt like he did. "It was some bullshit OMC sting to fight police corruption in the big city." The OMC was the Office of Management and Control—formerly called Internal Affairs, the department that policed the police.

"You being an ex-cop," McDougal said, "you'll be amazed to hear that sometimes it's hard for us street guys to pay for coffee, snacks, like that. Seems like people we're out guarding their stores, they feel grateful sometimes. They make us a sandwich, pour us a cup, forget to ring it up."

"I'm shocked to hear it," Visser said. "That's almost as bad as gambling."

The officers both chuckled. From over by the entrance to the gun room, Bellew took it up. "Yeah. So anyway, OMC gets a bug up their

ass that guys are abusing their public trust. Taking a goddamn sandwich. So they put a couple of their guys behind counters and one son of
a bitch gives us both doughnuts . . ."

McDougal: "Which—get this—I offer to pay for. And he says, 'No,
that's okay, don't worry about it.' "

"And they bust you guys for that?"

Bellew answered. "They hit maybe twenty of us in one day, said we
ought to take it as a wake-up call. Yada yada."

"But they sent you down here?"

"Six weeks, no overtime."

Visser took in the immediate surroundings—institutional clutter
ruled here in the sign-in area. The walls were lined with green metal
shelves to the ceiling. Stained and rusted metal tables sagged with
the weight of cardboard boxes filled with junk that had lost its case
number—confiscated cell phones, batteries, radios, bicycle tires, tools.
From his time in the police department, he knew that the rest of the
place was an enormous cavern, nearly a city block on a side, a home to
the records and evidence in every crime committed in the city and
county over the past ten years.

There were miles of case files. There was a freezer for blood, soiled
clothes, the occasional body part. There was an entire room for bi-
cycles, another for computers. A locked walk-in safe for narcotics. And
the gun room, adjoining the sign-in.

"And how much time have you already put in?" he asked.

"Four weeks. Two to go, but who's counting?"

McDougal stood as a homicide inspector—Marcel Lanier—appeared
at the window with a yellow folder bulging with stuff. When the two men
had been talking a minute, Visser leaned over the table and interrupted.

"Marcel, how you doin'?" Lanier stopped his paperwork, nodded
with a question in his face, and Visser answered it. "I'm just waiting for
Dash Logan, doing some baby-sitting. How's the murder biz?"

"A little shaky at the moment. Glitsky had a heart attack. You hear
that?"

Visser chatted about that for another minute or so, establishing still
further to McDougal and Bellew that he was really in the club—buds
with Keene, friendly with Lanier in homicide, familiar with Glitsky, a
sympathetic guy about their beef with the OMC.

At the counter, they went back to logging in Lanier's evidence. Visser, already standing, turned to Bellew. "That box full of pieces still here?" he asked.

"It never goes away," Bellew answered.

"You mind if I look at it?" He turned back for a minute. "Gary?" He pointed. "Guns? Okay?" •

McDougal waved him in. "Sure."

Nonissue.

Like the sign-in area, the gun room was floor-to-ceiling shelves and files, packed with yellow storage envelopes identified by case numbers in black permanent marker, and each of which held a gun. Four or five hundred file drawers, with a minimum of, say, forty handguns in each one. Several of the file drawers gaped open, possibly—Visser thought—because they were too stuffed with hardware to allow closing.

On the wall behind Bellew's station, rifles and assault weapons threatened to flow over onto the floor. Another large box of rifles sat open on Bellew's table. Below the table, a wooden crate was open on the floor, half filled with assorted confiscated handguns—unloaded, of course, but fully operational, unassigned to any specific case. The police found them in the streets, in hedges, garbage cans, Dumpsters and dope houses where all the occupants had fled out the back. They were destined to become manhole covers, and good riddance.

The "piece box" had been in the same place under the table here in the evidence lockup—albeit with a continuously changing assortment of guns—at least since Visser had started with the force twenty-some years before. And probably for a long time before that. When a gun came in, they put the serial number into "the book," a set of records going back almost seventy-five years. And on the last day of the month, every gun was logged into the computer, dumped into a crusher and destroyed.

Now, on February 9th, Visser estimated that the crate held about forty handguns—everything from little .22 or .25 caliber derringers to Uzi-style repeating pistols, from tape-handled Saturday night specials to shining new Glock .38s. Visser knew that by the end of this month, every month, the weapons would be spilling over the top of the crate, clattering onto the tiles. Guns guns guns.

Bellew was delighted with the company—anything to break up his enforced boredom. He and Visser were a couple of kids in a candy store. Picking up one piece, then another, clicking off a bunch of non-rounds, checking actions, dropping the cylinders out of the revolvers, the clips from the automatics. Telling the occasional story behind one of them.

Time was flying they were having so much fun. Then, suddenly, McDougal was at the table with them, delivering the message that Logan and Keene were signing out.

"Eugene!" Logan's voice, calling in. "Let's roll it out of here." McDougal, next to Visser, picked up a random revolver from the table, spun the cylinder, pointed it at the "Safety First" poster on the wall and pulled the trigger, smiling as it clicked.

"Fun stuff, isn't it?" he said.

"I almost feel bad about it." Visser was fastening the seat belt in Logan's Z3. "I keep telling myself it just can't be this easy every time."

The lawyer looked over at him. "Hey, Eugene, please. The cops let you go. Remember that? You weren't good enough for them."

"I know, but still. Metal detectors at the doors to the Hall so you can't get a gun in, except you can stroll right out, armed to the teeth. I mean, who's thinking here?"

Dash Logan nearly fishtailed getting into traffic out of the parking lot. It wasn't convertible weather by a long shot, and he had the top on. His nasal attack appeared to have kicked in again, and he was in high spirits. "Here's a little well-kept secret, Eugene. You can stroll right in, too."

"How do you do that?"

No signal, and Dash changed lanes, accelerating to fifty. He passed two cars, ran a red light, swung back into his original lane. He pinched his nose with his thumb and forefinger, sniffed back. "How do you think all those guns in the lockup get inside the Hall?"

"They're evidence. I've brought a bunch in myself in my time."

"Right. And what defines evidence?" Dash let him work it out.

It didn't take him long. "An evidence tag."

"Correct. A little piece of paper that says evidence on it. You want to bring a bazooka inside the Hall, you put a tag on it, walk right around the metal detector, tell the guard to have a nice day. If we weren't the good guys, I'd say it really wasn't fair. Whoa!" Suddenly, he braked hard and pulled into a spot at the curb. "Jupiter already." He flashed a grin at his passenger. "No wonder they call me Dash."

• • •

Gabe Torrey hung up and immediately started to punch in the numbers for Sharron's direct line, but decided this was important enough to warrant a visit. In half a minute, he was in the anteroom outside her office, where Madeleine, Pratt's secretary, waved him in as a matter of course.

The district attorney of San Francisco was hard at work—even Pratt's enemies conceded that she was a tireless workaholic. The complaint, if there was one, was that often her work produced no tangible results. But she put in the hours, no one denied that.

She was sitting at the computer next to her desk, her fingers flying over the keys. Hearing the door, she looked over. Torrey saw the telltale ghost of displeasure and impatience playing on her features, but then it flitted away. She didn't like being interrupted, but since it was him . . .

He closed the door behind him. "Interesting news," he said.

"I hate that word, interesting." With a sigh, Pratt pushed back from the computer. "You might as well just say bad. Somebody tells you about a movie and says it was interesting, do you want to go out and see it? Never. And if you do, guess what? It sucks."

Torrey heard out the tirade. "Is this a bad time?" he asked mildly.

"Not particularly. I'm just trying to get this article written for *American Lawyer.*"

They had discussed this over the weekend—the magazine was getting input from D.A.'s around the state on the question of how various communities were handling the problem of so-called victimless crimes, such as prostitution and drug abuse. Sharron's position was that, basically, you didn't prosecute them, and since the legal community in the state was aware of this, Torrey had been under the impression that he'd convinced her to farm the task out to one of her junior staff people.

"So you *are* writing it yourself."

There was no defensiveness in her answer. She had made her decision and it was the right one and that was that. "I told you I thought it would be better me . . ."

". . . than somebody else who couldn't express it as well."

"Exactly. I'd just wind up doing it over myself anyway. And if my name's going to be on it . . ."

"I know. We've been over this. You're wasting your time with this detail work. That's why you have a staff."

"I'm wasting my time reading incompetent drafts, Gabe."

"So hire a good writer."

"I'm a good writer," she snapped. "I know what I want to say and I say it well."

He was never going to win. He nodded with resignation. "We agree to disagree, okay?"

"Fine." She bit off the word.

This wasn't the best start for what might prove to be an important and controversial meeting. Torrey considered taking her dismissive tone to heart and making his exit. Leave her to her damned article.

He could come back to it tonight, when she'd be more receptive after a drink or two. But he didn't get a chance to move before she said, "So what's the interesting news?"

Torrey had no choice. He willed all trace of the earlier tone out of his voice and delivered it flat. "Dismas Hardy called me ten minutes ago. He wants to deal."

Pratt looked at him. "Actually," she said, "that is interesting. What does he want?"

"Murder two."

"Murder two?" Clearly, it surprised her. She barked a cold laugh. "He wants to go from death to murder two? The man's got a tremendous imagination. What did you tell him?"

"I told him I had to talk to you."

Pratt fixed him with a hard eye. "That's a nice flattering answer, Gabe. But what did you really tell him?"

"That's really what I told him." He pulled a chair around and sat. "I said that since you'd made this particular case a campaign issue, it wasn't going to be that simple."

She frowned. "But it is that simple," she said. "There's no way."

In fact, Torrey had told Hardy that they would have to work out the details, but in general he thought a reduced charge in return for a guilty plea was a workable idea. After the election, of course. Hardy could waive time for a few months and then, after the dust had settled on the results, they would do the deal. Pratt's administration had grown infamous for its willingness to plead out cases rather than take them to trial. In this regard, it had by far the most lenient record of any jurisdiction in the state. Torrey saw no reason to let the campaign change the basic policy.

So Pratt's refusal here hit him like a broadside. "There's no way, what?"

"There's no way we cut a deal on this. I've gone on the record saying

I want the death penalty in this case." She came around in front of him and leaned back against her desk. "I can't believe I have to explain this to you. There's no other option, I hope you see that."

Her adamance here was what surprised him. Perhaps she just needed him to explain a little further. "Well, I told Hardy it couldn't be 'til after the election, of course, but . . ."

"Even then!" She brought her face down directly in front of his. "Gabe, you of all people. You're the one who came up with the idea. I'm expecting our friends at the *Democrat*"—a small, alternative newspaper sympathetic to Pratt—"to start beating the drums for it any day now. People hate the death penalty all right, but I'm confident they'll come to hate this kid more. And this crime."

"Well, all that's fine, Sharron, but after the election it won't matter anymore." He still had to try to bend her. If she would allow Cole Burgess to plead guilty on a lesser charge, then it would be over. And trials, even an apparent no-brainer like this one, were always uncertain. That was their nature. Anything could happen. He got up from his chair, took a half lap of the room. He came to rest and faced her. "But we've still got Hardy. What if he'll take murder one with specials, LWOP?" This was life in prison without parole.

But the D.A. wasn't budging. "We still ask for death."

"Sharron." He put his hands on her shoulders. "Listen to me. You can't ask for death if he pleads guilty and says he's sorry. You'll come across as bloodthirsty. If it gets to there after a trial, it's different. The kid's unrepentant, shows no remorse, okay. Otherwise . . ." He let the word hang.

It was her turn to walk to the window, separate the blinds, look down onto the street. She stood there a long minute. "I want to go to trial on this one, Gabe. The evidence is rock solid and it's all with us. The boy did it and people don't like him. When we send him down, they're with us. Even if we don't get the death penalty, and we probably won't, we still get LWOP and look tough. Your instincts were right."

He stood in the at-ease position, his head bobbing as though he were in thought. "All right," he said.

She looked back out the window for an eternity. Setting her mouth, she directed a steely gaze once around the room, then finally over to her chief assistant. Her voice had a raspy quality, but it was firm. "That bastard Hardy has impugned the integrity of this office and accused me personally of playing politics with a man's life. No deals."

Torrey kept himself from showing any reaction. He knew the look. Argument would be futile. She had made up her mind. Her eyes went back out the window, to the dull-gray afternoon. Torrey looked at her for a moment, then bowed slightly from the waist and turned on his heel.

The attorneys' room at the jail was a good deal more pleasant than the general visitors' room, where Cole would meet his mother behind a barrier with a dozen other inmates on either side. At ten by twelve feet, it wasn't exactly spacious, but there was room for a table and two chairs with some floor left over for pacing. The far wall was made of opaque glass block, and this seemed to brighten up the room, although Hardy realized that this was possibly an optical illusion—more likely it was the glaring fluorescents overhead.

Cole sat across from him in his orange jumpsuit. His face was troubled, his brow clouded, his eyes clear. "But I didn't kill her."

He went through it all, as he had with Jody—the difficulty of getting a not-guilty verdict, the seriousness of the special circumstances allegations, the strong physical evidence against him, his own confession.

His client listened until he'd finished. Then he shook his head. "No," he said, "I didn't kill her. I won't plead guilty."

Hardy started over quietly, hummed along in low for a while before he blew it out and got loud. He paced the room, slammed his fist on the table a few times, damn near threw a chair. He would have done cartwheels if he thought they might have had an effect.

"I'm sorry," Cole said when he finished. "I can get a public defender if you don't feel you can stay in. But I'm not pleading guilty. I didn't do it."

For which, ultimately, there was no argument.

The events of the day had beaten Hardy down. He told himself that his biorhythms were low now in the early dusk. He'd perk up any minute. When Torrey got here, his adrenaline would kick in, as it had with Rich McNeil this morning, then with Glitsky at the hospital. As it had a couple of times in his grueling session with Jody Burgess, and then again with Cole, to say nothing of each of the three times he'd left increasingly curt messages for Dash Logan to please get back to him if his busy schedule allowed.

He brought a hand up to his eyes. Had all those disasters occurred during this one day? Did he have any adrenaline left?

And now he had to face Gabriel Torrey and tell him Cole wouldn't plead. He was sitting in front of the chief assistant's power desk in the same old room he used to love back in his own prosecuting days during the Civil War. He'd come in here just at this time of the evening and sit around with his boon colleagues, arguing the law and their strategies with his old mentor Art Drysdale.

The good old days.

This wasn't them anymore.

After Jody, he'd felt cocky. If he could convince her, he could convince anybody. He could just wriggle out of this entire dilemma. Cop a plea for Cole, get the boy in a rehab program in prison, collect a nice fee for his efforts and move on. It was an impossible case to try anyway. So he'd called Torrey and set up this meeting before discussing it with his client. A mistake.

And now he was on the D.A.'s turf, in an entirely different mode than he'd intended.

A side door opened and here was the man himself, professional, even cordial. "Diz," he began, proffering a hand. "I want to start out by apologizing for the other day in court." A self-effacing smile. "I've got a short fuse. I was protecting my boss. I'm sorry."

Hardy was on his feet, shaking the man's hand. "It happens. I got a little emotional myself."

Sometimes—and this was one of those times—it bothered him when he went along with his natural inclination to be a pleasant person, to adhere to social conventions. He didn't remember this as one of his primary character traits when he'd been younger. Now, he tended to be rude only when it served a purpose. He wasn't sure this was an improvement over the earlier model.

He took his seat while the chief assistant went around the Desk and got himself settled. "So," Torrey began without any more preamble, "I was in with Sharron after our phone call."

"Well, about that . . ." Hardy didn't want to waste any more time on this. Cole wasn't dealing. There was nothing to talk about. If Torrey hadn't appeared cooperative as he made the appointment, he'd have phoned it in. Now, though, he felt as if he at least owed him a personal explanation.

But before he could say anything else, Torrey kept on. "I'm afraid she wasn't inclined to deal."

This was a far cry from what he'd been led to believe. Torrey had told him he was sure they could work something out, and he had to wonder what had happened. He cocked his head. "At all?"

Torrey shook his head.

"She won't even go to life without?"

No response.

"This from an administration that has never even asked for LWOP before, much less death?"

"Right."

Hardy brought a finger to his jawline and scratched at it. "That's pretty raw." The offer didn't matter at all, of course—Cole wasn't going to take anything that involved a guilty plea—but Hardy felt his blood beginning to boil. He turned down the volume on his voice. "So me coming here to see you tonight, this was in the line of a joke? I'm supposed to go back to my client with that?"

Torrey spread his hands. Hardy found himself thinking of the William H. Macy character, the slimy car salesman in Fargo. "Sharron has strong feelings about this case. She said it was a matter of principle."

Hardy's bile continued to rise. His pulse pounded in his ears. He knew that if he remained seated here across the desk from this liar, his commitment to *la politesse* was going to be tested. And found wanting.

He didn't believe he could endure any more conflict today.

He knew where they were coming from. It didn't matter anyway. He noticed that his knuckles were white on the sides of the chair as he stood up. "Well," he said, "as long as it's a matter of principle . . ."

20

Glitsky thought they certainly liked to keep those beds empty in the ICU in case somebody got admitted who needed one.

He hadn't had a heart attack in all of about a day and a half, so by hospital lights he guessed he was out of immediate danger, although it didn't seem so to him. They moved him to a semiprivate room at a little before five in the afternoon. He had been sharing his thoughts about this with his new roommate, Roy, an elderly gentleman who was getting over pneumonia—trying not to sound too querulous, but voicing the opinion that maybe it was a little soon to be off the monitors.

Roy chuckled drily. "Last time I was here—I got COPD," he explained, tapping his chest, "bad lungs, so I'm in here all the time now. But last time, I passed out at home just after I punched 911. It took the paramedics a while to pick me up, and so anyway by the time I got admitted to the emergency room, I was DOA. Dead, right?"

"Dead?"

"Right. So they slapped me around with some CPR, got me breathing again and gave me a new oxygen bottle. So I called my brother to tell him where I was, and by the time he got down here, they told me to go on home. Home! I'm dead an hour ago and they send me home. What's that about?"

This was all new to Abe, but he was getting the hang of it—bemused resignation seemed to carry the day. "Managed care. That's my guess."

Roy shook his head. "My brother wouldn't let them do it. Made a big fuss, wondered if anybody thought it possible I might stop breathing again, since I just had. Eventually they let me stay overnight."

"One night?"

A shrug. "Hey, I lived through it. No hard feelings, because what would be the point? Is anybody going to care? So my doc comes in and says, 'See?' I could have gone home after all."

"Nice of him."

"Hell of a guy," Roy agreed. "Probably figured a little guilt never hurts. Maybe next time I get admitted dead I wouldn't push so hard for a bed."

"You were actually DOA?"

"Yeah, I saw it on my chart. Admitted two-nineteen. DOA. I love that, telling people I died." He broke a smile. "I'm in my resurrection phase now, though I've been disappointed to discover it's pretty much the same as last time around."

They fell into a silence for a while, until Glitsky shifted in his bed and sat up straighter. "You mind if I ask you something, Roy?"

"Shoot."

"Did you see any white light or anything like that while you were dead?"

He thought about it briefly. "You know, I can't say I did. One minute I'm dialing 911 and then I'm in the ER here with a tube down my throat and somebody pushing on my chest. How about you?"

"No. I wasn't dead. Heart attack," he explained. "I didn't see anything either, though."

"My wife died of a heart attack," Roy said. "They gave her all the tests and everything and told her it hadn't been a bad one. She was fine. She ought to come get another checkup in a week, but meanwhile she didn't need to be in a hospital. She should stop smoking and lose a little weight, change her lifestyle, which she didn't get much of a chance to do, seeing as she died about two hours after she got home."

"I'm sorry," Abe said.

"Hey." Roy lifted his shoulders. "Mangled care."

Glitsky hadn't seen his oldest boy, Isaac, for the winter break. With a group of his friends, he was skiing at Mammoth for the first week, then they were all going to the Grand Canyon until school started again. He told his father he'd try to make it back up for spring break, but everybody was talking about a road trip up to Chico State, a college in the northern foothills of California which was getting itself something of a reputation for throwing a weeklong revelry—Lauderdale West. Naked chicks, loud music! Dancing and fights and all-night raves. Vandalism, riots, rivers of beer!

Or Isaac could come home to the spring fog and watch TV in their duplex while his dad went to work.

Tough choice.

But now, no planning for it, here he was coming through the door to Abe's room. He seemed bigger somehow, but then he always did after an absence. His head was shaved—a shock—but Glitsky realized at a glance that it looked powerful and terrific. There was a lot of his mother in the face, though without her coloring—Isaac was a few shades darker than Abe or the other boys. The words came without warning, as did the gloss over his eyes. "Oh my beautiful boy."

Isaac either didn't hear or chose to ignore the remark. The handsome face wore a smile, concern all over it, a completely adult expression. A tiny gold Star of David glittered in one ear. The black body shirt said he'd been working out a lot. Abe almost felt whiplashed by the impressions—but above them all rode the flood of emotion and relief. He and Flo had raised a fully formed, civilized, wonderful person. Isaac might not be a finished product, but he was certainly no longer any kind of a child.

He leaned over the bed and rested his head a long moment on his father's chest, gripping him tightly. Abe kept an arm over him, patted a few times, hugged him closely a last second. Then Isaac pulled up and looked in his dad's face. "What is this bullshit?" he asked.

By the time Hardy arrived with Frannie and the kids at a little before eight, it was a full-fledged party. Orel and Isaac were on chairs on either side of Abe's bed. Rita, his housekeeper and Orel's daytime guardian, hovered near his head, ready at any opportunity to get him more ice or refill his cup of tea. Nat, Roy and Roy's brother Fred had struck up their own conversation about forming an Infirm Old Men unit for the Bay to Breakers race in May.

Glitsky was all the way up to a full seated position. He'd removed the morning's plastic tube from his nose. To Hardy, it appeared that he'd been up out of bed. There was a gloss to his hair as though he'd washed it. Any trace of the morning's pallor was gone—beyond that, he simply looked good, talking with some animation to his boys.

"Dr. Diz," he said by way of greeting. Then to Frannie. "Mrs. Dr. Diz." Because Abe's own children had been trained that it was proper to stand when a woman entered the room, they stood up. If Hardy didn't know from years of experience that it was physically impossible, he would have sworn his friend was smiling. "And these would be the young children of Dr. and Mrs. Diz."

"Uncle Abe!" The ever-flamboyant Rebecca ran to his bedside, put her arms around him. "I've been so worried."

"There's nothing to worry about." He gave her arm a welcoming squeeze. "People have heart attacks all the time."

Orel snorted a laugh. "Good one, Dad. Pretty reassuring."

The glare. Watch it, junior. "I mean they have heart attacks and get better."

Frannie had moved up behind her daughter. "Completely better, Beck."

"Sometimes even better than when they started," the older son said from the other side of the bed.

Hardy took the opening. "That wouldn't be too hard."

Frannie was staring over Abe's bed. She put a hand to her face. "Oh my God. Isaac?"

A smile played at his mouth. "That's me."

"I wouldn't have recognized you."

The smile broadened. "I think you just did." When Flo Glitsky had died, Abe's boys had lived with the Hardys for a month. Isaac and Frannie had become especially close, even if they hadn't seen each other now in three or four years.

"Isaac!" Beck shrieked, coming around the bed, hugging him. "I didn't know who you were."

"Just me, girlfriend, same old me."

"Like . . . not," she said.

"Okay, maybe stylin' a bit more." He picked her up with one arm, kissed her on the cheek, put her back down, then narrowed his eyes at Hardy's son. "Yo, Vin."

"Cool hair, Isaac." Vincent, eleven years old and the quiet one in the family, finally logged in.

"What hair?" Hardy put in. "He doesn't have any hair."

Vin ignored him. "Can I shave my head, too, Mom?"

Hardy answered for her. "The next time Uncle Abe smiles, Vin."

"He's smiling now." Vincent thought he had him.

"This time doesn't count. In fact, tonight doesn't count."

"Your father means the next separate time on another day."

"That's not fair."

"Why not?" Frannie asked.

"Because Uncle Abe never smiles."

"He does sometimes," Hardy said. "And when he does, you can shave your head. Promise."

"Promise?"

Glitsky joined the discussion. "You remind me, Vin, and I'll make a special effort."

Hardy turned to him. "It's got to be a sincere smile. Not one of those phony 'I'm going to rip your legs off in a minute' smiles like cops make."

"You can't change the rules," Vincent said. This was serious stuff. "You said a smile, Dad, just a smile."

"Sometimes he smiles at home." Orel was a hero to Hardy's kids. "I could call you at home, Vin."

"This whole discussion is pathetic," Isaac said. But he was clearly enjoying it. "I go away for a few years and the level of discourse devolves to this point?"

"Discourse?" Hardy said. "Devolves? What is that? Is that college?" He turned to the bed. "Abe, you've got to help us here."

But suddenly, Glitsky had lost all interest in the conversation. He was staring over Hardy's shoulder. He was wearing his old face, his everyday face. The smile gone. All trace of it gone.

"Abe?" Hardy repeated.

And suddenly everyone else became aware of something, a different vibration. Heads turned. The silence was profound.

Just inside the doorway, Treya Ghent had stopped where she stood. She was holding a large mixed bouquet of winter greenhouse flowers— daisies, daffodils, carnations. Her daughter shifted nervously beside and a half step behind her. "I'm sorry," she said. "I don't mean to interrupt. I just wanted . . . I thought . . ."

Glitsky cleared his throat and the awkwardness held until Frannie turned completely, broke a wide and genuine smile, moved toward her. "Those are beautiful," she said. "Abe loves flowers. I should have brought some myself."

• • •

It was nothing like Treya thought it would be. It hadn't really occurred to her that he had a family, friends, a life. Since he had never functioned as a father to Elaine, she'd assumed he didn't have that gene. Until he'd collapsed yesterday morning, he'd only been a cop to her, not a person.

Now here was Glitsky's father, an old Jewish man of all things, yarmulke and all. Two well-behaved and good-looking boys. That awful attorney Hardy—Elaine's killer's lawyer—from the arraignment, and his pretty wife and sweet children.

She'd heard the conversation about one of them shaving his head before they'd seen her. The obvious, warm connection between everybody. It was the last thing she expected. The tough and heartless Lieutenant Glitsky. Uncle Abe?

People.

And now here she was in the midst of them. Introductions to Frannie, Dismas, Isaac, Nat.

A Hispanic woman, Rita, taking her flowers, exclaiming over them. Raney and Orel checking each other out, but cool about it. Fast eyes.

"We can't really stay," she said. "I just wanted to see if you were all right." She felt she had to continue. "About yesterday, Lieutenant."

"It wasn't you," he said.

But she shook that off. "I didn't think . . ."

The lieutenant raised a palm. "Please. Stop. Okay? It wasn't you," he repeated. He turned to his Frannie. "Somebody needs to tell Ms. Ghent she didn't make this happen."

"Yes, sir." Frannie went with it. "You didn't make this happen," she said to Treya. She made eye contact, somehow making her feel welcome. Then back to the lieutenant. "What, though?"

"I'm starting to think it didn't happen at all." Frannie's husband was being inclusive, too. There was none of the anger Treya had seen from him in the courtroom. He spoke matter-of-factly to her, humor in the tone. "Abe will sometimes do this kind of thing to get attention. He lives a sad and lonely existence."

"We all feel sorry for him," Frannie added.

The little boy, Vincent, couldn't follow the irony. "We do? I don't. I like Uncle Abe."

"Thank you," Glitsky said.

His mother patted him on the head. "We're kidding, Vince. We like him, too. We don't really feel sorry for him."

"I do," the attorney said, smiling. He, too, rubbed a hand in his boy's hair, gave him a wink.

Treya could see that no one was going to acknowledge that she'd played a role in the lieutenant's collapse. She realized with some surprise that these were good people, protecting her while supporting him.

Glitsky spoke to her. "I appreciate your coming down, I really do. But this would have happened anyway."

She didn't believe it for a minute. "Well," she said, "I'm still sorry."

Treya's plan—apologize, drop the flowers and run—disintegrated in front of her. Dr. Campion came in and Frannie Hardy took control and dispatched Nat and Rita with the two teenagers and the younger kids down to the gift shop to get ice cream. So Treya's daughter, now part of the gang, was gone and so they were staying at least until she returned.

When Campion left, the four that remained clustered around the bed. Treya and Frannie had the chairs, with Frannie's husband and Abe's son standing. Now without all the people diffusing the energy, Treya much more acutely felt like an outsider.

She sat listening to them all talk about Glitsky's release, which the doctor thought would be Thursday, although everyone else seemed to think that would be too soon. But the lieutenant was explaining that was how they did it nowadays. "Besides," he said, turning to Hardy, "if you're doing the hearing a week after that, I've got some work to do."

"Dad, you're not going back to work."

"Well . . ."

"Grandpa said you were on leave anyway."

This was news to Treya. What did that mean, he was on leave? And if he was, when had it begun and why had he interviewed her?

But he was telling Isaac that he'd take it easy. He wouldn't push things. Then he came back. "So Diz, did you ever talk to your client about the gun? The snitch who said he gave it to him?"

Hardy slapped his forehead. "I would have if I wasn't brain-dead. But we just talked plea."

Glitsky sat up straighter. "What about his plea?"

"No deals," Hardy answered. "We go."

The scar in the lieutenant's lips went white. He was sitting forward now, his back off the mattress. "Why would you do that?"

"What do you mean, 'why'?" Hardy asked.

Frannie spoke up. "I don't think we need to talk about this now."

She was on her feet, up from the chair by the bed, the color high in her face. "I really don't."

Glitsky turned his face to her. "It's okay, Fran, it's fine. Just a little business."

"It is *not* fine." Flint in Frannie's tone. "And I know you two. It's not a little business." She turned to her husband. "This can wait, Dismas, okay? This is *exactly* what the doctor meant five minutes ago when he said to avoid stress."

"No." Glitsky was trying to keep it light, normally not his strong suit. "He meant physical stress. I shouldn't lift heavy objects, like that. This work stuff," he indicated Hardy, "it's just a job. It rolls right off me."

Isaac piped in. "I don't think so."

He turned to his son. "You haven't been around, Ike. I'm much more mellow now."

"Dad, five times as mellow would still put you in the top ten percent of uptight."

Treya had to smile at that, but then Glitsky was looking at her. "But I did want to talk to you about Elaine, though. Before you leave?"

She looked to Frannie, as though for permission. A silence clamped down again over them all.

"Who's Elaine?" Isaac asked.

Hardy jumped in, too fast, out of rhythm. "Elaine Wager. The victim in this case we were talking about."

But it hung there. Everyone but Isaac knew, and they were all aware of it. Finally, Glitsky looked over to his son. "I've got to talk to you about Elaine, too."

"What about her? I didn't know her."

"No, but—"

Frannie started. "Abe, I don't know if now is the time . . ."

But he held up a hand. "If anybody should know." He turned back to his son. "When I was about your age, Ike, I went out with Loretta Wager."

"Who became the senator. Mom mentioned that you dated her. We all knew that."

"Yeah, well, what maybe didn't get mentioned is that we were pretty serious." He hesitated, then came out with it. "Anyway, to make a long story short, a few years ago I found out I'd gotten her pregnant."

"You didn't know back then? When it happened?"

"She never told me. Suddenly she dumped me and married Dana Wager."

"But it was your kid?"

He nodded. "Elaine. Yeah."

Isaac ran a palm over his skull, looked around at the assemblage. "Wow." But Isaac was an intelligent young man, and the other ramifications began to kick in. Treya could see him beginning to process them. "I mean . . ."

Footsteps and high-pitched laughter outside in the hallway stopped him. Then Rebecca exploded through the door at a dead run, a step or two ahead of her brother. "I win! I win!"

Treya thought that the lawyer and his wife gave a damn good example of what zero tolerance for inappropriate behavior really was. It did her heart good, since she'd just about come to believe she was the last of the breed. With no hesitation, both of them were laying down the law in tandem. Unheard of. "Beck! Hey! Vincent! Enough."

"What are you doing? Don't you know people are trying to sleep?"

"This is a hospital, get it? Sick people."

"Think! Use your brains! Have a little respect, all right?"

By the time they were through and had marched both kids over and had them apologize, Nat, Rita and the teenagers were back, and Frannie was up by the bed, bussing Glitsky's cheek. "That's enough excitement for one night. We'll be back tomorrow, maybe without children."

"It's Date Night," Hardy said. "Definitely without children."

Treya was standing, too. Raney had come back over by her side, put a hand on her shoulder and squeezed. Visiting hours weren't officially over, but everybody was heading out, Rita and Nat shooing Orel over to his dad to say good night.

Although Isaac wasn't quite ready. "What's the earliest I can get back in here tomorrow?" he asked.

"Morning might be tricky," Abe said, mentioning angiograms and perhaps some other testing. "But anytime after that." He turned his head. "And Ms. Ghent?"

"Treya, please."

"All right. Treya then. About Elaine. If you get a little time . . ."

She nodded. "I'll see what I can do."

With all the bedlam, Glitsky found it hard to believe that Roy had gone to sleep. He'd pulled the sheet around his bed, though, and the light was off on his side of the room. More tellingly, so was the TV, which had been gently droning for the entire rest of the day. If it was off, Roy was sleeping.

He wasn't even slightly tired, but he turned the room light down, lowered the back of the bed slightly and settled himself against it. Nat had brought him a book by Patrick O'Brian called *Master and Commander*. According to his father, this was the first in a long series of seafaring tales that he was sure Abe would love. He'd loved Hornblower as a young man, and Nat thought this stuff was better, although Abe was skeptical. What could be better than Hornblower?

But the gift also delivered the subtle hopeful message that Abe would be around to read more books in the series, which had been running now for nearly thirty years. That Abe had never heard of it nagged slightly at him, but you set your priorities and he'd had other things he'd been doing. Reading was even among those things, but most of his reading over the years had been to improve his mind or to feed it more facts, which he consumed like the peanuts in his desk. The few novels he read tended to be mysteries, and with a few exceptions, more often than not he put them down halfway through, the law people who populated them bearing little or no resemblance to anyone in the real world of cops and killers in which he lived.

So books about the Royal Navy set a couple of centuries in the past? He couldn't take the time.

Now, holding this new book in his hands, he wondered why that had been so. He closed his eyes, remembering. He used to love stories like this one promised to be—pure adventure, with the fore-t'gallant sails and the mizzenmasts, whatever they were, and the salt spray in your face as shot and ball peppered the quarterdeck.

"If Vincent were here, Mr. Hardy would have to let him shave his head."

He started back into awareness, on some level equally thrilled both at the sound of the contralto laughter that accompanied his surprise and at the unexpected sight of the woman who'd produced it. "I didn't mean to startle you," Treya said. "You looked so happy." She pointed. "I love those books. Are you just starting?"

Sheepish, he looked down at the book in his hand. "I haven't read a page yet. I was remembering Hornblower."

"And smiling."

"And smiling, I suppose. Don't tell Hardy."

"I won't." She was sitting in the chair, now moved up close to the head of the bed. Her hand rested on the railing. "Hornblower was great, too, wasn't he?"

"Still is, I'd bet." He looked at her, a question. Why was she here?

"On the ice cream run, your dad got the kids talking, even the teenagers."

"Nat," Glitsky said. "The guy's a miracle."

"Apparently. Anyway, it turns out my daughter and your son both play basketball for Washington. We, you and me, live about five blocks from each other. So I'm trying to work out with Raney when I could get back and talk to you about Elaine, and your dad overhears and asks me why don't I just stay now while I'm here. He'll take Raney home, make sure she's locked in." She shrugged apologetically. "It seemed like a good idea. I hope you don't mind. Were you going to sleep? I could come back another day if you're tired."

"I'm not tired."

"Good," she said. She looked down. "I also didn't really want to leave until I told you I was sorry. I mean, yesterday. And before even. I don't think I've been fair to you."

"It's all right."

"No it isn't." She took a breath. "I was sitting up last night, worrying about all this, not able to sleep. I told a little of it to my daughter, why I'd jumped all over you, and she said maybe you felt the same way Elaine had. Why she didn't feel she could come to you."

"She felt like it wasn't her place. I was busy enough with my own life. I didn't need her in it mucking it up. If it was important enough, I'd come to her."

"Right."

"Genetics."

Her mouth softened. "Maybe that."

"Funny how I've got all the excuses down pat."

"It's like you practiced them."

"Plus, there was always tomorrow. I could always just decide it was time. Maybe if I'd known that she knew . . ." He shook his head regretfully. "How stupid we are."

She let a moment go by. "Can I ask you a question?"

"No." At her reaction—a fractional clouding of her brow—he realized he'd hurt her somehow. He reached out his hand, touched hers on the railing, then withdrew it quickly. "I'm kidding. I'm a great kidder, famous for it, in fact." He met her eyes. "You can ask me anything you want."

"Your son mentioned you were on leave, but when you came by to interview me—"

"That was before." He recounted enough of the story to give her the idea.

"They're not going to fire you, are they?"

"Unlikely. Maybe knock me down a grade, which wouldn't be the worst thing in the world. Back to doing cases. Or transfer me out of homicide, which would be worse."

"But you were investigating Elaine?"

"That was because it was Elaine. Normally I don't get involved with investigations." A bitter chuckle. "Which is for the best if the hash I made of this is any indication. They're all probably right. He just made a bad confession, but there isn't any doubt. He did it."

"But you're not sure."

Again, her eyes drew him. "No, not that exactly." Then. "No. Not as sure as I want to be. In a lot of ways I just . . . I can't accept it." He shook his head, stopped.

"What?" The eyes pleaded with him. "What?"

And he gave in. "This will sound strange, even downright weird, but it's as though she's finally talking to me, telling me there has to be a better reason than a chance encounter with some junkie. And after all the denial I've had with her up to now, I just can't make myself ignore it." A pause. "Dumb, I know."

She pondered a moment. "Why did you come to me first?"

A shrug. "As opposed to who else?"

"I don't know. Maybe Jonas? Her fiancé?"

"I would have gotten to him. But you were close by. I talked to Clarence Jackman and he told me that if she was involved in something squirrelly with her work or any of her projects, you'd probably know about it."

A rueful expression. "Probably."

"But you said there was nothing."

Treya shook her head. "That was that first day. I was so furious at you, at who you were, that I wasn't going to help you, period. No matter what you were asking. I didn't believe you were working for Elaine's interests."

"I was. I am."

"I see that now."

"And? Was she working on something?"

"Honestly, I don't know. Nothing's jumping up at me." She gave him a hopeful smile. "But at least now I'm disposed to look."

"There's progress," Glitsky said. "But before you even start that, why did you mention her fiancé? Were they having problems?"

Treya made a face, hesitated. "Maybe you should talk to him?"

"I intend to, but you're here now." He waited.

Finally, she came to the decision. "Well, a couple of things." She told him about the argument in the Rand & Jackman conference room on the day of the arraignment, how Jonas had been so adamantly opposed to any discussion of the validity of Cole's confession. "He just didn't want to go there at all."

"And this meant what?"

She shrugged. "I don't know. I thought it was pretty understandable myself. But other people thought it was funny. They said if Cole didn't do it, shouldn't Jonas want to find Elaine's killer? Whoever it might be? Of course, this was a room full of lawyers and law students, so we're not talking about a typical cross section of humanity."

"Or humanity at all."

"Well . . ." But she acknowledged his point with a nod. "Still, everybody seemed to think he should have cared more somehow."

Glitsky pondered that a moment. "What's the second thing?" he asked.

"Well, this is more . . ." She hesitated. "He told me she was leaving him."

"Did you already know that?"

"No."

A questioning look. "Wouldn't that be odd, you not knowing? Her not telling you?"

"I thought so. Maybe she hadn't finally decided. Maybe she was too embarrassed to admit it to me."

"Why would that be?"

"Maybe because when she was first getting together with Jonas, we were kind of conspirators together—Elaine and I—to keep anybody from finding out. Then, after that, when they were together, Jonas changed a little."

"Changed how?"

A shrug. She didn't like these revelations, but they seemed relevant.

"A little more impatient." Then she added, "Like I was the help, not a friend anymore." Another small pause. "If I ever had been. Anyway, Elaine saw he hurt my feelings, and she tried to smooth it over a few times, make excuses for him. So then if she was thinking about leaving him after all . . . I could see where she'd feel embarrassed with me."

"But Jonas told you?" Glitsky asked with an air of disappointment.

"Yes. Why does that bother you?"

A shake of the head. "Because if it was a motive for murder . . ."

"A motive for murder? You mean Jonas?" She shook her head in surprise or disbelief.

"That's who we're talking about, right? Her fiancé."

"I know, but I never thought he killed her."

"You may be right," Glitsky said. "At least if she was leaving him and that was his motive for killing her, I can't see him telling anybody about it."

She came forward on her chair. "Except if he thought I already knew. Then his *not* mentioning it would be significant, right? So he had to say something about it to cover himself."

Glitsky allowed himself a smile. "Not a bad point."

Suddenly, her eyes opened wider in surprise. "Are you wearing contact lenses?" she asked.

"No."

She was staring at him. "You've got blue eyes," she said.

"I do? You're kidding me."

"I'm not. It's not all that common for a black man to have blue eyes."

"It's not all that uncommon when the black man's father has them. Actually, I like to think of them as the color of cold blue steel. That's a good color for a cop's eyes, don't you think? Ice in the veins, steel blue eyes . . ." He narrowed his gazed, fixed her with one of his hard looks. "How can you be smiling right now?" he asked. "That look strikes terror into the hearts of hardened criminals."

"It's terrifying," she admitted. "It's very good. If I didn't know you were putting it on for show, I'd be very scared at this moment, Lieutenant."

He relaxed the scowl. "By the way, you can call me Abe," he said.

"Al. The song is 'You Can Call Me Al,' not Abe."

"The cop is Abe, not Al."

The loudspeaker came on announcing the end of visiting hours.

Treya looked at her watch, frowned. "Did you say you were getting out on Thursday? I could have a good look at Elaine's files by then, now that I know what I'm looking for."

"Thursday's the plan. If all goes well tomorrow."

"What's tomorrow?"

He shrugged it off. "Just some tests, make sure my arteries are working. So should we make an appointment, say Thursday, your lunchtime, your office?"

She stood up. "That sounds good. I'll be ready."

"If I get hung up here for some reason, I'll call and leave a message."

She was just saying good-bye when a thought struck her. She got her wallet and a pen from her purse. Withdrawing a business card, she wrote on it, handed it to him. "Save you from having to look it up. And that's my home number, if you need anything else."

He used the card as a bookmark. "Thanks. While you've got your pen out . . ." He gave her his telephone number as well and she wrote it on another card.

"Okay, then . . ." She shrugged awkwardly. She lifted a hand slightly, Abe did the same, and she turned to go.

As she reached the door, Glitsky called after her. "Treya." She stopped and turned. "Thanks for coming back. And for the flowers."

"You're welcome." She pointed to the bedside table. "Enjoy your book. Good night, Abe."

21

An excellent French restaurant, the Rue Charmaine, occupied the ground floor of David Freeman's apartment building. Freeman sometimes ate there as often as four times a week, after which he'd walk up the flight of stairs to his own spacious one-bedroom flat. Last night, he'd had dinner there with a forty-year-old female attorney named Gina Roake. They'd shared an extraordinary bottle of Romanée-Conti, talked law and politics, law and the theater, law and the recently concluded football season. After dinner, Gina had asked if David would mind her staying over, and he said he thought that would be very nice.

Now, just after dawn, Freeman was whistling tunelessly, puttering about his cluttered kitchen in an ancient and threadbare maroon bathrobe and his lounging slippers. Normally, his battered and pitted kitchen table sagged with documents, law books and files on his cases, but this morning he'd cleared all that away, covered the wood with a white linen tablecloth and laid out a formal coffee service—sugar, cream, butter, jams and jellies, and a still-warm and crusty morning baguette from the Rue Charmaine's morning delivery.

Freeman paused and smiled appreciatively as the strains of Mahler's Fifth began to emanate from his living room at a barely audible volume. A moment later, Gina made her appearance, combing out her still-damp hair, delightfully filling out the still-plush bathrobe he'd once purchased from the Bel-Air hotel.

"You look lovely," he said.

She crossed the few steps over and leaned up to kiss him. Then she withdrew to arm's length, smiling up at him. "I feel lovely," she said.

"For a moment there, I had this awful feeling that you were going to tell me I looked lovely, too."

She laughed. "Actually . . ."

He wagged a finger. "I don't think we want to go there. Come, sit down, coffee's hot."

He poured for her, then for himself. When they were settled, Freeman took his first sip, nodded approvingly and put down his spoon. "All right," he said, "if you still want to talk about it, I suppose I'm as ready as I'll ever be." The previous night during their dinner, in one of their law discussions, Gina was talking about one of her cases, and suddenly—atypically—Freeman had stopped her, saying he'd prefer not to ruin such a fine evening by talking about Dash Logan.

Now he made a face. "This is the second time he's come up in the past two weeks. Or maybe I should say crawled out from under his rock or wherever it is that he lives. I'm taking this as a bad sign for our profession." He sighed. "So what's the case again? Last night my mind was on other things."

She smiled at the compliment, then briefly sketched in to the point where he'd stopped her last night on the Oberlin proceeding. The district attorney was bringing criminal charges against Gina's client, Abby, who had taken care of her mother for the past several years, and who had inherited the vast percentage of an eight-million-dollar estate. It was obvious, Gina said, that Jim, the no-good brother, was behind the charges, and simply was extorting his sister for a portion of the take.

Freeman listened, chewing absentmindedly on a crust of baguette. "So let me get this straight—the D.A. is filing charges. What are they alleging?"

"I gather elder abuse all the way to manslaughter. They haven't filed them yet."

This brought a frown. "Why not, if they've built the case?"

"I don't know for sure. I think Gabe Torrey might just be dragging his feet." Her tone conveyed some skepticism. "He said he didn't want to try this case, although elderly abuse is high on Pratt's agenda. Apparently he didn't like Jim, the brother . . ."

Freeman nodded impatiently. He'd heard the name once and of course didn't need to be reminded. "So what's like got to do with it. Your client committed a crime, or she didn't."

"She didn't, David."

He held up his bread hand. "I'm not saying she did, Gina. I'm saying that's got to be Torrey's position."

But she was shaking her head. "And evidently it will be. He will green-light the investigation and get to the charges pretty soon, but he wanted to give me a chance to settle, maybe save Abby some grief."

Freeman had stopped chewing, stopped all movement. His eyes bored into emptiness somewhere between himself and Gina. "My Lord," he said.

"What?"

He answered her with another question. "And if memory serves, this humanitarian brother Jim is our connection to Dash Logan?"

"He's his lawyer."

A nod. "Right, and already on board, *n'est-ce pas*? You see anything wrong with this picture, Gina?"

She stalled, sipping some coffee, finally shook her head. "To this point, not really." She leaned forward. "Except it felt funny somehow. It's why I brought it up to you."

"I'll tell you why it felt funny. *Because the D.A. doesn't do that.*"

But she didn't agree. "I think Gabe did it on his own. My take was that Gabe was trying to do the right thing off the record."

"The right thing?"

"It does happen."

"Not as often as you think, Gina. Not as often as you think."

"Well, maybe this time, though."

But he kept at it. "And this right thing, this time, would be to make your client give away a million of her dollars?"

"That wasn't exactly the spin he put on it. He was talking about saving her half a million, a couple of years of hassle and a lot of trouble."

"And he just happened to find this particular case out of the blue, out of the hundreds the D.A. is prosecuting? And felt sorry for your client, whom his office is about to charge?"

Gina fidgeted with the crumbs on her plate. "Maybe that's why it made me uncomfortable."

"Because you have good instincts, that's why." Freeman stood up, walked over to the window, looked down onto the street. "So the next step is Gabe tells you to call this guy's lawyer, is that it?"

"Essentially." She saw his reaction. "What? That seemed to make sense. It still does."

"How's that?"

"I'm a lawyer. I'm not going to talk to the brother. I'm going to go through channels, through his counsel."

"How do you know he has one? How does *Torrey* know he has one."

"He's talked to the guy, remember? That's how. He probably mentioned it."

Freeman had paced back to the stove. He leaned back against it, arms crossed. "Okay, ask yourself this. A guy thinks a crime has been committed, he goes to the police, right? Right. Then the crime gets charged, and he's working exclusively with the D.A.'s office, with the prosecutors. Are you with me here?"

Catching on, Gina nodded. "He's already got an office-full of lawyers working for him, who also happen to work for the D.A."

"Exactly," Freeman said. "The D.A.'s office. So what does he need his own lawyer for? I mean, handling the same case. He's not a defendant so he doesn't need a defense attorney. Hell, he's not even a plaintiff in a civil case. He's just a guy reporting a crime. He goes to the D.A. He doesn't need his own attorney."

"Well." The light was coming on, but Gina still couldn't quite see. "People have lawyers, David. Abby—my client—she told me they'd been fighting over the will."

"She and her brother, or you and her brother's lawyer?"

"Well, no. The first."

"But now dear old Jim's got a lawyer who's ready to settle." Freeman had switched into his justly famous flamboyant courtroom mode. He took a couple of steps forward, toward the table. His voice took on a note of urgency. "And then Torrey says old Jim will withdraw the accusation he made. Torrey tells you he knows this. He holds it out to you as pretty much guaranteed, a done deal. Well, answer me this: How can he possibly know that unless he's talked to Jim's lawyer, who—I might add—shouldn't even be in the picture around these criminal charges? And who happens to be the most unsavory person practicing law in the great state of California?"

Freeman grabbed his breakfast napkin and wiped it across his forehead, leaving a couple of damp crumbs in its wake. Then he sat down with a satisfied expression, returned to his normal voice, spoke as though to himself. "God, I wish just once he'd try something like this on me." He looked across the table. "Do me one favor please?"

"Of course, if I can. What?"

"Don't settle. Don't talk to Logan. See what Torrey does next."

She thought about this for a long moment. "But what if he files the charges? He's holding all the cards here, David. If the investigation even begins, my client loses."

"Did she do what they're alleging? Did she commit this crime?"

"No."

He leaned back in his chair, pulled at his bushy eyebrows, scratched the corner of his mouth. "Well, people hate me for saying this . . ."

"I won't hate you."

He touched her hand. "If I were you, what I'd do is trust in the wisdom and fairness of the law."

She studied his face, saw he was completely sincere. "A person could get to like you a lot," she said. Then, a cloud crossing her visage. "About settling . . . I'll try to hold out."

Just after eight in the morning, she stopped him as he was crossing the lobby on his way to the staircase and his own office. "Mr. Hardy."

He stopped on a dime, turned ninety degrees to his left, marched across to her station and looked her in the eyes. "Phyllis, my love. How are we this fine morning?"

"Very well, thank you. If you're free, Mr. Freeman would like to see you in his office right away."

"Well, that makes this both of our lucky days. I wanted to see him, too, but I didn't know if you'd let me."

"Anytime you need to, Mr. Hardy. You know that."

"As long as I have an appointment."

"Those are Mr. Freeman's rules, not mine."

"Well, thank you, Phyllis."

"You're welcome."

As he closed Freeman's door behind him, Hardy was grinning. "I've got it."

Chewing on the nub of a pencil, the old man sat at a desk completely littered with case files. He looked up. "Got what?"

"The automated voice on all those phone message menus. You know the ones." He put on a voice. " 'For security and training purposes, and to help us serve you better, this call may be monitored for your convenience.' I especially love the convenience part. But that voice."

Freeman put the pencil down. "What about it?"

"It's Phyllis." He'd put his briefcase down and was over at the side counter pouring himself a cup of coffee. "I can't believe I didn't recognize it until this morning. I think it's probably because we don't talk as much now as we used to. But it's her, David, I'm sure of it—that same girlish enthusiasm, the clarity of purpose, the joie de vivre humming through every syllable. Why do you think she hasn't told us? A celebrity in our midst, imagine."

Freeman let him go on in the same vein, waiting until he'd taken the seat in front of his desk, had his first sip of coffee. "I've got a friend who's got a client," he began without preamble. "The client's name is Abby Oberlin." He went on for a few more minutes, outlining the case as Gina Roake had done for him that morning, ending with a question. "And who would be your guess for Abby's brother Jim's attorney?"

"At least I know why you wanted to talk to me," Hardy said.

"I assumed it would occur to you. That asshole." Freeman almost never got truly upset, although the mention of Dash Logan was one of the things that could do it. He was spinning his pencil rapidly between his fingers. "I've been living with this thing for an hour now, and I wanted to bounce it off a decent legal mind before I decide what I'm going to do with it."

However the phrase "decent legal mind" sounded, Hardy knew that Freeman meant this as high praise. "Okay, hit me," he said, and Freeman told him what was on his mind.

In his office upstairs, Hardy removed his coat and hung it over the back of his chair. The come-and-go fog had this morning gone again, so he raised the blinds in both of his windows, letting in a feeble winter light. For a few minutes, he stood looking down at the traffic on Sutter Street, then he whirled and went over to his desk, where he punched the buttons on his telephone.

Rich McNeil's secretary told him that her boss wasn't expected in until midday. Could she take a message? Hardy considered for a moment and said he'd be at Sam's at one o'clock. He had some news. If Rich couldn't make it, he should call—otherwise, he'd expect him there.

He had just hung up, intending to call next to check on Glitsky's progress, when the telephone rang. Perfect, he thought. Here's the son of a bitch now, calling him back at precisely the wrong moment. Well, he'd let his machine answer. Except it wasn't Logan. It was Glitsky himself, saying something about the Burgess case. Hardy grabbed at the receiver.

Glitsky started over. "You'll never guess who I just talked to."

"Don't tell me," Hardy said. "Joe Montana?"

"Allison Garbutt."

"I'm proud of you. Who is she?"

"She's the inspector on the case where Elaine acted as special master. They just turned the seized documents over to Judge Thomasino."

"Okay? And this is important because . . . ?"

"I don't know if it is."

"And yet you're telling me about it?"

"It's a fact we don't know anything about, that's all. I know you and Thomasino get along all right." This was true enough. Hardy and Thomasino weren't close friends by any means, but they knew each other from the courtroom and shared a mutual respect. "There might be something there."

Hardy wasn't going to look a gift horse in the mouth. Glitsky was giving him a free fact—possibly just another in the endless accretion of them surrounding a murder case, and experience had taught him that all facts were worth collecting. You simply never knew. "You're right," he said. "There might be. What was the name of the case?"

"*Petrof.* Insurance fraud of some kind."

"And what do you know about it?"

"Completely nothing beyond that, except that Elaine was around it, working on it the day she died. It occurred to me as I was lying here. I thought it might give you something to do to while away your many idle hours."

"I appreciate it."

"Don't mention it."

The two men traded health and beauty tips for a few more minutes, talked logistics about Glitsky's eventual release from the hospital. After they hung up, Hardy paced his office for a while, unable to say why his adrenaline was flowing. He realized that it made little sense. He hadn't even been thinking about Cole Burgess, but suddenly here at least was something to do for his client, a lead to follow. Finally he picked up the telephone again and punched some numbers he knew by heart.

It wasn't yet nine o'clock, and court wouldn't be in session until nine-thirty. In a perfect world, Judge Thomasino would be in his chambers right now. Or at least his clerk would be in. As it transpired, for an instant all was perfection.

"Judge," Hardy said after their greetings, "I understand you signed off on a warrant on an insurance fraud case. I don't even know if it's been settled or tried. *People v. Sergei Petrof.*"

The judge sounded weary of it. "No. It's not been settled. Yes, they're still doing motions. Bunch of Russians faking car accidents. What about it?"

"You appointed Elaine Wager special master in connection with it."

"Yes. And then she gets herself killed in the middle of it, as I'm sure you've heard." The judge's tone reflected his frustration. "That's the way the entire investigation has gone. You wouldn't believe—one delay after another. Some cases. Now it seems I'll need another special master for more warrants before we can proceed, and I don't know . . ." His voice brightened up. "You wouldn't be on the list, would you, Diz?"

In fact, he was, although he hadn't been called to serve in years. He told that to the judge. ". . . but my plate's pretty full right now, your honor. And I've more than heard about Elaine's death. I'm representing the accused in that case. Cole Burgess."

A dissatisfied grunt. "So I can't use you. All right, what was your question?"

"Well, I'm afraid it's not too specific. I was curious because Elaine was involved in it. Wondered if it might somehow be related to anything I could use."

"In your murder case?"

"Stranger things have happened, Judge. I thought you might be able to tell me a little about it. See if something might be worth pursuing."

Thomasino gave it a beat. "Well, all right. It isn't any secret." He began. "The fraud unit starts getting calls from insurance companies about a rash of similar accidents in the last six months—all Russian surnames, same doctor, same type of car, same lawyer for half of 'em. So I sign a warrant to pull the records, and Elaine's got to go along and supervise. Normally, you know, a piece of cake. Except if one of your colleagues is particularly uncooperative, won't give the special master any direction, won't even tell her where any of the files are. Says 'Find 'em yourself. This whole investigation is bogus anyway.' The belligerent son of a bitch."

"What do you mean, one of my colleagues? Is this a friend of mine?"

"No. Sorry. I just mean it was another lawyer, not to lump you all together. Certainly not in this case."

Hardy went with his hunch. "You wouldn't be talking about Dash Logan, would you?"

"Maybe. With my apologies if he's a friend of yours."

"He's not," Hardy replied.

"No." The judge sighed. "Somehow I didn't think he would be."

On his way down to the Hall, Hardy decided to stop by the *Chronicle*'s main office and see if Jeff Elliot was in, a virtual certainty at this time of the morning. He'd just gotten into the reporter's office and said hello when the building began to shake. Reflexively, Hardy backed up under the door, said, "Earthquake. Get under a beam."

Elliot was in his wheelchair. He kept his hands on his keyboard, cast an amused, tolerant look across the room. "Okay, sure, I'm on it."

The shaking—really no more than a quick minor jolt—passed. Hardy stayed under his beam, and Jeff held out his hands as though feeling for raindrops. "Two on the Richter," he said. "I don't move 'til we get to six." He indicated a chair on the other side of his desk. "You can stay in the doorway if you want, but it might be five years before another good shake. You'll get pretty bored. The seat's more comfy."

Hardy waited another moment for the possible next temblor. When, after a few seconds, it didn't come, he moved forward. "It's good to see a man with no fear of nature's wrath."

Elliot glanced out into the city room, where the small quake had pretty much passed unnoticed. "My computer didn't even blink, Diz. I'm not going to die in an earthquake, I promise you. Way less chance than lightning, and that's the rule in our house."

"You have a rule about lightning in your house? Us," Hardy said, sitting down, "we just flat don't allow it."

"No. Not lightning, getting killed by lightning."

"You have a rule about getting killed by lightning?"

Jeff sat back, pulled his hands off his keyboard and rested his arms on the sides of his wheelchair. "Actually, yes. Ridiculous as it may sound, we have a rule about not worrying about something unless it's more likely than getting killed by lightning."

"I like it," Hardy said. "Let me guess—your girls are plagued by the occasional random fear?"

"Ha! Occasional. I'd pay large dollars for 'occasional.' It's everything." He tried a smile to make light of it, but Hardy could see it was about as funny as his own daughter's constant fears, which was not at all. "Everything, I swear to God," Jeff repeated. "Plane crashes, AIDS, the hantavirus, terrorists, zits, snakes, nuclear accidents, spiders, child molesters on every street corner, the dark—Lord, the dark!—walking home alone . . . everything."

"You left out heart attacks," Hardy said. "The Beck's afraid of getting a heart attack now since Glitsky did."

"Don't worry," Jeff replied. "If Nicole hears about that, it's on the list."

"I tell the Beck that twelve-year-olds rarely die of heart attacks. She doesn't care. It *could* happen, couldn't it? And no warning. Abe didn't have any warning. I tell her Abe isn't twelve. Ask me if she cares. This until eleven-thirty last night." Hardy was leaning back, an ankle on his opposite knee. He dragged a hand across his eyes. "Sometimes I think it must be us, always telling them to watch out for this, watch out for that, especially the girls. So this rule—how's it work exactly?" Whatever it was, if it worked Hardy wanted to know about it.

This time Jeff got all the way to a smile. He scratched at his beard, perhaps embarrassed that it had come to this, but it had, damn it, it had. "Well, we finally had to come up with some lowest threshold for paranoia that we could take seriously. I mean, there are legitimate fears she should worry about once in a while, I suppose. Right?"

"Right."

"Although I doubt if either you or me or our wives ever had them. Maybe it's a new millennium thing."

"Maybe," Hardy agreed. "Although I remember worrying during the Cuban missile crisis."

"I hate to say it, Diz, but there were adults who worried then, too. And you know why?" He raised his voice. *"Because there was some real goddamn thing to worry about!"*

"Or, as it turned out, not."

"Exactly. So, anyway, we finally had to tell Nicole that whatever she was worried about had to be more likely than getting killed by lightning, which for some reason she's not afraid of. If it was less likely, we weren't going to talk about it, especially after lights-out at night."

"And what are the odds of that, dying by lightning strike?"

"Thirty-two thousand to one in a seventy-five year life span, more or less."

Hardy whistled, impressed. "That's a good statistic."

Jeff shrugged. "It still leaves a hell of a lot to be afraid of—you'd be surprised—but at least it gets rid of death by earthquake, spiders, snakes, plane crash, atomic bomb blast. None of them make the cut. It's really helped, actually."

"I'm bringing it home tonight," Hardy said. "It's a great concept."

"It is," Jeff agreed, "but I don't believe that's why you're here, and if it's about Cole, he's not my topic today." He indicated his terminal screen, half filled with words. "Gironde again. Due in two hours. I wish they'd invent a program to actually write the words."

"I'm sure it's on the way," Hardy said. "So what's new at the airport, aside from that it's never going to be finished?"

Jeff looked at his screen, fixed something, came back to Hardy. "The way it's going, Diz, they may never even start this last phase, given all the subs who supposedly didn't have their minority quotas on board. It's been seven months and everybody and their brother has had their personnel records subpoenaed. Gironde can't start work, will probably even lose the contract, and the D.A. hasn't brought one charge yet. Not one. Three subs have already gone under because they've lost the work. It just sucks."

To Hardy, this was an old song. "That's how Pratt works, Jeff. Make a big public stink, then drag on the follow-through. Are you on Gironde's side on this? I thought they were the bad guys."

A shrug. "All I know is that apparently fair and square they won the biggest contract this city's seen in ten years. Now everybody hates them. The supes are asking for another round of bids. And it's all based on Pratt's office deciding to very publicly look for minority-hiring irregularities, which now, it's turning out, may not exist." He made a face. "It smells, Diz. It really smells." He looked back at his terminal. "And I've got to write it. So? Cole?"

"It's not specifically about Cole."

"Specifically. There's a good word. So more specifically, what? And we do have to make it fast."

"All right," Hardy said. "You know everybody in the city, right?"

"Oh yeah," Elliot said flatly, "me and everybody else, we're all pals."

"How about Dash Logan?"

The by-now-familiar reaction, a faint line of distaste. "What about him?"

"That's what I was going to ask you."

"Has he got something to do with Cole?"

"I don't know." Hardy broke a small grin. "Not specifically."

But the topic had gotten Jeff's attention, and he reached for a cup on his desk, sipped some coffee, beginning to concentrate. "The only thing that comes to mind is that Logan represents a lot of dope cases. A lot. People say he takes fees in trade."

"Then he sells it?" This was close enough to Cole to get a rise out of Hardy. "Heroin?"

"No. Cocaine. Evidently he's got his own . . ." Jeff paused. "I was going to say habit, but I don't know if it's to that point. Probably just recreational. He functions, evidently."

"Not well," Hardy said, "if returning calls is any indication."

"Well enough to make a good living," Jeff replied. "He drives a Z3, wears nice clothes, keeps up an office."

Hardy sat up straighter. "His office? That's the other connection."

"To Cole? What was the first one?"

Hardy glossed over that. "Elaine was working at Logan's office the day she was killed."

"Okay?" Jeff sat back in his wheelchair. "And this means?"

Hardy shook his head, spoke with a weary tone. "I don't know. That's what I can't figure out. It's making me crazy."

"Why was she there?"

Hardy briefed him on Elaine's special master duties, the Russian insurance scams, Logan's lack of cooperation on the earlier search at his place. When he finished, Jeff was still interested, but saw no point of connection. "So these insurance scam cases, did they have drugs around them? Am I missing something?"

"We've got to be," Hardy said. "There's too much Logan."

"But maybe not enough." He sat back in his wheelchair and looked over the desk that separated them. "You know, Diz, we run into this all the time in journalism. You're on a story, and if this one last little piece falls into place, they can start printing up the Pulitzer citation for you. I mean you want it so bad. And then guess what? What you want to write didn't happen. It's not true, just coincidence. Good story, no facts."

Hardy considered a second. His jaw was set. "That's not this. At least I don't think so."

"Okay."

"How about Gabe Torrey?"

"How about him? In what sense?"

"David Freeman has a theory about a connection between Torrey and Logan. What I want to know is, are they old friends? Did they go to school together? Maybe they're gay, having an affair?"

Here Jeff stopped him. "They're not gay. Logan's a notorious cocksman, in fact. And Torrey's sleeping with Pratt."

This intelligence nearly knocked Hardy off his chair. "What?"

Jeff laughed. "You didn't know that? We're off the record now— they try to keep it quiet 'cause Pratt's happy to let the feminists think she's a lesbian, but the Shadow knows."

"My God. See? You do know everything. You ought to print that."

"In due time, say nearer the election, when it might do a little more good."

"I can't believe it." San Francisco was a small town, but apparently not so small that there were no secrets. "Okay, so they're not gay. Maybe they're bi. Maybe their mothers were pen pals? I don't know, Jeff. You're the ace reporter, finger on the pulse of the city."

"And if there was something, I would have heard it, right?"

"Right." Hardy came forward expectantly.

Jeff met his gaze, a hint of humor in his eyes. "As far as I know, they have no personal relationship."

Hardy sat back. "That's the wrong answer."

"I thought it might be."

Cole was the first person in Hardy's experience whose looks and demeanor had actually improved while he was held in the county jail. He'd asked for and received a short haircut. Some of the scrapes and bruises from his life on the street, to say nothing of the night of his arrest, had begun to clear up. He'd shaved off the wispy, downy growth of beard. Three squares a day for only these few days had already added a visible overlay of flesh to the bones of his face, eradicating the intimations of skull. He wasn't yet anyone's idea of robust, but neither was he heroin chic.

Hardy sat across the table from him in the attorneys' visiting area, the light room with the glass block walls. Cole's speech would lapse into hazy around the edges from time to time, but today it seemed more a habit than an impediment. That he spoke clearly for long periods of time meant, to Hardy, that he could do it anytime he thought about it. He had simply gotten into the habit of mumbling to fit in on the street, where he had grown used to a numb mouth and no reason to enunciate words, to communicate anything beyond his most basic needs.

Well, Hardy thought, he had a reason now and he was rising to the occasion. "Glitsky? Are you kidding me?" His eyes were clear as well. He was on methadone and had, in fact, asked for an accelerated detoxification. All to the good if he stuck with it. But at the moment, he wasn't on that page—he was mostly angry. "We're talking the same Glitsky that dropped me on my head."

"He couldn't catch you in time is what I heard."

A snort. "He tell you that? 'Cause it's a lie."

Hardy had a haunch on the edge of the table in the visitors' room, and now he leaned forward, hovering over where his client sat. "How do you know what happened? You were unconscious."

"Well . . ." Cole's hard gaze gradually gave way. "But there's no way he's trying to help me."

"No," Hardy agreed. "I don't think he is. Not for your sake anyway. The thing is, Cole, he's a good cop. An honorable person."

Another dismissive grunt, the concept for him obviously difficult to believe. "I'll tell you what it is. He's worried we'll decide to charge him with brutality after all. He's trying to cut you off on that. Figures if he pretends to be on our team, it'll all go away."

Hardy sat back. "You got it all worked out, huh?"

"It's not rocket science."

"No. You're right. So we don't want his help, is that your position?"

For an instant, Cole's expression sharpened. "He's not offering any help. He's covering his ass."

Hardy nodded, stood up, cricked his back. When he spoke, his tone was harsh. "See if you can wrap your brain around something, Cole. There's nobody else in the entire police department who's looking for anything about this case, let alone anybody else who might have been involved in Elaine's death. But Glitsky is. He's doing it on his own for his own reasons, and you'd be smart not to care too much about what they are. You want to know the truth, yeah, he's covering himself." He felt his voice getting away from him, his anger building. "Glitsky doesn't want your conviction overturned because you made a stupid, stupid confession. That's where he's coming from, Cole. He wants to nail you on righteous evidence. That's what he's about—he doesn't give a shit about your poor sorry ass." He almost added that he didn't much either. If it wasn't a death penalty case, he'd have been long gone.

"But anything he does find is going to be against us."

Hardy, still wound up, whirled on the boy. "What he's trying to find, Cole, is the truth. Which, correct me if I'm wrong, is supposed to help us."

Cole's eyes bounced around the corners of the room.

Getting his tone back under control, Hardy sat on the edge of the table again. "Look," he said. "I don't care at all really what Glitsky's motives are. If he wants to convict you, that's fine by me, and it ought to be by you. He doesn't want the confession in because as soon as that happens, we've got grounds for appeal."

"Appeal is after I'm convicted. I don't want to talk about appeal."

"Oh, okay, let's not then." Hardy brought a palm down sharply on the table. "Get a clue here, Cole. You're in deep shit and Glitsky's the only one doing anything that might help you, whether helping you is his intention or not. That's assuming the truth helps you." He'd challenged Cole a minute before with the same point, and now he waited again for a response—denial, outrage, something—but none came. He sighed. "Now, listen, Glitsky's a fact. We'll use him if we can. If you can't live with that, then I'm gone, too."

Cole met his gaze. "I don't trust him."

Hardy dropped his trump. "Well, he's been my best friend for like thirty years, so I'd have to say I do. Now you've got two options. You can live with it, trust my instincts and talk strategy." He threw a little edge into it. "Or you can tell your mother to hire another lawyer."

This brought a rise. "It's not my mother."

"Yeah, Cole. Yes it is. Don't kid yourself. Unless you want to take responsibility on your own. But that's not what you do, is it?" He waited, surprised that it had come to this. He hadn't intended to have any of this discussion, but now that they were in it, he'd follow it until it ended, even if it meant terminating his involvement with the case. Hardy thought that his client needed a dose of some hard life truths almost more than he needed a good attorney.

Cole swallowed rapidly, a couple of times in succession. He set his jaw, finally raised his eyes. For the first time, Hardy saw something like resolve in them. "All right," Cole said. "I'm listening. We'll do it your way. What's the plan?"

Hardy felt the tension break in his shoulders. He was still angry and frustrated, he still didn't much care for his client. But for now at least they could work together. Maybe. He leaned back, arms folded over his chest. "The strategy is two-pronged. First, if you did it—"

"Wait a minute. I said I'm not sure if . . . I mean I didn't—"

"*You* wait a minute." Hardy came forward, fed up to here with objections and interruptions. Here, in all probability, sat the man who had killed Elaine Wager. Maybe he didn't deserve the death penalty, but Hardy didn't have to endure his self-serving excuses. "I don't want you to tell me whether you did or didn't kill Elaine anymore. Do you understand me? I don't care about your denials or your admissions. That's not why I'm defending you. And right now I'm talking. You listen, that's the deal. Maybe you'll learn something."

Cole's eyes narrowed. Any hint of his methadone lethargy had vanished. He slumped back in the chair, his arms crossed. Pissed, dissed and dismissed.

Hardy ignored it all. He picked up in a relaxed voice. "Our first line of defense is unconsciousness. The facts here are going to make it very difficult, if not impossible, to even get to reasonable doubt about whether you did it."

"I—"

Hardy held up a palm. "Not interested. Of course we argue that you didn't do it. But what's really going to matter is if we can prove that even if you did, you were so drunk that you couldn't have realized what you were doing. With six or eight drinks in you, you're legally drunk. With twenty and in withdrawal, you're comatose."

"What about the gun, though?"

"I was going to ask you the same thing."

"I didn't get any gun from Cullen. He's lying."

"Why would he lie? I thought he was your friend?"

"Yeah, right." A shrug. "He's out on three separate probations for selling rock. He's got three or four strike convictions—robberies. They pull him in another time, he figures this time they've got to keep him. So he makes this up and they trade. Hey. You know this stuff happens all the time. And in this case, somebody wants to see me fall more than him, so they go for the trade."

"Who would want that? And why?"

"I don't know. Somebody with the D.A. Some cop. Maybe your friend Glitsky. I don't know."

Hardy felt his blood heating up again, but tried to ignore it. "You know anybody either place? Have you had any run-ins I ought to know about? Screwed around with some cop's daughter, anything like that?"

"No." He shook his head, then decided the denial wasn't strong enough. "Hey, I swear to God, no. Nothing like that."

Hardy was fairly sure that he was telling the truth. And the fact was, Cole didn't need to have a personal enemy in the D.A.'s office. There might be nothing personal in it—Pratt had to win this case, that was all. To fill a hole in the prosecution's theory of the crime, a witness needed to appear to account for Cole's possession of the murder weapon.

And lo, it had come to pass.

Hardy knew he needed to have a few words with Cullen Leon Alsop, get a better feel for that situation before too long. But first he needed Cole to understand his strategy, to be on board with it. "So Plan A is unconsciousness. You don't remember."

"But I *do* remember." He pushed ahead over Hardy's warning expression. "Seeing the gun. I don't know why it's just that, like a snapshot. I didn't have the gun. It was in the gutter, next to her. She was already down, I swear."

Hardy was almost tempted to believe him.

"I swear," Cole repeated.

"All right, Cole, you swear. But moving along, I'd also like to address the point that if you didn't kill Elaine, someone else did." Hardy didn't really think so, but mentioning it to Cole would serve as a pop quiz for his credibility. As he sat across the table from him now, he would have given about eighty percent odds that in the next few days his client would develop another "snapshot" of Monday night. And this one would feature the proverbial one-armed man.

"I'm surprised Jeff would even talk to you about me." Hardy had told him about his visit to the *Chronicle* that morning.

"Why's that?"

"I haven't exactly been like the perfect relative to those guys."

"So I hear."

"So . . . why?"

Hardy started gathering his documents, his legal pad, his pens. He stood up and had an acute flashback of Cole's mother in his office yesterday, the later years of her life now reduced to pain and guilt because of Cole. Even if he hadn't killed Elaine. Hardy looked across the table at him. "Maybe with Jeff it's like your friend Cullen, Cole. Something else is going on. You're in it, but you're not it. You know what I'm saying? There's a whole universe out there, and guess what?"

"What?"

"It doesn't all revolve around you."

22

I think I was a little hard on him." Hardy clinked his martini glass against David Freeman's.

In theory, he'd given up martinis at lunch about ten years before, but he always made an exception at Sam's. He'd walk through the door, there would be the old, tiny dark-wood bar, the male waiters in tuxedos, the buzz of busy people fortifying themselves with honest food for a productive afternoon. And suddenly the thought of not having one martini would always seem to be an unnecessary denial of one of his life's great pleasures.

Hardy hadn't missed a day of work because of alcohol in half a dozen years, and a martini wasn't going to slow him down this afternoon. So he ordered—Bombay Sapphire gin, up, very dry, one olive, and ice cold in a chilled glass.

Freeman didn't agonize half as much as Hardy. Hell, he didn't agonize at all. He was standing, waiting at the bar, when Hardy entered. Nodding in approval at the order, he said he'd have the same, and raised his glass when Hardy raised his own. "I'm sure he had it coming."

Hardy broke a cragged grin. "So here's to tough love, huh?"

"Or failing that, just plain tough."

Both men sipped appreciatively. A waiter informed them that their booth was ready. He would carry their drinks for them.

Sam's was already a popular San Francisco lunch spot by the turn of the twentieth century, and though it had changed some, it still retained a bit of the feel of a private men's club, with a public dining area in the main room. A side room provided more privacy, with booths along both walls that could be closed off by curtains, and it was to one of these that the men repaired.

McNeil hadn't arrived yet. It was possible that he might not show up at all, although Hardy had kept his invitation vague enough to whet his client's curiosity—had Manny Galt agreed to a settlement already? McNeil had been so anxious for it that he'd called a postdawn meeting yesterday. He would want to know right away, but he might also wonder why Hardy couldn't just leave a message. He would make the meeting if he could.

But in the meantime, there was plenty to talk about, and Hardy tried to keep the excitement out of his voice as he filled Freeman in on the unexpected appearance of Dash Logan again, this time in his murder case.

The old man, pensive, twirled the stem of his glass. "Russian insurance fraud?" He was frowning. "Sounds like the kind of work he'd like."

"The guy is everywhere. I find it pretty intriguing."

"Depressing is more like it."

"Maybe more than that." Hardy sipped gin, put his glass down. "I can't shake the feeling he's going to show up around Cole Burgess."

Freeman was shaking his head from side to side. "I doubt it."

"I'll give you a scenario. Logan wasn't being cooperative—the judge told me this—when Elaine came to do her special master work. Dash wouldn't show her where his files she needed were. If she wanted to pull them, she'd have to find them first."

"Have I already called him an asshole?" Freeman muttered.

Hardy nodded. "Several times. So Elaine just turned herself loose in his office, going through everything. And she found something she wasn't supposed to see."

Freeman almost choked on his drink. "You're saying you think Logan killed Elaine because of that?"

"Or one of the Russians. Or another of his clients."

"You've been watching too many movies."

"All I'm saying is we can make the argument and drag our friend Dash through the mud pretty good, and I know that would make some people at this table very happy." He shrugged. "At least it's somebody to point at, David. Something the jury might want to think about."

Freeman wasn't convinced. "Don't get me wrong, Diz, I love the concept," he said, "but it's pure speculation. Maybe she saw something and then maybe somebody killed her because of it. I don't think so. No judge would let you introduce it at trial."

Hardy didn't pursue it further, though—his client had arrived. As McNeil slid in beside him in the booth, it was clear he was both surprised and unhappy to find another guest at the table. Freeman had no real business being there, and when McNeil realized that he wasn't one of Hardy's old friends he'd spontaneously asked to lunch—no, he wanted to talk about McNeil's case!—he was as close to hostile as Hardy had ever seen him.

As always at Sam's, the waiter came by immediately. McNeil saw the other two glasses and ordered a martini, too, vodka. If not for that—the brief defusing hiatus—Hardy thought he might not have stayed. The pressure he'd been under recently threatened to escape in an explosion—the blood was up in his face. When he turned to Hardy, there was nothing but anger. "You're trying to bring somebody else into my case at this stage? What kind of bullshit is this? I thought I told you it was over. We were settling. And whatever, it was all confidential."

"It is, Rich. David knows nothing about the facts of the case itself."

"He'd better not."

Freeman wasn't inclined to stop himself from jumping in, and he did. "I'm here to tell you about one of *my* cases. Not the facts. The way it's being handled."

"And I'm going to care?"

"Yes, sir, I believe you will."

McNeil's florid face showed no sign of softening. He shot a glare again at Hardy, then took in Freeman with his rheumy basset eyes, his rumpled brown suit, the shaving stains on his shirt collar, the tufts of hair growing from the tops of his earlobes. "This pisses me off," he said. Unexpectedly, he grabbed at the curtain and violently pulled it closed. "All right, I'm listening."

Hardy let Freeman talk and as always he was impressed by the man's brilliance. Although Hardy had tried to leave out specific facts in his recital of McNeil's problems to David, he was sure he'd let a few slip out in the telling. By contrast, Freeman told his own client's story completely without reference to the details of the case.

It was a masterly performance. Freeman told Rich that he had a client with both civil and criminal cases pending. The leverage of one against the other. The offer to drop the criminal charges in return for a cash settlement. Finally, the name Dash Logan. The similarities in the *logistics, not the facts,* of his—McNeil's—case. And Hardy, by the way, would never have mentioned anything at all about Rich if Freeman hadn't first acquainted him with everything he had just recounted.

By the time the story ended, McNeil had cooled. A long silence followed, during which the waiter returned, drew back the curtain, delivered Rich's drink and took their lunch orders—sweetbreads for Freeman, sand dabs for Hardy and McNeil.

"Wine?" Freeman asked. "ABC? Everybody okay with that?"

"Don't know it," McNeil said.

"Anything but chardonnay," Hardy explained.

And finally his client smiled, Hardy thinking Freeman the goddamned genius. "Yeah," Rich said, "sure, sounds good."

"Is one of you gentlemen a Mr. Hardy?"

He looked up. "Yes." He hated this—someone tracking him down at lunch. It could only be bad news, an emergency, a disaster. And he wondered where the Beck got it?

The waiter was the soul of professional deference. "Your office called. Do you know someone at St. Mary's Hospital? They're trying to get in touch with you. You left your pager at the office, and evidently your cell phone is turned off."

"Thanks." He used his napkin. There was no need to panic. "I'll be right back."

Hardy followed the waiter through the main dining room—empty tables now for the most part—up to the bar. A large delivery truck had pulled into the alley by the front door, blocking any view, casting the room in shadow. As they handed him the phone, a large pallet of something fell outside with a tremendous crash. Even the bartender jumped.

Glitsky was dead. He knew it.

He called information for the number, let them connect it for him for an extra thirty-five cents. He didn't trust his brain to hold the number for the time it would take him to punch it in. "You have a patient named Abraham Glitsky."

"One moment, please. He's in the ICU. I'm not sure he'll be able to take your call. Please hold."

His heart was clogging his throat. He cleared it. It made no difference. They were playing "Feelings" in his ear while he was on hold. It didn't make the wait any shorter.

The operator came back on. "I'm sorry, sir, what was the name again?"

"Dismas Hardy," he said, tempted to add, "What's yours, Phyllis?"

"No," she said, "the patient?"

"Abe Glitsky. He wasn't in the ICU last night. He had a room with another man."

She couldn't have cared less. "The computer has him in the ICU. It doesn't say he's left it."

"Do you think you could maybe call the nurses' station there and check? Maybe someone would remember where they moved him if he's not still there."

"Oh, that's a good idea," she said brightly. "Please hold again. Sorry."

. . . feelings, oh, oh, oh . . .

Then, finally, a tone, a ring. Someone picking it up. "Glitsky. Hello."

For a minute, he felt light-headed with the rush of relief. "Did you call me?"

"Yeah."

"I thought you were having all kinds of tests and stuff today."

"That was this morning. It all went like a top, in case you were wondering."

"I haven't thought about anything else all day," he said. "Except just now I was sure you were dead."

"Nope," he said. "But somebody else is."

"Who's that?"

"Cullen Leon Alsop, former famous snitch. Diz, you still there?"

"Yeah. How?"

"OD. Uncut heroin. He got OR'd"—released on his own recognizance—"yesterday afternoon and I guess he thought it'd be fun to go out and celebrate."

"How did you find out?"

"Ridley Banks called me here. He was slightly upset. This kind of majorly complicates Cole Burgess for him and it's been a mess from the beginning. He didn't like it when Cullen came up with the gun story before and he doesn't like this even more."

"I don't, either."

"I didn't think you would. Which is why I wanted you to know right away."

"Would he talk to me? Banks?"

"He's a public servant. I don't see why not."

"Perhaps because the last cop who talked to me got himself suspended? That would be one reason."

"Maybe you can wear a disguise?"

"Or fake a heart attack, appear feeble and harmless. Speaking of which, I appreciate the call, but are you sure you should be working already?"

Glitsky didn't say anything for a long while. Then: "Maybe somebody else did kill her, Diz. I'm going to find out."

"Not if you die first."

"Then I'll make sure I don't."

The thing about Freeman that Hardy found so continually impressive was not only that his personal arsenal was so huge but that he could pull out any weapon from it at the moment of its peak effectiveness. At the precise instant, he'd managed to become both Rich McNeil's drinking buddy and his father confessor, even going so far as to pull the curtain again to shield them.

After Hardy pulled it back, he saw that Freeman had ordered a second bottle of Pinot Grigio and they'd already put a significant dent in it, the two of them having moved from hostility to something approaching intimacy in about a quarter of an hour. McNeil was leaning back into the wall of the booth, the earlier tomato-red flush of anger having softened to a rosy glow. He'd loosened his tie, undone his top button.

Hardy got settled in next to him and poured himself some ice water.

"Rich was just telling me an interesting story," Freeman said. "Do you know Gene Visser?"

"Used to be a cop? Sure, though I don't know what he's doing lately."

"Now he's a private eye. You'll never guess who he works with."

Hardy could figure it out. His eyebrows went up. He turned to Rich. "How did you meet him?"

McNeil lifted his glass, drank off another half inch. "He came to me one day last week at the office. Said he'd been doing some work for Mr. Logan, didn't want to see us get involved in a lot of ugly accusations."

Freeman chuckled without mirth. "We can bring this to the bar, and I'm going to. But I'm sorry, Rich, you go on."

The expression was apologetic. "I should have told you, Diz. I just thought it would be easiest to bail out. I'm just so tired of all this."

"What?"

McNeil sighed from his shoes. "Fifteen, eighteen years ago, I fucked up, got involved with another woman. My secretary. Stupid, stupid, stupid." Pure disgust. He sipped wine. "Anyway, I did it. She got pregnant, had the child. Sally found out. It was awful, but we worked it out. It was awful," he repeated. "And the girl, Linda . . . hell, it wasn't her fault . . . anyway, I wound up having to let her go, essentially paid her off out of our own savings, got her set up with another job . . ."

"And now she's blackmailing you?"

McNeil shook his head. "Not her, Diz. But the main thing Sally and I wanted to do was keep it from the kids, you know. I'd made a mistake and I was paying. Believe me, I was paying. But it wasn't going to ruin our family."

"And Visser found out about it?"

A nod. "He must have gone digging around in my old company for dirt on me. There had been rumors, probably some resentment. I left a couple of years afterward, but people remembered. And now . . ." He shrugged helplessly.

"So Visser threatened to tell your kids and drag Linda and her kid through it if you didn't settle." Hardy sat back, considering. "You know, Rich, it's not as though this kind of thing is going to make headlines. You had an affair, you and your wife worked it out, you're sorry."

McNeil looked across the table. "I know. That's what David was saying, too. It was just that after all this time, hearing it from Visser, knowing the kind of person Manny Galt is, what else he might do . . . I panicked, I guess."

"Totally understandable." Freeman was controlling the moment and this was precisely where he wanted McNeil. "Anyway, Diz, I suggested that he and Sally just gather the family together—maybe not the grand-children, but the kids. They should just—simply, honestly, humbly—lay it all out for them." He poured out his heart across the table. "They'll understand, Rich, I promise you."

"You know. I see it now. I think they would."

"Of course they would."

McNeil had his hand on his forehead as though rubbing away a headache. He wore his feelings like a billboard—it was all going to work out at last. Finally he looked up. "So both of you guys, you think I should just wait?"

"A few weeks, that's all," Freeman said.

Hardy added, "You can always settle. It never has to get to the criminal trial."

"That I really don't want. I'd sell the building before that."

"That's the right decision," Freeman said forcefully. "Nobody could blame you. But let's not breathe a word of it until when . . . let's say March first? Three weeks. How's that sound?"

McNeil gave the decision its due, then nodded. "I can do that."

Images, smells, feelings were beginning to break through the fog.

Cole didn't remember the last time he'd felt any kind of hunger except the craving for "g." But after this morning's meeting with his hard-ass lawyer, they took him back to his cell and he realized he was ravenous. He'd gotten his pill from the orderly, then had his four slices of white bread, glass of milk, orange juice, two sausages, two eggs for breakfast only three hours before, but now he was counting the minutes until eleven-thirty, when they'd bring up lunch.

As a capital murder defendant, he was still separated from the general population, in a sort of wing with six cells, three on each side of a ten-by-twenty-foot common area which they were not permitted to use. He was in front right, with only one "neighbor." Cole didn't know his name. He thought of him as Jose, a tattooed rail of Mexican steel who spent all of his time doing push-ups, then watching the public television which was left on sixteen hours a day above the common area in the center of the pod of cells.

There was some game show on now, and he stood at the bars for one of the segments between commercials, then gave that up. Jose was doing push-ups again, and Cole watched him for a while before deciding that this wouldn't be the worst way to spend some time. He dropped himself and ripped off ten before it got a little difficult. By twenty he was done, his biceps and chest muscles, such as they were, screaming at the exertion. He looked over and Jose was still methodically pumping, his head craned up to the side to follow the TV.

Cole lay on the cold concrete, catching his breath. Loathing what he'd become.

It didn't even feel like a memory. He could close his eyes and recall it perfectly, the sense that he was sixteen—yesterday—he and Steve Polacek in his garage, their huge twenty-dollar bet over who'd be the first to press his weight. A hundred thirty-one pounds, that was Cole. Polacek was seven pounds heavier, wanted a handicap.

For a while, he remembered, their *warm-up* had been fifty push-ups. Fifty! He couldn't bring back who'd won the bet—if either of them had ever made it to their weight. Probably both—that was the way they were back then.

But he remembered the garage. They never parked cars in it, not even in the winter. Just his dad's tools on the wall, the workbench, the Ping-Pong table in the middle. Bikes and skates, skis and balls and sports equipment all over the place. Pretty good jock family up 'til his dad died. His sister Dorothy training with him that whole last summer she was home before she went to college. They were going to ski cross-country from Des Moines to Iowa City when she came back on Christmas break.

Cole lifted his cheek off the floor, pulled his arms up to beside his shoulders, pushed. This time, even the first few were hard. Eight.

Turning onto his side, he sat up, then pulled his mattress off its concrete pad, onto the floor. He rolled onto it, hooked his hands behind his head, tried a sit-up. Once upon a time he could really do sit-ups—sixty in a minute. Polacek couldn't touch him.

Again he started fast. Again he faded quickly, but he forced himself through fifteen and on to twenty. He wasn't going to accept less than twenty, although the last couple felt like they ripped something inside him. But he got to it, turned on his side away from Jose, gulped for breath, closed his eyes.

The clang of the outer door to the common room jolted him up. Cole had dozed through the twenty minutes that inmates were allowed out into the common room every morning. Two guards with the trolley holding the lunches banged again on the outer door. "Back in your rooms, girls!"

When everyone was back where they belonged, the guard entered his code into the box outside and all the cell bolts slammed into place. Seeing the mattress on the floor with Cole cross-legged now on it, the guard distributing the trays couldn't resist a little moment of clever repartee. "Having a picnic, Alice?" he asked. "Nice day for it." He slid the tray under the door.

Cole barely heard and didn't care.

Eric was the social worker who passed out the pills—he stopped at the door. This was the first dose Cole had told him he was going to miss—he'd get his usual come dinnertime again—and Eric wanted to check to make sure Cole was comfortable with the idea. He was.

Then, finally, the food. If Cole thought he'd felt a jab of hunger before, it was nothing compared to now, with another of the jail's full-fledged meals actually in front of him. All the meals he'd had so far included four slices of white bread and four pats of butter. The butter was soft, warm, and he smeared one of the pats onto a piece of the bread, folded it over and put it all, whole, into his mouth. While he chewed, he looked down at the tray. Today, lunch was two thick slabs of meat loaf with gravy, mixed peas and carrots, mashed potatoes and more gravy, canned peaches in a plastic bowl, milk and two chocolate chip cookies.

The bread went down. Cole stabbed at the meat loaf so hard that he broke his plastic fork. It didn't matter. He used his spoon, shoveled in a few more bites, began to savor, to taste—prodded by the mnemonic smell of the gravy, to remember.

Polacek's kitchen. A winter day, late afternoon, snow outside. An after-school-snack before hockey, Polacek's mom pouring reheated gravy over bread and cold meat loaf.

Polacek. He hadn't thought of him in years, and now he found himself wondering where his old best friend was. Certainly no place like here. He probably had a job someplace, maybe even was married. Polacek with kids? Imagine.

The last year of high school they had stopped being friends over the dope—marijuana, then. Polacek really believing it was the killer weed. Didn't want any part of it. So Cole started hanging with the other guys—Reece, Baugh, Neillsen, Parducci.

Baugh was the best of them. He had even been friends with Polacek before, as Cole had. The good students through grade school, Little League, Boy Scouts. Then, after Cole's dad died, when Cole had been trying to get through that darkness, Baugh turning him on the first time. No doubt he had good intentions—that was who Baugh was—trying to make Cole feel better about life with his sister gone away to college, his dad gone for good. Hey, life isn't easy. People need to laugh, get high, forget themselves. It was an unbelievable bummer, his dad dying.

"Marijuana, BFD. Come on, Cole, it's totally harmless. Marijuana never killed anybody."

Baugh was dead now four years, though.

Polacek trying to get him to stop a few times, coming around the house, worried about how much Cole was changing.

Yeah? Well, people change. Cole wasn't hooked on anything. He could stop anytime he wanted. The other guys—Reece, Neillsen, Parducci—his mom kept up with their moms. Last Cole heard, Reece had become a cop back home. He knew Neillsen worked at GM. Parducci was still playing ball, second year in Triple A, might make the bigs.

Telling himself, soaking up his gravy, "Didn't hook any of them. Didn't hook me either. Not the marijuana."

Another flash—the last time he saw Polacek. A party at Notre Dame. Cole had dropped out after a semester, and his mom sent him up to visit his old friend, subliminal message that maybe he'd see how great Steve was doing and clean his own act up. Subtle as a cherry bomb. But he'd gone. Cole in his own mind nowhere near any kind of junkie. This is recreation, that's all—the only kind he knows anymore, constant doping. But he can quit anytime.

He's shocked at Steve, in a frat now, with his alligator shirt, drinking beer, dancing to Hootie. Just like so *unaware,* so naive. Whereas Cole that night, he was the king . . .

There was this girl, somebody somebody. By now he was into cocaine whenever he could get it, dealing a little to cover costs. So he and this girl, they're upstairs in the bathroom. They've got lines laid out and one of the dorks comes in and next thing there's Polacek, angry but calm, laying some trip about him being a *guest* and abusing their friendship. Cole's got to leave *right now!* They can't have cocaine in their house. The college could close them down. They could lose their charter.

Cole's temper out the window—half the blow wasted now, scattered

in the commotion. "Who gives a shit, Steve? About any of this?" Screaming at him.

"Everybody here, Cole. Everybody who's trying to make a life."

Polacek, the dweeb. Never saw him again, and good damn riddance.
The best friend, though, that he'd ever had.

"Hey, Alice! You done? What's a matter? They put too much pepper
in that for you?"

23

Ten years ago, when Sharron Pratt had been a city supervisor, she had lobbied to pass an obscure change in the city's law regarding business announcements in the community's newspapers. Previously, if you wanted to file a Fictitious Business Name statement, a Notice of Application to Sell Alcoholic Beverages, a Notice of Foreclosure or any number of other legal notices, the law required that you publish this information in any newspaper with a paid circulation of at least one hundred and fifty thousand.

Sharron had persuaded the other supervisors that this law unfairly discriminated against the smaller, more "community-based" newspapers that proliferated all over the city, and which could receive no revenue from this lucrative market. Largely as a result of her efforts, the law was changed to require the filing of these notices in any newspaper with a *print run* of over ten thousand copies, of which the most well-known in the English language was the *Daily Democrat*.

As a practical matter, this change in the law made a millionaire out of Chad Lacey, the *Daily Democrat* publisher, a friend and political ally of Sharron Pratt. Suddenly Lacey's community bulletin, distributed for free on racks or as a throwaway on driveways mostly in the Haight-Ashbury district, found itself on the receiving end of almost $300,000 per year in city money alone. Lacey could now afford to hire a few well-known guest columnists and to pay several full-time reporters. With the paper's new respectability, distribution went into three more districts in the city—the Sunset, the Richmond, Twin Peaks—and the *Democrat* became the city's premier free newspaper.

Its print run had grown to twenty-five thousand, and it positioned itself as the voice of the people—the downtrodden, the disenfranchised—the political pals of Lacey and Pratt. Before any papers had been filed in the matter, for example, the *Democrat* had run a five-thousand-word piece on the tragic plight of a powerless and law-abiding citizen named Manny Galt, who'd trusted his landlord, paying advance rent in cash while he'd gone to care for his dying mother for a few months. He returned from this errand of mercy only to find himself evicted from his longtime residence, in flagrant defiance of human decency and the city's rent control laws, by a grasping, crooked and heartless developer named Rich McNeil. They'd run a picture of poor Manny on the front page and he had, indeed, looked very sad and downtrodden, sitting there on his motorcycle.

Now Sharron Pratt stood over her desk and punched numbers on the phone so hard that her whole desk shook. She had the speaker on so her voice would boom slightly on the other end. "I need to talk to Mr. Lacey right now. Yes, a personal matter." This was their code phrase—Pratt wouldn't call the *Democrat* under her own name and appear to be giving orders to its publisher. To do so would do fatal damage to the credibility of his objective editorials. She waited impatiently, looking at her watch.

Less than a minute elapsed. "I'm here," Lacey said. "How are you?"

"I'm not well, Chad. Not well at all."

"What's the matter?"

"The matter? Oh, let's see. Perhaps it's the fact that last week we talked before my speech at the Commonwealth Club. Do you remember that?"

"Sharron—"

"Do you remember telling me you'd make sure this death penalty decision I announced would get a lot of favorable press, editorial coverage, like that?"

Lacey didn't respond.

Pratt took a breath and softened her tone. "And yet I notice you have rather loudly stayed silent, while your colleagues over at the *Chronicle*, particularly Jeff Elliot, have been having a great deal of fun at my expense." She picked up the receiver, spoke in a still more measured tone. "I certainly don't mean to tell you how to run your paper,

Chad, but I was under the impression that you were in my camp. Have I offended you in some way? If I have, I'm sorry, but I've kind of been waiting for you to step up."

She heard his sigh over the line. "Well, we've had some problems, Sharron. I suppose I should have called you sooner."

"About what? What kind of problems?"

The publisher paused. "Well, frankly, some of my reporters . . . as you know, Sharron, we haven't been much in the death penalty camp here over the years."

"Well, neither have I, Chad. But this is a special case."

"I know it is, Sharron. I am on your side. The thing is, we're having some trouble figuring out how it's so special and then what kind of spin to put on it. I had to personally kill the first article I got on it. You know why? Because it sounded a lot like Jeff Elliot's 'CityTalk.' "

"Who was it? Whoever it was, he works for you, doesn't he? If he doesn't write what you want, it seems like you'd have some leverage."

"It doesn't matter, the individual. He's a good reporter, he's been on your side a lot. He doesn't like this, that's all."

Pratt pursed her lips, stripped off a piece of Scotch tape from the dispenser on her desk, began dabbing at imaginary spots on her skirt. "I've got an idea, Chad," she said. "Why don't we do an exclusive interview, you and me, one on one. The spin is that while in general the death penalty is the wrong penalty, it is the only remedy for a hate crime such as this one. This was a hate crime, make no mistake. And I believe, Chad, that a hate crime like this calls for blood vengeance."

She could almost swear she heard him thinking about it. "That might play," he said at last.

"Damn straight," she replied. "The two of us, we can *make* it play. It *has* to play."

Treya was supposed to start on Mr. Jackman's project—the *Grayson* matter—on Monday morning, but the firm had been excused to attend Elaine's memorial. In the aftermath of Glitsky's collapse, she had been unable to make herself come in for the rest of the day. She knew that under other circumstances, this would have been inexcusable. She herself would not have condoned it. And to make matters worse, the time she'd spent at home had been wholly unproductive. Now it was Wednesday afternoon.

Mr. Jackman, at least, seemed to understand, but she felt awful about it. Yesterday she did come in, but she worked only about six hours, all of it on *Grayson*. Mr. Jackman had been right, it was about the most tedious number crunching she had ever experienced. After her sleepless Monday night, she had made almost no headway and finally she realized that if she was going to call on Lieutenant Glitsky at the hospital that night—which after her behavior seemed a sacred duty—she would need some rest first. So she'd signed out early again.

She'd come in this morning with a new resolve, went directly to the abandoned associates' room that was her work space for the new project—seventy-four cardboard boxes filled with data stacked along the walls, in the bookcases, everywhere—and began where she'd left off the night before—on the third manila folder in the first box.

And could not do it.

In four and a half hours, she estimated that she'd done twenty minutes of useful work. At twelve-thirty, she checked her watch, looked at the pages spread out before her, and got out from behind the desk.

His secretary was at lunch, the gatekeeper's desk deserted. His door was open a crack. She heard him talking on the telephone. The conversation wound to a close and she knocked on the door and pushed it open slightly further.

"Mr. Jackman? Excuse me? Can I bother you a minute?"

He looked up, surprised. His hand was still on the phone and now he stopped, placing the receiver back into its cradle. "Ms. Ghent? What can I do for you? How's *Grayson* coming along?"

She steeled herself and told him the truth—that it wasn't the project, it was her. She was wasting the firm's time these past few days, and after he'd been so kind to her . . .

He stopped her. "What's really bothering you?" he asked.

She drew a long breath and stared across at him. "That I can't seem to get focused on anything. Except Elaine." The rest of it—Glitsky and her feelings there—was too nebulous to mention. She pressed on. "The talk you and I had last week about her enemies, that you knew about some of them." She paused, looked down at her hands, back up at him, told him she'd gone to visit Glitsky at the hospital. "I felt like I'd made it happen somehow."

"What? His heart attack?"

A nod. "It sounds ridiculous, I know." She shrugged. "I just felt I had to make sure he was all right."

"And was he?"

"He seemed fine." Wonderful, in fact, but she merely nodded again. "But he's still worried about the case."

Jackman's face grew grave. "Did he say why? Or give any reason?"

She thought of what he'd said—it was as though Elaine were finally talking to him—and knew there would be no way to communicate that. "Nothing specifically, but the reason is all wrapped up around Cole's confession—he thinks it's internally inconsistent, maybe inadmissible."

"To the point that it's completely invalid? Not just inadmissible but untrue?"

She shrugged her shoulders. "I don't know."

He cocked his head, intent. "But what do you think, Treya?"

She hadn't worked it through completely yet, although she found it compelling that a veteran cop like Glitsky would believe it enough to get laid off over it. "I think it's a gap worth closing."

"And that isn't happening with the police? With Glitsky?"

Treya still resisted giving it up. Glitsky's position as a lieutenant of homicide was the font of his power and she found herself reluctant to undercut that. So she temporized. "Well, you know. They've got a suspect in custody who's been charged with the crime . . ." She left the conclusion unstated. "The point is, he's doing it on his own."

"Eliminating any other possible suspect but Burgess?" Jackman rocked in the chair behind his desk.

"Yes." She hesitated, leaned forward. "Which brings me to what I wanted to say."

He waited.

"I'm probably the best source of what Elaine may have been working on."

"And this means?"

"I think I could be valuable to an investigation, if the lieutenant's interested."

Jackman drew in a lungful of air. "Interested in what, precisely?" he asked carefully.

"If you'll forgive me speaking up, sir, Elaine was one of this firm's premier assets. It seems to me that it's in the firm's best interests to make sure that her murderer doesn't get off."

"The firm's best interests," he said dubiously. "In what way?"

"Cole Burgess took something from you, sir. The lieutenant doesn't want him getting away with it, and I don't believe you would stand for it, either."

She knew that she'd hit the right chord. Someone had stolen from him, from everything he'd built up from scratch, and nobody was going to get away with that. For a moment, her boss's eyes were alight with intensity, and she realized that it had become personal now—somehow she'd made him see that. "You do what you have to do," he said finally. "Bill it to admin."

She stood up. Her employer, too, got out of his chair and came around the desk. Now he stood perhaps a foot in front of her. She looked up into his face. "What bothers me," she said evenly, "is that I didn't even know she had enemies. I know we confided in one another. I think she would have told me."

Jackman drew back half a step. He folded his arms and stared out at something beyond her right shoulder. "Maybe enemies is too harsh," he said. "More like competitors. She was strong-willed, vibrant. She wanted her way and got it. People were jealous of her, thought her aloof and arrogant. That she was unaware of that reaction—maybe even of the people themselves having it—only made it worse. Perhaps you've experienced some of the same thing yourself? Even here at the firm?"

And, of course, he was right. She acknowledged the truth of it with a small smile.

"I know she could rub people the wrong way, so in that sense, yes, she had enemies." Jackman's face suddenly set itself in ice. "I was one of them."

24

It was closing in on dusk, and Ridley Banks was back at the same crime scene to which he'd been summoned just after dawn.

He'd had a busy day, putting a greater concentration of investigative fieldwork into the past ten hours than he normally would get to in a month. The results were mixed, as they almost always were in homicides anyway. But they were also, in his opinion, provocative in the extreme.

The victim had been found dead in room 412 of the Excelsior Hotel at Sixteenth and Mission. In spite of its name, the Excelsior is not a hotel in the usual meaning of the word. Rather, its clientele rent rooms by the week or the month, and these tended to be casually bartered by its inhabitants mostly for drugs, but also for sex, booze, clothes, money.

There was no current guest registered to the room containing the body of Cullen Leon Alsop. The door had not been locked when he'd been found. Still, the homicide team upon its arrival had little trouble identifying him—his wallet bulged in the back pocket of his jeans, which he was still wearing. He also had his jail release and OR papers on him, stuffed into the front pockets. So it was Cullen, all right, and Ridley's name was on one of the sheets, so he got looped into the call.

The inspector spent a few hours at the scene, asking questions of the crime scene investigation unit. He then decided it would be instructive to wait for John Strout's arrival. He wanted to talk to the coroner before things moved too far along. Because while people died quite often from heroin overdoses in the city—especially in this neighborhood—there was too much coincidence in this case for Ridley's liking.

The sergeant with the CSI team was of the opinion that somebody else had been with Cullen and then, not too surprisingly when he realized what was happening, fled. He was surprised, though, that he'd left the Baggie with a reasonable amount of white powder still in it on the small table next to the bed. This stuff was far more valuable than gold to any addict—it was unprecedented in the CSI sergeant's experience that this much would be left behind, regardless of what had occurred in the room. Cullen also had six hundred and fifty-four dollars in cash, a couple of joints and a matchbook from a bar called Jupiter jammed into his other front pants pocket.

When Strout came, he was his cautious, but helpful, self. After he'd examined and autopsied the body and all forensic evidence relevant to it, the coroner would eventually release his opinion on the official cause of death. Before that, Strout wasn't going to be hurried, nor was he inclined to make any official pronouncement before he had time to analyze all of his facts. But there were a few informal opinions he could share with an inspector of homicide to guide him in his investigation.

The first was that the residue left in the bag appeared to be an unusually pure form of heroin, possibly almost uncut China White. Strout told Banks that if this was a representative sample of the latest stuff to hit the street, they could expect half a dozen overdoses, maybe more, in the next couple of days. Neither Strout nor the CSI team could see any sign of struggle, and that, combined with the probable cause of death, suggested to Strout that this was mostly likely an overdose situation. An accidental suicide, not a homicide.

Banks couldn't shake the feeling that in this the coroner was mistaken.

Over the next two hours, he talked to everyone who'd been in the building and who hadn't managed to escape before the word got out that the police were on hand. Of the twenty-seven people he interviewed, fourteen admitted to knowing Cullen at least by sight, but none of them had seen him come into the building. None admitted to knowing he'd been there last night.

The "manager" was a toothless mid-fifties gnome in a lime green bathrobe and combat boots. He had no idea how that poor boy had gotten into the room. It was vacant. See? He still had the key! Far more concerned with getting reimbursed by the city for the room's rent during the time the police kept it closed off as a crime scene than he was with the death, the manager had not seen or heard anything unusual in the past couple of days. Of course, he would have said the same thing if he had personally witnessed the Second Coming.

In the next four hours, Ridley had first called his old mentor Glitsky in the hospital. After that, cursing himself for everything he was and everything he'd done in the past ten days, he'd gone back to the beginning, and remembered the matchbook from Jupiter. Armed with a mug shot, he got to the bar at around two-thirty, and five people, including the bartender, a lawyer, a private investigator and two random daytime drinkers recognized Cullen's face. Yes, he'd been there, had a few drinks, seemed impatient, but didn't cause any trouble.

Ridley was glad to run into some cooperative witnesses. The five of them had been helpful, sitting in a circle around him at the bar trying to help him connect the dots. The lawyer and the private eye—Logan and Visser—were sure that they had left the bar before the victim had, so they couldn't vouch for when he left, but the other three witnesses came to an agreement that Cullen had left at a little after dark.

Now Ridley was back where he'd begun, on the streets surrounding the Excelsior. He pulled his shirt out, untied his shoes and adopted a slouch. In a half hour, he'd made a friend who directed him to one of the neighborhood's salesmen—Damien was parked in an alley a block and a half from the Excelsior, selling prewrapped, packaged, brand-name dime bags of heroin out of a shiny Buick Skylark.

In another five minutes, whatever streetlights still worked in the city would come on. Ridley looked around to be sure nobody was watching. He reached under his jacket and pulled out his gun and badge and walked up to the car. "Lucky for you, dirtbag," he said, "I'm in homicide. Get out real slow."

Backing up to let the door open, Ridley nearly had his own heart attack. To his right, at the back bumper of the Skylark, stood another bum—his face in the dim light vaguely familiar. He, too, had a gun in one hand. In the other, he held out a badge. He was smiling dangerously.

Damien had one foot on the pavement when the other man sprang forward in one long step. Grabbing him by the collar, he dragged him the rest of the way out of the car and threw him to the ground.

"Hey, man," Damien whined. "My clothes, you know."

Both men kept their guns trained on him. "Damien, Damien, Damien," the bum with the badge clucked sympathetically. "Some people are just never going to learn. Do you not have brains, is that the problem? Are they defective? Can't you tell a cop yet after all this time? Haven't you and I done this enough?" He shook his head dishearteningly. "I swear, it's depressing."

He looked over at Ridley, still holding his badge up to avoid any misunderstanding. Then he went back to Damien, still on the ground. "This man here," he said, indicating Ridley, "is Inspector Banks from homicide." He flashed a smile, speaking over his own shoulder. "Jan Falk. Narcotics. I tried to get you coming out of Jupiter, but you were too fast. Sorry if I spooked you just now."

Ridley was coming back to earth, finally recognized Falk as one of the daytime drinkers from Jupiter. Undercover, and fooled him clean. "I'll get over it."

"You guys going to kiss now or what?" Damien asked.

Falk smiled at him again, put on a mincing voice. "If we want to, Damien. In fact, we're going to do anything we want to, and I get the feeling Inspector Banks wants to ask you some questions. Is that right, Inspector?"

"That's right."

"Well, you can ask my lawyer. I didn't do no homicide."

Banks gave Damien a heartless little grin of his own. "I didn't say you did now, did I?"

"I'll tell you what," Falk said. "I'm going to make a phone call now to some friends of mine and meanwhile let you fellows get to know each other a little better. How's that sound, Inspector?"

A half hour later, Damien was leaving the alley on his way downtown in the back seat of a squad car. Inspectors Banks and Falk waved good-bye, then went to lean against the bumper of the Skylark to wait for the police tow truck to come and impound the vehicle. By now, they were laughing about it.

"You were damn lucky I didn't pop you where you stood," Banks said.

"I know. I realized that about a second too late. It just seemed too good an opportunity to pass up. I hate that little pecker. Haven't seen him in a couple of years."

"How'd you know where I was going?"

"You said Excelsior. Drug overdose. I guessed. I'm made here, so I don't hang much about, but I saw you and thought it would be fun to stroll through the old neighborhood. And what do you know, we both run into Damien."

Ridley phrased it carefully, not wanting to step on a fellow officer's toes. "He wasn't very hard for me to find, you know."

"No, we figure it takes maybe a half hour for a new guy, one of us, to make one of them. Then we leave 'em alone."

"But you just busted him."

"That was purely for fun, Inspector. We got twenty Damiens in this square mile. If you hadn't connected with him, I wouldn't have done a thing. They're just literally holding the bags, not worth the trouble. Their only value is maybe leading us to their source, and even at that next level . . ." He shrugged. It was terrible, but it was reality. Every policeman knew that arresting the intermediaries in the drug trade was at best a stopgap measure, a nuisance for all concerned. Between Damien and his ultimate supplier (whom Damien would never meet, or know, or possibly even hear of), there were probably six to ten layers of intermediaries, each taking their money, most cutting the product. "Anyway, you wanted something from him. I thought I might put him more in the mood to be cooperative. You find what you wanted?"

It was Ridley's turn to shrug. "I have trouble believing insurance salesmen are telling me the truth. And Damien scores a little lower than they do."

"What did you want to know?"

"If there was something new, super pure, on the street. That's what my guy died of."

"What did he say, Damien?"

"He said no. Same stuff all the time lately. Guaranteed. You know, I've got to say, I can't believe they put brand names on this stuff. Those bags Damien had on him. Heavenly Daze. Jesus."

"Sure. There's all kinds of great shit—Nirvana. China Sleep. Tar Babies. But your guy had something else?"

"The coroner said—unofficially of course—that he thought it was nearly pure. And it wasn't in any container, just a plain Baggie."

Falk took his heel off the bumper and walked off a few steps. He stood there a couple of moments, nodding his head as though reaching some conclusion. Then he turned back around. "This is why I came out looking for you after you left."

"Why?"

" 'Cause I'm on a thing out of the Jupiter. There's a lot of cocaine in and out of there, and since it's mostly a law crowd, people want to see it cleaned up before it gets busted. Am I making it clear?"

"Yeah."

"Okay, so yesterday, I'm passing a slow afternoon and your man Cullen comes in, just like we all said today. But he's not like a *little* impatient—he's climbing the walls. So he's halfway through a beer, and he gets up and goes to the bathroom. Couple of minutes later, one of the guys today—the PI, Visser?—he gets up and goes to the bathroom. Now I been in there, the bathroom, and it's one stall, one pisser, and those two guys are in there, swear to God, ten minutes, before Visser comes out first and sits back down in his booth. Of course, it's Jupiter, late afternoon, nobody's paying any attention. Except me."

"So what?"

"Not what you're probably thinking. Another minute and out comes your guy, Cullen Leon Alsop. Now he's Mr. Mellow. Sits and finishes his beer, has another one while Visser and his lawyer friend leave."

Ridley shook his head. "I must be missing something. This wasn't cocaine. This was heroin."

But Falk had a scent. "Either way," he said. "Visser was in there and gave him something. Then this morning the guy's dead? I never thought of it until you came in today asking questions, but as soon as I saw that kid's face, I'm going click click click, you know?"

"I know the feeling," Ridley said. "I'm getting it now."

25

A decent legal mind?" Frannie whistled, impressed. "David actually said those words?"

"Every one of them, in that order."

Behind the bar of the Shamrock, Moses McGuire slid a black and tan—half Bass ale, half Guinness stout—across to his brother-in-law. "He's buttering you up," he said. "I'll bet he raises your rent in the next few weeks. You watch."

But Hardy was shaking his head. "It was a sincere compliment. You had to be there. I doubt if he even realized he said it."

"We're talking David Freeman?" Frannie said flatly. "If he said it, he realized it."

"Shameless flattery," Moses said. "And not much of it at that."

Hardy sipped at his brew. "Mose, I once heard Freeman say he thought Oliver Wendell Holmes wasn't too stupid. If the greatest jurist our country has produced is not too stupid and I've got a decent legal mind, you see where that puts me."

"At least in line for the Supreme Court," Frannie said. "I can't wait."

"In line for a rent increase, is more like it." Moses wasn't to be persuaded. "I wouldn't go anyplace expensive for dinner tonight. You're going to need the money."

It was Date Night. Normally they didn't do the Redwood Room at the Clift followed by Charles Nob Hill. On a typical Wednesday, they would meet—Hardy from downtown and Frannie from their house out on Thirty-fourth Ave—at the Little Shamrock midway between them at Ninth and Lincoln. They would have one drink, usually at the bar with Moses behind it, and then repair to dinner wherever the mood took them.

A young couple had seated themselves at the bar by the front window and Moses walked down to wait on them. Hardy covered Frannie's hand with his own, gave it a gentle squeeze, put on an apologetic face and reached for the beeper on his belt. "Sorry. I meant to leave it in the car."

"Now, though, since you didn't . . ." But she was used to it—the constant interruptions were always unwelcome, but they had ceased to be an issue. When they got to wherever they were going for dinner, she would remember to have him take the beeper off his belt, leave it in the glove compartment. She put her hand over his now, kissed him lightly on the cheek. "It's okay, go ahead."

He used the phone behind the bar, which he figured was the last working rotary in California. The callback number wasn't immediately familiar to him, and this was in itself a bit unusual—Hardy's legal mind might only be decent, but he had almost an idiot savant's knack for remembering telephone numbers, and this one seemed new to him.

"Banks," he heard. "Homicide."

"Inspector. This is Dismas Hardy. Thanks for getting back to me."

The voice wasn't enthusiastic. "Sure. I try to return calls. What can I do for you? You said the lieutenant . . ." He didn't finish the sentence.

"I talked to Abe this afternoon. He said maybe this Cullen Alsop thing is related to Elaine? To Cole Burgess."

"Maybe." The voice wasn't any more inviting.

"I understand the gun story felt a little funny to you. And now the overdose the day he gets out . . . ?" At some point, Hardy hoped Banks was going to catch up and run with it, but he also knew the cause of the reluctance and respected it. "Somebody might have wanted to shut him up."

"Possible." Banks was noncommittal. "Strout's leaning toward calling it an accident."

"What do you think?" Hardy let a silence develop. This wasn't working. He wasn't getting through to the young man. Professionally, they were still on opposite sides. He had to find a way to bridge the gap.

Banks said, "Well . . ." About to end the call.

Hardy cut him off. "Remember the other day at the funeral, Inspector? Asking Abe if there was anything you could do?"

No response.

"This might be it. All I'm asking is give me a half hour."

Another long pause. Then the voice more matter-of-fact, a decision reached. "I got an appointment coming up I've got to make. It's on this. After that I thought I'd go down and see the lieutenant around the end of visiting hours, maybe nine, nine-thirty."

"As it happens, I was going to stop by and see him after dinner myself."

It was a way for Ridley to justify what he was about to do. That appeared to be what he needed. "So it would just be a coincidence if we both got there around the same time?"

The weather had cleared and warmed up slightly. Not that it was balmy by any stretch, but the biting damp wind of the past week or so had abated, and now the air was calm, the stars bright overhead.

Hardy and Frannie had miraculously gotten a table without advance reservations at Pan Y Vino, a longtime favorite Italian place just up from the Marina, and when they finished, they decided to take a walk. They'd already discussed what seemed to be every possible permutation in the lives of their children, Frannie's progress with her school applications— she'd gotten them all off—the terrific food they were eating, Moses, Abe, his health and his children. Even Treya Ghent. And what had that been about, the degree of personal involvement in her showing up at the hospital. This was what Date Night was for—to catch up, to stay in touch. Personal lives.

They were holding hands, strolling with the mass of other pedestrians up Union Street. It wasn't yet eight-thirty. Occasionally, they would stop and look in a window at something. Eventually, Frannie squeezed her husband's hand. Smiling, she looked over at him.

"I'm sorry? What?" he asked.

"I was saying, '. . . and then my grandmother died.' I think that must have been what you heard that woke you up."

"Sorry," he said again. "I guess I'm a little distracted."

But she didn't want to criticize him. "All right," she said, "you've been the soul of patience. We can declare the date over if you want, talk about whatever it is."

Out of the topics they could talk about, in the first years of Date

Night, one had come to predominate—Hardy's work. From time to time, he would become so involved in his cases that he would suggest they drive together to crime scenes, or maybe stop by the jail to interview his client. They would theorize cases to death over meals that neither of them tasted.

Finally, they had outlawed discussing his cases during Date Night. It still did creep in but generally the law was respected and, in fact, treasured.

But she was right. Tonight Hardy's input to the various family and personal discussions was minimal at best. Distracted was hardly the word. She already knew that he and Freeman had made some crucial strides on one of his cases at lunch. There was some inkling that much of his involvement in several cases might be related somehow. He would be seeing Glitsky within the hour, getting new information from Ridley Banks. The connection between the relationships might become clear. It was all he could think about.

"I just don't want to waste Ridley's time with stupid questions," he said by way of explanation. "He's not going to want to help me without Abe anyway. I don't want to wind up threatening him, getting him all defensive, scaring him away."

"How would you do that?"

"I start talking about the videotape on Cole, the confession, and he's gone."

"Why?"

"Because Ridley's the one who got it. He's still standing by it, but this new overdose makes it a little funky. He doesn't really know why and neither do I, but it's there. And also, Abe's lost his job over it and then nearly died. All that may or may not be related, but either way, Ridley's conflicted."

"And you hope to straighten him out?"

Hardy nodded. "With my decent legal mind, at least identify the issues. Maybe."

"Which are?"

He stopped walking and stepped out of the stream of foot traffic. It was still chilly enough that his sigh produced a visible plume of vapor. "That's the problem. I don't know, Fran. I've been racking my brain all day, especially since I ran into Dash Logan connected with Elaine, which of course is Cole's case. But I'm not convinced he's killed anybody. And I really don't see any connection between Elaine and Rich

McNeil. None of it makes any sense. None of it relates except for Logan, who seems to be in the middle of all of it."

"Well," Frannie said, "if Abe's got the doubts, and now Ridley—and neither of them are exactly pro-defense—then maybe you'd better start considering that Cole is telling you the truth."

"It wasn't unconsciousness? He just happened upon her after somebody else did her?"

She shrugged. "It could have happened."

" 'Could have happened' doesn't meet much of a legal standard, Fran. I can't argue that in front of a jury."

"How about just a judge? How about at the hearing?"

Hardy didn't even have to think—he shook his head no. "The hearing's a formality. The standard is probable cause, not reasonable doubt. Torrey demonstrates that—and the confession alone ought to be enough on that score—and that's it. We go to trial."

"I know, I know, but listen . . ." Her eyes were alight with the idea. "There's something about this particular case that's causing all kinds of confusion even among you professionals, right? You've got to admit that. I mean, Abe getting put on leave over it? Come on, that is not normal. Now Ridley Banks agreeing to talk to you. Even you yourself and your decent mind."

"Decent *legal* mind. The rest of it's often pretty indecent."

"Okay, still. I'm saying you might be able to get a judge to feel that way, too. Not a jury, but one person. If you could get all the questions out in front of one of them."

His eyes had turned inward. A couple of times he seemed about to speak, but the thread eluded him. Finally, he looked at her. "The problem is, Fran . . . that presupposes that he didn't do it after all, and I think he did." He put up a hand to stop her from breaking in. "I'm not saying he meant to. I don't think he planned it. Maybe even as he did it, he didn't *get* it. But I'll tell you something: he sure had means, motive and opportunity. He's got the opposite of an alibi." His voice was becoming harsh, unyielding. "He's exactly the kind of pathetic loser who makes mistakes and ruins lives and then really, truly wishes he hadn't done it. Maybe even to the point of believing his own lies. But frankly, I think he deserves to be punished for it. Not death. Not even life without since nobody else in San Francisco gets it. That's why I took the case at all. But he ought to get a good long spell in the slammer, during which maybe he'll come to have a little bit of a clue."

"But probably not."

"Probably not," Hardy agreed. "Law of averages, probably not."

"So you're going to try for unconsciousness?"

His eyes flashed impatiently. "And that, Fran, would be a major triumph."

"Even if he didn't do it?"

"He did do it!"

"He says he didn't, doesn't he?"

"Everybody says they didn't. Smart lawyers don't even ask."

"But if the best defense the law allows is proving he didn't kill Elaine, that he's telling the truth after all, don't you have to try for that? Otherwise, maybe you should give him to somebody else."

"I'm not giving him to anybody else!"

She let him live with that for a second. "When you talk to Abe and Ridley, maybe you ought to really listen to what they say."

"That was my actual plan, believe it or not. What did you think I was going to do?"

She looked into his eyes. Her voice was gentle, without any threat in it. "I thought you might be looking for something to argue, not something to believe."

She rarely saw any sign of her husband's Irish temper. It surprised her that he was on the edge of losing it now. Over Cole Burgess? It made no sense unless the boy had come to represent something beyond himself.

She reached a hand out and touched his arm. "What's going on, Dismas?" she asked.

"I'm not looking for something to believe, that's for sure." His voice was harsh.

"Then what are you arguing against? What's so terrifying?"

"What's so terrifying?" he snapped back. "How can you even ask me that? That's what I want to know. You can't envision our sweet little Vin where Cole is someday? Or even the Beck? You don't think that's terrifying?"

She tightened her grip on his arm. "That isn't going to happen, Dismas. That doesn't make any sense."

"That's my damn point, Frannie. It doesn't have to make any sense. It just happens sometimes. It just happens."

And suddenly the source of his terror was clear to her. Educated, white, middle-class, raised by caring parents, Cole Burgess was Dismas's own private vision of the devil, the personification of everything he feared and could not control. Their own children might turn out just like Cole if they weren't ever-vigilant with them, and maybe even if they were. And beyond that, the dangers everywhere in the modern world—the threat of random violence, terror out of the dark night. The tragedy inherent in every moment of temporary weakness—why the struggle must never end, not for an instant.

She lifted her hand up to touch his face, and he backed off, by all signs angry at her. During his little speech, his color had gone progressively to a deep red. To the Union Street crowd, it probably seemed that they were having a fight.

"Dismas?" she said softly.

He was furious. Tears of rage had come to his eyes and he was determinedly blinking them back. She stepped into him, put her arms around his back, held him. "It's all right," she said. "Everything's going to be all right."

It was Old Home Week around Abe's bed again. Isaac had picked up Jacob after his arrival from Milan, and the two of them came straight from the airport to the hospital. Nat and Orel were already there—the first time the whole family had been together in nearly two years. There were only the five of them, and that was just as well. Since the word was out about Elaine, there was a lot to talk about.

At a little before nine o'clock, Hardy and Frannie showed up, looking a bit the worse for wear. They had both cheered slightly at the sight of Jacob, as they had with Isaac the night before, but after a while the edge between them appeared again. It didn't help that Hardy was expecting Ridley Banks to come and talk about Cullen Alsop, and that he never appeared. And with the boys and Nat there, it wasn't a good time to talk murder cases anyway.

By nine forty-five, everyone had gone home.

Glitsky leaned back into his bed and closed his eyes. Tonight, he was tired. His groin throbbed where they had inserted the angiogram into his femoral artery. The blisters on his chest—mementos of the defibrillation—itched uncomfortably. They had him on some blood-thinning medication and he still felt wiped out from sedatives.

He fancied that he could feel his heart, that the presence of all of his sons and his father tonight had filled it almost beyond its capacity. Early on, before the Hardys came and after the first flurry of questions and answers about Elaine, he'd asked Jacob if he would sing them all a song with his newly trained Italian voice, then surprised him not by asking for anything from the opera repertoire, but for "Unchained Melody." He'd sung it so beautifully that the nursing staff and other visitors seeing patients had come into the room, applauded when he finished.

The melody came back to him now. It had been Flo's song, but the image now was not of his past wife. He opened his eyes, grabbed his book, took out Treya's card and reached for the phone.

26

Still in his scrubs, Jonas Walsh commanded his own table in the St. Mary's cafeteria. His newspaper was spread out over every inch of the available surface area, all the sections separated. His tray held the remains of his midmorning snack—the empty bowl that had held his mixed fruit, the plate for the dry toast, three empty juice glasses. He sat back at some distance from the table, an ankle resting on a knee. He held his cup of coffee out at arm's length. For one man, he took up a lot of room. It was ten-thirty in the morning and his four scheduled hernia surgeries had all gone without incident, as they always did.

Nevertheless, his posture reflected a great deal of frustration. He hated being out here, but the idiot operating-room schedulers had been unable to book in all his patients, even though he had them lined up waiting. There'd been a couple of cancellations and the hospital hadn't been able to fill the damn time; and when you only have two surgery days a week, you'd better make sure you pack them in. But now, instead of ten hernias today, he had only eight—which meant thirty-two hundred dollars out the window. Plus he had to endure a much-despised break for a couple of hours before he could start making more money with another four in the afternoon. At this rate, he was never going to pay off his loans.

At least you'd think they could have moved up two of the late afternoon jobs, let him get off early. But no. No thought. He was going to complain to the administrator. Get somebody else on scheduling who had some kind of clue.

He finished sports and grabbed at the business section, where he noticed that his stocks remained in the tank. Shaking his head in disgust, he brought his cup to his lips, sipped. The coffee had gone tepid and he swore.

"Is this chair taken?" A large black man with a hatchet nose and a scar through his lips hovered on the far side of the table. He stood casually, his expression relaxed, his hands resting in the pockets of his windbreaker. He was in need of a shave and Walsh thought he detected a slight pallor under the pigment, an almost jaundiced quality to the whites of his eyes.

Was the man sick?

Whatever, he wasn't welcome. Jonas looked around ostentatiously. There were maybe ten other people in the entire room, forty unoccupied tables all around him. "Sorry. I'm busy," he said. "Not here, pal, okay?" His eyes went back to his newspaper.

"You're Jonas Walsh?" The man had taken the seat, cleared a space on the table in front of him.

A dark glance. "I'm *Dr.* Walsh, that's right. And I just told you I'm busy."

"I can see that," the man replied calmly. "And I could take out my badge and show it to you, but maybe you'd find that embarrassing."

Walsh snapped the paper down, stared for a while. Then: "You're Glitsky."

"That's right."

"Elaine's father." Walsh fixed him with a challenging look.

"I guess the word's out. How'd you find out about it?"

"How do you think? We didn't have secrets. We were engaged, you know—you also might have heard that."

Glitsky nodded. "That's why we're talking right now. And you were happy? Everything was fine with you both?"

"Yes." A pause. "Of course." He waited for Glitsky to pursue it, and when he didn't, added some more. "Sure, why not?"

"No reason." Glitsky stared across at him. He wore his most bland expression and it finally wore Walsh down.

"What?" the doctor asked. "What do you want?"

"What I want is to fill in a few blanks. You know we've got a suspect in custody, but we don't know why Elaine was downtown at that time. We don't know who she was meeting, if our suspect knew her somehow." A shrug. "All of that. If you two didn't have any secrets from each other, maybe you could help."

"Of course I'd like to help if I can." Walsh pursed his lips tightly, cast his eyes briefly to the upper corners of the room, came back to the lieutenant. When he spoke, he'd found his professional, courteous, bedside voice. "I'm sorry if I was rude just now. It's been a difficult couple of weeks."

"I would imagine so. I'm sorry." He took a minute. "So on the Sunday, the night she didn't come home, did you expect her to be out late?"

"More or less. Yes, I guess. She called and left a message."

"You weren't in?"

"No. We had breakfast in Sausalito and then she went into work and I took a long bike ride over Tamalpais, back through Lucas Valley. It's the only exercise I get."

"Did you go with anybody?"

Walsh hated the question and seemed tempted to reply angrily, but in the end he just shook his head with resignation. "No. I went alone."

"So you got back home—Tiburon, right?—and there was a message? What time was that? When you got back?"

"Five-thirty or six. Just dusk."

"And the message was that she wouldn't be home until after three in the morning?"

The question slowed him down. "Well, no, not specifically. Just that she had an appointment and she'd be a little late. Where does three o'clock come into this?"

"That was when we got around to notifying you." Glitsky made an effort in the direction of a smile. "She said she'd be a little late, though?"

The doctor sat back again, took a measured pause. "Where are we going with this, Lieutenant?"

Glitsky thought it was a fair question. "Well, if you thought she was only going to be a little late and she didn't get in by, say, three . . ." Surely Walsh understood what he was driving at.

"I would have called the police by then. I would have been worried."

"The question came up, that's all."

Walsh took another minute deciding whether or not he was going to answer any more stupid, leading questions posed by the police. When he did, the frustration was back in his voice. "First, I went to bed at nine-thirty. I'd ridden many, many steep miles that day. I was tired and had to work in the morning. Second, Elaine's meetings often ran late, sometimes very late. So no, I wasn't worried."

"And she didn't say who she was meeting?"

"Not then. But I knew who she was meeting earlier in the day." Suddenly, something else struck him. "You know, it seems like this is an awfully long time after the fact to start asking these kinds of questions."

"You're right. If we didn't have a suspect, we'd have moved on it faster. Now we're not really looking for anybody. As I said, we're filling in blanks. We might not need any of it, it's just gravy. Still, we'd like the case to be as tight as it can be. Does that make sense?"

"Obviously."

"Good." They were making progress. Glitsky brought his hands together, a kind of clap of approval. "So the meeting earlier in the day, who was that with?"

"You really don't know?"

"How would I know?"

"Because it was you guys." Glitsky showed his surprise. "The police." Walsh explained about Elaine's special master duties on the Russian insurance fraud case. She had gone in with a team of police officers to serve a warrant on the law offices of Dash Logan.

"On Sunday?"

A shrug. "Evidently the first time they'd all come by, Logan had really been a pain. He didn't want anybody looking at his files, wouldn't tell Elaine where anything was, if he even knew."

"Why wouldn't he know?"

"Because—this according to Elaine—there wasn't any order to it. Elaine said she'd never seen another law office like it ever. She thinks . . . she thought . . . he must be on drugs or something. Logan."

Glitsky shrugged. A lot of people did drugs. If they didn't kill people because of it, it wasn't homicide, and wasn't his job.

"Anyway," Walsh continued, "then they found another couple of these Russian guys, cases Logan was handling. They figured this time it would be easier to do the search while nobody was there but him. So they woke him at his house, brought him to the office and served the warrant."

"They actually went to his office? That Sunday?"

"I don't know, Lieutenant. I assume so. That was the plan. You could probably find out easier than me."

This was the truth, and Glitsky accepted it ruefully. "And you didn't hear from her again?"

Walsh bit down on his lower lip. Suddenly Glitsky got some sense of emotion. "No. Just the last message. You know, it's funny, I haven't been able to bring myself to erase it."

Which was all well and good and perhaps sad, Glitsky reflected as he walked away from the table, but all in all not as interesting as the fact that Walsh had lied about the current state of his relationship with Elaine. He also had no alibi for the time of her murder.

On the other side of the cafeteria, Glitsky's father and the two older boys were at their own table, reading different sections of the newspaper. Glitsky got to them and pulled a chair around, straddling it backwards.

Nat looked up. "Not to nag, Abraham, but maybe you want to sit like a normal person? Maybe now you go home and get in bed and rest. Enough already with talking to people on this thing."

Glitsky looked at his kids. "Not to nag, he says." Back to Nat. "It's my job, Dad."

"Except last I heard, they put you on leave. Am I wrong here? Tell me I'm wrong. Also tell me I'm wrong you had a heart attack three days ago, maybe you noticed."

"I noticed. But Ms. Ghent told me that he"—he pointed across at Walsh—"that he worked here Thursdays. I was right here. It was too good an opportunity to pass up. Besides, they wouldn't let me out of here if I wasn't okay."

"Famous last words, Abraham. Don't worry, this parachute opens every time."

Glitsky threw a half-amused glance at his two boys, both of whom had stopped reading to follow the exchange.

"And enough with that look!" Nat shook a finger at him. "That same look your mother had that she was okay, too. So she goes home and does a load of laundry and dies. God forbid she dies with dirty clothes in the hamper."

Abe held up a hand. "Okay, Dad, okay. We go home."

Nat nodded his head violently, included the boys. "Finally, your father says a smart thing." He pointed a finger at his son. "And rest."

A nod. "Rest is good," Glitsky admitted. Although he had no inclination to get any.

Acting on the information Treya had given him on the phone last night about the doctor, Glitsky had called Walsh's office first thing and learned that he had a break in his surgery schedule. It turned out that it coincided with the arrival of his father and sons with his clean clothes, here to take him home. Glitsky had put on the clothes, but didn't take the time to shave. Hospital rules mandated that they use a wheelchair to take him outside, so they had wheeled him out the front door where he'd stood up and turned around and walked back in to corner Dr. Walsh, his family in tow, Nat kvetching all the way.

Now they were finally in the car, Isaac driving, his father next to him in the passenger seat. "So how did that interview go?" he asked.

Nat started to mutter an objection from the backseat, but Abe spoke through it. "Pretty good. He only told one little fib."

Jacob, interested, leaned over from the backseat. "Is that normal?"

"What? That he told a lie, or that he only told one?"

Nat, still unhappy, interjected again. "Your father's line of work, nobody tells the truth. I don't know how he stands it."

Glitsky spoke over his shoulder. "Are you kidding? That's the best part."

"But he really lied? Knowing you were a cop? I mean, he's not some criminal," Isaac said. "He's a doctor."

Glitsky got a kick out of that. "They've done experiments," he said. "You can be both."

Jacob piped in. "So did you call him on it?"

"Not yet. Maybe never."

"Why not?" Isaac asked. "If you tell a lie, you're hiding something, right?"

A nod. "That would be the general rule."

Jacob again. "Well?"

"Well, you can *call* someone on a lie, or you can *catch* someone in a lie. And the second one's way more fun."

"Fun?" In the backseat, Nat sounded disgusted. "What do you know from fun, Abraham?"

Hardy had had enough of waiting for Ridley Banks to get back to him. He was reasonably friendly with a fair number of homicide inspectors, and not a one of them—Glitsky included—had as his first priority a callback to a defense attorney. But that didn't mean he couldn't pursue an investigation of his own. He killed time at his office for an hour while he waited for the phone to ring, then finally decided to walk the half mile or so down to the jail and the Hall of Justice.

When he got there, force of habit made his first stop the homicide detail, but without an appointment with Banks and in Glitsky's absence, the reception he got was a little bit cool. Inspector Sergeant Marcel Lanier knew Hardy fairly well, but he was handling the administrative overflow left in Glitsky's wake, and, stuck at his desk, he was neither a happy camper nor inclined to chat. No, he didn't know what was happening with Abe, but he hoped whatever it was wouldn't take too long. No, he hadn't heard from Banks. So what? No doubt he'd check in when he got far enough behind on his paperwork.

John Strout, the coroner, was in the middle of an autopsy, "up to his elbows," and couldn't see him either. Hardy left a message, asking him to call when he could, and walked across the corridor to the jail's entrance, where he couldn't make himself go inside. He still tasted a kind of bitter residue from his ruined Date Night with Frannie. Although he was certain that his client would be thrilled to have any visitor, Cole Burgess was the last person he wanted to see.

He walked back through the Hall, out the other side, and jaywalked across Bryant Street. Lou the Greek's was a bar located there in the basement of a bail bondsman's building. Lou's served food, too, for lunch. Since Lou's wife hailed from Hong Kong, these were mostly Chinese-Greek combinations—hot and sour lemon egg-drop soup, egg rolls stuffed with hummus—the culinary equivalent of colors not found in nature.

It was a dark and somber bar, pure and simple, its popularity now on the wane due to the young, hip legal crowd's attraction to loud, jumping, music-filled meat markets such as Jupiter and, just down the street, the Circus. Today, though, still early in the morning and deserted except for Lou behind the bar, the place fitted Hardy's mood perfectly.

"Hey, Diz." The bartender slid a napkin across the pitted wood.

Hardy nodded. "I've got a question for you, Lou."

"You want a drink while you're asking it?"

"No. I'm good. Maybe some coffee."

He waited while the Greek turned and poured a cup into an old ceramic mug, came back and placed it on the napkin. Even in the dim light, Hardy could make out a faint lipstick stain on the rim— cleanliness was never a big issue at Lou's. He turned the cup around to drink from its pristine side, nearly burned himself on the bitter brew. "Let's say you're a lawyer . . ."

Lou crossed himself backwards, smiling. He said something, but it was Greek to Hardy, who pressed on. "You've got a client you think is guilty. The evidence says he's guilty. He—the client—even starts out by saying he's guilty. He confesses to the cops. Now, get this, the cop who arrests him comes to you and says, 'No wait, I don't think the confession's any good.' Then the other cop, the one who took his confession, he starts to have doubts . . ."

"This guy, your client—is he a hypnotist or something?"

"He's a heroin addict. He's been known to take a drink, too."

Lou nodded. "My kind of guy—not the heroin part, though. So what's your question?"

"Wait. I'm not there yet."

Lou raised his eyes and scanned his dark and empty bar. He raised his voice. "Anybody need another round?" He came back to Hardy. "Okay, I've got a couple more minutes, but my rates are going up fast."

"Here's the problem. My client is charged with robbery and murder. I believe I've got a better than decent chance to get him off by arguing to a jury that he was too drunk or stoned or both to have planned to tie his shoes, much less rob or kill anybody. You with me?"

Lou guessed that he was.

"Okay, but if I argue that, best case he gets years in prison. Whereas if I argue that he didn't do it at all, and the jury believes that, he gets off completely. The problem is, no jury is going to believe it, since I've got no alternative suspects. Hell, I don't believe it myself."

Lou, a lifelong bartender, knew that Hardy wasn't drinking alcohol, but he also knew that any conversation with even a sober customer that lasted over five minutes was somehow bad for business. He cut back to the chase. "I hope we're closing in on the question."

"Almost. So I'm supposed to do what's best for my client, give him the best defense the law allows. Now, the question is, what do I do?"

Lou cocked his head. "You're kidding me? That's the question? What's best for your client—prison or walk out the door?" He jerked a thumb. "Out the door, no contest."

"But I've got no chance to win. I can't prove he didn't do it."

Lou hadn't worked in the Hall's watering hole for a lifetime without picking up some rudimentary knowledge of the law. "I thought they had to prove he *did* do it."

"They do."

"Well, don't let 'em. It doesn't matter what you believe. Besides, ask your client. He's not going to think prison is winning." Lou thought another minute, picked up a glass from the counter under the bar and began to wipe it with his rag. For the first time in the conversation, Hardy had the feeling that he'd engaged his mind. "You got any idea what you're going to be doing in ten years, Diz? If you're even going to be alive? Ten years."

"Nope."

Lou nodded. "Same with most people, I bet."

Hardy worked as a defense attorney, but as he walked the second-floor hallway in the public defender's office, he felt very much out of place. Although it had been nearly a decade since he'd been a young assistant D.A., in his heart he still considered himself very much in favor of the prosecution. If it wasn't for the politically misguided and extralegal idiocy of Sharron Pratt and her administration, he had no trouble envisioning himself working hard and long to put bad people behind bars.

Here in the public defender's building, however, two blocks from the Hall of Justice, the ethic was the diametrical opposite. Just walking to Saul Westbrook's office gave Hardy a strong sense of unreality, as though he'd suddenly made a turn into an alternate universe. It seemed to extrude from the very plaster in the walls. It shouted from every bumper sticker, cartoon or poster on the doors and bulletin boards—"He's NOT GUILTY until you prove it!!" "3 Strikes = Bad Law!!!" "No Victim, No Crime!!!" "Alternative Sentencing Works!!"

The vibe, Hardy thought, so different than his own. It was disorienting.

From Lou's, he'd gone back to the Hall and discovered the name of Cullen Alsop's lawyer. Saul Westbrook had been in his office when he called him and said, "Sure. Come on up."

Now he knocked at the open door. The office was about the same size as those of his prosecutorial counterparts over in the Hall of Justice—ten by twelve feet crammed with two desks, overflowing file cabinets, cardboard boxes bulging with three-ring binders, metal bookshelves to the ceiling.

"Mr. Westbrook?"

He was the only person in the room. The other desk was empty. Westbrook didn't look as though he was old enough yet to shave. He wore blue jeans and tennis shoes, a white shirt with a collar but no tie, and either had just won the Masters Golf Tournament or had his own green jacket from another source. He looked up, stood, extended his hand. "Saul."

"Dismas Hardy."

"Dismas? So we're both named after a couple of early Christian saints, huh?"

Hardy cracked a grin. "I think my guy was first."

"I think you're right." Saul had an open, angular face with a sincere smile. A shock of surfer-length blond hair flopped across his forehead. The smile faded briefly. "Maybe between us we can try to put a word in to God about poor Cullen."

Hardy was tempted to like him right away, but he couldn't duck the truth. "I'll need to wait until I find out if poor Cullen screwed my client before he died."

"Cole Burgess," Westbrook said, and it wasn't a question. The expressive face seemed to sadden. "I don't think he did."

"You think he had the gun?"

"I don't know. Why would he make it up? Burgess was a friend of his."

Hardy wanted to tell Westbrook to give him a break—the list of good works by addicts to protect or save their friends was short indeed. In his experience, addicts did not have friends in the usual meaning of the word. They had sources, but no friends. But he didn't wish to antagonize Westbrook, so he was matter-of-fact. "Maybe somebody made it up for him. And it got him his OR"—out of jail on his own recognizance—"so he could stay high. That's why."

The idea was distasteful, and Saul shook his head. "Who would have done that? I'm his lawyer. If I was sharp and crooked, I might have dreamed up something like that. But I'm the only one who would have been motivated, and I'm not and I didn't."

"How about someone who wanted to strengthen the case against Cole Burgess?"

"But that would be . . ." He stopped, then spoke carefully. "One of the D.A.'s?"

Hardy shrugged. "It's Torrey's case."

"But that would mean, if Cullen was killed . . ." The young man's voice trailed off. It was the kind of moment, Hardy knew, that would eventually put some age on Saul's face.

"It's a long shot," Hardy admitted. "I don't have any idea if Cullen was an accident or a suicide or what he was. I was hoping you might have an opinion."

They shared a look. Saul sat back in his chair, picked a paper clip off his desk, opened it up. "You know Ridley Banks?"

"I talked to him last night."

A nod. "He came by yesterday, asking about the same thing. Which, for a cop, I thought was a little weird. What did he say to you?"

But here Hardy was stymied. He'd had the impression Ridley was going to tell him something about his suspicions, but with the no-show, he never did. "He kept it pretty vague." Hardy could do vague, too. "But I got the strong impression the coincidence made him nervous."

The discussion was threatening Westbrook's worldview, and his reply came out sounding defensive. "But coincidences do happen."

Spoken like a true defense lawyer, Hardy thought. But he said, "Undoubtedly. This would be a particularly unlucky coincidence for my client, though, so I'd like to be a little more sure it was one. I'm waiting for Banks to get back to me now, which I'm sure he will. But listen, in the meanwhile, if you don't mind, I wanted to ask you how this whole plea thing came down." At Saul's dubious look, Hardy prodded. "I don't see how it can hurt your client now."

The face softened. "You're right." Still working the paper clip, he rocked back in his chair. "Actually, the first I heard of it, I got a call from Cullen, from the jail. And it was already pretty much a done deal."

"This was over the weekend? He just remembered?"

"Yeah, maybe Monday."

"So he'd been in jail how long on his own thing?"

Westbrook came forward now, opened a black calendar book on his desk and leafed through it briefly. "He was arrested on the second." His expression became confused. "So he started trying to cut the deal on . . . I guess the eighth."

"Six days in jail," Hardy said. "I wonder what made him think about it? Or more to the point, made him forget it for so long?"

"That's a good question."

"Has he ever snitched before? How'd he know who to go to? How'd he know the gun was the missing link in my case?"

Suddenly, the young man's face looked miserable. "I don't know," he said at last. "I think you've got to talk to Banks."

27

They dropped Nat off at the synagogue, where he liked to spend his mornings. After that, Isaac drove them home, where Glitsky climbed into bed and told the boys they should go out and enjoy the city. They'd have dinner together tonight—maybe Rita could whip up some of her famous enchiladas. As soon as the door closed after them, he was out of bed. He shaved and changed into slightly stylish clothes— pressed slacks, a beige merino collared sweater, tasseled brown loafers. Then he called a cab and took it downtown, arriving at Rand & Jackman well before noon.

At Elaine's office, he knocked. Treya sat behind a stack of files piled high on the desk. Checking her watch, she looked up in surprise. "It can't be lunchtime already?" Then, apparently concerned for him: "How are you feeling?"

"I'm moving a little slow, but I'm moving."

She tilted her head fetchingly to one side. "Are you sure you're all right, being out like this?"

He made light of it. "I don't think it's much more strenuous than laying in my bed." He pulled up a folding chair and sat in it. "See? I walk a few feet and sit back down. Don't even break a sweat. I could do this all day." She'd hung the gray jacket to her business suit over the back of her chair. She was wearing a thin gold chain around her neck, gold stud earrings, a sleeveless teal silk blouse and under it, he couldn't help but notice, a black bra. He felt the beating of his heart—under the circumstances both comforting and scary.

Last night on the phone, they had discussed Elaine and the case, both pretending that there was nothing personal in Abe calling her at home at ten o'clock. Then, just before they hung up, Treya had said, "If you're not feeling well enough tomorrow, promise me you'll stay there. Don't feel like you have to come down to the office just because you said you would."

"But then I won't see you."

"I could call and tell you what I've found."

"That's not what I meant."

There had been a long pause, after which, in a different tone, she'd whispered, "I know. I know what you meant. But first you need to take care of yourself."

"That's my plan."

"It's a good one. Stick to it."

"Yes, ma'am."

Then she'd added, "Please, Abe. If you need to stay there longer, you can just call me and I'll come, all right?"

Now, a foot away from her, his arm resting on the desk between them, he wanted to say something personal—how nice she looked, how grateful he'd been for her visit, for talking to him last night, the scent she was wearing—but he found he couldn't take the step. It was too soon, too uncertain, too perilous.

Instead, he straightened up, his back against the back of his chair. "I did connect with Jonas Walsh, by the way. At St. Mary's."

"You talked to him?"

"Two hours ago. He seemed to think he and Elaine were doing fine."

Her brow clouded. She pursed her lips. "Well, that's not . . . he told me . . . I don't think that's true."

"I don't either." Now that they were on his business, talking came more easily. "But I don't know it means anything. Maybe he's convinced himself they were going to get back together, so nobody needs to know."

"But he told me."

"You're different. You were a friend. I'm a cop. Plus, he didn't know I'd talked to you. It might be something, but by itself it isn't much. Not as much, for example, as the fact that he had no alibi for the time of her death. You told me that Elaine had this appointment Sunday night, after which she was going home. Do you remember that?"

"That's what she said."

"Okay. Did you get any idea at all that the appointment might have been with Walsh? That then they would go home together?"

She reflected for only a second. "No, I don't think so. It was somebody else."

"Dash Logan maybe?"

She shook her head. "I doubt it. She really wanted to avoid him. When she got back from his office, she told me how glad she was he had been in better shape than the first time, how the search was so much easier. He still refused to help, but she didn't even have to talk to him."

Glitsky drummed his fingers on the desk. "And there's nothing in her calendar?"

"No." She touched his hand for an instant, then quickly, instantly, pulled hers back. "I would have told you." Frustration was written all over her. "She just said she had a meeting, then she was going home. That's all she said."

"But when we first talked, you said you thought she was a little detached."

"Maybe, yes, a little. But I don't know what from. It could have been anything."

He indicated the mass of stuff on the desk. "So how's all this coming?"

"I'm only just starting on the G's."

" 'G'? Maybe she had a file on me." Meaning it as a joke.

"She did." She raised her eyebrows and gave him a half smile, then rummaged for a minute, found what she wanted, and handed over the thin manila folder.

Glitsky opened it up and was startled to see an eight-by-ten glossy of himself—a copy of his Police Academy graduation photo. He couldn't believe he'd ever been so young. Where had Elaine ever gotten her hands on this? Glitsky didn't even have one himself.

As though reading his mind, Treya said: "She was pretty good at getting what she wanted."

He nodded dumbly. Behind the photo, there was an envelope and he removed the letter from it and scanned it quickly. It was from her mother, delivered after her death, informing Elaine of her true paternity. Refolding the letter, he put it back where it had been.

Then there were twenty or more clippings cut from the newspaper—the few times in his career that Glitsky had been hailed as a hero, his promotion to lieutenant and head of homicide, various community-involvement moments, including one featuring Glitsky as a private citizen—standing as the proud father with his arm draped around a beaming Orel when his son was chosen Pop Warner Player of the Month a year ago. Glitsky was the coach of Orel's team—the same picture still hung on the bulletin board in their kitchen. It was more than strange to see it here in this setting.

Here was a picture of himself and Elaine together, seated at the head table at Gino & Carlo's during a "Champion of the People" roast they'd had when Art Drysdale had left the D.A.'s office a couple of years back. Abe looked up quickly, flashes of that night coming back to him. It had been the closest he'd come to telling her since the first days after her mother had died. He remembered they'd laughed a lot—for Glitsky a rare enough event in itself. Funny, there was Gabe Torrey on the other side of Elaine. Abe had no memory of his presence, but that wasn't really surprising. He'd only just come on as chief assistant and Abe had had few dealings with him to that point. Also, with Elaine next to him, he wasn't much aware of anyone else.

Closing the folder, he let out a long breath. "Well . . ."

This time when Treya put her hand over his, she left it. "Let's go have lunch," she said.

"God. Real food." They were reading the menu at the window bar at Glitsky's favorite deli—David's, an old no-frills establishment on Geary. He looked at Treya. "You ever wonder what they do to food in the hospital to give it that special bland quality?"

"It's a secret spice"—she didn't miss a beat—"that makes everything taste like cardboard. It's really good for you. Promotes healing ten ways."

"But tastes awful."

A shrug. "They tested it on mice," she said. "They loved it."

"And this is why health food tastes like cardboard?"

"Only the real good stuff," she said. "The rest is pretty bad."

Glitsky, chuckling, was back at the menu. "There's nothing I can eat here anymore. You wouldn't believe the list of what I'm supposed to avoid from now on."

She looked over at him. "I would bet the chicken soup here is good."

And that's what he decided upon, along with a toasted bagel, no butter, and a slice of kosher pickle. She ordered a pastrami and cole slaw on rye.

"And to drink?" the waitress asked.

"I'll have a celery soda," Treya said.

"Wait a minute." Sitting back, Glitsky nearly fell off his stool. "You can't order celery soda. I was going to order celery soda."

Treya patted his hand. "I bet they have more than one."

"No," Glitsky said, "what I mean is that nobody I know drinks celery soda."

"Well, you know somebody now."

The waitress put in her two cents. "Actually, it's fairly popular. I've never had one myself, but I'm sure we've got tons in the back."

"See?" Treya was smiling triumphantly. "Tons." Then, to the waitress: "We're living large today. Can we get a whole bottle each? You might even try one yourself—they're really pretty good."

By two-fifteen, Hardy had left a message with Dash Logan to call him. He'd left another message with Ridley Banks—a callback at any old time would be fine. Glitsky at home. Strout. Even Torrey to ask for further discovery in *Burgess,* specifically any transcripts that might have come in on the Cullen Alsop interviews with the police or with prosecutors.

Since it appeared that no one was ever going to call him again, he decided to get some work done in his office. He did have other clients, after all. So he reviewed some documents in a few of these cases, reached his party three phone calls in a row and decided to run a victory lap down the stairs and across the lobby to the coffee machine.

The phone rang, stopping him, before he'd reached the door. He crossed his office in a couple of strides and picked it up before it rang a second time.

"Diz."

"David," he said. "What's up?"

"I wondered if you could spare me a minute."

"Have you cleared it with Phyllis?"

"She'll be holding the door open for you."

"I'll be right down."

Phyllis was not in fact manning the door, but she waved him by the reception area with barely so much as a glance. When Hardy entered the office, he saw that Freeman wasn't alone. There was some kind of associates' meeting in progress. Hardy knew all three of them, although none of them very well. Jon Ingalls, Amy Wu, Curtis Rhodin. Since Freeman didn't offer partnerships in his firm, his associates didn't tend to stick around for long. They did, however, tend to work like slaves and learn a lot of law in very little time.

The old man cleared his throat. "I've made a decision about the *Burgess* matter," he began in a gruff tone, "but I'll need your permission before I proceed."

Hardy glanced at the associates, back to his landlord. "I'm listening."

"Here's the situation. I'm beginning to believe that this case is going to dominate the news once it gets to court. I know that after the hearing, you'll be handling the guilt phase." In California, a capital case such as this had two components—a guilt phase and a penalty phase. Typically, each phase had its own, different lawyer. The lawyer in the penalty phase was termed "Keenan counsel" after the appeals decision that had created the precedent. Freeman was going on. "I want to offer my services as Keenan counsel. With the profile the case has already achieved, the advertising value alone is priceless. I want to be involved."

Hardy's fondest dream had been to ask Freeman to fill this role all along if it came to it. He'd hesitated up to this point because of money—Jody Burgess had retained him, not Freeman, to represent Cole. And Freeman's standard rates were nearly double his own, nearly triple for courtroom time. Jody could never afford him. And now the city's most famous lawyer was volunteering for the case's advertising value.

Not that Hardy for a minute believed advertising was the reason. But he'd certainly accept it. "That's a generous offer, David," he said. "I'll take it under advisement."

Freeman kept up the charade. "I do have one demand. I will insist on using my own able associates to help investigate Factor K elements, if any." This included other potential suspects or anything else that might produce lingering doubt in a sentencing jury. "They can be under your immediate supervision and direction, but their time will be charged to the firm, for my administrative oversight." He kept it up straight-faced, a sales pitch. "I really believe this partnership could be beneficial to both of us, Diz. It's just too good a business opportunity to pass up. I hope you agree."

Hardy glanced at the young and eager associates, the Three Musketeers, apparently ready to go to work immediately. He nodded. "I think I could live with it," he said.

Glitsky went back to Rand & Jackman with Treya after their lunch and spent the afternoon looking through miles of files. Near the end of the day, he checked his messages at home, got Hardy's and called him at his office. Treya had a meeting with Jackman planned for after close of business, and Hardy volunteered to swing by and drive Glitsky home, which he was doing now.

Abe wasn't in high spirits. "I am such a horse's ass."

"I've been telling you that for years."

But he didn't come back at him with some clever riposte, and this was worrisome. Whatever it was, it had gotten under Abe's skin. At the moment, though, it was difficult for Hardy to feel anything but pumped up—if not elated, then at least thoroughly heartened. "But enough about you," he said cheerily, "I want to talk about this incredible offer. Do you realize if we need to, now we can interrogate half the state."

"I don't think half the state hated Elaine."

Hardy stopped at a red light and looked across the seat. "Okay, what?"

"Nothing."

"Oh, right, nothing. Let's see why this doesn't scan. You're trying to carry on your own investigation without manpower, money or time. We just get given about a hundred grand worth of our own damn dream team. And yet, and yet—you're even *less* than your usual cheerful self, which isn't much to begin with."

Glitsky looked over at him. "It bothers you so much, you can let me out here. I'll get a cab."

"I'm not asking you to be wildly enthusiastic. But you've got to admit that this is a positive development."

"I'm thrilled," Abe said. "Honest."

The light changed and Hardy moved ahead. "It's the woman, isn't it?"

"Her name's Treya." He could barely say it. "She's with Jackman. Idiot that I am."

"I thought he was married."

"Oh, then it couldn't be. Married men don't have affairs, I forgot."

Abe was brooding and Hardy, tired of it, decided to let him. But after a few blocks, he spoke again. "How do you know? Did you ask her?"

"I didn't have to. It was obvious."

"So one of them was wearing a sign? One of those sandwich board things, maybe?"

Glitsky nodded. "Might as well have." He paused. "We're sitting in the window at David's and Jackman comes walking by down Geary. He sees her and they both light up like Christmas trees. He comes inside, she's off her stool, next to him . . . then it's like, oh yeah, this is that cop I was telling you about. Jackman sticks around, orders a sandwich. Then after I leave tonight, she's off to his office."

"Obvious," Hardy said.

Another shrug. "You had to be there."

"I was at the hospital the other night. I thought that was obvious, too."

A glance. "What? Me?"

"And her."

"Well, we both read it wrong, then."

"If you say so. But if it were me and it mattered even a little, I'd ask her." They'd come out along California Street and were getting to the turn for Glitsky's block.

"How am I supposed to do that? What am I supposed to say? She's with him."

"Okay," Hardy repeated, making the turn. "Fine."

"She is."

"I'm not arguing with you. I hope they're happy." He pulled up in front of Abe's duplex, turned in his seat. "You pick up the telephone, dial her number, ask if she wants to go to dinner or something. We call this a date. If she's involved with somebody else, she says no. If she likes you, she says yes. It's a simple concept. Even in your enfeebled state, I think you can grasp it."

Glitsky shook his head, disagreeing. "We've got to work together in the next few weeks, Diz. It would be too awkward. She'll say no anyway."

"And I wouldn't blame her. But you never know, and you won't if you don't ask." Hardy saw that Abe was suffering with it, and his voice softened. "You know how you told me the other night how you wished you'd talked to Elaine when you had the chance?"

"That was different."

"Only in the sense that everything is different from everything else. It's also a lot the same. I know it's not your preferred means of communicating, but talking isn't so bad once in a while. What's she going to do, laugh at you? I don't think so. Worst case, she'll be flattered you asked." He brought a palm down on the armrest between them. "All right, that's my spiel. I'm done. You want me to swing by in the morning?"

For another beat, Glitsky didn't move. Then he bobbed his head and pulled the latch for his door. Out in the street, he leaned back in. "Okay."

Hardy had a small patch of grass in front of his house. It grew behind a white picket fence and was bordered on the back by a flower garden that they tried to keep up, even during the winter months. A short walkway bisected the lawn and led up to an inviting porch. His house was the only single-family dwelling on the block, and its curb appeal, to Hardy, was enormous. Tonight, though, after the four-block walk in the fogbound darkness from the nearest parking place he'd been able to find, he considered tearing out the whole thing and paving it over.

He really thought he might do it except, of course, that the downside— other than the loss of his lawn—was that someone someday would park in his own private spot, maybe even by mistake. It wouldn't matter— Hardy would have to kill him.

The porch lights were on, as were those in the front window—their living room. He opened his door, smelled the oak fire burning in his fireplace, put his heavy briefcase down.

"Daddy!"

Rebecca came flying out around the corner and had her arms around him. Then Vincent, nearly knocking him over. He enfolded them both in his arms, dragged them laughing a few steps, roughhousing. Frannie was coming up the hallway with a glass of wine in one hand and what looked suspiciously like a martini in the other. "What did I do?" he asked.

As it turned out, he'd done nothing special. Frannie had lit the fire and the kids were lying on the floor in front of it writing up their Valentine's Day cards for everyone in each of their classes. She'd called out for Chinese food, which would be there any minute, so she wasn't cooking. She'd like a glass of wine. If her husband got home at his normal time, she thought he'd enjoy a martini, too.

Handing him the glass, she kissed him. "Sometimes it just works."

It continued to work. The phone didn't ring once. The dinner arrived punctually and was delicious. Neither Rebecca nor Vincent had any kind of crisis, and they were both in bed by nine-thirty. The name Cole Burgess never came up.

In the age of mangled care, Dr. Campion proved himself extraordinary. He had called three times during the day and, receiving no answer, finally got worried enough to decide to see for himself. He got to Abe's duplex at a little after dark—it turned out that he made about one house call a week. The three boys and Nat were already home, which made all the Glitskys except the one he wanted to see. The doctor was probably more angry than all of them, but it was close.

Campion couldn't believe his patient wasn't home, but when that message finally made its way through, he reiterated his instructions, underlining them for everyone's benefit. This was no joke. He'd released Abe from the hospital, yes, but he wasn't out of danger. His instructions had been that Glitsky could walk around inside his house, but should take it easy and avoid all stress. There were no circumstances the doctor could imagine that could justify Abe being outside, presumably stressing about a murder case. The walk down his twelve front steps alone . . .

His heart had been seriously weakened, the muscle damaged—it was still not clear how badly. There was a reasonable chance of another serious, even fatal, attack. He should *religiously* be taking the blood-thinning medication that was on the table next to his bed, its seal unbroken. Campion waited around for half an hour, then finally left his cell phone number and left.

When Abe did finally walk in the door, it was to the riot act. They all wanted to know what he thought he was doing? Did he want to die?

Nobody considered that what he'd done was even remotely defensible. They spent fifteen minutes repeating all of Dr. Campion's horror stories, then marched him into his room, where they watched him take his pills, made him get into bed. Much to everyone's surprise, he admitted to complete exhaustion and fell asleep almost immediately. The rest of the family had a powwow in the kitchen and decided that they'd spell each other keeping an eye on him.

He wasn't going anywhere. Not without the doctor's permission.

Frannie kissed him. "You might not be as good as you once were, but you're as good once as you ever were."

It was sometime a little after ten o'clock. They were in their relatively new upstairs bedroom. It gave them privacy they would have considered unimaginable in the old configuration of rooms—theirs adjoining their two children's downstairs. Now they still might not be able to scream with rapture, but the occasional sound of pleasure could occur without it being followed by one of the kids knocking at the door, asking if they were okay. Did somebody get hurt?

"Thank you, I think." He took her earlobe between his lips and gave it a tug. "You're not so bad yourself." Then, after a moment, quietly: "You're my one."

They lay contentedly in spoon fashion for a while, then, when her breathing had become regular, he kissed her again, extricated himself and turned onto his other side. The last embers crackled in the bedroom fireplace. He closed his eyes.

Somewhere far away a siren screamed. It was coming closer.

Abruptly, his heart racing, he sat up and threw off the covers. It wasn't a siren. It was the phone on the desk across the room. Frannie, still asleep, shifted behind him, made some noise. He got to it before it rang again.

"Yo."

"Mr. Hardy? This is Jon Ingalls."

It took a moment. One of his new team. The clock in front of him read 11:11. "What's up, Jon?"

"I'm in the car now. I just left Jeff Elliot's."

"His house?"

"Yeah. He was talking about quitting. He's super pissed."

"Quitting what? The paper? What for?"

Ingalls told him. This afternoon, the *Democrat* had come out with a story suggesting that when Cole had been staying with Jeff's family, he had undoubtedly used heroin there in Jeff's presence, if not with him. It was the most crass and unsubstantiated attack—ridiculous to anyone who knew Jeff—but the *Chronicle*'s editor, Parker Whitelaw, had called Jeff right in. He wasn't to write another word on the Burgess case. Jeff had tried to explain that his connection to Cole was aboveboard and strictly as family. Whitelaw didn't care. Jeff's credibility as an objective reporter, he said, was compromised. With this kind of accusation in the city's political atmosphere, a simple denial wasn't going to be enough—there would have to be some show, at least, of an investigation. The entire future of his column might be in jeopardy.

"Anyway," Ingalls went on, "Jeff thinks Pratt set this up."

"I think I'd agree with him. So what's he going to do?"

"He doesn't know."

Hardy sat holding the phone. Getting involved with this case seemed to be bad for job security. First Abe, now Jeff. It was intriguing, maybe even a little scary.

"Mr. Hardy?" Ingalls asked. "I didn't wake you up just now or anything, did I?"

Hardy laughed. "Are you kidding? I was just suiting up for my midnight run."

Halfway to morning Hardy was still awake.

The D.A.'s interference in what was increasingly becoming every part not just of the *Burgess* case but of what seemed like his whole life had become a real issue.

Now, sitting downstairs at the kitchen table, he was writing names and drawing circles and arrows on a legal pad. McNeil, Torrey, Alsop, Burgess, Logan, Elaine. He wasn't anywhere near yet to taking notes—it was all too ephemeral. Still . . .

He looked down at the paper and wrote another name. Freeman's girlfriend's client—Abby Oberlin, had definitely received a settlement offer from Torrey, and that settlement would profit Logan. But so what? Lawyers profited from settlements every day. Except that Logan was also connected to Elaine, and therefore to Cole. And since Logan represented Manny Galt, he was involved with McNeil, too.

God! Hardy wished that Logan had been Cullen Alsop's lawyer, but that had been that nice kid this morning, Westbrook. He didn't know what it would mean—Logan knowing Cullen—but the symmetry of it was appealing as hell.

Reluctantly, he drew a line through Cullen's name.

Another thought struck him and he hastily scratched out his own client's name. If, as appeared to be the case, they were working on the assumption that Cole was innocent . . .

McNeil, Oberlin, Torrey, Elaine, Logan.

It was a small town, circling back on itself. Rather like a noose.

28

Isaac Glitsky was adamant. "He's not going out anywhere. Doctor's orders."

"But yesterday . . ."

"Yesterday," Jacob interjected from behind his brother, "he snuck out. Made believe he was going to bed, sent us out to have a nice day, then went out and tried to kill himself. Can you believe that?"

Hardy nodded. "Sounds like your father."

"He's been asleep for twelve hours," Isaac said. "His body wants to recover even if he doesn't."

Hardy was confused. "I thought . . . he told me . . . I mean, they let him out."

"To go home, maybe putter around in the house, avoid stress. That's all." Isaac had his arms crossed over his chest. "Let me guess, he left that part out."

"He said he was fine. Cleared. Ready to rock and roll."

"Which he is not," Jacob said. "Maybe in a week . . ."

"Maybe." The older brother wasn't making any promises. "The heart's got to heal before he stresses it again. You'd think that would occur to him."

"You'd think so," Hardy agreed. He shook his head, frustrated. "I love your father, but the man can be a moron. Tell him I said so, then sit on him if you have to."

• • •

Glitsky might be reluctant to call Treya, but Hardy had no problem with it. It had occurred to him that since everybody was essentially working to the same end, it made sense that everyone do it in the same place. He'd called her at Rand & Jackman first thing this Friday morning and she had agreed. She'd be delighted to come to his offices and help facilitate the work of the associates. She might even have some ideas of her own. Hardy told her he'd be happy to use them.

Amy Wu stood an inch over five feet tall. She had large enough breasts so that people rarely noticed the bit of thickness at her waist. Half Chinese and half black, she had an unusual and extraordinarily compelling face. Under a small and flattened nose, her sensuous lips might have been collagened but were not. Her complexion was dark honey, small-pored, unlined. She was twenty-six years old and had never bought a drink in her life without someone asking for her identification. There was a heaviness to the lids under dark brown, almost liquid eyes, although she was rarely taken for an Asian. Thick, straight, shining black hair cascaded a few inches past her shoulders. At the office, she dressed in a woman's business suit, but today she was in jeans and hiking boots, a black turtleneck sweater.

She'd already spoken to five students who had been in Elaine's moot court class. They had all directed her to a single student. Muhammed Malouf Adek was more than happy to talk to her, as what young man would not be? He was sitting on the floor in one of the hallways at Hastings, a book open on his legs. He was eating an apple. Amy hovered over him until he looked up. "What are you studying?" she asked, smiling down.

In fifteen minutes, they were in the cafeteria. She told him a version of the truth about who she was and the general reason she was here—to talk about Elaine. It didn't seem to bother him.

"People say that you and she were close at one time."

He shrugged. "She was my teacher."

"I'd understood it was a little more than that." Her eyebrows went up ingenuously.

"All right. They have a mentor program here. I signed up for that. I was doing poorly in my other courses." Muhammed looked at her with a kind of challenge in his eyes.

She pegged his age at perhaps a year older than she was—maybe he was even thirty, which was slightly old for a law student. But his eyes were too bright, too hard and piercing. His beard was short, extremely thick, almost like wool. His teeth were white, but very uneven, and his hygiene was poor—he hadn't washed his hair in a while; his jeans looked as though they would stand up by themselves; it appeared he'd worn the brown shirt for most of the week.

"And you became friends?"

"I don't know about that. We did not go out."

Amy wrinkled up her face, confusion all over it.

He couldn't take his eyes off her. "What's the matter?"

"Only that I've heard differently. I wanted to talk to somebody who knew Elaine pretty well, and if that's not you . . ." She made to get up.

He gripped her arm above the wrist. "We had coffee a few times," he said. "But there wasn't anything . . . between us." Realizing what he'd done, he released his grip. "What do you want to know about Elaine for, anyway? She was not what she pretended to be."

"And what was that?"

He hesitated, decided against answering.

"Muhammed," she said. "You've heard she died last week, haven't you?"

He nodded. "It was the will of Allah."

"Well, yes, but it was maybe a little more than that. Somebody killed her."

He sat up abruptly. "That was not me. They arrested that other man."

"I know. No one is saying it was you. I'm not saying that." She smiled again. "Please, Muhammed, we're just talking, all right?"

"But what are we talking about?"

"We're talking about who she was." She leaned in closer to him. "We were thinking of some kind of a memorial, maybe a statue, some-thing like that. It will be very nice, out in the lobby, as a tribute to her."

"To Elaine?" Amy realized that Treya had chosen a perfect cover story for them. Clearly infuriated, Muhammed's eyes were burning.

"Yes. Elaine. But you know, it's political. We would not want to go to all that trouble and expense if there was some embarrassing . . . if she—"

"She was a whore. A liar and a whore. She believed in nothing."

"Well, surely—"

He slammed the table. All around the room, other students looked up, startled out of their studies. Muhammed was oblivious to it. "She pretended to be coming to Islam. I would read from the Koran, and she would nod, pretending. 'Yes,' she would say, 'that's interesting. That's good.' But it was all false. She was white inside. She sold her body for their money, for her doctor's money." There was spittle on Muhammed's lips. His breath came in ragged little gulps.

"When was the last time you saw her?"

"She was here," he rasped. "She was always here."

"Here at the school?"

"Yes."

"But I mean alone? Did you see her alone after she got engaged?"

"I told her she had to stop. It was all a lie. She was tormenting me."

"Stop what? You mean call off her marriage?"

"No. Teaching here. Coming here."

"That was tormenting you?"

He nodded. "Every time I saw her. I knew she was laughing at me that I had believed her. I told her she had to stop."

"When was this?"

"This new semester. Just now." He gripped her hand again, so hard that it hurt her. "You must not make this thing, this memorial. She was a whore. She was laughing at Allah and, of course—" The eyes. The eyes were crazy. He laughed. "That is what happened, you know. He put an end to that."

"Abe? Are you all right?"

"I'm under house arrest. My boys."

"Dismas said you were in bed."

"That would be accurate, but the prescription wasn't bed rest. The doctor just doesn't want to see me out walking the streets, but he'd actually like me to move around a little here."

"But today? Your heart . . . ?"

"Is pumping away even as we speak. I'm sorry I didn't call you earlier myself. I just woke up."

"That's a long sleep. It's almost eleven o'clock. Are you sure you're okay? Something else didn't happen, did it?"

"No, nothing happened."

"Really?"

"Really. How are we doing on our work?"

"It's moving along, but I'm not calling about that. I'm calling about you."

"I'm fine. This is routine. Honest. A couple more days and I'm dancing."

"But not 'til the doctor says so, okay?"

"My jailers will see to that."

"But you yourself?"

"Me myself, too."

"Would you promise me?"

"I promise."

It seemed forever before she spoke again. "All right, then," she said. "All right."

Treya knew that Jonas Walsh took Friday afternoons off, so she had called him at home Thursday night to prevail upon him to let somebody from the firm come by the condo he and Elaine had shared in Tiburon and look at Elaine's things the next day. She wasn't demanding as a matter of law, but requesting as a favor, as a friend. Elaine might have left something lying around that might prove useful to their investigation.

He didn't like it, but the question of what he was going to do with Elaine's belongings was still unresolved. And Treya knew that after his apology in the R&J offices here last week, she had some leverage. He'd let them look.

She was right.

But that didn't mean he had to be pleasant about it. Walsh shook hands perfunctorily with Curtis Rhodin, but made no effort to try to be friends. "This is a total waste of some very valuable time."

Treya had briefed Rhodin about what to expect from Walsh. In any event, it was unlikely the greeting would have thrown Curtis, who was no wimp, off his stride. He exuded confidence and *savoir vivre*. At six-three, he towered over the other man. There was no sign of fat on his body, although he carried two hundred pounds to Walsh's one-seventy. The charcoal Brioni suit had set him back nine hundred dollars but it fit him so perfectly that it might have been his day-to-day lounging attire. His face was long and slender, his eyes somber. If Modigliani had painted men, Rhodin could have been one of his subjects.

"If you've got somewhere else you need to be, Doctor, I'll be fine here on my own." They were in a large, bright living room with sparse, almost antiseptic modern furnishings and floor-to-ceiling windows. The condo was set on a hillside overlooking the yacht harbor. The sun was out brightly here twenty-five miles north of the city, and from where they stood in the living room, the panorama was breathtaking—the Marin headlands and Mount Tamalpais on the right, Angel Island and the graceful though largely unsung Richmond Bridge in front of them, a glittering white-capped bay under a robin's egg sky. "This is beautiful," Rhodin said. "I couldn't get any work done if I lived here."

"This isn't where I work," the doctor replied, "and I hope the view won't be too distracting today. I don't really understand all this continuing investigation into Elaine's murder. They've got her killer in jail, for Christ's sake. I'd like to see an end to it."

Rhodin nodded understandingly and tried to sound prosecutorial. "We're on the same page, then. But we need to make sure some surprise doesn't come up during the trial. To tell you the truth, I don't even know what I'm supposed to be looking for. If you've got other plans, that's fine, but if not and you'd like to show me where to look, it might move the process along."

Reluctantly, Walsh led him into the back of the condo, past the gourmet kitchen—a granite countertop with dishes piled on it, more dishes stacked in the sink, a strong odor of garbage. There was an office to his left down a short hallway—two desks, two computers, some file cabinets. The bedroom was a few steps further along on the right and Walsh showed him in. He hadn't made the bed and made no apology for it. "That's her closet," he said, pointing. "The near one is her dresser. I'll be in the office."

Left alone, Rhodin went to work. In spite of what he'd told Walsh, he had received a reasonably specific laundry list from Hardy and Glitsky the day before. Mostly, it was stuff he'd expect to find in the office—a Rolodex file, maybe, or old checkbooks and financial records, perhaps a diary. But there might be something elsewhere—it was worth looking everywhere.

Curtis Rhodin was a methodical man. He had known Elaine only slightly—she was older and a partner at Rand & Jackman and light-years from him on many levels—and it felt strange to be going through her things, but he knew what he was supposed to do, and he was going to do it.

She had a lot of dresses, thirty pairs of shoes. There was a smaller, built-in set of drawers in her closet containing sweaters, blouses, exercise clothes. At the bottom of the lowest one, under a pile of sweat-shirts, he found a smallish, flat white box. Taking it out and opening it up, he recognized it for what it was—Elaine's collection of meaningless memorabilia from her past.

Rhodin smiled to himself. He had a similar stash himself, although his was a cigar box in which he kept twenty or thirty stupid items he just couldn't bring himself to discard—a jade rock he got diving off Big Sur, a guitar pick from a B. B. King concert he'd gone to in college, his first pocketknife, a diamond tie tack in case they ever came back in style, a signed Willie Mays rookie year baseball card. Junk. But priceless junk.

Elaine's box wasn't all that different really, considering she was a woman. There were several pins for various political campaigns—her mother's, Chris Locke's, Sharron Pratt's. A man's college ring. A garter. A .38 caliber bullet. A packet of business cards with a rubber band around them. Many coins from different foreign countries. He closed the box back up—this was coming back with him.

A framed picture of Elaine's mother rested on top of her dresser next to the lamp. In the drawers, he found underwear, socks, foldables. Condoms. The top right drawer, however, contained nothing at all, and this straightened Rhodin up in surprise. He walked across to the office and asked Walsh if he could come in for a minute. Sighing, putting down his magazine, the doctor labored up and followed him. "Do you know what she kept in this drawer?" Curtis asked.

Walsh looked, shrugged. "I guess not much. Did you just take something out of it?"

"No, it was like this. Was it always like this?"

Another shrug. "I don't know. I didn't go through her drawers."

"No, of course not," Rhodin said, "but there was nothing at all in this one. That seems a little odd, doesn't it?"

"I don't know," Walsh repeated. "I didn't take anything out of it."

"But it sure seemed like he might have." He was back now at Freeman's office, in the Solarium reporting to Treya and Amy. He'd eventually left Tiburon with a cardboard box now about a quarter filled with what he'd collected from the office and the rest of the house, including a copy of the Koran and, of course, the white memento box. On a whim, at the last moment, he'd also thrown in the framed photograph of Loretta Wager. But it was the empty drawer that had captured his interest. "Any of you guys have a completely empty dresser drawer?"

"Drawers don't get empty," Amy said. "They get full about ten minutes after you move in someplace. Then too full. It's a law of nature. He must have cleaned it out."

Treya disagreed. "He would never have done that and left it empty knowing we were coming to look through her things. He would have put something back in before we got there."

Rhodin had his own suggestion. "Maybe he didn't really imagine that it would make any impression? I mean, it was just an empty drawer. Doesn't mean anything."

"No." Treya was sure of it. "If he emptied it, he would have remembered and it would have seemed significant."

"Then she emptied it," Amy said. "Elaine."

They were all with their thoughts a moment. Treya finally spoke up. "If she was leaving him, if they'd had a fight and she walked out one night, she might have just taken a handful of underwear."

"I've got another one," Rhodin said. "In the bathroom, she had a couple of months' worth of birth control pills, but in her dresser she had maybe a dozen condoms."

Amy had an answer for that. "So she *really* didn't want to get pregnant."

"Or she wasn't being faithful," Rhodin said.

Treya looked at both of them. "Or she knew he wasn't."

"Dash Logan?"

The lawyer looked up from the newspaper he was reading, which happened to be the *Democrat*. Jupiter was beginning to hop in the long slide of a Friday afternoon, but he was sitting alone in his usual back booth, a bowl of pretzels on the table next to him, a half-full glass of beer growing warm at his elbow. The look on his face was welcoming, untroubled. "You got me." He ran his eyes down the man who'd addressed him, extended his hand. "And you'd be Mr. Hardy, I presume. Dismas? Was that the name, Dismas?"

"Still is." Hardy took the hand—a firm grip—and slid in across from him. "You are one tough man to get a hold of."

Logan nodded sympathetically. "I hear that a lot. Sorry. I must be having some kind of midlife crisis or something. My motivation's just gone in the toilet. I got your calls, though."

"That's nice. I was starting to think the phones weren't working."

"Didn't I say you could always get me here?"

"Yes, you did."

"Well, then." He flashed a smile. It seemed genuine enough. Hardy didn't have to remind himself, though, that the greatest con men oozed sincerity—it was their stock-in-trade. "Hey, listen, let me buy you a beer for your trouble. If it's any consolation, I would have called you Monday, but I figure now, Friday afternoon, nobody's in when you call them anyway. It'll wait for the weekend, right?" He raised a hand, flagging the bartender. "Wally, a couple of cold ones, see voo play. What do you drink, Dismas?"

Hardy made an apologetic gesture. "I've got to stick with water. I see a client at five."

"And they wouldn't want their lawyer to have a drink in the afternoon? I hear you. Wally? Just one. And some of that stuff fish fuck in." A grin back at Hardy. "You know, I'll tell you, that's why I stopped working out of my office."

"Why's that, Dash?"

"Why? 'Cause when clients come to an office, they see the trappings, you know? You've got the secretary and the law library and the phones and all that shit—which is just what it is, shit—and they get so they expect the rest of the package that goes with it. Hey, thanks, Wally. Here's looking at you, Dismas." He held up his new glass of beer and touched Hardy's glass. "So anyway, I'm not that guy. Used to try to be, but it didn't work. So people would come in with these expectations and I'd *dash* 'em. They wanted a different kind of lawyer and God knows there's enough of 'em. But if they want me—and a lot of folks do—they can come down and meet me here and they know what they're getting. No frills, maybe, but no bullshit either. And most of 'em, end of the day, they go away happy. So"—his limpid blue eyes fixed Hardy over the rim of his beer glass—"I'm assuming you've reconsidered on settling with McNeil?"

"Actually, not." Hardy sat back and enjoyed Dash's reaction, the quick snap in the mellow facade—a blink of an eye—then the impressive return to how he'd been. "I'm here on another matter entirely. Do you know a kid named Cullen Alsop?"

Logan appeared to think about it. "Some cop—Banks, I think his name was—was asking about him in here the day before yesterday. OD, wasn't it?"

"Yeah. Looks like."

"So this boy Alsop," Logan asked, "was he your client?"

"No," Hardy said. "My client's Cole Burgess." If the name registered, Logan didn't show it. "Elaine Wager?"

His face fell. "Oh, Elaine." Logan had sympathy down pat. He clucked. "Such a shame about her."

"It was," Hardy agreed. "Though I'd understood the two of you had had some problems."

"No, noth—" The smile. "You don't mean that special master thing? That was nothing to do with Elaine."

"Really? I heard she might have taken it that way."

He shook his head back and forth. "No. That was all for the benefit of the cops. They call me down here . . ."

"The police do?"

"No, no. My office."

"I thought you didn't have an office."

"Hey, what am I, stupid? No, I keep an office. I just don't use it much. So anyway, I'm down here having a couple of brewsks, my girl calls all in a panic. The cops are there, they got a warrant, they're doing a search. Well, I go a little ballistic and who's gonna blame me?"

Hardy lifted his shoulders ambiguously.

"So I'm smack in the middle of something in the female line here and I've got to run uptown, rush hour. Time I get there, I'm not feeling my most cooperative. Now Patsy, my girl, she's makes a nice presence at the door—you know what I'm saying?—but she's a little weak on the business side, filing stuff, like that. So I say to the search party, 'Fine. You're showing me this kind of respect, you're treating me like I'm vermin, you can go find the shit yourselves.' " He wore his apologetic look again, his voice back to calm and reasonable. "So that's all it was with Elaine. She got in the middle of it, that was all. 'Nother couple of weeks, I would have gotten back to her and told her I was sorry. If she hadn't gotten herself shot."

The recitation seemed to tire him out. His expression went strangely blank, then he recovered, grabbed a pretzel, picked up his beer glass and drank. "But how'd we get on Elaine? You were asking about the OD."

"Cullen."

"Right, Cullen, okay. And the guy who killed Elaine. Your client."

"Cole Burgess. Cullen snitched him out. He was the source of the murder weapon."

"And I'm supposed to know these guys? How do you get to that?"

"I don't, really. I went by the Hall today to see if I could get my hands on some early discovery on Cullen since Cole's prelim is next week. Cullen had a matchbook from here on him."

"Yeah, that's what Banks said."

Hardy shrugged. "You'd told me you hung out here. I thought there was a chance you might have known him."

Logan couldn't believe it. "Dismas, turn around, would you?"

Hardy did.

"How many people you see here?"

Hardy did a quick count. "Thirty-five, forty."

"That's about right." Logan popped another pretzel. "At four o'clock. You know how many people are jammed in here come nine or ten? You can't take a deep breath 'cause there's no room to put it. So the odds of me knowing one guy . . ." He let the sentence drop, shook his head at Hardy's optimism. "Forget it."

"Well, I thought I'd ask," he said. "Couldn't hurt. Thanks for your time." He started to get up.

Logan stopped him. "But the McNeil thing. You're really going ahead on that? My guy still might settle, but who knows for how long? I think you're missing a bet."

"That could be." Hardy conveyed that clearly he believed it was the least of his worries. And in spite of all his talk about Cole and Cullen, carrying that message to Logan was the primary reason for his visit here. Maybe the news that McNeil wasn't going to settle would flush something. He smiled politely. "It wouldn't be the first time."

Driving up from Jupiter to his office, he stopped on Seventh Street and this time got lucky with Strout. The coroner, lanky and laconic, knew Hardy from several trials as well as his days as an assistant district attorney. It didn't matter that he was doing defense now. Generally, Strout had no ax to grind over which side the courtroom you called home. He was a scientist who dealt in medical facts, equally useful—or not—to both the prosecution and defense.

It was near the end of the workday and he came out himself to the lobby to let Hardy back into his office, a large room filled with medical books and a famous collection of murder weapons from antiquity to the present. Many were under glass, but an equal number—including a reputedly live hand grenade on a candlestick pedestal on his desk—were out there for anybody to grab, wield and use. Hardy could read the upside-down title of the book that was open on Strout's desk: "The Golden Age of Torture: Germany in the 15th Century."

"There's a sweet-looking little tome," Hardy remarked. "Keeping up on the old research, are you? Are they teaching that in med school now?"

Strout lifted the book, ran a finger fondly over the open page, put the volume back where it had been. "If you ever wonder why cruel an' unusual punishment made it to the Bill of Rights," he drawled, "you don't need to look any further'n this. The stuff people was doin' to one another back then, just as a matter of course."

"Slightly cruel, was it?"

The coroner chuckled. "I tell you, Diz, the *least* of 'em is more'n most people would believe anybody without serious mental problems ever did to one another. And here we got our judges splittin' hairs over what's cruel and unusual, what the Foundin' Fathers meant. They all ought to read this book, settle their minds on the matter. I mean, this tongue clamp here, for example . . ."

"John." Hardy held up a hand. "Maybe another time, huh?"

"Not your area of interest today?" Strout settled into the chair behind his desk, chuckling contentedly. He reached for the hand grenade and threw it gently from one hand to the other. "No. Lemme remember. Cullen Alsop."

"Ten points."

Strout nodded and came forward. His hands hovered an inch above the desk and he bounced the grenade nonchalantly on the blotter. "Well, it was pretty much what I thought it might be. Heroin overdose all right, as expected. I asked the police lab to do a quick analysis of the heroin left at the scene, and it's really their report I'm drawin' on more'n anything in the blood itself. But let's just say in laymen's terms that if he used one syringe, which needle marks indicate—he's only got the one fresh one, relatively speaking—then it was very pure stuff."

"And there's no doubt that was the cause of death?"

"No." He was bouncing the grenade again, thinking. "There was some trace alcohol and if we ran down to the C-scan level, odds are we'd find other drugs. But this was heroin."

"And higher-quality than what's on the street?"

Strout lifted his shoulders. "I don't know. It might be what's *on* the street now, although with each passin' hour, that becomes less likely."

"Why is that?"

"Because if stuff this pure is out there, we'd have seen at least a few more overdose deaths. You may 'member late last summer, one week-end one of the dealers brought up a new load of brown tar that hadn't been cut? No? Well, it killed seven kids in four days." Strout clucked in dismay. "But now, we got Mr. Alsop so far and that's all."

"And that means . . . what?"

"By itself, nothing definite. But it could mean a few things. One"— he let the grenade fall to the blotter and held up a finger—"the boy was dealing himself, checking out the product, guessed wrong on its po-tency. Two"—another finger—"he knew what it was and decided it would be a painless way to kill himself. And three, somebody else knew what it was and gave it to him."

"Which would have made it a murder."

A shrug. "Out of my domain, Diz. Absent any sign of struggle or motive or anything else, I'm listin' cause of death as accident/suicide. Have you talked to Banks?"

"Ridley?" Hardy shook his head. "Not since Wednesday night, and not for lack of trying. He hasn't returned my calls. But even Wednes-day," he added, exaggerating slightly, "I know he didn't like the timing of Cullen's death. The day he gets out, he's dead, he can't testify. So what's the deal, do you think? Somebody set Cullen up to sink Cole, then somebody killed him before he could. It doesn't make any sense."

"Yeah, but so little does anymore, Diz." Strout picked up the grenade again, hefted it casually. "Maybe Banks'll come in with some-thing," he said. "I'm sure he's looking."

Hardy sat with it a minute, then got to his feet. "Well, thanks, John, you've been a help."

29

Glitsky eventually persuaded his sons that he could probably take a shower, get dressed in his jeans and a light sweater, and make it to his favorite chair in the living room without stressing out too much about it. They didn't have to watch him continually—he gave his word he wouldn't go outside or do the long version of his tap-dancing routine around the duplex.

But both of them wanted to stay near him, and Abe couldn't say it bothered him. More, their obvious concern for him touched him deeply. It was good to have his family back together. Who could say when it might happen again? They gave Rita the afternoon off, then called Nat and asked him what he was doing. He came over with Chinese food—chicken chow mein and Happy Garden—and after lunch the three generations played hearts at the kitchen table for three hours. For the first time in years, the small kitchen echoed with actual laughter. Everybody caught up with each other, their lives in the last couple of years, swearing genially at bad play or bad luck, reconnecting.

When Orel got home from school, Nat left for the synagogue and the boys decided they'd get outside and shoot some hoops at the park down the street until it got dark. Glitsky had taken out his book and sat in his Barcalounger in the living room. In five minutes he had transported himself to the Mediterranean, where he prowled the shipping lanes off the Costa Brava looking for prize ships and booty.

The duplex had a west-facing front, and on clear days there was a short window of time just before dusk when the sun sprayed the room with light before it sank into the buildings across the street. The sudden glare made Abe look up from his book. He closed it.

Motes of dust hung in the room's air.

Elaine was walking with someone she knew. It was very late, nearly one o'clock in the morning. She'd left Treya that Sunday at Rand & Jackman in the late afternoon and, if Jonas was to be believed, hadn't come home to Tiburon. So she had stayed in the city—the two of them had probably met for dinner downtown.

Six hours? A very long dinner. Much to discuss, or one topic that consumed them? Perhaps cocktails afterwards.

She was leaving Jonas. It may not have been a dinner after all, but a romantic tryst at a hotel, or even the new man's place. That would at least account for the hours.

But at some point, they left together. Why? They could have stayed the night either at a hotel or the man's place. He assumed that some other nights she would stay in the city after a late meeting—Jonas would not need to suspect anything.

But she was going home this night, which again seemed to make a restaurant more likely. Her car was parked under the building in the Rand & Jackman lot, so she had walked to wherever it was, meeting him there. She must have thought they had settled whatever it was. He was accompanying her as she walked back to get her car . . .

Had any policeman looked in her car?

Probably not. There would have been no reason to. From the first minutes, they'd had a suspect. No one was looking for a killer.

Glitsky had a city map out on the coffee table and was hunched over it. The sun was down behind the buildings now. He had switched on a couple of floor lamps and drawn a circle with Rand & Jackman in its center. There were a finite number of restaurants—and perhaps bars afterwards—in the circle from which to choose.

The fact that it had been a Sunday night would eliminate those few that closed on that day. More importantly, the others would have been far less crowded than on the other weekend nights. Ten days had passed since the shooting, it was true, but a waiter, a maître d', someone would remember.

This was police work. It was way past time for him to get proactive here. If Cole hadn't killed Elaine, then someone else had, and there would be some positive trace of it. He would supply Hardy's Three

Musketeers with a photograph of Elaine, and between them they should have no trouble covering every restaurant within the circle over the weekend. It would be a start.

Folding up his map, he walked into the kitchen to call Ridley Banks. When the young inspector had called Abe in the hospital on Wednesday, he'd sounded as though he'd begun to suspect that he'd made some kind of mistake with Cole Burgess. He still hadn't admitted any wrongdoing in his interrogation, but the door was open. Clearly, Banks understood that Cullen was tied to Cole in some way. Evidence at the scene of Cullen's death might bear upon Elaine's, and if that were the case, Banks would be a critical source.

It was no surprise that he wasn't in, but Abe was sure he'd check his messages and get back to him in a matter of hours.

They stopped where the dark alley met the dark street. Did Elaine think she was about to be kissed? Certainly the killer was close beside her, one hand at the nape of her neck. He checked the street in either direction, the alley off to his left. The shot rang into Union Square on the cold night. Someone—a bellman at one of the hotels?—would have heard it.

Then he'd caught her. Brutally, cold-bloodedly taken her life, knowing he was going to do it at least since they'd left dinner, but walking along with her, perhaps chatting easily, ostensibly satisfied with whatever conclusion they'd reached. And then gently broken her fall.

Suddenly, another terrible conjecture, but so compelling it immediately felt like fact. He'd apologized as he let her down! Glitsky could hear it, could hear the son of a bitch. "I'm sorry, Elaine, but you made me do this."

Outside, it was now dark. Glitsky was standing, leaning over, resting his weight on his hands on either side of the kitchen sink. His face, reflected in the window in front of him, had broken a light sheen of sweat. His jaw trembled, and the scar between his lips stood out fresh as a new wound.

"Dad? Dad?"

He hadn't heard them come up the steps or open the door. Turning on the water quickly, he filled his hands and threw it into his face. When they got to the kitchen, he was drying himself with a dish towel. "Hey, guys," he said easily. "How'd it go?"

• • •

"All right, all right," he said. "I'll see if I can get the number."

Hardy and Rita both showed up independently in the half hour after the boys arrived, and now the two men sat at the kitchen table while Rita put together a tuna fish casserole on the counter behind them. The boys were down in their "wing," taking showers and watching television. And Abe finally conceded that he ought to try Ridley Banks at his home.

Sergeant Paul Thieu was manning the homicide detail and gave Glitsky the number he needed off the top of his head.

"Scary," Glitsky said to Hardy. "The guy knows everything." He was punching at the phone, listening, leaving another message. "Rid, it's Abe again. Still trying to reach you. Sorry to nag, but whenever you get any of these . . ." He left his own number, hung up, looked at Hardy. "He's a bachelor. It's Friday night."

"Swell," Hardy said. "I'm married. It's Friday night. Speaking of which, did you ever talk to Treya?"

"How's that connected to you being married and it being Friday night? But yeah, she called this morning, wanted to make sure I avoided the near occasion of stress."

"Which, I notice, you're not."

"Close enough." End of subject. "So what did you have her doing?"

"Directing the kids, mostly, but I also wanted to see if she had run into any files Elaine might have kept on Dash Logan."

To Glitsky, this was clearly an unexpected direction. "Dash Logan? What about him?"

Hardy ran it down for him, including suitable disclaimers about how far-fetched it all was, how coincidental. "But," he ended hopefully, "as Saul Westbrook told me just this morning, coincidences do happen."

"It's not whether they happen," Glitsky said. "It's whether they mean anything. Who's Saul Westbrook?"

"Cullen Alsop's public defender, who knew nothing about Cullen's deal."

Glitsky was still trying to find some thread. "And he's somehow with Logan, too?"

"No," Hardy admitted.

"Then I'm officially confused." Abe touched his head. "Must be the drugs."

Hardy tried to explain it again. When he finished, Glitsky was nodding as though it made sense. "And you spent your whole day billing some client for this?"

"Most of it, yeah."

Abe's voice was filled with admiration. "I'm in the wrong field," he said. Rita interrupted things, shooing them away so she could set the table for dinner, but as the two men went to the living room, Glitsky kept talking. "So you're working on one case against Logan, who is, after all, a lawyer like yourself. And another lawyer, your friend David Freeman, completely apart from you, has got another one. Right so far?" They sat on either end of the couch. Glitsky threw his map and notepad onto the coffee table and continued. "And Elaine, another lawyer, went to Logan's office on a completely different group of cases? And finally, the clincher—Cullen Alsop had a matchbox from Jupiter, a bar where Logan hangs out."

"Right," Hardy agreed. "What does it clinch, though?"

Glitsky fixed him with an amused look. "Remember last night when I said I was a horse's ass? I was wrong. That wasn't me. It was you."

Hardy took the criticism in stride. He lifted his shoulders. "Still, I felt like I had to follow it up. Shake his tree a little. But nothing fell out. Not today anyway."

No surprise there, Glitsky was thinking. But he'd gone galloping off after wisps of nothing himself. There was no point in tormenting his friend over it any further. "Well, listen, tomorrow maybe we go a different direction. We might get luckier." He picked up the map and his notes and went over some of his reasoning about Elaine's last evening. He was in the middle of it when Isaac came in and sat down.

Glitsky stopped and looked up at him. "This is not strenuous," he said. "I'm allowed to think and talk."

"Stressful." Isaac wasn't budging. "The doctor said stressful, not strenuous."

"He's right," Hardy said, standing up. "Sorry, Ike. We just get to talking."

Glitsky looked from one to the other. "Two more minutes."

"I'm timing it," Isaac said, checking his watch.

Glitsky shook his head. "Then I'd better hurry. So, Diz, we get our three helpers out canvassing the area, checking out the restaurants and bars. Then if Ridley ever calls back, we have him check the lab reports again for whatever they found in Maiden Lane that we didn't look for last time. Also, Rid can follow up on Cullen's scene—he said he had something on this, didn't he? You were assuming he meant Elaine and Cole, right?"

"That's the impression I got."

"One minute," Isaac said.

"All right, then somebody ought to look at her car. And her house . . ."

"We already did that today. Curtis went up there."

Abe nodded in satisfaction. "Already? Good. And Walsh let him in?"

"Treya called him first, greased the wheels. She's good."

"Did he find anything interesting?"

Hardy shook his head. "Not at first sight. He brought a box back, but I only got a glance at it. I'll give it a closer look over the weekend. And while we're on it, Amy found that guy at Hastings, too. Not an Elaine fan anymore, though once upon a time he was a big one. According to her, definitely a possible."

"Did she ask him where he was that night?"

"I don't know."

"All right, then maybe Rid can go talk to him . . ."

"Time!" Isaac called out, standing up. "That's it, gentlemen. Time is called."

"Dinner!" Rita yelled from the kitchen.

"Okay." Hardy was on his feet. He had the map and notebook in his hands. "Never let it be said I can't take a subtle hint." He started moving to the doorway.

Glitsky sidled along with him. "One more time," he said, "for the record. As far as you've been able to find out, Logan isn't any part of this."

"Hey!" Isaac said. "Time's been called."

"We're just saying good-bye, Ike," Glitsky yelled back.

Hardy had gotten to the door. "In code," he added.

"So no Logan?"

"I guess not. Unless something turns up on him in Elaine's files. Which won't happen because she didn't have any." Hardy spoke with finality and disappointment. He'd put in a lot of hours on some Logan connection, and it was starting to look as though they'd all been wasted. He was at the door, on his way out, closing it behind him.

Glitsky stood a moment, frowning. Suddenly, he pulled at the door and stepped out onto his landing. Hardy was almost to the sidewalk and he called down after him. "What do you mean, Elaine didn't have any? You mean files on Logan?"

Hardy turned on the bottom step. "Yeah."

"But she must have."

"I don't think so. Nothing labeled that way, anyhow."

"Then what did she give Treya when she came back to the office on Sunday? She'd just been to Logan's office and gave her some files."

Hardy considered for a long beat, then broke a grin. "He just won't go away, will he?"

The weight of the world settled on him as soon as he opened the door to his home. Had it only been last night, he thought, that it had all worked so well here? Tonight, like an animal in the moments before an earthquake, he felt the tension before he could have been consciously aware of it. He walked back through the dark and silent house, turning on lights as he went. "Anybody home?"

A distracted voice answered—Vincent's. Before the remodel, their old bedroom had been directly behind the kitchen. They had turned it into a family room with their entertainment center, a couch, some reading chairs. Vincent sat in one of them, the room dark around him, playing with a handheld Game Boy. "Hey." Hardy flicked on that light, too. "How's my guy?"

Vincent barely looked up. "Hey."

"What's the matter?"

"Nothing."

He stood looking at his son, debating whether he should try to break through, but he decided not. Vincent was all right, into his game, which Hardy thought probably wouldn't harm him for life. He knew from long experience the probable reason why Vincent was here, doing what he was doing. It was a refuge.

"Where are the girls?" he asked, although he was sure he knew. The door to Rebecca's room was closed and a light showed under it.

Frannie was sitting on the Beck's bed, a stricken, exhausted look on her face. His daughter was lying across the comforter, her head on her mother's lap. Frannie was stroking her hair. They both looked up and he saw exactly what he expected—that the Beck had been crying again.

He felt his own shoulders sag. Another crisis. My God, he thought, would it never end? Without a word, he crossed over and sat with them on the bed. His eyes met his wife's, he put a hand on the Beck's shoulder. "How's my sweetie?" he asked.

She shook her head. "Not too good."

"I guessed that." He rubbed her shoulder, looked a question at Frannie.

"They had a suicide workshop today."

He would have laughed if it hadn't made him so furious. He couldn't keep the comment in. "Well, there's something every seventh grader sure needs to know all about. What did they do, give tips on the top ten favorite ways?"

Frannie gave him a signal to hold his temper, but he couldn't do it. This was at least the fifth such workshop in the past couple of months, and each one had traumatized his already fragile daughter. Since Thanksgiving, in the name of God knew what, the Beck's school had subjected her and apparently the rest of its students to perhaps forty hours of "awareness training," and it was playing havoc with her life.

She was, Hardy hoped, still a good five or six years away from sexual activity, but her school had given a *five-day* course on every possible malady and consequence that could ever be associated with sex. A few weeks later, all the girls had been enlightened on the growing incidence of anorexia and bulimia in the age group. Rebecca tended to "pick" at certain foods, and the fact sheet that the school had sent home with her listed this as a possible indicator of trouble. Although the Beck weighed ninety-odd pounds and ate with a healthy appetite, the eating disorder bug had even infected Frannie over the holidays, and that had been a lot of fun. Then, in January, came the drills in case a group of terrorists, or some of their fellow students, broke into the school and started shooting or throwing bombs—how they should pile their desks a certain way, strategies for exiting the campus.

Hardy rubbed his daughter's back. And now suicide prevention. For the life of him he couldn't imagine how any amount of precounseling was going to have any appreciable impact on the rate of teen suicide. The Beck sniffed and sat up. "Why would somebody my age want to kill themselves? I didn't even know they did that."

"Not very often, Beck. Really."

"But why?"

Maybe, Hardy thought, because all these awareness courses made kids so fearful that they no longer had the guts to live, or even wanted to, in such a treacherous and unstable world. But, of course, he couldn't say that. "It's really not very common, Beck. It's not like it's something that happens to you. You've got to decide that's what you want to do, and very very few people feel that way, especially kids."

No doubt Frannie had been mouthing the same truths for the past hour, and gradually, getting them from her dad as well, they were beginning to sink in. She was perking up slightly. "I don't think I'm going to want to commit suicide. Do you?"

"No. Of course not."

"But they made it seem like if you have a boyfriend and he breaks up with you, then that's one of the things to do." She brought a little fist down on her thigh. "But that would be so *stupid*. I mean, I never would have thought of that, even if I ever did have a boyfriend to begin with."

"You're right," Frannie said. "That would be stupid."

"But how great that they teach this and give everybody the idea." Hardy couldn't keep the disgust out of his voice. He pulled his daughter closer. She wrapped her arms around him. "Bad things happen sometimes, Beck, but not as often as you think. Not even close. You don't have to worry about all of them, or even any of them."

"I know," she said. "Worrying doesn't do any good, ever. You always say that."

"I do, you're right."

"Your father's right, Beck. It really doesn't do much good." Maybe, they hoped, if she heard it enough from people she trusted, she'd start to believe it.

Suddenly Hardy remembered the talk he'd had with Jeff Elliot yesterday. "Do you know anybody who's ever been hit by lightning?"

The Beck didn't know where this was coming from, but she was curious. "No. That almost never happens."

"How about you, Fran? No? Me, neither. Now . . . you know all these things you're learning about in school? Well, guess what?"

Vincent was standing at the door, bored beyond words with all of this. "Are you guys done? Are we having dinner tonight? I'm *so* starving."

Hardy wanted to check his messages before he turned in for the night. He hadn't been at his desk since before he went down to Jupiter to see Dash Logan, and there was enough hanging fire that he knew he wouldn't get to sleep if he didn't.

His answering machine gave him the time and date of his messages. The first two calls came in within five minutes after he'd left his office for the day, and he clenched his teeth at the perversity of fate. He might even still have been downstairs, sharing a few end-of-the-week bon mots with the lovely Phyllis.

The first call was from Jon Ingalls, wanting Hardy to know that he'd remained unlucky with witnesses. Jon left his number, telling Hardy to call anytime. What was on tap for tomorrow? He'd be waiting by the phone.

The next message was from Jeff Elliot: "I wanted you to be among the first to know that I just resigned. If they want me back, and they will, they'll have to beg and then pay me more for all the trouble they put me through. Also, anent our other recent discussion, something did finally occur to me. That connection you were talking about between Torrey and Dash Logan—I might have one. There's a private investigator named Gene Visser. You might know him. He used to be a cop."

Hardy felt a small surge of electricity. At Sam's the other day, Visser's name had come up as the heavy who'd tried to blackmail Rich McNeil.

Jeff was going on. "When Torrey started at the D.A.'s, Visser worked for him almost as his own personal investigator. They were pretty tight. I don't know if they still are, but I have seen Visser and Logan together a lot. So if Torrey and Visser still talk . . . anyway, for whatever it's worth."

Hardy thought it might be worth a lot, but he didn't get any time to celebrate. The last call, from Torrey himself, was made at 4:41—about ten minutes after Hardy had left Logan at Jupiter.

Torrey's message was that since he and Hardy were getting to prelim on Cole Burgess next week, they were both going to be swamped. So he was just looking through some other prosecutions that were coming up through the office in the next few weeks and happened to notice Hardy's name on one of them as the attorney of record. It seemed to Torrey that this case, *People v. McNeil,* was one where a judge was likely to try to get the parties to settle so it wouldn't clog up the docket, and certainly neither Torrey nor Hardy needed the extra hours when their plates were so full. If Hardy wanted to settle the case, he could probably save his client both time and aggravation, and Torrey would be happy to consider alternatives. At least the two of them should discuss it, see what they could work out.

The small surge of electricity had turned to an insistent hum.

Frannie came into the room as he was hanging up. She came up behind him, put her hands on his shoulders and dug her thumbs into the muscles along his backbone. His head fell forward as though he'd been clubbed. "Don't ever stop," he said.

She kissed the top of his head, massaging around his neck. "You know why the camper got a migraine?" she asked.

"No, and I don't care." His eyes were closed. He was in heaven.

"Too tense." Then, relief and fatigue in equal parts. "They're both down and out."

Hardy straightened up. "Did you double-check for molesters lurking outside the Beck's window? Maybe we should do nightly drills, the best ways out of the house just in case . . ."

She brought a palm up against his head. "Stop."

"She strikes him," he intoned. "A clear case of domestic violence, spousal abuse . . ." He turned back to her, took the hand that rested on his shoulder. "Sorry. I know, enough. I'll be down in a sec. Two phone calls. Short. Promise."

"I'm pouring wine and will start without you. You've been warned."

"Fair enough."

He called Jon Ingalls back. He appeared, in fact, to have been waiting by the phone. Hardy told him about Glitsky's idea to canvass the restaurants and bars in the area around Maiden Lane. Ingalls was in, whatever it was. He'd be there. What time should they start?

He didn't expect anything when he called Ridley again, but you never knew. Cops worked strange hours. Friday night bachelor or not, he might be in catching up on paperwork. But no such luck. The machine answered again.

Ridley's machine was the kind that beeped before the tone. Every beep was a call, and since he'd started trying to reach him, Hardy had been subliminally aware of the increase in the number of calls. Now he sat at his desk and waited, counting through ten, fifteen, twenty.

When the tone finally came, Hardy left his message and hung up. He scratched at his stubble, his face a brown study. In the two days since Hardy had last talked to him, twenty-eight people had left messages for Ridley Banks, and apparently he hadn't even checked them to clear his machine.

It was almost eleven o'clock, and bitter cold.

Treya climbed the steps up to Glitsky's door, then stood for an eternity on his doorstep. In the dark. Unable to knock.

Earlier, Treya had been to Raney's basketball game. After that, she and her daughter went out for a pizza. Then they went back home, where Raney got ready for bed. And Treya told her she had to go out. She'd be back in a little while.

No light showed from within. It was still as death.

Finally, finally, she tapped on the glass three times with her fingernail, a sound infinitesimally small, tentative, gone. No one could have heard it, but that was all she would do. She'd wait here another little while and . . .

Something was moving inside the flat. The landing light came on. The door opened. Abe was barefoot, still wore his jeans, the black sweater.

"Does your doctor want you awake this late?"

"I'm bad with authority. You might as well get used to it. It's a little cold." He backed up to let her enter.

"Where is everybody? Your boys?" she asked. Then: "What's that noise?"

Glitsky listened intently for a minute. "I don't hear . . ."

"There. That."

"Oh." His face softened. "That's Rita. She snores sometimes. I'm so used to it, I don't even hear it anymore. She's behind that screen."

"She sleeps in the living room?"

Glitsky gestured simply. It was a small place, homey, crowded with furniture. "Only until we finish the guest wing."

She grimaced. "I'm sorry, Abe. I didn't mean . . ."

He touched her arm softly. "It's okay. Anyway, the boys are out someplace. They made me swear on my mother's honor that I wouldn't budge. I was to sit and read my book, then go to bed, preferably early."

"Which you haven't done."

"I know," he said. "It's bad of me. That authority thing again. It's lucky I'm a boss. When I have a job, I mean."

A long moment. "So how's your book? The high seas. Good as Hornblower?"

"I think so. It's amazing how deeply he makes you feel it all."

He was staring at her. She looked back at him. The silence settled.

Glitsky cleared his throat. "Hardy says I should just ask."

"What?"

"I should just say something, like I never did with Elaine." He hesitated. "I can't have anything like that happen with you."

She waited.

"If you don't want to hear . . ." He took a breath, nearly choked out the words. "I don't know what to do with this, but I need to have you in my life."

Closing her eyes, she nodded. A sigh of what might have been relief. Then she looked at him again, and a smile played at the corners of her mouth. "I was hoping that was it," she said.

Then they were in each other's arms. Under his sweater, beneath the burns where they had shocked him back alive, his ribs ached with the pressure.

PART
THREE

30

At 8:00 A.M. on Wednesday, February 17, Dismas Hardy stood at the head of the huge oval table in the Solarium and looked with satisfaction at his assembled team of investigators and associates. Three weeks ago, no one could have predicted this assemblage. Certainly, on the day of Cole's arraignment only two weeks ago, several people in the room would have counted themselves among Hardy's opponents. At that time, only he and David Freeman had been in Cole's corner, and even they were reluctant at best.

Now he still had Freeman, who would continue on as Keenan counsel if the death penalty case did in fact get to full trial, which Hardy desperately hoped it would not. But there was also Treya and Abe, the Three Musketeers, Jeff Elliot in his wheelchair. The team had also acquired another defense attorney, who simply wanted to be part of it. This was David's friend Gina Roake, who seemed to have her own slightly unarticulated bone to pick with Torrey and perhaps Dash Logan. The case had touched a lot of nerves in this room and around the city, and now they were within hours of the opening gavel.

The hearing was beginning with a high enough profile, and would have kept it because of Elaine's notoriety alone. Pratt's political posturing, which had led to Elliot's much-criticized reprimand and highly applauded resignation, had raised the stakes. But the events of the last two days had brought things to a fever pitch.

On Monday morning, Inspector Sergeant Ridley Banks, the primary officer in the case, the man whose interrogation of Cole Burgess had led to his confession, was declared a missing person. Authorities suspected foul play, but no body had turned up—Ridley was still missing. As the last person known to have spoken to Banks, Hardy came forward with the information that the inspector had told him he was going on an interview related to both Cole Burgess and Cullen Alsop.

At this news, Gabe Torrey effectively withdrew the olive branch he'd extended to Hardy on the McNeil matter by calling a press conference covered by every print and television journalist in the city and publicly accusing him of lying. There was no proof of this alleged phone call. This was one of the sleaziest defense tricks he'd ever seen. Hardy was stooping to new depths, obviously trying to use a missing, perhaps dead, man's voice to imply that the police had doubts about the man who'd confessed to the crime. There were no such doubts.

At the same time, Torrey chose to ratchet things up significantly by floating his own reason why the former chief of homicide had prematurely delivered prosecution evidence to the defense—and lost his job for his efforts. It wasn't really because he had any doubts about the guilt of Cole Burgess. No, Glitsky's defection and the subsequent betrayal of his fellow officers was merely a self-serving effort to avoid prosecution for police brutality himself. Torrey had several witnesses who would testify that the lieutenant had illegally manhandled the defendant on the night of his arrest.

In the meanwhile, the sidebars and other human interest stories kept up the heat. As promised, John Strout declared the death of Cullen Alsop an accident/suicide. An overdose on the day of an inmate's release was nowhere near unknown in the city. The police crime scene investigation unit found no evidence that supported any other finding.

And all the while, the seriousness of the crime itself leant a gravity to the case. This was murder in the commision of a robbery, a capital case. The headlines had screamed it anew just yesterday morning; the anchors chimed it throughout the day. The D.A., as she'd promised, was going to ask for death.

Now, surveying the scene in front of him, Hardy felt that they had worked like galley slaves for the past week and done all they could. They were not unprepared, but he remained a long way from confident. The probable cause standard of proof in a preliminary hearing, after all, was nowhere near the reasonable doubt standard of a jury trial. All the prosecution had to do was demonstrate enough to bring a "strong suspicion to a reasonable mind" that a crime had been committed and that the defendant had committed it.

During all the time in the past week that he'd spent organizing the efforts of the rest of the people in this room, he'd been unable to completely shake the fear that his strategy—bringing out all his guns at the prelim rather than saving them for the trial—was misguided. What, he kept asking himself, was the hurry?

And indeed, one of the clichés lawyers spouted to their clients about why it was always better to delay—"look, if we put this off long enough, you never know, the cop who arrested you might die and won't be able to testify against you"—had already come to pass. If Hardy waited longer, maybe Torrey would die, Pratt would be voted out of office, someone else with a guilty conscience or a slight case of schizophrenia could come forward and admit to the crime. Anything could happen.

But he was committed now, and finally satisfied that his decision was the right one. Jury trials brought with them their own insecurities, and they were of a subtly different nature. With a panel of citizens in front of you, the proceeding inevitably became slightly less intellectually rigorous. This was not to say that both sides didn't need to cover their factual bases, but a human element always came into play, and thus there was an opportunity to play to emotion, to feelings.

A jury of twelve was going to hear a horrific litany of Cole's uncontested actions that night—ripping off the earrings, breaking Elaine's finger to get the ring, and so on. They would know that he'd fled from the police. He'd fired the gun—perhaps once, possibly twice. They would likely witness the videotape of the confession despite Hardy's motion. After all that, try as he might, and no matter how brilliant a defense he was able to mount, Hardy could not believe that any jury would acquit. It could simply never happen in the real world.

So in a true sense, the prelim was Hardy's best chance. Judge Hill was a crotchety old fart, sure enough, but he was careful and conservative. Perhaps the judge's brain was not one that ascended to the exalted heights of "decent legal mind" as Hardy's own apparently did, but the Cadaver had a reputation for intelligence nevertheless. He was also an experienced jurist. He would be fair-minded, although after Hardy's intemperate outburst at the arraignment, there might be a hump to get over at the outset. Ironically, though, Hardy thought it even possible that the judge would cut him more slack in the courtroom precisely *because* he was angry with him—he wouldn't want it to seem that his personal pique affected his judgments.

In fact, he would have to give Hardy tremendous latitude. A preliminary judge would admit evidence that a trial judge would exclude as confusing or irrelevant or too time-consuming. In the name of making "a complete record," Hardy could ask Judge Hill for almost anything and the court would at least hear it before, inevitably, holding his client over for trial. Indeed, Hardy was virtually compelled to advance every single fact and theory in support of his client, no matter how tenuous. He wasn't going to open himself up to an appeal based on incompetent counsel that the Ninth Circuit would uphold in ten years.

The burden of proof was on the prosecution to show, affirmatively, that Cole Burgess had "probably" committed the murder. Hardy's team had uncovered some alternatives with motives and perhaps means and opportunity that he might be able to argue with a straight face. The police hadn't investigated thoroughly enough. Too many questions remained unanswered. There were too many other possible suspects. The waters were too muddied by politics and self-interest.

Yet Hardy knew that, even so, the judge was going to hold Cole to answer. Using the "reasonable man" standard, even if Hill might be persuaded that a trial jury might not in good conscience reach a verdict of guilty beyond a reasonable doubt, he would still order Cole to stand trial. These charges would never be dismissed.

Hardy more than halfway still believed that Cole had killed Elaine. If he himself were the judge in this hearing and knew everything he now knew, he would still have to say that Cole had "probably" done it.

The conclusion was all but foregone, but in a death penalty case, Hardy had nothing to lose. And this was the moment for the battle to be joined.

One of the surprising and wonderful things about San Francisco is that summer is not a real season in the normal meaning of the word. In any given year, there were perhaps sixty days that would classify as belonging to summer by virtue of general balminess, but these would almost never occur consecutively. Four days doth not a season make.

But the necessary corollary to the lack of seasonal continuity was the fact that a random summer day or two could occur at almost any time, willy-nilly, during any month. This morning, as Hardy mounted the steps outside the Hall of Justice, it was such a day.

The smell of roasting coffee hung in the air and he stood a moment outside in the unnaturally warm sun. A small shift in the soft breeze brought an overlay of sweet decay—the city's wholesale flower mart around the corner, he realized. A news truck pulled up and double-parked across the street. The cars behind it honked their displeasure, then pulled around in a near unanimous flow of obscenities. Hardy lingered, knowing that once he passed inside these doors, all of this, the vibrant life of the city, would cease to exist.

He had given some last-minute instructions to David Freeman, then had driven on down alone before the rest of his "team." He wanted to have a few minutes with Cole before the circus began. To reassure him. To settle himself.

Then he was passing through the metal detectors and on his way across the lobby. At this time of the morning, there was no one else around. Here on the opposite wall were the names of policemen who'd given their lives in the line of duty, and he stopped a moment, wondering if Ridley Banks was going to be there before long. He ascended to the second floor by the internal stairs rather than the elevator.

It wasn't usual, but Hardy had asked for and been given permission to "dress out" his client for the hearing. To that end, Jody Burgess had gone shopping and bought Cole several pairs of slacks, some nice shirts, a couple of sports coats. In the holding cell behind Department 20, he was wearing one of the new outfits now, and Hardy was again—continually—surprised at how well the boy cleaned up. From a tactical standpoint, this was to the good, of course, although it would have meant even more if they were in front of a jury. Still, Hardy believed that there was value in a presentable appearance in the courtroom, even at a hearing. The orange inmate jumpsuits were all too familiar in the Hall of Justice, and all too associated with guilt.

A bailiff admitted Hardy behind the bars of the holding cell and lawyer and client got through the amenities. Cole's eyes were clear now, his skin didn't exactly glow, but it looked healthy. And though he would never be mistaken for Demosthenes, his speech had continued to improve as well—the slur was all but gone, the rambling quality to his earlier answers a thing of the past.

To all outward appearances, Cole was an earnest young man of adequate means and a decent education. If anything, Hardy thought, he projected an ingenuous naïveté, a sincere human innocence. He was sorry for everything that had happened. He was getting himself back on track. He'd do everything he could to help.

"I don't really know if there's anything more you can do right now, Cole," Hardy told him. "Just don't change your story from now on. That would be the best thing. Beyond that, try to react appropriately to what you hear in there, and some of it's going to be awful, I warn you. But don't overreact. And don't act." Hardy put a hand on his shoulder. "How are the push-ups coming along?"

"Twenty-five." A trace of pride. "Four times a day. Thirty sit-ups, too. Four sets."

"And the pills?"

This wasn't as happy a topic, but Cole kept his head up. "Getting there, slow but steady, though that's not exactly been my style."

"Styles come and go," Hardy said. "Check out your clothes. A couple of weeks ago they weren't your style either. Now you look like you were born in them."

"That's outside," Cole said. "Inside's another thing."

"So what's inside?" Hardy asked.

A look of quiet desperation. "The feeling that I'm not going to beat it. It's just got too good a grip. And that's not just a style."

"You're right," Hardy said. "That's not a style. It's a choice." He flashed him the hard grin and squeezed Cole's shoulder. "You know what Patton said, don't you? 'You're not beaten until you admit it. Hence, don't.' "

Hardy saw it in Cole's eyes—the remark had hit home. He indicated the courtroom through the adjoining door. Noises had begun to leak through as the time for the session drew nearer. He gave the boy a last pat on the shoulder. "Keep your chin up, Cole. See you out there."

He had to walk around Torrey at the prosecution table, and this time there was no repartee. The chief assistant was talking to one of his own acolytes, a young woman, and pointedly ignored Hardy as he crossed the courtroom in front of him.

At the defense table, Freeman had arranged some folders and a couple of yellow legal pads in preparation for the first shots. On the other side of the bar rail, the gallery was filled to overflowing, and the crowd buzzed expectantly. Missing, though, was the almost palpable sense of anger and polarity that had marked the arraignment. Hardy attributed this partly to the passage of time, but mostly to David Freeman and Clarence Jackman, who between them had somehow gotten the word out to the various interested communities that this was not a racial crime, nor necessarily as clear a case as it had first appeared.

Hardy hadn't even made it over to Freeman when a bailiff intercepted him. "Mr. Hardy, the judge would like a word with you."

"Right now?"

"Yes, sir. This way, please."

Hardy was truly stunned. This was a peremptory summons and couldn't possibly bode well. In a capital case such as this one, every meeting between the judge and any of the attorneys had to be on the record, with a court reporter present. Hardy hesitated. Freeman, from the defense table, looked up with concern and started to come around, but Hardy held him back with a hand. "Will Mr. Torrey be joining us?"

"I don't know, sir. The judge asked for you."

There was nothing to do but follow him—back behind the bench, down the hallway in front of Cole's holding cell, where his client sat dejectedly, elbows on his knees, head down. The bailiff knocked once and did not wait for an answer, but pushed open the door to Judge Hill's chambers. A firm hand on Hardy's back all but pushed him inside.

The Cadaver sat in an upholstered armchair reading the *Chronicle*. There was another chair next to him, but Hill rather pointedly did not ask Hardy to sit. Instead, the bailiff informed his honor that Mr. Hardy was here, and the judge nodded, finished his article in a leisurely fashion, then finally closed the newspaper. Out of his judicial robes, Hill appeared far more formidable than he did on the bench—any notion of caricature was displaced here. In his tailored suit, impeccably groomed, he could have been an ancient titan of business. The ascetic and angular face, which when perched over his robes suggested a disembodied skull on the bench, here was very much alive. The pale blue eyes seemed to float in little pools of malice. Tiny capillaries coursed the parchment skin of his cheeks. His mouth was a harsh line.

He took another minute before he spoke, and when he did, his voice had a rehearsed quality, although the delivery itself was dry, uninflected. He did not address Hardy by name but, looking up with a challenging dismissiveness, simply began. "I've called you in here before this proceeding begins because I want to tell you something personally, outside of the context of this hearing."

Hardy noticed that the court reporter was indeed taking this down.

"Yes, your honor."

"Please don't say another word. This is a one-way communication. I wanted to make it explicitly clear to you that any outburst such as your display at the arraignment on this matter won't be tolerated in my courtroom. Any such outburst will get you fined, and if it's serious enough I'll put you in jail for contempt. If you think I'm kidding, we can find out real quick. I have not invited the prosecutor here since I did not think it necessary to admonish you in front of him. This is the very last latitude I will give you."

"Yes, sir," Hardy said.

Hill nodded, an expectation confirmed. "Here's a word about precision, Mr. Hardy. I told you not to speak to me again and you just did. Further, I don't know how long you've been practicing law, but a judge is 'your honor,' not 'sir.' I'll see you in the courtroom."

Hardy, his blood running hot, started to say "Yes, your honor" but caught himself in time. The bailiff nudged him out of his shock, and he turned and left the judge's chambers.

"You look like you just saw a ghost," Freeman said.

Hardy's legs would not hold him as he got to the defense table, so he sank into his chair and reached for the beaded pitcher to pour himself a glass of water. His hands were shaking in a palsy of rage.

Freeman reached over and covered one of Hardy's hands with his own gnarled one. "Diz?" With his other hand, he poured a glassful and slid it over. "Talk to me. What happened?"

Still unable to speak, Hardy's breath was ragged and came in deep through his nose. A muscle worked in his jaw. His eyes rested on a fixed point somewhere in front of him. Eventually, he saw the glass of water and drew it nearer, but did not pick it up.

"Hear ye, hear ye! The Superior Court, state of California, in and for the county of San Francisco, is now in session, Judge Timothy Hill presiding. All rise."

Pratt had come in and joined Torrey and his young assistant at the prosecution table. Hardy glanced across at her—an elegant, statuesque carriage in a dark blue business suit—and thought he detected an almost a gloating confidence. For an instant he wondered if she'd fixed things with Hill somehow, put the bug in his ear to reprimand him so humiliatingly. No more than ten minutes had passed since he'd reentered the courtroom, and he still felt physically sick with spent adrenaline. And certainly he felt totally inadequate to muster any kind of rational argument.

In normal circumstances, he might have called for an immediate recess citing the call of nature, but here he knew he didn't dare. His relationship with the judge was bad enough already. If Hardy did anything to antagonize Hill any further, he risked being charged with contempt, and any hope of making headway would be dashed before he'd begun.

Watching the Cadaver take the bench, he wondered anew about his benighted, misguided strategy, marveling at how badly he'd misjudged the situation: reasoning that Hill's anger would be a "little hump" to get over in the first minutes. Now it loomed as an impenetrable, unscalable escarpment. And he had based all on this "reasonable man," this fair-minded jurist. Now where would be all the judicial leeway he'd expected on so many critical issues? What were the odds of even getting past the videotape of the confession?

But there was nothing to be done at this point. They were here, committed.

At his side, Cole nudged him and whispered, "Patton." His client was obviously reading his thoughts, which meant that he was telegraphing them. A bad sign to go with his bad feeling, but the advice was well taken. He forced himself to summon some of the general's fortitude or control, to direct his anger and despair into something constructive.

Hill got himself settled, rearranging his robes. He greeted his clerk with a familiar if stilted geniality, then asked him to call the case. Hardy listened with half an ear as the Cadaver arranged some paper in front of him, swept his eyes around his courtroom. When they got to Hardy, there was not the slightest sign of animus—no momentary squint or pursing of his lips. It was as though their exchange had never taken place. And then the clerk had finished and the judge was talking. "Mr. Hardy, Mr. Freeman. Good morning. Ms. Pratt, Mr. Torrey. Are the People ready to proceed?"

Torrey stood up. "We are, your honor, but if it please the court, sidebar?"

Hill frowned deeply, shook his head in apparent disgust, and sighed. "All right," he said at last. He motioned with one hand. "Counsel will approach."

Hardy's legs held him as he stood—a blessing. He and Torrey got to the bench at the same time and looked up at the judge, who was still scowling. "What is it, Mr. Torrey?"

"Your honor, with all respect, you just had a private meeting with Mr. Hardy."

Hill's face held a terrible blandness. He waited and waited a little more. "Was that a question?"

"Yes, your honor."

"I'm afraid I didn't hear one. Maybe you could try again."

Torrey, aware that he'd already committed a tactical error, cleared his throat. "Well, your honor, as you know, in a capital case such as this one, all communication between the parties has to be on the record."

"You don't say, counselor." Hill was breathing fire, a controlled burn. "As a matter of fact, I was aware of that." Another wait. "I'm still waiting for a question."

Hardy suddenly became aware of unrest in the gallery behind him. Hill looked out, then back down to Hardy and Torrey. As he'd shown at the arraignment, this judge seemed comfortable allowing some limited reaction among the spectators. In Hardy's experience, this was unique. At very little volume, the low, white-noise hum added a kind of subliminal tension to the tone in the room. He wondered if Hill had some reason for allowing it.

Torrey finally found his question. "Very well, your honor. The People would like to inquire. What was the purpose of your meeting with defense counsel?"

"It was a personal issue, Mr. Torrey. This case had not yet been called. We did not discuss it in any manner." Hill shifted his eyes. "Is that completely accurate, Mr. Hardy?"

"Yes, your honor."

The judge wanted unassailable clarity on this point. "Mr. Hardy, did you say even one word about this case in my chambers?"

"No, your honor."

"Did I?"

Again, Hardy said that he did not.

"Does this satisfy you, Mr. Torrey?"

The prosecutor swallowed, clearly feeling that if he could get out of this without any further damage, it would be a victory. "Perfectly, your honor."

Hill nodded brusquely. "Then if you'd be so good as to call your first witness."

Another of the many ways that a preliminary hearing differed from a trial was that there were no opening statements from either side. The prosecution simply began by calling witnesses (whom the defense could cross-examine) and introducing evidence, as they would at trial. When the D.A. was finished, the defense could then present its own witnesses and evidence.

Torrey took his chastised self back to the prosecution table. Hardy returned to his chair, thinking that at least the judge was equally intolerant of both sides. All things considered, this was terrific news.

Earlier in the week, Freeman had bet two hundred dollars that he could predict every witness in the order that Torrey would call them throughout the day, and—perhaps foolishly, given it was David—Hardy had taken the bet. Now the old man leaned across Cole and whispered, "Strout."

Two seconds later, Torrey stood on the other side of the room. "The people call John Strout."

The coroner rose from one of the wooden theater seats on the prosecution side of the room and made his long-boned way up the now frankly talkative center aisle, through the bar rail, to the witness chair. Strout appeared as a witness in a courtroom no less than once a fortnight, and as he took the oath, he projected his usual relaxed confidence.

As Torrey stood to begin his questioning, Hill lifted his gavel and touched it down lightly. The decibel level dropped a few points, Torrey greeted Strout, and the hearing had begun.

"Dr. Strout, for the benefit of the court, can you tell us briefly your occupation, as well as the training and experience that qualify you for that position?" Strout quickly qualified as an expert and gave the preliminary information about the case. In about ten questions, Torrey got to the point. "Doctor, what killed Elaine Wager?"

Strout leaned back in the witness chair and crossed his legs. "She was shot once in the back of the head at point-blank range with a .25 caliber bullet. Death was instantaneous."

"And the manner of death?"

"Death at the hands of another—homicide."

As Hardy listened to the uncontested testimony, his spirits continued in their downward spiral. The prosecution, after all, only had to prove two things and it was already halfway there in less than five minutes. But, he thought with relief, that's over now. Homicide has been established. The second half, as Yogi Berra would say, was ninety percent of it. But if he thought that things couldn't get more depressing from here, he was mistaken.

Torrey: "Now, you carefully examined the deceased body in your forensics laboratory, did you not?"

"I did a compete autopsy, yes sir."

"And during this autopsy, did you discover any other injuries to the body?"

"I did."

"Would you please describe them for the court?"

Strout, in his element, turned slightly and spoke directly to the judge, describing in homespun terms the gash on Elaine's neck, the broken ring finger, the damage to her earlobes where the pierced earrings had been pulled out. By the time he'd finished the short recitation, the susurrus in the gallery had ceased. Torrey introduced the eight-by-ten color photographs of Elaine that documented all of this testimony and Judge Hill spent several minutes examining them minutely, leaving Strout on the stand while he did so.

When he finally got the pictures back and entered as People's Exhibits, Torrey told Strout he had one more question. "These injuries, Doctor, were they administered before or after the decedent's death?"

Strout replied, "From a medical standpoint, it's impossible to say with certainty in the cases of the neck and ear injuries. Certainly near to the time of death, say within an hour. The finger, however, was broken after the decedent's heart had stopped pumping blood."

"In other words, after she was dead?"

In his laconic drawl, Strout granted that death usually went along with when the heart stopped and stayed that way. A ripple of amusement—tension breaking in the gallery—greeted this reply. Torrey let it die out, then passed the witness.

Hardy stood up. "Dr. Strout," he began, "the injuries you described earlier, including the gunshot wound, the pictures we've seen—was that the extent of damage to the decedent's body?"

The witness considered for several seconds. "Yes, sir," he answered with finality.

"Were there any other broken bones, physical marks, bruises, abrasions?"

"No."

"Did you examine her extremities, Doctor?"

"Yes, of course."

"And were there any scratches or scrapes on her knees, or elbows, or on her hands?"

"No."

"Aside from the bullet wound, was the same true of her head?"

Another wait while Strout considered carefully. "Yes."

"Doctor, was there *any* abrasion, no matter how slight, that, in your expert opinion, would be consistent with her dropping dead—instantaneously, as you said—and falling directly with gravity onto unyielding concrete or asphalt?"

"No, there was none."

Hardy thought he'd nailed down his point succinctly enough. The Cadaver had listened intently, even had taken a few notes. He'd have to let the information—and inferences to be drawn from it—hang fire for a while, but when the time came, it might be persuasive.

In the gallery, the noise bubbled up again. Hardy didn't know if the Cadaver used it for the same purpose, but suddenly the waxing and waning of the background sound struck Hardy as a kind of barometer. While he was asking his questions of Strout, the room had been almost completely silent. Which told him he must have been getting somewhere, making people think. Even if the majority of them, like Cole, were ignorant of where he intended to go, what his questions meant.

But he knew.

And the gallery would remember them, waiting for an answer, for closure. So, Hardy believed, would the judge.

He bowed his head slightly to Strout. "Thank you, Doctor. No more questions."

By the time Hardy was back at his table—six steps—Hill had directed Torrey to call his next witness. As he sat down, Cole whispered, "What was that all about?" and Torrey stood and asked Steven Petrie to come forward. Hardy looked around Cole to Freeman. The old man pointed to the yellow legal pad on the desk in front of him. In block letters, he'd written "PETRIE." He smiled helpfully.

"What?" Cole asked again.

Hardy patted his arm, whispered to him. "It's like a movie, Cole. You pick it up as it goes along."

Petrie, the officer who'd been first on the scene, was in uniform today. Blond and crew-cut, he had a runner's body and a military air, and seemed nearly as uncomfortable as Strout had been composed. He gave his name, his rank, his duties and time on the force. Torrey was up, standing in front of him. "Officer Petrie, would you please describe your actions on or about twelve-thirty a.m. on the morning of Monday, February first, of this year?"

Hardy conceded that this was a good way to loosen up the stiff cop. Petrie seemed to sag in relief—he wasn't going to be answering a barrage of questions, at least not right away. He glanced up at the judge, then back to Torrey, and began his recital in a normal voice.

The details were familiar enough to Hardy, but he knew that a straightforward chronology of events would be helpful to the judge. Eventually, also—he hoped—it would serve him. But for now, he sat forward, listening for factual error, taking notes.

Petrie told it clearly. He and his partner, Daniel Medrano, were cruising downtown on their regular beat when they saw some suspicious movement at the head of Maiden Lane, at Grant. As they pulled closer, they brought their squad car's spotlight to bear, and saw a man squatting over a fallen figure. He turned and began to run. Petrie's partner Medrano got out and gave chase while Petrie first called for backup, then got out to see to the fallen figure, a young African-American woman, who appeared to be dead.

He took under a minute satisfying himself that he could do nothing to help the victim, but he called the paramedics anyway. By the time he finished, Medrano was returning with the suspect, whom he'd apprehended at the Union Square end of Maiden Lane. Medrano told him that, in the dark, the suspect had run into a fire hydrant and fallen down.

Shot out of a cannon, Hardy was on his feet with an objection. He heard Freeman call his name hoarsely, but he was already up, committed. "Hearsay, your honor."

Hill's eyes narrowed with displeasure. "Absolutely," he replied. "And as such permitted in a preliminary hearing when offered through an experienced officer, as you no doubt remember from your days in law school. Mr. Torrey, please continue." But another thought struck him. "Oh, and Mr. Hardy, try to refrain from frivolous objections like this as we go along here, would you. We've got a lot of ground to cover. Thank you. All right, Mr. Torrey, you may proceed."

Hardy sat down heavily and Freeman reached around Cole to pat his arm. "I tried to tell you," he said. It wasn't any solace.

Torrey brought Petrie back to where he'd been and he continued. "So Dan—Officer Medrano—came back down Maiden Lane with the suspect. He also had a gun that he said the suspect had dropped when he fell."

More hearsay, though Hardy didn't doubt its truth.

"Let's stop there for a moment, Officer Petrie. Do you recognize the suspect that you and your partner arrested that night in the courtroom today?"

"Yes."

"Would you point him out to the court, please?"

Petrie raised a hand, pointed a finger. "In the middle of the defense table over there."

Torrey had the record reflect that Petrie had identified the defendant, Cole Burgess. "Now, this gun . . ." He introduced the murder weapon into evidence, and evidently the size of it made an impression on the gallery. It truly was a tiny weapon—no more than two and a half inches long, perhaps half an inch wide. Petrie identified it as the gun from the scene. "All right," Torrey said, "you've arrested the suspect and recovered a gun. What did you do next?"

"I should say he was already handcuffed. Dan had handcuffed him after he caught him."

"Okay, thank you."

"Then we brought him over to the squad car and patted him down. His pockets, his coat. He was wearing an old jacket."

"And did you find anything on his person?"

"Yes, sir. Several items."

"Would you describe them, please?"

Petrie identified them—the necklace, diamond ring, pair of earrings, a wallet belonging to the deceased containing her identification as well as eighty-five dollars in bills and a dollar sixteen in coins.

Prosaic as this was, no one in the courtroom was unaware of the significance of this testimony. This made it murder in the commission of a robbery. It's what made it a capital crime for which Cole Burgess could be put to death.

If there had been a jury present, this would have been the opportunity for Torrey to play to it, to underscore the importance of this testimony. But there was nothing for him to do in that regard now, no theatrical business to attend to, so he had to press on ahead.

"Officer Petrie," he said, "was the defendant intoxicated when you arrested him?"

Hardy stood. "Objection, your honor. Calls for a conclusion. Officer Petrie is not an expert witness."

But Torrey was ready with an argument. "Your honor, a layman can offer an opinion in this area and every policeman on the street is intimately familiar with apparent intoxication."

Hill nodded in agreement. "Objection is overruled."

Hardy wanted to keep going, but he'd been warned. The judge had made his ruling. Besides, it was the correct one. There was nothing to do but sit back down and listen to Petrie's answer.

"I smelled liquor on his breath, but he was conversant and coordinated."

Torrey smiled, obviously pleased at how well his witness had taken to his coaching. "Conversant and coordinated," he repeated. "Thank you, Officer. No further questions."

If Hardy had been prosecuting, he would have had a lot more, so he was surprised—his rhythm off—as he stood to begin his cross. "Officer Petrie," he began, "you smelled liquor on Cole Burgess's breath, is that correct?"

"Yes, it is."

"Was this a strong odor?"

"I could smell it, yes."

"Did you give him a Breathalyzer test?"

"No."

"No." Hardy paced a few steps to his left, deep in thought. "Officer Petrie, in your years as a police officer, have you ever pulled over a car for a driving violation?"

Petrie reacted with a bit of impatience. "Yeah," he said. "Of course."

"Of course," Hardy repeated. "And on any of those occasions, if you wanted to know if someone was drunk, what was your procedure?"

"Usually we ask the person to get out of the car and administer some field sobriety tests. Saying the alphabet backwards, or standing on one foot with their eyes closed, like that."

"So basically walking and talking, right? And other basic tests of coordination?"

"Yes."

"Now you saw my client staggering when he walked, isn't that right? When he came back with your partner?"

"Well, yeah, but he had fallen down."

"That's right, Officer. He not only couldn't walk when you saw him, but he was too uncoordinated to escape, right? He plain fell down when he tried to run, isn't that correct?"

"Well, he ran into something."

"And fell down, didn't he?"

A reluctant nod. "Okay. Yes." Petrie tried to sneak a glance over Hardy's shoulder, pick up a cue from Torrey.

Hardy took a step toward the witness box and to his right, hopefully blocking the line of sight. "Now, how about his speech?"

"I don't know," Petrie said grudgingly. "It varied."

"Did he speak at all, Officer," Hardy asked, "or was he too incoherent to say much?"

"He was pretty incoherent."

"And passed out in the back of the patrol car?"

"Yeah." Petrie squirmed. "He did that."

Hardy backed away a step, took a beat, then came back to the officer. "People who act as you've described here might be drunk, correct?"

"Yes."

"Another alternative would be if they were injured, is that right?"

"Yes."

"And in fact, Mr. Burgess was bleeding slightly from a head injury, correct?"

"Yes, sir."

"Well, since you've testified that there were paramedics at the scene and your policy and procedure is to have injured prisoners evaluated by paramedics, isn't it true that the reason you didn't show Mr. Burgess to the paramedics was because you could tell that the only thing wrong with him was that he was drunk? Falling-down, incoherently drunk?"

Petrie was stuck. "He was."

Hardy nodded, satisfied. "No further questions."

During the recess, Freeman left for the bathroom. Cole pushed back from the defense table. He was not cuffed in the courtroom, and had crossed his arms over his chest, rested an ankle on his knee. "I can't believe you didn't ask him anything about the shot," he said.

Hardy wasn't much in the mood for criticism at the moment. "Like what? He's not our witness."

"Why not?"

Hardy, pretending to read from some notes in front of him, finally gave that up and turned to face Cole. "Because I talked to him early in the week. He says he didn't hear any shot. And we need that shot as much as they don't need it."

"Why didn't Torrey bring it up, then?"

Hardy had wondered about this, too. Certainly, it was an important point. If Cole had only fired the gun once, and *not* when he fell during the pursuit in the alley, then the only handy explanation for the gunpowder residue on his hands was that he'd fired the gun before the police arrived. Presumably to kill Elaine. Petrie's report of the incident never mentioned a shot, although Medrano's did. So Hardy had put Medrano on his own witness list. He assumed that when Torrey had seen this, he chose Petrie for the prosecution version of the story. Then, in the flush of having demonstrated his special circumstance—robbery—he'd decided he had gotten enough out of him. He didn't need what the officer didn't hear. Hardy hoped this would prove to be a critical omission, but he downplayed it to his client. "I don't know, Cole," he said. "My honest feeling is that he just plain forgot."

Freeman guessed right again on the next witness—the crime scene lab technician. Lennard Faro was a small man in his early thirties with a thin mustache and thick, pomaded black hair. He wore a blue blazer over a tangerine shirt. A tiny gold cross earring dangled from his left ear. He verified that the slug ballistics confirmed that the bullet that had killed Elaine Wager had been fired from the weapon Cole had had in his possession. Faro had tested the defendant for gunshot residue, then analyzed the results. Now Torrey had come to the nub of it. "And therefore, based on the results of this test, it was your conclusion that the defendant had on his hands residue that could only have come from a discharged firearm."

It was a no-brainer. Faro had no doubt at all. "Yes, sir." And Hardy got the witness.

"Mr. Faro," he began, "did you find any fingerprints on the gun?"

"No, sir."

"Is this unusual?"

The lab tech shrugged. "It's common enough, sir. The surfaces of the gun had been treated with Armor All, the car upholstery cleaner? So it didn't hold fingerprints."

"I see. And when you say this is common enough, roughly how frequently do you see it?"

This was an unexpected direction, and the young man paused to reflect before he answered. "Every few months, I'd say."

"Every few months? So it's not an everyday finding?"

"No, not at all. I didn't mean common like everyday."

"That's all right. I'm just trying to get a sense of when you would see this Armor All used on a weapon to avoid fingerprints. It seems like an esoteric bit of knowledge."

Faro had no reply. Hardy realized he hadn't asked a question. Torrey was objecting behind him. "Relevance. What's the point here, your honor?"

"That's a good question, counselor. Mr. Hardy?"

It was not a pleasant moment. The Armor All was one of dozens of details that possibly meant something, but it didn't prove a damn thing either way. Cole was more likely to be ignorant of its usefulness in avoiding fingerprints than, say, a member of law enforcement or a hardcore criminal, but it certainly was possible that he knew all about it, and had put it to good use.

Hardy apologized, took another tack. "Mr. Faro, how many bullets were in the gun when you examined it?"

"Well, it's a five-shot revolver. There were three live rounds and two spent casings."

"Two casings?"

"That's right."

Hardy looked at the judge, turned in a half circle, came back to the witness. "Now, Mr. Faro, did you take the GSR swabs from Mr. Burgess yourself?"

"Yes, I did."

"And you've testified you found gunpowder residue on the swabs, is that so?"

"Yes."

"Did you find a lot of it?"

"No. Very little."

"Very little," Hardy repeated. "If a person fires a gun more than once, Mr. Faro, does he leave increasing amounts of residue with each shot?"

"Yes, of course."

"Of course. And yet Mr. Burgess had very little?"

"Yes."

"Are you able to say that this residue came from one or more than one discharge?"

"No."

"In fact, you can get GSR on your hands from picking up a recently discharged firearm, isn't that true?"

"Yes."

Hardy wasn't going to get any more out of that well, so he decided to move on. "And when did you swab the defendant's hands, Mr. Faro? Wasn't it in the middle of the night?"

"Yes, sir. The defendant was handcuffed and brought to the homicide detail for questioning. I was at the crime scene, and came down when we were done there."

"Do you know what time you administered the test?"

"Yes, sir. I noted the time when I started. It was four thirty-seven in the morning."

"And during all that time that you were at the crime scene, was Mr. Burgess handcuffed in an interrogation room in the Hall of Justice?"

Faro nodded. "That's what the officers told me, yes sir. They didn't want to let him wash his hands. That's pretty standard," he offered helpfully.

"I'm just curious, Mr. Faro. Why didn't you administer the test in the field?"

"I guess they wanted to get him downtown fast. I don't really know."

Hardy paced a little, in thought. "All right, Mr. Faro, so you got here to the Hall of Justice after Mr. Burgess had been in custody for at least three hours. Would you describe his condition at the time you took the swabs?"

"Your honor, objection. Calls for a conclusion."

But Hardy was ready for this one. "Not at all, your honor. I'll let you draw the conclusions. I'm only asking Mr. Faro what he saw."

The Cadaver gave him one. "Very well. Overruled."

"Mr. Faro?" This wasn't the tech's usual area of expertise or testimony, and he shifted in the chair with a degree of discomfort. "Let me be more specific," Hardy offered. "Was Mr. Burgess asleep?"

"No, sir. He was in a chair."

"Was he sitting up straight, or slumped down?"

Torrey again. "Your honor, defendant's posture can hardly be relevant."

But again Hill overruled him, adding harshly, "I'm allowing this line of questioning, Mr. Torrey." The message was clear—object again at your peril.

Faro answered the question. "He was way down, slumped as you say."

"Did you talk to Mr. Burgess at all?"

"Yes I did. I told him what I'd be doing with his hands."

"And how did he respond?"

He considered a moment. "Incoherently. He was pretty out of it. I finally just pinned his arms down and took the swabs."

"Was his speech clear, or slurred?"

"Slurred. It was more like mumbling."

"Mr. Faro, did you smell alcohol on his breath?"

"Whew!" The witness finally showed some personality. "It was a brewery in there."

"A brewery," Hardy repeated, delighted with the phrase. "That would be 'yes,' wouldn't it? You smelled alcohol, is that right?"

"Yes."

"And was this a good three hours after he'd been brought downtown?"

"Yes, sir, at least."

"One last question, Mr. Faro. Did you see any video equipment set up in the interrogation room when you were there administering your tests?"

"No, sir." And another sentence slipping out. "When I passed the monitor next door, they hadn't turned the camera on yet."

"Thank you, Mr. Faro. Mr. Torrey, your witness."

The prosecutor honed in on Hardy's most salient point. "On the matter of the gunpowder residue, can it be wiped or washed off?"

"Washed, yes. Wiping, eventually, over time. Which is why we try to get to it pretty quickly."

"But in this case, as you've testified, you didn't get to it very quickly.

In three hours, might someone lose a great deal of residue if they wipe their hands enough on their clothing, for example?"

"Yes."

"But not all of it?"

"No. Not necessarily."

"So is it entirely possible that the defendant could have fired the gun more than once and still had only little or trace amounts of gunpowder residue?"

"Yes. Completely."

As soon as the witness stepped down, Hardy asked for a sidebar, and all the attorneys came forward to the bench. "Your honor," he began, "I'd like to make my motion to exclude my client's statement—his so-called confession—right now. It's clear he was drunk when he was arrested and equally clear that Officer Petrie was coached to say otherwise. Let's get this issue resolved right now."

This tactic didn't stand a chance and Hardy knew it. The prosecution could call their witnesses in any order and any coaching they were going to do was already done. But it might serve to disrupt the orchestration of the prosecution's case. At least making the motion would annoy Torrey and Pratt. And if the judge made them change the witness order, who knew? As a bonus, he might even win his bet with Freeman.

"Give me a break." Pratt, all scorn, addressed Hardy but was looking at the judge. "It was almost five o'clock in the morning, your honor. He was punch-drunk, maybe, with fatigue."

But David Freeman wasn't only there for his good looks. He took a half step toward the bench. "Your honor," he said. "Three hours?" He took in the whole circle of them. "They come upon Mr. Burgess on the scene, apprehend him there with the victim's jewelry and an apparent murder weapon, and *three hours later* they haven't even asked him a question? On the face of it, the confession is fatally flawed. The police overstepped." He was raising his voice. "They don't give him his phone call—"

"He called his mother," Torrey interrupted. "He waived an attorney. We've got that on the videotape."

"Bullshit!"

Hill, shocked at the language, couldn't find any response other than to point his finger. "Hey!"

"It's on the tape, David," the prosecutor shot back. "Deal with it."

Freeman implored the judge. "Where are we, your honor? In Turkey? In Iraq?"

"Jesus." Pratt did a little pirouette of disgust. "Your honor, no one has fought police misconduct more than I have. This was a murderer they needed to interrogate. He signed his Miranda notice. There was no overreaching here."

Finally, Hill caught up with it all. He slammed his gavel for order, since by now the whole room behind him had degenerated into chaos. When things had settled, the Cadaver turned a terrible face to both Hardy and Freeman. "I've said I will rule on these issues when the People seek to introduce the evidence. I've heard nothing to change my opinion," he said in clipped tones. "Mr. Freeman," he continued. "I don't allow profanity in my courtroom. Now I'm calling a five-minute recess and I want everybody calmed down by the time we reconvene. This is a court of law and not a goddamned circus act."

31

Pratt herself took over for the next witness. "The People call Anthony Feeney."

Hardy had known Feeney, a journeyman assistant district attorney, for over twenty years, and had always considered him a decent sort—honest, hardworking, cooperative. When Hardy had first interviewed him because he'd taken Cullen's information on behalf of the D.A., he'd gone home particularly depressed. The details that had eluded both him and the public defender Saul Westbrook about the mechanism of Cullen's snitching were not a secret. No one appeared to be trying to conceal anything. Hardy had hoped this would turn out to be a break in the case—against Torrey if nothing else—but his hopes had been pretty much dashed. Feeney wasn't a liar. Hardy didn't think he'd be lying now, and this was not good news.

He was Hardy's age, although sometime in the past decade he'd gone from looking younger than him to much older. His hair had turned snow white. He'd developed a middle and his clothes, once flashy, had become conservative, dated. The almost oddly shaped, triangular face had crumbled on itself somehow—the once-distinctive beauty marks on either cheek now lost in liver spots and mild eczema. Feeney had turned into a bureaucrat, an office worker—flat affect, squashed personality, perfectly competent and nonconfrontational. He aimed to please.

After establishing his credentials, Pratt got down to her business—demonstrating that Cole Burgess had the murder weapon at least a day in advance of the shooting, and therefore that premeditation was possible if not likely. "Mr. Feeney, do you know a young man named Cullen Leon Alsop?"

"I do, or did. He's dead now."

The familiar hum in the courtroom began again, low and ominous. Pratt turned full around and waited until it had died out a bit, then continued. "How did you know Mr. Alsop?"

"I prosecuted him for several drug-related offenses. He was a dealer of crack cocaine, and had been convicted on that offense several times."

"I see. When was the last time you saw him?"

"I had an interview with him on the afternoon of Tuesday, February ninth, at the jail."

"Would you please explain to the court what this meeting was about?"

"Sure." Feeney shifted in the witness chair. "I got a call from one of the guards at the jail that morning, saying that Mr. Alsop wanted to talk to me, that he had information that the district attorney would like to have regarding the Elaine Wager case. He wanted to trade that information for a reduced sentence, or even to get out of jail."

"So what did you do?"

"First, ma'am, per our guidelines, I brought the information to the chief assistant D.A., Mr. Torrey. He directed me to talk to the snitch—to Mr. Alsop—get his demands, and we'd see where that led us. So I went down and talked to him. He hadn't yet been arraigned and didn't have a lawyer up to that point, so I was free to talk to him directly."

Pratt looked good. There was no doubt about it. She held her head high, a tiny private smile playing with her features as she walked back to the prosecution table. There, she picked up a thin folder and turned gracefully, walking back up to the judge, handing it to him. The gallery, watching her, was silent. "Was your entire conversation with Mr. Alsop taped?"

"Yes."

"If defense does not object"—here she turned again, charmingly—"rather than put in the whole tape, perhaps we can hear the essence of the discussion from this witness."

Hardy was halfway to his feet to object in a big way. This was the rankest kind of hearsay, pure and simple. The witness wasn't a police officer, so it couldn't even come in at prelim. And even if it could, Alsop was dead. He couldn't be cross-examined at trial, so his statement would never be admitted there. No jury would ever hear about this tape in a million years.

Pratt was just playing to the crowd, the judge, and not least the reporters—reminding them that, admissible or not, they had a statement tying Cole to the gun. There was no doubt, reasonable or otherwise, as to who had killed Elaine Wager. Pratt must have expected the objection to be made and sustained. She had all but invited Hardy to step up.

So he wouldn't do it.

If he did the expected and put up a good, even brilliant technical defense, Cole would go down. His client would die in prison, sooner in the death chamber or later of old age. Better to change the rules. Suspend the rules of evidence. Everything would come in. Maybe Pratt and Torrey, sloppy lawyers both, would do something so gross that it would actually damage the case, or maybe—this just a glimmer—they'd let slip something Hardy might have missed.

He stood. "For the purposes of this prelim only, no objection, your honor."

Clearly puzzled, the D.A. hesitated, then inclined her head graciously. "Thank you. Mr. Feeney?"

Hardy had heard the whole thing almost word for word a couple of days before, and there were no surprises. He'd read the transcript and listened to the tapes of Cullen's talks with both Feeney and Ridley Banks. The story was simple and consistent enough. At the heart of it, though, lay Cullen Alsop's credibility.

When Pratt gave him the witness, Hardy rose and approached the box. "Mr. Feeney, when you went over to the jail to meet Mr. Alsop, was it the first time you'd seen him in connection with this information he was offering to trade?"

Feeney thought for a minute, then nodded. "Yes."

"And this was on Tuesday, February ninth, was it not?"

"Yes, it was."

"Did Mr. Alsop tell you how he had learned of Elaine Wager's murder?"

Behind him, Hardy heard Pratt's objection. How was this relevant? And Hill asked him the same question.

"Obviously, your honor, if Mr. Alsop's story is true, it strengthens the prosecution's case immeasurably. On the other hand, Mr. Alsop was a desperate man, facing a long prison term. The mechanics of this negotiation—who approached who, who told who what, is critical to Mr. Alsop's credibility. If the District Attorney approached him and fed him this story—"

"Your honor!" Pratt was up again behind him, moving forward. Hardy half turned to face her. "I'm outraged by this accusation. He's implying that we have suborned perjury to strengthen an already airtight case."

Hardy sprung the trap. "If it's so airtight without the gun, your honor, why did Ms. Pratt bring it up? This evidence is clearly and totally inadmissible at trial. Unless counsel is prepared to admit she's just pandering to the press, it must have relevance. And I'm entitled to explore Mr. Alsop's credibility."

"Your honor, it's completely absurd."

Hill drew himself up in his chair. His eyes had become slits. He raised a bony finger at the D.A. "Please return to your seat." He stared her down until she obeyed, and then he continued. "Ms. Pratt, you wanted it in, you got it in. Now he can attack it." He turned to Hardy. "You may continue."

Hardy inclined his head. "Thank you, your honor. Let me withdraw the question about how Mr. Alsop learned of Elaine Wager's murder for the moment and ask another." He went back to his table. Freeman was ready for him, and handed him what he wanted, the transcript of the Ridley Banks interrogation of Cullen Alsop. Hardy had it marked as an exhibit, then returned to his witness. "Mr. Feeney, at the time of your visit to Mr. Alsop, had you read any part of Defense Exhibit A?"

"No."

"And why was that?"

Feeney frowned. Hardy knew, of course, that the assistant D.A. hadn't even received the transcript before his own interview took place, but if Hardy could somehow make him feel as though he'd done something wrong, he might get defensive, and that would be to the good. "Because Inspector Banks had only talked to Mr. Alsop the night before. It hadn't even been typed yet."

"So you hadn't gotten around to reading it?"

Pratt objected, as Hardy knew she would. "Asked and answered."
Hill sustained her.

But Feeney wore a cloud on his brow. He was paying close attention
now, on his guard. The gallery was producing a low-level hum. "Had
you heard about Inspector Banks' interrogation at all?"

Feeney threw a glance over at Pratt, then came back to Hardy.
"Yes?" he answered.

"I'm asking you, Mr. Feeney. You said yes, but it sounded like a
question."

"I'm sorry. Yes. I had heard about it."

"But you didn't hear the tape itself?"

"No."

"Or talked to Inspector Banks? Or read a transcript?"

Pratt slapped the table in anger. "How many times are we going to
hear this question, your honor?"

Hardy made an apologetic gesture to the judge. "I want it to be clear,
your honor, that Mr. Feeney didn't know anything about the talk
between Inspector Banks and Cullen Alsop, other than that it had
occurred."

"You've succeeded there, Mr. Hardy. Move along."

"Mr. Feeney, didn't you testify that you hadn't spoken to Mr. Alsop
in connection with this case until your meeting with him on Tuesday,
February ninth?"

"Yes."

"And you were the first and only D.A., to your knowledge, to have
talked to him up to this time?"

"Yes."

"And wasn't it also your testimony that, after talking with him, you
left him to discuss his information with Mr. Torrey?"

"Yes, that's true."

"During your discussion with Mr. Alsop on February ninth, did
you offer him any deal in connection with the information he was
providing?"

"No."

"Did you suggest any deal might be in the works?"

"No."

"No?" Hardy expressed surprise. He raised his voice over the background din. "Mr. Feeney, didn't you in fact offer him release on his own

recognizance in exchange for his testimony about this gun in the Elaine Wager case?"

Now he'd riled Feeney up good and proper, as had been his intention. "Absolutely not! I offered him nothing. We have procedures about this kind of thing and I followed them exactly. I took his information, that's all! Then we analyzed and discussed it upstairs and came to a decision. We didn't offer him any deal of any kind until the next day."

"February tenth? The day he was released?"

"Absolutely."

Hardy lifted the exhibit and handed it to the witness. "Mr. Feeney, would you be so kind as to read aloud the first few lines of this transcript after Inspector Banks' introduction."

It didn't go very far. Feeney got to the words "I got a deal going here with the D.A." and Hardy stopped him cold. "How do you explain that, Mr. Feeney? On the night before you saw Cullen Alsop, he told Inspector Banks that he already had a deal with the D.A.?" A pause. "What was that deal? Who did Mr. Alsop have it with?"

The witness tried to figure it out, then gave it up. "I can't explain it. He must have been mistaken, or bluffing."

Hardy knew he'd be rebuked for it, but he had to get it on the boards. "Or somebody else with the D.A. had already cut him a deal."

Pratt exploded up again, and the gallery noise reached a level where Hill slapped his gavel and called for order. Sternly, he told Hardy that he should know better. He was to refrain from that type of editorial comment.

"I'm sorry, your honor," he said. "But this does lead back to the question I asked earlier. I'd like now to revisit that issue if the reporter would read back the question."

After only a small hesitation, the judge so directed, and the reporter found the spot. "Did Mr. Alsop tell you how he had learned of Elaine Wager's murder?"

Hardy added. "Or my client's arrest?"

Pratt's voice behind him was firm. "Your honor, I still object. The question remains irrelevant."

But something had sparked Hill's curiosity. "Overruled," he said simply, and directed the witness to answer.

Feeney, wrung out, shook his head. "I have no idea. He didn't say."

"Did you ask him?"

Another accusation of oversight. Feeney sighed at the burden of it. "Mr. Hardy, as you know, San Francisco has newspapers and the jail's got a grapevine. Somebody like Elaine Wager dies, it gets around."

"Perhaps it does. But you didn't answer my question. Did you ask Cullen how he knew that Elaine Wager had been killed by Cole Burgess using his gun?"

"No."

"Did you wonder how he could have put all that information together?"

Feeney shrugged. "Maybe he read a newspaper, saw it on television, I don't know."

"All right," Hardy conceded. "Maybe he did." He walked back to the defense table and, stalling, took a drink of water. He needed a last connection, and didn't know where he was going to get it. The first rule of questioning witnesses is never ask a question for which you don't know the answer. But Hardy had Feeney on the ropes now, defensive and doubtful. He might let something slip. It might be a knife that would come back and stab Hardy, but he felt he had to take the risk. "Mr. Feeney, just a few more questions. You've told the court that you knew Cullen Alsop from previous arrests and prosecutions, isn't that true?"

"Yes, it is. Three to be precise."

"But you had never spoken to him personally, correct?"

"Yes, correct."

"But you'd seen him in court before many times? Perhaps a dozen or more?"

Weary, wanting to get it over with, Feeney was bobbing his head with resignation. The gallery was a tomb behind Hardy. "Yeah, sure, something like that."

"And in those cases, before last Tuesday, did Mr. Alsop ever appear with a codefendant?"

The bobbing stopped. At the prosecution table, Torrey was leaning forward, his elbows on his knees, shoulders hunched, and he raised his head. "In two or three of the narcotics offenses, he had a codefendant," Feeney answered.

"And who would that have been?"

Feeney didn't like it. "The defendant, Cole Burgess."

"So they were friends," Hardy said, "or at least knew each other well. "Now, Mr. Feeney, please try to remember. This is important. When you heard about the arrest of Cole Burgess, did you recall his friendship with Cullen Alsop?"

"Your honor, please. What is this about?"

Hill raised his glance and directed it behind Hardy. "Is that an objection, Ms. Pratt?"

"Yes, your honor. Relevance?"

"Overruled."

But this time, Pratt wasn't going to let it go. "Your honor, if it please the court . . ."

"Well, it doesn't, Ms. Pratt. I've ruled on your objection. We're not under the same strictures as a formal trial here, and this is a capital case. I see an argument that Mr. Hardy is trying to complete here, and I'm inclined to let him keep trying."

Still, Pratt couldn't sit down. "It's taking him a very long time, your honor."

"Not as long as the appeals if I get it wrong, counselor. Now, please." He turned to the court reporter again and had her read back the last question. When Feeney had heard about the arrest of Cole Burgess, did he have occasion to recall the name in connection with Cullen Alsop?

The witness answered in a quiet voice. "Actually, no, not until I heard of Mr. Alsop's arrest a couple of days later. Then I remembered."

"You remembered that they were friends? That there was a connection between the two young men?"

"Yes."

"Did you mention this connection to anyone?"

A look of chagrin. "I'm sure I did. Burgess was a hot case. I remember I was in the coffee room and Mr. Torrey was in talking about it, just generally, Ms. Pratt's new policy plans. I made some wise-guy crack about all this interconnected drug culture, that we'd just arrested this other kid Alsop again. It just came up."

Hardy glanced up at Hill, said he had no further questions.

It had been an exceptionally long morning, and Hill finally called the lunch recess, and a bailiff came over immediately to get Cole. "You guys aren't having lunch with me?" He seemed pathetically sad, and Hardy understood why. During trials, he'd usually try to eat lunch in one of the holding cells with his clients, keep them informed of what was happening, try to keep them from freaking out any number of ways. Hardy said he was sorry and promised Cole that it wouldn't happen again.

Cole gave his mother a quick wave over the railing, and then he was marched out. Hardy spent a couple of minutes consoling Jody, then making lunch plans with Jeff and the musketeers. Glitsky and Treya had already gone. Gina Roake was leaning over the bar rail, discussing something with Freeman.

Hardy started gathering his papers, and Freeman pushed out his chair, stood, stretched and came around the front of the table. "How'd you get that with Feeney?" he asked. "It was a thing of beauty."

"I had a vision."

"You didn't know?" A rebuke.

"I knew they'd been arrested together. I just couldn't prove that Torrey knew." Hardy shrugged, nonchalant. "Easy, David. It worked out. Sometimes you take a risk. It seemed worth it." He plopped his stuff into his briefcase. Over to his right, he noticed a little conference continuing at the prosecution table.

He lowered his voice. "You know the other complaint we been talking about?"

This was Freeman's letter to the state bar association complaining about Torrey. David, Hardy and Gina had discussed it over the past weekend and decided that they really had nothing. Compelling coincidences, but nothing resembling real evidence. Reluctantly, they'd decided to table the issue until after the Burgess hearing at least.

"Maybe we want to move on that after all."

Freeman moved in closer. "Move how? We agreed we don't have anything."

"Not quite true, David. We've got the bare facts. Torrey's screwing with at least two cases."

"Maybe, but we can't prove it yet. And we can't prove he's getting anything for it. The bar's going to need . . . what?"

Hardy was shaking his head. "Forget the bar. We've got to have Hill see it. He's never going to believe the D.A. suborned perjury to win this case as long as he thinks Torrey plays by the rules. It's just too big a leap. But if we can convince him that they fudged one piece of evidence, then he's going to have to take a hard look at the rest. We've got to get him to consider what we know."

"Or think we know."

"Close enough, yeah. We can't convince the bar, but maybe we can use it here."

This appealed to David, but he didn't see how it could happen. "So what are you saying? We're not going to get our two cases introduced here. There's really no relation at all."

"I'm not suggesting that, and we don't need it anyway. There's other ways Hill might get the message. He might read about it, say, in the papers." He gestured toward Jeff Elliot, still talking with Gina in the row of seats behind them. "We've got a guy here who's been known to get the word out."

Freeman being who he was, Hardy didn't have to draw him a more detailed diagram. David's eyes took on a sparkle with the possibilities. This was his kind of game, playing all the angles, in and out of the courtroom.

"All we've got to do," Hardy continued, "is plant the seed. Hill doesn't have to believe it. He's just got to acknowledge it's something Torrey's capable of."

David still didn't think so. "Even if he were convinced of it personally," he said, "without some kind of proof he's never going to let it affect his ruling."

"Probably not," Hardy said. "But on the other hand, how could it hurt? It's something, and otherwise we've got nothing."

Freeman considered for another moment. "You put it like that, it kind of grows on you. By the way," he added, "I should be happier about it, but I'm afraid you owe me the two hundred."

Hardy looked up. "Not 'til the end of the day."

"No, I bet not. Torrey's not calling any more witnesses."

Hardy studied his partner as though he'd lost his mind. "Of course he is. He's got another twelve names on his list. He hasn't even touched the crime scene."

"He's got the crime, he's got in his specials. He's got Cole at the scene with Elaine's jewelry and wallet and the murder weapon. Guess what? He's done. He doesn't even need the confession, although he'd be crazy not to use it. And I think you rocked him a little with Feeney. He doesn't want to walk into any more walls."

Hardy flatly couldn't buy it. "You want to go double or nothing?"

Freeman, sadly, shook his head. "Diz, I wouldn't take any pleasure in taking your money. If this were the grand jury, it would be over. I still don't know why he didn't go to the grand jury, in fact."

A shrug. "I didn't fight him on timing. He figured it was a toss-up. Either way we were going to trial."

The old man clucked in disapproval. "Ah, hubris."

32

Glitsky chewed on an ice cube, moving his glass of iced tea through the ring of condensation on the table. He was in a booth in the far back at Lou the Greek's, facing away from the entrance, waiting for his appointment. He couldn't shake the thought that it had been unwise to decide to meet here. It was too close to the Hall, to the homicide detail. People he knew would see him. Word would get out.

The window at his ear was half below the level of the street outside. He could look up and see a line of blue sky between the buildings. With the nice weather, Lou had opened the windows a crack to let the place air out, get some fresh oxygen into the mix. All Glitsky could smell was Dumpster, though. He lifted his glass, sucked in another cube, chewed some more.

Treya had gone back to Hardy's building. The big box from Elaine's condominium was there in the Solarium and she wanted to catalogue everything in it on the chance that something might jump out. The slim chance.

At this point, Glitsky felt they were all grasping at straws. Hardy and Freeman doing their legal hocus-pocus, Treya making lists, Jeff Elliot wanting to take down the district attorney. The kids remained enthusiastic, fascinated by the whole procedure. But they were, after all, lawyers. Hardy had them writing more motions about unconsciousness, temporary insanity, police misconduct. They were more interested in the courtroom strategies that might save Cole Burgess than they were in discovering who might have killed Elaine.

For Glitsky, this remained the focus. Someone had killed his daughter. He owed it to her—and to himself—to discover who it was.

What had begun as simple remorse over his own excesses had ripened into a genuine concern that a combination of malice and stupidity might possibly have ensnared the wrong man. And if it had, it was up to him—he was the only trained investigator on Hardy's dream team—to run down the right one.

Try as he might, he couldn't develop any warmth for the idea that it had been Jonas Walsh. The doctor had no alibi, true. He'd fibbed about the state of his relationship with Elaine. He was abrupt, distracted, uncooperative. In short, Glitsky had come to believe, he was in a state of grief, something of which he himself had a visceral knowledge. He recognized it intuitively, and while he would change his mind in an instant if any evidence came to light linking Jonas Walsh with Sunday night in San Francisco, he really didn't expect that to happen.

Likewise with Muhammed Adek. Glitsky had fifteen years' experience interviewing killers, and he came away from his Monday interview with the law student convinced that he wasn't involved. If he'd been less angry, if the sense of betrayal he obviously felt about Elaine had been less acute, maybe he would have felt differently. But even after he identified himself as a cop—administrative leave or not, that's what he was—Muhammed hadn't attempted to downplay any of his feelings as killers tended to do. The boy had been in love with her and she'd chosen another man, and while this could be a motive for murder, it didn't comport well with what Abe thought he knew about the last night of Elaine's life.

Plus—and this was key—from everything Treya had told him, Elaine would have been far more specific with her on Sunday afternoon if she had been going out to meet with Muhammed. "But she would never have met with him in the first place, Abe. And if she'd somehow gotten talked into it, she wouldn't have just said she was going to a meeting, believe me. She would have mentioned him by name, and not flatteringly. There was no way."

Glitsky agreed with her. His theory was simple. Elaine's killer was at least a cordial business acquaintance, maybe a good deal more than that. They'd had dinner, or perhaps done something more intimate. But Abe believed in his guts that the crime wasn't one of passion. It wasn't about jilted love or domestic upheaval. It was a cold-blooded contingency that had become a necessity, then been acted on decisively.

He crunched another cube, drummed his fingers on the table, checked his watch. "Come on, Paul," he said aloud.

"I'm here." Inspector Paul Thieu, with another man in tow, slid into the booth across from him. "Sorry I'm late. Lieutenant, this is Jan Falk. Narcotics."

"Abe," Glitsky said. He reached across the table, shook hands. "Nice to meet you. I assume Paul told you I'm on leave at the moment, maybe forever."

Falk badly needed a shave and the Dumpster smell seemed suddenly stronger. He wore a roguish grin. "Sometimes I wish I was. No, *always* I wish I was. Except now, maybe. So what's goin' down?"

Glitsky turned to check the room another time. It had filled up nicely for lunch. There was camouflage in the numbers and the noise. Still, he leaned in across the table so he wouldn't have to speak too loudly. "Paul says you know something about Ridley Banks."

Falk shrugged. "I don't know what I know, tell you the truth. Monday I heard he'd gone missing and I remembered him from last week, some OD case in the Mish. Long story how we got together, but he was on to something and I thought you guys—homicide—might be interested, but maybe not. I couldn't even get a callback."

Thieu piped in. "The place is a disaster, Lieutenant. You wouldn't believe it."

"I bet I would."

Thieu felt he had to give Glitsky some feel for it. "They haven't put anybody in your chair, even temporarily. Nobody's fielding calls, everybody's out all the time. The car's driving full speed and nobody's at the wheel."

"You're breaking my heart," Abe said. Then, back to Falk. "So what happened?"

But he couldn't get right to it. Lou came by for their orders, recommending the special, which today was a dish called Yeanling Clay Bowl. Thieu looked up at him. "Yeanling? What's a yeanling?"

"I don't know," Lou admitted. "It's got rice noodles with lamb and some kind of sauce. Really good, though. I'll put you down for three of them, okay?"

Glitsky saw they had consensus. "Okay, three bowls," he said.

"It doesn't come in a bowl," Lou explained. "That's just the name of it. Yeanling Clay Bowl. From back where they originally made it someplace. My wife could tell you all about it, but she's busy right now."

"I got an idea, Lou," Glitsky said.

"What?"

A tight smile. "Go make her busier, okay."

Lou got the message and disappeared. Abe looked at Falk. "You were trying to talk to somebody in homicide."

"Right. So after a day, nobody's called me back and I ask around and Banks is still missing. So I decide I'll go down to the Hall in person and see what's the problem."

"The problem," Thieu interjected, "is that nobody's in charge. Sorry, go ahead."

"So I go in and there's Paul and I start to talk to him a little about this . . ."

". . . and I take it upstairs, the chief's office himself, and what do they tell me?" Thieu's voice had thickened in outrage. "That Banks is a missing person. He's not a homicide. Go back downstairs and do my job. If it turns out he's dead, then I can worry about it. Can you believe these guys? So anyway, Abe, this is about when I remember you'd called me about Rid, wanting to reach him at home. I figured maybe you'd know something."

Falk picked up. "Then they're talking about Ridley on the news. What he's working on, about him being the main witness in this Elaine Wager case, and this OD is part of that, too."

"That's true," Glitsky said. "So what was he on to, you think?"

Falk finally had a clear field to run on, and he took off. The operation that narcotics had been running out of Jupiter, Cullen Alsop's appearance at the bar, Falk and Banks bopping Damien together, Gene Visser the ex-cop possibly being a source of heroin. "That's what Banks really sparked to. If Visser had been there in the flophouse with the kid."

"Then what?" Glitsky asked.

"I don't know," Falk replied. "But if this kid was a snitch . . . the thing about being dead is it's a lot harder to change your story."

"A lot harder," Thieu agreed.

"But you can't testify either, so what good's the snitch to begin with?" Glitsky was chomping more ice now, thinking. When he swallowed it, he spoke. "I got a question, Jan. You hear on TV that this is part of the Wager thing. You know the hearing's going on right now. How come you don't go to the D.A.?"

Falk almost spit his tea across the table. "You know how many times me and my guys are putting something together for like a year, wrapped up nice and tight? Righteous busts, dealers in the slammer, good shit. Then two weeks later it's all over. The case has mysteriously fallen apart. Or it's not charged. Or some fucking thing. My dealers are sprung and I'm made on the street and gotta start over someplace else. And half the time my snitches have been exposed and I'm on the line for that." He drank iced tea, calmed down slightly. "It's got so . . . you know what I do now? I go direct to the A.G."—the state attorney general. "If they don't want it, I've even been known to turn cases over to our generous brothers at the FB-One, even though they'll find some way I get no credit for the goddamn bust. But no way do I go to the D.A. No way!"

"That's who got the lieutenant busted," Thieu offered.

Falk broke a conspiratorial smile. "I think I heard something about that. I think I even heard you might be working on the other side."

"That's a vicious and ugly rumor," Glitsky said. "But if it's true, I got a friend you might want to talk to. Get on the same bus."

"And run over Pratt and Torrey? Where do I sign up?"

Glitsky nodded. "I think you just did."

"Here you are, gentlemen. Three Yeanling Clay Bowls."

Falk took Thieu's plate and passed it across. Then grabbed his own. "I hope it's rare," he said to Lou. "If there's one thing I can't stand, it's well-done yeanling."

This, Glitsky thought, was police work. Finally. This was how it was going to get done.

Astoundingly, no one had issued him a subpoena for the hearing—Torrey because he would be at best a hostile witness and had nothing to add that might help the prosecution case; Hardy because he simply figured Glitsky would be there anyway. He could call him as a witness at his pleasure.

When Glitsky left Falk and Thieu and got back into Department 20, the hearing had already resumed for the afternoon. From the little he heard, he gathered that the lawyers were yakking about how much of the videotape they were going to have to watch. As usual, it didn't appear they were going to get to an agreement anytime soon.

He tapped Treya on the shoulder and motioned that she should accompany him. She took his hand in the hallway, and they walked through the lobby and all the way outside to the steps of the Hall—the day still warm, without any breeze.

"God." She inhaled with pleasure, her face up to the sun. "You know what this reminds me of? I had a teacher—Mrs. Barile—in junior high in lovely Daly City, where we'd get a day like this about every seventeen years, and I remember one time we did. For just one period, English, this time of day, right after lunch, Mrs. Barile, she took us all outside and we sat on the grass and she read out loud to us. The shirt scene from Gatsby. You know that one? Where Daisy cries? Anyway . . ." Treya suddenly looked embarrassed. "Sorry. I just had that same feeling again. That's not what you wanted."

"Actually, it's pretty close to exactly what I wanted." Glitsky felt he could have listened to her all day. They could stand here on the steps of the Hall of Justice and she could tell him all the good feelings she'd ever felt in her life. For the first time in half a decade, he was feeling them himself—a wash of something other than duty, persistence, cold honor. He still didn't trust them entirely, couldn't talk about them. But they were there. Warmth, hope, the future.

He wanted it too badly, and this, he believed, would guarantee that it would never last. So he returned to what he could live with, his comfort zone. "But it's not why I called you out from in there." He told her he was going to go try and have a talk with somebody, so he wouldn't be around if Hardy decided he was going to call him as a witness.

"This is from your meeting at lunch?"

He nodded, almost smiling. "I'm happy to report that the unit seems to be falling apart in my absence. Nobody's covering any bases except Paul Thieu and he's on my side. He's getting me copies of the lab stuff and crime scene report on Cullen Alsop. Meanwhile, there's this ex-cop that Ridley thinks might be involved somehow."

"You saw Ridley Banks? He's okay?"

This erased any sort of animation from Abe's face. "No. He told this to a guy in narcotics, and Thieu put us together."

"So who is this person? Did Ridley go see him?"

"No one knows, Trey."

"But he might have been the appointment he told Diz about."

"That's what I'm hoping."

Treya took a half step backwards, crossed her arms over her chest. She spoke with a slow precision. "That would have been the last time anybody heard from him."

"That's right." He knew what she was thinking. It was one of the fundamental moments. You got involved with a policeman, you accepted an elevated level of risk. Some people couldn't do it. Some people found out too late. But sooner or later, it always had to be dealt with.

"What's his name?" she asked.

"Gene Visser."

Another pause. "Maybe your friend Paul Thieu could go with you."

"Then nobody's watching the shop at all. Besides, I haven't even located him yet." He touched her arm lightly. "Trey, this is what I do. It's okay. How'd it go with your lunch?"

A shine had risen in her eyes. She spoke again with exaggerated care. "Please don't change the subject, Abe. What if this man killed Ridley?"

"Then he'd be a complete fool to try anything with me, wouldn't he? The first thing I'll do is tell him everybody knows where I went. I even logged it in."

"And that will protect you?"

"Well," he said, "you know, protection, the whole concept. There's really no such . . ." He stopped, his eyes suddenly filled with a kind of panic.

"What?"

"Nothing. I think maybe my yeanling didn't agree with me." He took a heavy breath.

"Abe? Are you all right?"

"Yeah," he said automatically. "Just a little . . ." Another breath. His hand went to his chest. "I think I'd better sit down."

In the courtroom, Judge Hill was about to rule on the admissibility of the confession. Hardy had been arguing that they should watch all six hours of interrogation on videotape. He wanted to get to the coercion issue now, before trial.

Torrey objected. "Your honor, the movies are full of wonderful performances by people who are apparently drunk or high on drugs. We can watch Mr. Burgess on tape all day long and still never get to anything approaching proof that he was in fact under the influence of anything. He was never tested for drunkenness. Perhaps, as you say, he was in the early stages of heroin withdrawal . . ."

Hardy chimed in. "And as such, your honor, would have said anything, he would have done anything . . ."

Hill used his gavel. "Don't interrupt the bench again, counselor. I've read your arguments in motion form. Just because defendant perhaps had motivation to lie does not demonstrate that he did in fact lie. If you have nothing new to add, I'm standing on my ruling. You can take it up again if this hearing results in a trial."

The bad blood between Hardy and Hill was so thick that Freeman felt compelled to intervene. "Your honor, if I may approach."

Hill sighed in frustration. This argument had already been going on for more than a half hour. He'd made his ruling. And suddenly now the old lion was coming out of his cave. "All right, Mr. Freeman."

David stood up slowly. As protocol demanded, all four attorneys made their way to the front. "Your honor," Freeman began, "as you know, we have prepared a brief outlining internal inconsistencies within the alleged confession itself."

"As you say, counselor, I know that. I have read it."

"Then, your honor, with all respect, we'd like to object further to the confession on foundational grounds. Who can say if this is a complete, unaltered copy of the tape unless Inspector Banks will testify?"

"Your honor!" Pratt and Torrey, in unison.

Hill held up a peremptory hand and glared at them. "Mr. Freeman, the defense has just been arguing for the better part of an hour that the court should sit through six hours of the defendant's videotaped testimony on the coercion issue. Now you're saying we shouldn't see any of it? Am I getting this right?"

Freeman's calm was unnerving. "Even if it weren't so fatally flawed," he said, "the officer who took the confession isn't available to swear to the tape's authenticity and completeness."

The prosecution fumed and sputtered. Other officers, including several homicide inspectors, had been around and even in and out of the interrogation room. They could say the tape was accurate. The tape looked full and complete. It was self-authenticating. A technician could say the tape was unedited. Behind them bubbled a cauldron of static. For a second, it seemed that everyone in the courtroom was speaking at once. Then Hill's gavel—*bam, bam*—cracked through it all like a gunshot and created an equally deafening silence. Hill had had enough. He glowered at all the attorneys, out over them to the crowd beyond the rail. He spoke brusquely. "The court will take a half-hour recess to consider these and other matters."

Without another word, he stood and left the room.

•   •   •

"Diz!" Jeff Elliot was wheeling himself furiously up the hallway.

Hardy had his hand on the door to the rest room and stopped. "What?"

"Did you hear that siren before that last argument?"

"I didn't hear anything."

"I did. I went out and checked. It was Abe."

"What was Abe?" Though of course he knew. Uttering an oath of despair, he broke for the lobby at a run.

33

Glitsky wasn't on anybody's witness list. He wasn't part of the hearing. He wasn't a member of Hardy's immediate family. So Hill would not excuse Hardy for the afternoon.

Aside from that, the session picked up more or less where it left off. After a series of suitable disclaimers, most notably that he was *not* ruling on the claim of police coercion, and that he most specifically was *not* ruling the tape inadmissible if the case went to trial, Hill announced that they would not in fact be viewing the videotape. Freeman's argument had merit, he said, and he didn't want to get into an open-ended discussion on the form and content of the tape. And if he didn't admit the tape for lack of foundation, he wouldn't have to deal with the coercion/intoxication issue either. He had plenty of other evidence to hold Burgess over for trial.

Torrey and Pratt kept at it for ten minutes, and finally settled for the court's unspoken but unmistakably clear intention to hold the defendant to answer without the tape. All in all, Hardy wasn't sure that Freeman had done their client a service by getting the judge to leave out the tape. Now, from the hearing's point of view, nothing in the record contradicted or even mitigated the force of the circumstantial evidence. And they didn't have the tape issue for appeal. Hill had come to his decision to keep things moving along here. Up to now, the evidence presented was plenty to send Cole to trial.

But Hardy was finding it difficult to keep his mind on the hearing, and he had to trust Freeman's instincts. He knew nothing about Glitsky, not even where they'd taken him. He didn't know where he'd gone for lunch, whom he'd met. He didn't know where Treya was, although he assumed she had gone with him in the ambulance.

Jeff Elliot was going to find out about Abe. He'd know soon enough. He had to put it out of his mind.

There was no time. The prosecution had rested. Hill's latest mistreatment had him in high dudgeon, a whiteout of a rage. He didn't trust himself to speak. But *right now* he had to begin the presentation of his affirmative defense. *Right now* he had to call his first witness.

He was looking at the notes in front of him and heard himself croak out the first name he read: Sergeant Billie Oh, who'd supervised the crime scene unit in Maiden Lane. As she came up through the bar rail and took the oath, Hardy's couldn't muster his thoughts to remember what he'd intended to ask her.

He was still seated at his table. Everyone was waiting.

"Mr. Hardy?" The Cadaver appeared all out of patience himself—if he'd had any to begin with.

"Sorry, your honor." He was on his feet, moving toward the bench, the witness. Words were coming out of his mouth. "Sergeant Oh. Can you describe for the court, please, the position of Elaine Wager's body when you came upon the scene of her death."

The prosecution immediately and vociferously objected. The defense could only present evidence that went to an affirmative defense or contradicted the prosecution case. This was not a deposition, they argued. How could this possibly show that the defendant was not guilty?

Hill had cut Hardy as deeply as he was going to, however. The confession was out, the defendant was going to trial, and Hill wasn't inclined to risk any assignment of error. Hardy could do his damnedest within any reasonable or unreasonable limits. It wouldn't matter. Hill overruled all the objections.

Ms. Oh was a precise and careful witness, and briefly recounted her facts and impressions without inflection or comment. This was what she saw; this was how it was. When she'd finished, Hardy had recovered enough of his bearings at least to be able to begin. "Was Ms. Wager wearing hosiery, Sergeant?"

"Yes, she was. Black nylons."

"And what was the condition of these nylons?"

Oh thought for a moment. "They were in good condition. Damp

where they touched the pavement as the body lay there and of course in the crotch where she'd lost her urine."

"Was there any damage to the fabric itself?"

"No."

"No runs in the nylon? No threads coming loose?"

"No."

"They were in very good condition?"

"Yes."

"Sergeant Oh," Hardy continued. "Did it occur to you that the victim fell heavily after she was shot?"

"As opposed to what?"

"To being, for example, let down easily by her assailant?"

"Objection. Calls for a conclusion."

"Sustained. Another line, please, Mr. Hardy."

He was racking his brain for anything else. He certainly hadn't gotten any rhythm established with Sergeant Oh, and now couldn't remember why, in fact, he'd wanted to call her at all. He believed that whoever had shot Elaine had laid her down, and that this once had seemed incompatible with the rough treatment she'd received when Cole had taken her jewelry. But now that distinction seemed tenuous at best, frivolous at worst.

He walked back to his table, consulted his notes, hoped David would come to his rescue with some suggestion, anything. But the old man simply shrugged. Win some, lose some.

Hardy turned around. "Thank you, Sergeant." To Torrey's table: "Your witness."

The prosecutor stood up and walked to the witness box, taking his time, but Hardy didn't have the sense he was stalling. Certainly, as soon as he stopped walking, he asked his question. "Sergeant Oh, from the position of Ms. Wager's body, as well as the state of her hosiery, would you rule out the possibility that her assailant had forced her to kneel down before he executed her in cold blood?"

"No, sir, I couldn't." Then she volunteered her first sentence. "That was the impression I had from the beginning."

He had to remain in court, but he wasn't doing his client any good with inept questioning of his own witnesses. With the myriad of details he'd been trying to absorb over the past week, to say nothing of his immediate concern over Glitsky, he'd overlooked at least one other very much more obvious and ominous interpretation of the facts.

At the beginning of it all, Glitsky had put the bug in his ear about Elaine's killer breaking her fall and he'd come to accept it as the truth. And Torrey had just killed him on it. He had to be more careful, but he wasn't sure that he had it in him.

Again he stood. Again he called a witness. "Daniel Medrano." This time he wondered if he should pass the questioning off to Freeman, but before he'd made any conscious decision, he was moving toward the witness box.

"Officer Medrano, you and your partner were the first unit on the scene, were you not?"

The policeman could have been Stalin's twin—the square and swarthy face, the heavy black mustache. He appeared nervous on the stand, possibly because of his inclusion as a defense witness. Hardy knew from his earlier interview with him that this was the most notorious crime he had worked in his years as a cop. But there was no help for that.

"Yes, we were."

"Can you tell the court exactly what you saw?"

"Sure. My partner, Officer Petrie, and I were cruising downtown and we came upon a figure hunched over another one in Maiden Lane. We hit him with our searchlight, and a man turned and began to run. I was on the passenger side and got out, identified myself as a police officer and took off in pursuit."

"Go on."

"He had maybe ten yards on me, but it was pretty dark, and he ran into a fire hydrant and went sprawling and I was able to apprehend him and put on handcuffs."

"And do you recognize the man you caught that night in this courtroom?"

"Yes. The defendant Cole Burgess, over there."

"All right. Now, Officer Medrano, in the course of this chase, did you hear anything unusual?"

"Yes, sir."

"Would you please tell the court what that was?"

"Well . . ." This was the part Medrano hated. It disagreed with his partner's report (although not his testimony, since Torrey had neglected to ask him about it), but to his credit he delivered it straight. "There was a gunshot about when the suspect went down. Then I heard the gun clatter on the street, and I eventually saw it and brought it back with me."

"Are you saying the defendant shot at you?"

"No, I don't think so. He didn't stop or turn. He was just running and hit the hydrant and went sailing and the gun went off, like, when he hit the ground."

"Are you certain it was a gunshot, and not a car backfiring or something like that?"

"It was a gunshot. I saw the flash. I even heard the ricochet. It was a gunshot," he repeated.

"All right, Officer Medrano. Thank you."

For some reason that Hardy couldn't fathom, Pratt rose this time for the prosecution's cross-examination.

"A couple of small clarifications, Officer," she began gently, with a welcoming smile. "You and your partner, Officer Petrie, discussed this gunshot, didn't you?"

"He didn't hear it. He was in the—"

Pratt held up a hand, stopping him. "You discussed it?"

"Yes."

"And he said he didn't hear it?"

"Yes."

"Thank you." Another smile. "Now. When you came upon the defendant hovering over the body in the alley, did you see him reach to pick up anything in the street?"

Medrano was back visualizing the moment. "No."

"You don't remember him reaching down into the gutter and picking up any object. Say, the gun, for example?"

"No."

"So he must have been holding the gun already, isn't that so?"

"He must have. Then he just stood up and started running."

Hardy spoke up. "Objection. Speculation. Calls for a conclusion."

The Cadaver sustained him, struck the answer.

Pratt went sailing right along. "Did the defendant run well?"

A genial grunt. Medrano was back testifying for the right side, and he was much more comfortable. "Way better than me."

"In fact, Officer Medrano, was the defendant pulling away from you when he ran into the fire hydrant?"

"Yes. He was fast."

"He wasn't staggering or lurching or anything like that then?"

"No. The guy was a bullet."

"A bullet. Thank you, Officer. No further questions."

Jeff Elliot had been working without any merit raise for the past three years, and he decided this was as good a time as any to demand one. He and his editor were already discussing things, and he thought he might be back at work as early as next week. In the meantime, though, the *Examiner* had delighted and surprised him by making him an offer to bring "CityTalk" to them. The *Democrat* notwithstanding, the *Examiner* was the *Chronicle*'s afternoon competitor, and Jeff thought a guest column or two in it would dramatically enhance his negotiations with the *Chronicle*.

Besides, Hardy and Freeman had handed him the column at lunch. Now, midafternoon on Wednesday, he was in the reporter's lounge on the third floor of the Hall of Justice, typing on a manual from the notes he'd taken a couple of hours before. The *Examiner* was paying him a full week's wages for the one column. He was smiling as he wrote.

CityTalk
By Jeffrey Elliot

In the interests of full disclosure, I hereby reveal that lawyer Dismas Hardy is a personal acquaintance of mine, even a friend. Currently he is defending my brother-in-law, Cole Burgess, in a preliminary hearing in Department 20 of Municipal Court. Cole is charged with the murder of Elaine Wager. The prosecution is being handled by the district attorney herself, Sharron Pratt, and by her chief assistant and majordomo, Gabriel Torrey. Mr. Hardy is one of the sources of some of the information contained in this column.

When he is not personally trying murder cases, Mr. Torrey's day-to-day work involves overseeing the flow of civil and criminal cases brought through the district attorney's office before the courts. In this role, he is in a unique position to assign cases to the courts' calendars, to settle disputes without reference to the courts, and to either dismiss criminal cases outright (for any number of reasons, including lack of evidence, police misconduct, inability to locate witnesses, etc.), or to negotiate plea bargains. His word is law to every D.A. in the office, except Sharron Pratt.

This reporter has learned of at least two instances where a criminal case has been brought by Ms. Pratt's office against an individual who was also being sued in a civil matter. In both cases, Mr. Torrey offered to broker a deal whereby the district attorney would drop the criminal charges in exchange for a large dollar settlement in the civil matter. The attorney handling the civil matters in both cases is Dash Logan, one of the city's more colorful and controversial figures.

(Regular readers of this column in the *Chronicle* might remember the story of Mr. Logan's brief arrest last year after a short car chase that ensued after his car ran a red light, narrowly missing two pedestrians in front of the Virgin Records building on Market. The district attorney declined to press charges related to this incident for two reasons: the brakes in Mr. Logan's car appeared to have been tampered with—he apparently could not have stopped if he wanted to; and the blood-alcohol report was mislaid.)

Today's column will describe the first of these cases. Tomorrow's will deal with the second case, and a set of circumstances startlingly similar to the first.

Rich McNeil is a sixty-four-year-old vice president of Terranew Industries here in town. He owns a six-story apartment building on the . . .

The open hallway outside the courtroom. Hardy double-timing to the phones. He had to find out. A young Asian man, vaguely familiar, tapping him on the shoulder. "Paul Thieu," he said, extending a hand. "Homicide."

It had been an excruciating fifteen minutes since Hill had adjourned court for the day. Hardy felt the heat in his face and knew that his blood pressure was off the charts, the endless minutiae made unbearable by his haste to get away. But he had had to stay around to give his client encouragement, instruct his troops. Freeman, Jody, Jeff Elliot.

He'd finally closed his briefcase, made excuses. He really had to go. Now.

And now this. He steeled himself to ask. "Have you heard from Glitsky?"

A nod. "I know where he is. They took him back to St. Mary's, even though it was farther away. They wanted him to have the same doctor."

"Any word beyond that?"

"The hospital couldn't tell me anything. I called the ambulance company—I called all the ambulance companies 'til I got the right one. He was alive when he hit the ER."

"Thanks." Hardy was moving again.

"Mr. Hardy!" Thieu closed the gap between them. "I had lunch with Abe today," he said quietly. "I'd be grateful if you could go with me out to my car in the back." He read Hardy's reluctance, his impatience. "Abe thought it might be important, and he's not going anywhere, you know."

The simple truth of it hit him. "You're right."

"This way."

They took the inside steps to the back door, walked the long corridor that took them by the jail and Dr. Strout's office, got to a beat-up old orange Datsun in the lot. Thieu looked around—they were the only people back here. He went to the passenger door and opened it up. "Hop in," he said.

Hardy did as he was told. Thieu was on the driver's side and started the engine. "If your car's around here, I'll take you to it." In the still-warm gathering dusk, they pulled out of the lot.

Thieu reached into his jacket and pulled out a few pages, folded into thirds. He handed them to Hardy.

"What are these?"

"Glitsky asked for them. It's the lab and crime scene report on the Cullen Alsop overdose. I'm afraid there's no smoking gun, though, at least not one that I see. But he wanted to go through it with a comb."

"Glitsky wanted these? Turn left up here. What for?"

Thieu hung the turn, glanced across the seat. "I'm not sure. Maybe he thought Visser would have left some trace, maybe a print, I don't know. But no such luck."

Hardy sat up. The jolt felt almost like electricity. "Visser? Gene Visser?"

"Yeah."

"What about him?"

Another glance, maybe to see if Hardy was teasing him. But Paul recognized genuine intensity when he saw it, and he thought maybe

Hardy's look at the moment could penetrate steel. "You don't know any of this?"

"I know Gene Visser," Hardy said, "but I don't know what he's got to do with Cullen Alsop."

Paul Thieu put his foot on the brake. "We've got to pull over a minute," he said. "Have a little talk."

34

Dressler's syndrome," Abe explained. "It's like a heart attack, only better, in the sense that it's not a heart attack."

"A lot better," Treya agreed. "Way, way better."

It was now just after six-thirty at night, and they were gathered around the kitchen table back at Glitsky's place. Raney and Orel were doing homework in front of the television set in the back room, and the laugh track filtered up to the kitchen.

When Hardy had finished with Thieu, his mind reeling with the possibilities, and finally got back to his car, he made it out to St. Mary's in twenty minutes only to find that Glitsky had been examined by Dr. Campion, given a few tests and then, after a couple of hours, released.

Hardy had called Frannie from the hospital and she told him that she'd heard from Abe and he was all right. He'd gone home. Even though it was Date Night, Hardy drove straight there and found Glitsky sitting up. Dressed. Finishing dinner. Hardy wanted to punch his lights out for all the worry he'd put him through. "I called," Glitsky said. "I left messages everywhere."

He was fine. His doctor told him that there was probably some inflammation in the membrane near the area of his heart attack, that was all. Dressler's syndrome, which mimicked the symptoms of a heart attack, was not uncommon in patients who'd had a real one. Glitsky was taking some new medication for it now, and the worrisome chest pain should be completely gone in a couple of days.

Meanwhile, the connections in this case had started to present themselves and a sense of urgency hung in the room. Hardy handed over Thieu's lab reports to Glitsky, saying, "You know those chemists who used to predict that an element should exist because it fit the theory? And then they find it? That's what I'm feeling like around this."

"With Visser?"

"No. With Dash Logan."

Abe and Treya exchanged looks. "I give up," Abe said.

Tightly wound, Hardy had been standing all this time. Now he pulled a chair around and straddled it backwards. "In one way, this ties up the whole package," he said. "This puts Visser with Torrey with Logan. They're all together."

Glitsky was half reading excerpts of the lab stuff, and now he abandoned them and sat back in his chair. "All together in what?"

Hardy, eyes alight with his enthusiasm, ran down the list of his suspicions. Torrey, Logan and Visser constituted a triumvirate that were working together to settle cases by coercion. Certainly, they had all figured overtly in Hardy's dealings with Rich McNeil. Hardy wouldn't be at all surprised to learn, and he intended to put one of the musketeers on it tomorrow, that the private investigator who'd dug up the alleged dirt on Gina Roake's client Abby Oberlin had been Visser as well. That case was Logan's, too—he was acting on behalf of Abby's brother on the will contest. And then Torrey comes up with a settlement offer on that. "Now finally we get Visser with Cullen Alsop."

"Okay, that's Visser, but I'm missing something," Treya said. "How is Logan with Cullen, then?"

A smile of triumph. "He was at Jupiter, drinking with Visser, when Cullen picked up his payment."

"The bag of heroin?" Glitsky said.

"Exactly. This all fits, Abe. They're together in this. They've got to be."

Glitsky the cop clucked, unconvinced. "That old 'got to be.' You'd be surprised how often it doesn't. Are you saying you think one of these clowns killed Cullen?"

"Visser supplied him with uncut smack. He used it. He died. I'd call that killing him."

"But why would they do that?" Treya asked.

"Because Torrey had fed him a false story about Elaine's murder weapon. My own belief is that Cullen never even had possession of the gun, much less gave it to Cole. But Torrey needed that fact. Then Cullen got greedy, or stupid, or they suddenly realized that as a witness, the kid was going to suck. He'd crack under any kind of vigorous cross. Maybe he'd sell them out as easily as he sold out Cole. Or maybe Torrey set up Cullen as a witness without telling Visser. And Visser vetoed the plan by helping Cullen OD. So, totally unreliable junkie, completely expendable, adios."

Glitsky remained skeptical, to say the least. "You're saying the chief assistant district attorney of the city and county of San Francisco had him killed?"

"Somebody did."

"Lord. Creativity thrives here in the new millennium." Glitsky's arms were crossed, the scar tight through his lips. "And the proof of any of this is . . . ?"

Hardy acknowledged the problem with a nod. "It's out there somewhere. We just haven't found it."

Abe flicked the lab report. "Well, it's not here. Not that I see. No sign that Visser was even there."

"Except for what Falk saw."

"Which was nothing. I asked. Falk saw Cullen go to the bathroom at Jupiter and then Visser go into the same bathroom, which, last time I checked, was legal."

"But," Treya interjected, "then why were you going to see Visser this afternoon, Abe? You must have thought something similar."

Glitsky answered gently. "I wanted to ask him about Ridley, that's all."

But Hardy couldn't let it go. "This would be the same Ridley who told me that wherever he was going on that last night, it was on this? Those were his words, 'on this.' On Cullen and, therefore, on Elaine."

"And it might have been, that last visit. But we don't know *that* was Visser either, do we?"

Hardy's face was set. "It's got to be."

"That's where we started here, Diz. Got to be, got to be. When the fact is it doesn't have to be at all. Listen," he continued, "it's not like I don't think it's well argued and provocative, but I haven't even caught a whiff of one piece of evidence."

A long silence settled, everyone in their thoughts. Finally, Treya broke it. "I've got a question, Diz."

Hardy looked into her face. "Six one, one eighty-three."

"A silly little grin coursing the features of his copper-lined face," Glitsky added. He covered her hand on the table with his own. "Never tell this guy you got a question. He always does that."

"Not always," Hardy argued. "Sometimes I say, 'I've got an answer,' and then you go, 'What is it?' and I say, 'Babe Ruth, 1927,' or 'The circumference divided by the diameter.' Something like that."

"It's really fun," Abe said in a monotone. "You'd be surprised."

"I bet I would," Treya replied. "That, for example, just now, was more fun than I've had all day."

"See what I mean?" Glitsky asked. "It's always like that. It never ends."

"Okay," Hardy relented. "What's the real question?"

Treya hesitated, but she had to ask. "Are you saying you think maybe one of these three people killed Elaine?"

And for this—finally, the crux of it—Hardy had to stop and think. "I think while she was doing her special master work, she found something incriminating at Logan's office. Logan, drunk or coked up or both, just turned her loose on his files. Both of you told me that, remember? Anyway, I think what she found was the kind of evidence we've been talking about here, the proof that Abe says we don't have about what these guys have been doing." He paused. "I don't know what happened then. Maybe she threatened Torrey with exposure, or asked Logan what was going on. Or they just realized she must have seen something."

"And what, then? Visser killed her?" Abe had his arms crossed again. He was at full length in the chrome-and-weave kitchen chair, his legs outstretched. A muscle in his jaw clenched and unclenched.

"I don't know," Hardy said. Then added somberly, "Maybe he killed Ridley, too."

"We don't know that Ridley's dead yet," Treya said hopefully.

Hardy looked at her levelly. "Yes we do," he said softly. "Abe?"

Glitsky nodded. "Probably."

"Well, then . . ." She looked from one to the other. "We should . . ."

"Same problem," Glitsky said. "We need evidence. And Visser used to be a homicide inspector. He knows the tricks. He isn't going to leave much."

Hardy stood, went over to the refrigerator and opened it up, then stopped and turned. "I've got one for you, Treya. Are any of the muske-teers on the special master list?"

She rubbed her eyes. "All of them, I think. We were talking about it. Why?"

"Because the case Elaine was working on in Logan's office is still open. I checked with Thomasino. It might be worth taking a look."

"Do it!" Glitsky came forward excitedly, up on his feet.

Hardy gave him a baleful look. "I've got to check for sure, but I think I've got other commitments over the next day or two." Then, to Treya: "But I'm thinking one of the kids . . ."

Hardy was gone at last and Rita kicked Abe and Treya out of the kitchen so she could do the dinner dishes. Together in the cramped liv-ing room with barely room to turn around without touching one an-other, they cast about for the better part of five minutes, looking for ways to ignore the sexual tension that hummed like a guy wire between them. Since the first night, they hadn't even kissed, and in those first moments, that is all they had done.

Treya found her purse and pulled out the two sheets of folded paper she'd torn from the yellow legal pad she'd been using at lunch. "You were talking to Diz about evidence, Abe, and you really haven't even looked at the box that Curtis brought back from Tiburon. There might be something there."

"I already looked in it."

"He said defensively."

"I'm not being defensive."

She gave him an expression he'd already come to think of as the thousand-year-old look, as though she'd known him that long.

"I did go through it, Trey," he insisted.

"And got to Loretta's picture and stopped, didn't you?"

In fact, he had taken it entirely out of the box in Hardy's build-ing and laid it facedown on the Solarium table. He didn't want to see Loretta's face, to be reminded of Elaine's mother, especially now that he was beginning to be involved with Treya. For the truth was, Loretta had been in his life more recently than a quarter century be-fore. Only four years ago, she had waltzed back in and from his per-spective tried to restake her ancient claim to his heart. And, starving for contact after Flo's death, he'd almost let her have it. It shamed him still—he didn't need the reminder of how close he'd come, how weak he'd been.

How for Loretta it had all been a calculated lie.

Treya was altogether different, he told himself. Nothing about her was the same. And she was right—he was being foolishly defensive. He held out his hand, the corners of his mouth up fractionally. "Okay, let me see the darn list." He opened the pages and stopped immediately. "What's this first thing? Empty drawer?"

Their legs happened to be close enough to touch when she sat on the couch. "I didn't want to forget that, so I just wrote it first." She told him about the discussion when Curtis had first mentioned it.

"But what does it mean?" Abe asked.

"We couldn't figure it out, but all new theories are welcome."

Giving it a minute, he finally shrugged and went back to her list. She got up then, saying she was going in to check on the kids, maybe help Rita with the dishes. Treya wasn't comfortable with somebody else waiting on her. So she was in the kitchen, an apron around her, speaking reasonable Spanish to Glitsky's housekeeper and drying a serving platter, when Glitsky appeared back in the kitchen doorway. "At the bottom of the first page," he said. "What's this unknown key?" He crossed the kitchen and showed her what she'd written.

"Oh, I've got that," she said. "It's in my purse."

With apologies to Rita, she put down her towel and reappeared a minute later. "It was in the glove compartment of Elaine's car, which was parked down under R&J in the garage. Jon found it, I think, and threw it in the box. Do you know what it is?"

"Yeah," Glitsky said. "I think I do."

"We shouldn't be doing this anymore, Abe. It's almost eleven-thirty. You need to get some rest."

"I doubt it. I'm not going to get any rest anyway. Not until we find where this key goes."

"Are you sure it's a locker?"

A brisk nod. "Yep." Then he looked over at her, reached a hand across the seat to touch her thigh. "I'm sorry," he said, and added in a reasonable tone, "I can take you home and come back and do this myself."

She gave him the thousand-year look again, the long smile. "In your dreams, Lieutenant."

"That's not what I dream." He looked at her. "Besides, we can blame Rita. She kicked us out. It's her fault."

"She only kicked us as far as the living room."

"Where you had me look at your list, which brings us here."

"But the kids . . . ?"

"The kids are fine. If this turns out to be something, Trey, we need it yesterday, you know."

She nodded, accepting it. "I know."

"Well, then . . ."

The bus station was closest to his home and had by far the largest bank of lockers downtown, but Glitsky thought a better first bet might be the Union Square garage, a hundred yards from where Elaine had been killed. But the key fit none of the lockers there. Then, since they were so close, they walked a block to the Downtown Center Garage, with the same lack of result.

Glitsky knew this search was quite possibly futile and even stupid. It was the kind of thing that, as a lieutenant, if it was important enough, he would assign to three or four teams of officers, and give them a week. The city must have a couple of thousand rental lockers, maybe more, and it wasn't even certain that this key was from a San Francisco locker. But he felt he had to try. They might get lucky at the bus station as they swung by on the way home.

Close to midnight on a Wednesday night and the area around the bus station, he noted as he illegally parked, was in its usual gala finery. He hadn't had occasion to visit the place in five years, but it looked, smelled and felt now as it had back then.

He took Treya's hand against the vagrants and the noise, the pervasive loneliness and desperation. The loudspeaker cut through the Snoop Doggy Dogg rap to announce the arrival of a bus from Bakersfield, and a baby started crying on one of the plastic chairs over to his left. He and Treya shared a look, and decided that this was it. They would try again tomorrow. He could probably just go to Paul Thieu first thing, who would take one look at the key and tell him it was obvious from the distinctive red plastic top, upon which was printed the number 1138.

Which was there in front of them on the bottom row in the third bank back from the entrance. And suddenly the rap music and the crying and the smell of loneliness was gone.

He put the key in and turned.

Inside was a small, black, anonymous flight bag of the kind used by flight attendants. On top of that was a sheaf of stuff bound by a thick rubber band. Glitsky reached in and took it out into the light, stripping off the rubber band. On top was a passport, and under that a rather thick booklet of hundred-dollar traveler's checks. Then documents in an airline ticket pouch from Alitalia Airlines. "Did she mention going to Italy?"

Treya was counting the money, but she looked up from that, thought a moment, shook her head. "No."

Glitsky paused in his search. "You know what this is, don't you? This is the empty drawer." He began to flip through the rest of the pile, which seemed to consist mostly of envelopes—bills mostly—to the phone company, PG&E, a couple of credit cards, Macy's.

And then at the bottom, one last envelope, stamped, addressed in a firm hand, to Abraham Glitsky, at his home address.

Dear Lieutenant Glitsky (Abe?) (Dad?)—

Funny, isn't it? You know what I'm talking about although we've never talked about it. Isn't that funny? Or perhaps it isn't. Not really.

There is no return address on this letter because by the time you get it I'll be gone and where it came from will have no meaning. But now that I am gone, I wanted you to know that I don't plan to return. At least not soon. Maybe never.

Why do I want to tell you any of this? Because you are my only blood relative? Does blood even mean anything anymore? I don't know. There's so much I don't know. It makes me wonder what all the education was about, if it's left me so ignorant on the important things. You didn't have any part in raising me. The person I knew as my father, Dana, was older and distracted, but I think he must have suspected something and I can't say we were terribly close. Maybe this explains some of my problems with men, mostly older men. Hoping to get the affection of the father I never had? Again, I don't know.

I've reread this to here and realize that it sounds a little like I'm attaching some blame to you about all this, but please, it's not that. I know you had no idea about me until recently. I believe if you'd known you'd have taken some role—I just believe that. It seems to be who you are.

After you found out, and I knew that you knew, at first I didn't really understand why you didn't come to me. That's true. And it hurt me as I suppose you might imagine. But then eventually it came to feel right, that it was okay. We'd see each other at work from time to time and got along pretty well. I admired you, and think you felt the same about me. At least I hope you did.

You had your own family, your boys. See? I know all about them, my half brothers. But I had my life—busy and public and personally a mess. You didn't need any part of it, believe me. I think you made a wise decision. And with all the older men I was searching to connect with, who I'd try to please at work and then need to go further, make it personal—Chris Locke, then Gabe, Aaron Rand—well, I don't have to give you the litany, but these and so many more. Half my clients. And all of them went nowhere. They couldn't go anywhere. I was too needy and demanding and screwed up. I think that's really why I never came to you, either. It was the one sacred thing.

A part of me wishes that we could have talked, at least acknowledged what we were to each other, although something else tells me that this would have been a bad decision, too. Like so many of the rest of them.

I could somehow just keep you best by not saying anything. I could watch how you kept your dignity and handled the losses over Mom, over your wife. All the losses. And maybe I could learn something from that. I came to see it as though you were talking to me that way. By example. And as long as we had no acknowledged relationship, I could keep you as mine and not make all my usual mistakes. Does this make any sense?

The truth is, Abe, that I don't really fit in my life here and I never have. Oh, I know it seems like I did. My mother the senator and her connections. It was all laid out for me, who I was and what role I'd play. The politics. Who I'd become. So I finished law school and went right to work here for the D.A. and Chris Locke and I . . . well, you knew about that.

I thought he loved me. I know I did love him.

But after that—after Chris and Mom were dead—the bottom

just fell out. I'd done everything to please Mom, then to please Chris, and suddenly neither of them were there anymore and all the reasons I had for doing what I was doing just disappeared.

And then the awful truth began to emerge that I wasn't who they thought I was after all. I'd never been that person inside. But I'd also never taken any time for myself, to figure things out that if I wasn't that, then what was I?

The only thing I knew, the only reference I'd ever lived with, was Mom's, and she was happy with it because it was who she was, this political animal. She got her identity and self-worth by her causes and issues, by keeping busy and connected. You volunteered, you did good works, you fought for the oppressed, and that was the secret to a happy life.

But Abe, it wasn't my life. It was Loretta's, and then suddenly she was gone and I was the heir apparent, having to live it, to be it. To be the reincarnation of my mother, full-time, full-bore. Everybody wanted me to step in, fill her shoes, continue her work.

It's not the kind of thing you realize right away, that you're living a lie, that the whole thing isn't you. But you get enough headaches and cramps and you stop sleeping because you're living two or three separate—no, contradictory—lives. And eventually, even if you're not the most insightful person in the world, a few years go by and you start to get a clue.

But what do you do? All the tapes are running. You can't just drop everything at once. Especially if your entire personality is that you aim to please. You tell some school where you volunteer to teach or a neighborhood council you're organizing or even your boss that you need to cut back on your workload and get some time and perspective, and it's like you're speaking a foreign language. Give us just one more class, Elaine, one more term on the board, one more high-profile client.

And if you're me, when it finally comes to it, you agree to stay on. Because you need their approval. All their approvals. In your deepest heart, you need them to like you. You're nothing if you're not pleasing someone. You need to be loved. So you tell yourself . . .

No, not you, I.

So I kept telling myself it would be soon. I'd stop for a while, step off the treadmill. Nothing so drastic as a complete change

*of career, but a long vacation to figure out a new plan, a different
approach.*

And meanwhile, every single day, so miserably unhappy.

*I'm cheating on my fiancé; he's cheating on me. My boss is betraying me. I find out that another one of my mentors, who in the
past I trusted, confided in, worked with, depended on, even, of
course, slept with—here's another betrayal, more cheating. Now
there was no integrity even in the system that I'd worked so hard
on behalf of, that I still wanted to believe in. But no longer could.
The whole thing—the career, my private life, the law itself, Abe—
none of it was working.*

*And suddenly I know I couldn't take another hit. I was in the
wrong place, doing the wrong things. It was going to kill me.*

I had to change it all.

*I couldn't tell a soul, not even my dear paralegal, a woman
named Treya Ghent—she'd be wise and tell me I could stay and
change and work things out, but I don't believe that's true. Not
anymore. I've lost all my faith in this life. There was so much I
couldn't even tell her. Cheating on Jonas. Other things. I couldn't
have borne her disapproval most of all.*

*So I'm gone. It is the right thing and I am happy. A clean
break, no explanations to anyone with their agendas for me.*

Except this to you.

It isn't anything to do with you.

*Love, your daughter,
Elaine*

They both read it in the bus station, then took the packet and the
suitcase out to the car. On the way home, they started to dissect the startling revelations. Elaine had been leaving the country anyway? The
Alitalia ticket was for a 6:15 A.M. flight the morning after she'd been
shot. Gabe Torrey? Aaron Rand, Clarence Jackman's partner? Half her
clients? But eventually, the weight of it all became too much and they
both fell silent.

The duplex was still. When they got in, they discovered that Raney
had crashed on the sofa in front of the tube. Orel had gone into his
room and now slept, fully clothed and openmouthed, on the top of his

bed. Out in the dark living room, Rita snored lightly on her fold-a-bed in the corner behind her Pier 1 Imports faux Japanese screen.

They read it again, this time together, at Glitsky's kitchen table, the one light on directly over their heads. When they got to the last line, Treya put a hand over Abe's and squeezed it. She read it aloud. "It isn't anything to do with you."

"I know that," he said. "My mind knows that." He let out a long breath. "Tell me it's too late to call Diz, would you."

She looked behind him at the clock above the oven—12:20. "It's too late to call Diz," she said. "Do you think the other man, the betrayal of the system she talks about, was Gabe Torrey?"

"Yep. I think she found something at Dash Logan's."

"Just as Dismas said."

"Maybe. Parts of it."

She tapped the letter. "So what do you want to do with this?"

Glitsky shook his head. It was a serious consideration. "I don't know."

"Well, it was addressed to you . . ."

"I know. If she'd dropped it in a mailbox and it got delivered, it would be my property and I could keep it." He sighed. "But she didn't get to do that."

"So it's got to be evidence?"

"Oh, it's evidence all right. If I was working as a cop right now . . ." He paused, pushed back his chair and turned toward her. "But forget the legalities, Trey. This is personal. I'd really like to know what you think."

She faced him and said, "If making it public would correct some of the problems she wrote about, she'd want you to show it."

The corners of his mouth lifted slightly. "I keep waiting for you to come up with a wrong answer."

"Raney does, too." Her tired eyes sparked for an instant. "You'll have to get in line. So meanwhile, what do we do?"

Glitsky knew the answer to that. "Diz has got to get it in front of the judge. If she was sleeping with half her clients, if she was leaving the country the next day . . ."

"Then it need not have been random."

"No," he said heavily. "It never was."

Abe stared at the floor between his shoes. A shiver went through him and he lifted his face, inches now from hers. "You know my problem?"

"What's your problem?"

"A lot of times, like with Elaine, I don't say things when I should."

She reached out and cupped his hands in hers. Met his eyes. Waited.

"But I've got to ask you . . ."

She brought her mouth to his, her hands to his face. When she pulled away ten seconds later, she whispered to him, "That would be a yes."

35

In the minutes before Department 20 convened, the Cadaver's chambers vibrated with anger and accusations. Torrey was on his feet, pacing in front of Hill's desk, the day's issue of the *Examiner* in his hand as a prop. "Never in my time as a prosecutor have I ever seen this kind of irresponsible slander. I thought I'd seen defense attorneys pull every outrageous stunt in the books, but this . . ."

"With friends like Dash Logan, I bet you have," Hardy interjected mildly. He was standing by the door. Both David Freeman and Sharron Pratt claimed pride of place and sat in the armchairs arranged on the rug in front of Hill. The court reporter—since every word uttered in a capital case is on the record—sat with her machine to the judge's right, tapping away.

Torrey turned on his heel, lashing out. "I'm not talking about Dash Logan! I'm talking about this libelous—"

"So sue me." Hardy moved forward, toward the judge. "Your honor, excuse me, but so what? A reporter wrote a factual story that doesn't bear on this case—"

"A factual story, my ass! There's nothing but—"

"Mr. Torrey!" Hill boomed. As with Hardy in chambers the day before, the judge projected a much more powerful persona here in his room than he showed on the bench. Again, he was not yet in his robes, and the business suit added to the aura of power. "I'm *goddamned* tired of listening to profanity day in and day out, so we won't have any more of it here, all right."

"I'm sorry, your honor, but . . ."

Hill held up a finger, spoke sternly with the volume still up. "No buts. I'm tired of it. That's the end of it."

Torrey, no place to go, threw a malevolent glance at Hardy, pulled himself to his full height and stiffly walked over to the one window. Sharron Pratt watched him with sympathy, then shifted in her chair and came back to the judge. Her voice all smooth reason. "What Gabe's saying has merit, though, your honor. Mr. Hardy is named as a source in this column. Surely he could have exercised a little restraint in his dealings with the press while this hearing was going on."

"How many times do I have to say it?" Hardy leaned against the bookshelves, arms crossed and casual, although it was far from how he felt. "The article doesn't have anything to do with this case, your honor. I had no idea exactly when Mr. Elliot was going to run it. And there isn't a word in it that isn't factual."

Torrey pounced again. "That's a lie. I *never* offered you a deal."

Hardy was mild. "The article doesn't say you did."

"Well, it damn well implies it." Realizing what he'd done, Torrey faced the judge. "Sorry, your honor." Hill waved it off.

"That's how you read it, of course," Hardy replied. "If the shoe fits . . ." A shrug.

"All right, gentlemen, that's enough." Hill arranged some pens on his blotter. "Ms. Pratt, I've given both you and Mr. Torrey more than a reasonable opportunity to vent your displeasure at Mr. Hardy. But he's right. This article has nothing to do with the case at hand. And we are here in chambers at his request, not yours. Do you mind if we proceed?" He turned to Hardy. "And what you have does—presumably—bear here. Is that correct?"

"Yes, your honor, it does." He leaned over and undid the clasp of his briefcase, then extracted several sheets of paper and held them tantalizingly. "Last night, Lieutenant Glitsky was reviewing some property of Elaine Wager's that had been brought to my office . . ."

"My Lord! Your honor!" Torrey exploded again, marching forward. "What does Mr. Hardy think he's doing now? By what right does he gain possession of Ms. Wager's property? Lieutenant Glitsky has already been placed on disciplinary leave for interfering in this case and cannot serve any kind of search warrant on her or anybody else. This is completely improper, totally beyond the pale."

Hardy calmly addressed the judge. "If Mr. Torrey could keep his well-pressed shirt on, your honor. There was no search warrant. We asked Ms. Wager's fiancé if we could take a look through her condominium. He said yes. Simple as that."

Torrey grunted with displeasure. "I don't think so."

Freeman jumped in. "Why not, Gabe? Why wouldn't he want to help us find some clue as to who might have killed her?"

"We know who killed her," Torrey snapped.

"No. I don't think we do," Freeman replied.

Pratt ignored that exchange and leaned forward. "I have a question for Mr. Hardy. You're the one who brought up Lieutenant Glitsky. Is he working for you on this matter?"

Hardy shrugged. "As you say, he's on leave. He can do what he wants and it appears he wants to know who killed Elaine Wager. Naturally, anything he finds will be made available to you."

"We already have a police file on that, Mr. Hardy. From Lieutenant Glitsky's own department."

Hardy shrugged. "Lieutenant Glitsky thinks the police may have made a mistake and that you've painted yourself into a political corner." He borrowed one of Freeman's smiles.

"So you contend that Lieutenant Glitsky's involvement here is what? Somehow to protect the police department from its own ineptitudes?"

"I'm sure there's a little of that, yes. But mostly something else."

"Oh, what's that?"

Next to Pratt, Freeman clucked. She'd just asked another question to which she didn't know the answer, and it was always—always—a bad idea.

Hardy looked at Pratt, at Torrey, finally at the judge. "Your honor, Lieutenant Glitsky is—was—Elaine Wager's father."

After several seconds of absolutely dead air, Torrey found his voice. "My God," he said, incredulous, "is there no end to it? It appears that Messrs. Hardy and Freeman will go to any lengths of fabrication to muddy the waters here. This has got to be the most ridiculous . . ." Words failing him, he made some dismissive noise, then turned to the judge for commiseration. "Your honor, please?"

By now, though, Hill was fully engaged. Whatever else was going on here, this was as unusual a set of facts as he'd ever dealt with. If they were facts. He turned to Hardy, ready to strike at the first sign of nonsense. "I'm very much hoping you have proof of this, counsel."

"Of course, your honor." He approached the desk with his papers.

"As I began to say so long ago now, last night Lieutenant Glitsky was looking over some of Elaine's property that had been brought down to my office. Among the items was a key that he recognized as belonging to a public locker." He kept talking, loath to give anyone a chance to interrupt him again. "As it turned out, this locker was located in the bus station, and Lieutenant Glitsky opened it"—he held up a hand, stopping Torrey before he could start—"he is her next of kin, your honor, and not acting as a police officer. There was no question of his needing a warrant. He was perfectly within his rights. In any event, the locker contained many of Elaine's personal items, but also a handwritten letter addressed to Lieutenant Glitsky—"

Torrey could restrain himself no longer. "Oh, please . . ."

But Hardy could see that Hill was still with him, and continued. "—a copy of which I have with me. The original is in a safe place and can be made available to the court at short notice. Several references in this letter bear strongly upon this case, your honor, and I wanted to bring them to the court's attention at the earliest possible moment."

"To what end, Mr. Hardy? If this is evidence, present it at the hearing in your case in chief. If it's not, I don't want to hear about it, here or anywhere else."

"Your honor." Freeman came slowly up from his chair. "With respect, I've seen the document and believe it raises issues that address whether or not the district attorney's office should recuse itself, or you should recuse it, entirely from this case."

Pratt, under her breath: "You've got to be joking."

"Not at all, Sharron." Freeman turned to her. "We believe the A.G. is much more objectively situated to prosecute this case, your honor. There is evidence of personal animus here that—"

"I've heard enough talking," Hill interrupted. "We've got a hearing in the real world out there and I'd like to get back to it someday. Mr. Hardy, let's see what you've got. You make a motion if you've got one, and I'll make a ruling."

"Of course I knew the judge wouldn't force them to recuse. The fact that Torrey used to have a personal relationship with her sometime in the past isn't enough, even if we could prove it without hearsay. As his honor astutely noted." Freeman was in high spirits, trying to bring Cole up to date at the defense table while they waited for Judge Hill to enter the courtroom again after the long adjournment to chambers. "Besides, we need a written motion, notice to the A.G., and a whole lot more than we've got." David displayed a slight edge of disappointment that Cole had felt he had to ask why they'd requested the D.A.'s dismissal from the case. But it wasn't enough to dull his pleasure in the result. "And there was no way Pratt was taking herself out of this."

"Okay? And yet you asked them both to do it anyway because . . . ?"

Saddened by the thickness of his slow student, Freeman went into teacher mode. "Because we needed the judge to see that letter, Cole. We needed him to know as a fact that Glitsky was Elaine's father—*that's* why him helping your defense, bucking his own police force, is so significant. We also needed him to know that our friend Mr. Torrey slept with her. But mostly it goes to his character, which we've been trying to get out for reasons that Mr. Hardy might be better able to explain. Because say what you will, Torrey outranked Elaine, and in our culture, that smells enough like sexual harassment to make Hill wonder. Also, just between you and me, it didn't hurt for Pratt to hear about his little indiscretion, either.

"Basically"—Freeman's smile was terrible to behold—"we're just screwing with them, Cole. Screwing with them because they screwed with us. We're showing them this case isn't going to be a political victory lap ending with you on death row."

And indeed, across the courtroom, the two prosecutors were studiously not talking, sitting as far apart as they could possibly get as they arranged their water glasses and other important items on their table.

"But the most important reason, by far, really wasn't any of that. Since we really don't have a shred of evidence that somebody else in fact killed Elaine, the next best thing is to prove that Elaine's life was at least troubled and complicated. She had man trouble, work trouble, law trouble. Personal issues. She might have been killed by an unlucky random event like a mugger, that's true, but now it's definitely in his mind, and very strongly, that she wasn't your average Jane Doe walking back to her office on a Sunday night. With so much going wrong in her life, so much obvious angst that she was actually leaving the country *on the next day*, what would you think?"

"I'd think it's a pretty big coincidence that she got killed that night."

"Right. It makes the odds a lot better that one of these people had a reason to kill her." He shrugged. "To tell the truth, though, Cole, I don't want to bring you down, but none of it proves anything really. Certainly, it doesn't prove that you didn't do it and that's the whole point here. But it's got to give the judge some pause at least, and that in turn will maybe give us a little more stage to dance on, and *that*, my friend, that's the name of the game."

Glitsky the cop had his own jobs this morning.

His vision had shifted since he'd read his daughter's letter, and suddenly Hardy's theory of the previous night played to all the unrelated variables. Elaine had discovered something. Someone she trusted had recently made her lose all faith in the law. She had once slept with Gabe Torrey. She was in the middle of an investigation involving Dash Logan, who hung with Visser, who'd been with Cullen Alsop.

This was no longer a universe of possibilities. They were no longer searching the city for an anonymous trigger man. Glitsky could concentrate his efforts on limited targets. Hardy's theory might yet prove unfounded, but before he would abandon it now, Abe was going to test its limits.

Neither comfortable nor welcome at the Hall of Justice, he set himself up in the Solarium. Everyone on the team, with the addition of Jan Falk, had checked in by seven-thirty. He'd passed around the letter, told the story. By eight o'clock, Amy Wu was off with Gina Roake to interview the various witnesses who'd come forward in the Abby Oberlin will contest. If Gene Visser had threatened any of these people . . .

Curtis Rhodin had a good friend in the attorney general's office. Hardy and Freeman thought that Curtis could talk to his pal and bring him up to speed with the confluence of all these events. Elaine had been looking at Logan's files when she'd been killed. The A.G.'s office didn't have even a remotely good relationship with the D.A. anyway. Based on Torrey's relationship to the murder victim, it might be disposed to believe that Logan's files held evidence of a D.A. cover-up of some kind that had somehow resulted in a murder. It was all nebulous and unfounded, but it was also provocative and tied to a capital murder, and these features tended to get a judge's attention. They were hoping for a search warrant on Logan's office—and this time a warrant directed not at a few folks who happened to be Logan's clients, but at Logan's whole practice. At Logan himself. This was a long shot since they had no active case—but at the very least, it might shake up the principals and force one of them to do something rash.

Jon Ingalls was going to find both Visser and Logan and serve subpoenas on them so that they would be in the courtroom if Hardy got to where he needed to call them. Then, accompanied by Treya and maybe Glitsky after he finished some phone calls, Ingalls was going to check with more restaurants and hotels. Glitsky was convinced that somebody must have seen Elaine that night. He didn't believe she'd been walking alone through a deserted downtown at 1:00 A.M. She'd been walking with her killer.

But Glitsky, Hardy and Freeman were all in accord that their best shot, not only of finding any evidence but of introducing this entire line of inquiry at the hearing, lay in the Cullen Alsop/Ridley Banks/Gene Visser/Jan Falk connection, whatever that might be. Falk was going over to court with Hardy and Freeman, a critical link should they need him. He hated Torrey and the whole D.A. apparatus and was on their side, an invaluable police witness who was hostile to the prosecution.

But hating wasn't going to be enough, and Glitsky was on the phone to Paul Thieu now, pitching his idea. Copies of the lab and crime scene reports on Cullen Alsop that Thieu had managed to get were in front of him. "Right," he was saying. "I know that. But the lab wasn't looking for any specific print, were they?"

"Abe." Thieu kept his tone reasonable. He wanted to help because he liked and respected Glitsky, but he had to keep an extremely low profile or his own position would be threatened. And going to the lab on a murder case to which he was not assigned and asking for a rush re-analysis of their data wasn't low profile. It would get around the building. "What am I supposed to ask them? It was a room in a flophouse. I read the report, too. They didn't clean the place too often. There were dozens of good prints. The maids, past tenants, you name it. They're not going to run every print in the room."

"But on the bag itself? Paul, I'm reading it right in front of me. There was another print that wasn't Cullen's. One."

Thieu's frustration came through the wires. "It wasn't computer quality, Abe, and it didn't match anybody who was around or lived nearby when the police arrived. No match."

"I know. But if a print was clear enough, it could be run against the database." This was the state computer file of people with criminal records, against which the lab compared crime scene fingerprints. It was a useful database that could produce matches quickly and cheaply. But you needed a nice, clean print. The print on the bag was partial and blurry. Enough for a skilled and trained human to compare, but not for the computer.

"You're telling me you want to do a hand search with this? It'll take a month and—"

"No. A single comparison. Visser. That's all."

This wasn't that difficult a request. Visser was a private investigator and a former policeman. His fingerprints would be on file. Thieu was sure he could find a set of them somewhere, possibly even in the homicide detail itself, and run them to the lab for comparison within a half hour, although how long they'd take to get to it . . .

"Don't ask," Glitsky commanded. "Tell."

In the courtroom, Hardy was taking all the time he could with the death of Cullen Alsop. On the stand was Saul Westbrook, the young public defender.

"So Mr. Alsop was in jail for six days before he informed you that he'd struck a deal with the district attorney with regard to this information about the murder weapon. Is that right?"

"Yes."

"And during those six days, did you have an opportunity to meet with him?"

Westbrook looked into his lap and consulted some notes he'd brought with him. "I met with him twice, once here in the Hall of Justice, and then again the next day, in the afternoon, at the jail."

"And were these long discussions?"

"The first one, here at court, wasn't too long. We talked about his plea, his parole situation, logistics."

"And how about the second one, at the jail? Was that longer?"

Again, the young man consulted his notes. "Yes. We talked for a little under an hour."

"And during that discussion, did the name of the defendant in this case, Cole Burgess, come up?"

"Yes, it did. The two men were acquaintances. Cullen heard he'd been arrested for murder and wanted to know if I knew anything about it."

"And what did you tell him?"

"Only what I'd read. That it didn't look too good for him."

"Did he mention a gun at all?"

"No."

"And yet, Mr. Westbrook, just four days later, you met Mr. Alsop again after his plea bargaining arrangement with the district attorney's

office. At that time, did you mention this oversight to him? That he
hadn't mentioned the gun to you before?"

"Yes, I did."

"And what was his response?"

"He said that he thought it might be incriminating if he told me
he'd ever had the gun. He didn't want to get involved with a murder
charge."

"But obviously, sometime in the intervening four days, he decided
that it would be all right to disclose this information after all, is that
true?"

"Well, apparently that was what he decided."

"But he never discussed this legal matter with you, his own attorney?"

"No, he did not."

Hardy walked back to his table and got himself a sip of water. This
wasn't going anywhere. He had been hoping something would occur to
Westbrook on the stand that would shake things up a little, but he'd
gotten to here and the well was dry. Hardy caught Freeman's eye, and
after only the slightest hesitation, David nodded. Hardy turned back
to the bench. "Your honor, my associate has a question or two for this
witness if it please the court."

Hill didn't like it, but then again, he didn't like anything. "Mr. Hardy,
you know the rules—one witness, one lawyer. And this is your witness."

"Yes, your honor. And if you wish I'll have Mr. Freeman write
his questions out for me to ask Mr. Westbrook, but in the interests of
time . . ."

Exasperation was Hill's middle name. "Once, Mr. Hardy," he said
wearily. "Just once, only once, as in never again once. Mr. Freeman, you
may proceed."

Freeman stood at the defense table. He spoke with an exaggerated
calm. "Mr. Westbrook. You've just testified that Mr. Alsop never discussed this rather significant legal matter with you, is that right?"

"Yes, sir."

And suddenly Freeman's head came up and he exploded. "WELL
WHY NOT?" He came around the table, charging. "Did you ever ask
your client who he talked to about this urgent matter? Weren't you concerned that he just decided on his own to subject himself to the possibility
of being charged with murder?"

"Objection!" The attack had come out of nowhere and caught Torrey flat-footed, so it took him a moment to respond, and now he stammered out, "Hearsay and speculation."

But Freeman was on his horse, galloping. His voice still boomed. "Everything about Cullen Alsop's deal with the district attorney, his release from jail and his death is supremely relevant."

The courtroom hung in silence. Freeman had his hands on his hips facing the judge. He was completely out of line and totally confident, and Hill bought it. "Objection overruled," he said.

Freeman bobbed his head curtly, thanked the judge, then turned and pointed to the naive, sweet, stunned Westbrook. "You met your client after he made his deal, did you not?"

"Yes, sir, I did."

Freeman moved up close to the witness box and pressed his attack. "Why didn't you ask him about it?"

"I don't know."

"You don't? I think you do, sir." The words flew out staccato fashion. "You knew that this deal stunk, didn't you? That it would come back and bite him. Didn't you?"

Flustered, unsure of exactly what the question meant, Westbrook stammered, "Well . . ."

Torrey was up, yelling "Objection!"

As though he'd proved an important point, Freeman spread his arms in triumph. "Yes," he said. "And now it has. No further questions."

"I don't know what you did just then, David," Hardy said, "but it sure was fun to watch."

The court was in a recess after Westbrook stepped down. They hadn't left their table, although Cole had gone back with the bailiff to use the bathroom, so they were alone. Freeman didn't show any sign of glee over his performance. He lowered his voice. "We need a fact here pretty soon or we're dead. If I were Hill, capital case or not, I would have called it already and our boy's going to trial."

Hardy turned around and surveyed the courtroom behind him. No Glitsky or Treya. No Logan, either. He thought he'd recognize Visser if he saw him, and didn't. The musketeers were out on their errands. He drew little circles on the legal pad in front of him. He thought he knew so much about this case, but for the life of him he couldn't figure a way to get his vital information in front of Hill. "We've got to start talking about these tenuous connections and hope the judge stays interested."

Freeman shook his head, disagreeing. "Nope. We need facts," he re-peated. "Now."

Hardy stopped scribbling. "Is Ridley Banks part of this yet, his con-nection to Cullen? Both of them either dead or missing. Those are facts."

Unconvinced, the old man clucked. "Slim pickin's," he said.

But until Glitsky or someone else hit some pay dirt, it was all they had.

Jan Falk was obviously a surprise both to the prosecution and to the judge. After he'd been sworn in and had described his position as an undercover narcotics officer, Hill stopped Hardy and beckoned him up to the bench. "Mr. Hardy, as far as I can tell, your last witness brought nothing of any substance to this party. Now I have been granting you extraordinary latitude up until now, and will continue to do so because of the gravity of this case, but I'm not going to tolerate any more fishing expeditions. If you've got something to get out of this witness, it had better become damn clear what it is in a short period of time, or I'll dis-miss him. Am I making myself clear?"

Hardy swallowed, although his mouth was sand. "Yes, your honor."

Treya opened the top left-hand drawer in her old cubicle at Rand & Jackman. It seemed so long since she'd worked there. Her face fell. "I know, I know, I know I didn't lose it. I'm just so tired, my brain's not working."

Glitsky put a hand on her shoulder. "Didn't you get much sleep?"

She turned in the chair and laid a gentle palm against his face. "Stop."

He kissed her, then straightened up and sat against the edge of her desk. "All right," he said. "Let's go back to where you were when she gave it to you."

"I was in her office."

"Where we've been looking at files all this time?"

"Yes." Treya got up abruptly. Glitsky followed her across the hall into the now-familiar room, where she went and stood by a low file cabinet. "This was where I was. She was carrying her leather shoul-der briefcase and came in and . . ." She closed her eyes, trying to bring it back.

Glitsky, content to watch the subtle changes in her face, let her be.

"I was holding—that's it—I had a stack of files I was holding and she threw the briefcase on the desk and took out a manila folder and handed it to me while we were talking. Her meeting. She had to run."

"So it was with your other files?"

She nodded. "But I was going home, too. It was almost dinnertime." She took a breath, closed her eyes. "And first thing next morning I heard about her, and then everything else . . ."

"You never filed it."

They crossed back to her cubicle, and she sat again, thinking. Suddenly she spun the seat and slid the chair across the small space to a horizontal bank of metal file cabinets. Opening the bottom tray, she sighed with relief. "Here we go." Reaching down, she pulled out a loose bundle of folders, perhaps twenty of them. She opened the top folder, sighed again and handed it to Abe. "This is the one after she got back from Logan's. It looks like a business ledger, a check register," she said.

Glitsky was flipping through the Xeroxed pages, twenty or thirty of them. At one of the pages, he stopped, a puzzled look on his face. "It's missing some entries here," he said, flipping to the following page. "A couple more here. What do you think that's all about?"

She took the pages and studied them. "I'm not sure. Voided checks, maybe," she said. "What do you think?"

"I think it's funny," Abe said. "A little bit funny."

36

Jan Falk's testimony had only the most tenuous relationship to Cole Burgess, but by the time Hardy was done with him, after three o'clock in the afternoon, he felt certain that he'd forged another link in the chain that bound all these disparate elements to the murder of Elaine Wager.

Over a near constant clamor of relevance objections from both Pratt and Torrey, Judge Hill let Hardy make his case. The Cadaver spouted a constant flow of overruling rationalizations, and all of them taken together assumed the force of a mantra.

"Mr. Torrey, this is a capital case. I'm going to let it all in and sort it out at the end."

"Mr. Torrey, this will go a lot faster if you just let Mr. Hardy do what he has to do."

"Yes, I realize that defense counsel is arguing his evidence, but you're the one asking for the death penalty, and if you get it, Mr. Torrey, *every single layer* of appellate court in this country is going to review it. They're going to want a complete record of all the issues and I intend to give it to them."

"Ms. Pratt, if as you say this line of questioning is irrelevant, how could it possibly hurt your case to hear it?"

"I know my job, Mr. Torrey. I will throw out what doesn't belong here. You'll have to trust me on that. But I've told you I'm allowing extreme latitude here, especially after this morning's revelations in Ms. Wager's letter to Lieutenant Glitsky."

Hardy knew that no judge had ever been reversed for giving the defense what it wanted. He couldn't say whether it was Jeff Elliot's *Examiner* article, or the judge's time-tested views of the integrity of the D.A.'s office, or Elaine's letter, but whatever had caused it, suddenly the Cadaver appeared compelled by the argument that events surrounding Cullen Alsop's overdose were somehow key to Cole's guilt or innocence.

Hardy had introduced no physical evidence—the judge had simply allowed hearsay and argument. Falk had put Gene Visser with Cullen Alsop at Jupiter on the day of his release from jail and subsequent overdose. He'd disclosed information familiar to narcotics inspectors that substantial quantities of cocaine and heroin seized in arrests of dealers were finding their way back onto the street again. He opined that perhaps the evidence lockup room under the Hall of Justice was not as secure as was generally imagined. A recent internal narcotics department audit had revealed, for example, that in the past twelve months, there was a discrepancy of nearly eighteen ounces between the amounts of opiates and cocaine logged into evidence and stored downstairs and the amount actually on hand in the case lockers.

More specifically, though, Falk had testified that Banks was going to interview Visser on the day of his own disappearance. With the inspector still on the stand, Hardy argued that since two critical witnesses in this case had died or disappeared within the past week, more investigation was called for. The burden of proof, always on the prosecution, demanded some explanation for these unusual events.

In spite of all the objections, the prosecution didn't even bother to cross-examine Falk. What were they going to ask? If he'd made up any of this stuff? They knew he hadn't. He was Hardy's witness and they were evidently happy to see the end of him.

Hill stood up and announced that he would be leaving the bench for fifteen minutes, the last recess of the day. Cole went for a pit stop with the bailiff and Hardy and Freeman started talking about whether they had enough to make a motion to bifurcate the hearing—put it on hold until some of these outstanding issues had been investigated and/or resolved.

But Abe and Treya had come into the courtroom during the last half hour, and Glitsky, finally having pushed through the gallery and inside the bar rail, listened for a minute, caught their gist and interrupted. "I don't think we want to do that."

•　•　•

As Hardy called lab technician Nikki Waller to the stand, suddenly he had the sense that the momentum had truly shifted—the lone fact that Freeman had so desired had finally appeared. The stocky, pretty young woman came confidently forward out of the gallery and took the stand with a kind of bright effervescence. Enthusiasm was rare enough in the courtroom, and Hardy found himself smiling at her, grateful for the attitude and also—mostly—for the information she possessed. He walked her through her introduction and credentials, then got directly to the point.

"Ms. Waller, did you have occasion recently to examine for fingerprints some of the contents of the room where Cullen Alsop died?"

"Yes, I did, just today."

"Hadn't you already done something like that?"

"Yes." She briefly explained the computer problem, concluding, "I didn't have a print good enough to compare to prints already in the system by computer, so not too surprisingly, I didn't find anything to match."

"Although there were a lot of fingerprints in the room, isn't that so?"

"Oh yeah." She almost giggled. "There was no shortage there. They were everywhere."

"And then what happened this morning to make you look again?"

"Well, Inspector Thieu from homicide came to the lab and asked that I check the fingerprints again against a specific individual, whose prints were on file."

"And did you do that?"

"Yes, I did."

"Ms. Waller, what was the object on which you found the fingerprint?"

She wrinkled her face fetchingly. "Actually, it was a piece of Scotch tape—the inside sticky part—which was used to close the Baggie that had held the heroin."

"And was it usable?"

"It was blurry, but usable."

"And did you get a match this time?"

"Yes, sir, I did."

Hardy straightened up and inhaled deeply. "Would you please tell the court the name of the person whose fingerprint was on the tape that enclosed the bag of heroin?"

Nikki Waller looked helpfully up at the Cadaver. "Eugene Visser."

• • •

On the stand, Visser was the picture of blue-collar cooperation. "Of course I can explain it. This was the junkie in the bathroom, right?"

Hardy shrugged. "You're telling the court, Mr. Visser. Not me."

"Well." Visser sat back, no sign of tension anywhere. "First you gotta understand that Jupiter is a party place. I mean, I heard what your last witness was talking about—Falk?—and you know, I've seen him in there, too. In the bathroom."

"We're not talking about Inspector Falk right now, Mr. Visser. We're talking about how your thumbprint came to be on a bag of pure heroin that was a vehicle for a young man's death."

"Okay, sure," Visser said. "The short answer, then, is I picked it up."

"You picked it up?"

"I'm in the bathroom, I'm standing at the urinal, it's the middle of the afternoon. I'm hearing some noise next to me in the stall, but you know how that is, you don't exactly go sticking your head over the top and asking how things are going." A nervous titter rolled through the gallery. "Anyway, next thing I know, I hear this person swear, like he dropped something, and a Baggie of white powder shows up at my feet."

"At your feet?"

"Yeah. I don't know. He must have kicked it grabbing for it or something. But like I was telling you, this isn't the first time I'd seen something like that at Jupiter. I mean, this is an adult place. There's a lot of law enforcement types, like myself. So I figure, the kid in the stall, maybe he's undercover—like your friend Falk, maybe, huh?—and he's trying to entrap me." The gallery found this amusing, too. "So I leaned over, picked up the Baggie, closed it back up with the tape. By this time, the kid's out of the stall, coming around, frantic. Going all like 'Where's my stuff? Where's my stuff?' So I hand it back to him."

"You handed it to him?"

Visser smiled. "All taped up. Which, now, take my word for it, I wish I hadn't."

Another ripple of laughter, and Visser acknowledged it almost as though he was doing stand-up. He began to rise out of the witness chair, but Hardy held up a hand and stopped him. "Mr. Visser, excuse me. We're not quite done here. Inspector Falk has testified that you went into the bathroom after Mr. Alsop and both of you stayed in there for quite a while, perhaps as long as ten minutes. Would you care to explain that to the court?"

Shaking his head at all this silliness, Visser plopped back down and gave Hardy a long and serious look. "You don't have to believe me, but I talked to him."

"You talked to him? Cullen Alsop? What about?"

He threw a look to the judge, then back to Hardy. "No, forget it. Never mind. You'd just laugh."

"I'm not laughing, Mr. Visser, I assure you. Please answer the question."

The private eye fussed with his jacket. He took another moment, then shrugged. "I told him he oughta go easy on that stuff. That it could kill him."

Behind Hardy, the gallery hummed again, but this time there wasn't any laughter.

"So we talked like a minute, five minutes, I don't know. He seemed like a good kid. He told me he'd just got out of jail, and the first thing he did was get hooked up. He knew he should get straight, but couldn't seem to do it. So I told him just why didn't he take that bag and flush it right then. Start now. And you know, for a minute I thought he would. I think he really thought about it. But then he just said he couldn't do it, not yet." The big man let out a convincing sigh. "It was that close," he said sadly.

To keep his temper in check, Hardy walked across the courtroom, then to his table for a sip of water. Freeman got his attention, mouthed, "Let him go." The old man sensed that Hardy was going to go after him some more, with no idea even of what questions he was going to ask, much less the answers to them. But Hardy ignored Freeman, and by the time he came back to the witness, he had himself under control. "Mr. Visser, did you talk with the police regarding this matter?"

"Yes, I did."

"When was that?"

Visser made a show of remembering. "I don't know exactly, last Wednesday or Thursday, I think. I told the inspector the same thing I told you."

"You talked to an inspector?"

"Yeah. Black guy, right? Banks? He had me at Jupiter with the kid, too. He came by there the next day after the boy died, asking questions then." A nonchalant shrug. "He was just following up."

"Where did you see him?"

"He came by my office, which is down on Pier 38. I was working late there and he caught me. He asked me the same questions, not so specific about the Baggie maybe—I didn't know I had a print on it—but the same basic idea."

"And then what happened?" Hardy was so angry, he couldn't stop himself.

"What happened when?"

"Next," Hardy snapped. "After you'd finished?"

Visser lifted his shoulders, let them down theatrically. "I don't know. He left."

Hardy raised his voice. "Are you telling this court that you don't know that Inspector Banks has been missing from that night on?"

The witness sat back in dismay. "Missing?"

Behind him, David Freeman exploded into a coughing fit. Evidently he'd choked on some water he was drinking, and now was hacking with a devastating and awful severity. He knocked his glass over on the table. There wasn't a person in the courtroom who didn't believe he could be choking to death. Cole was up, patting him on his back, the bailiff was moving over. Hardy remembered the judge, asked to be excused for a moment, then hustled over.

Freeman seemed to be recovering. He looked up, caught Hardy's eye, put a finger on his legal pad, upon which he'd written and under-lined a question.

The dog! Hardy thought. The sneaky, brilliant dog. Slowing him to a stop, getting him back into focus. He couldn't blow it now because he had been baited into losing his temper.

Hardy stayed a moment longer to make sure that David was breath-ing again. Finally, Freeman stood and apologized, and Hardy returned to the witness.

"Mr. Visser." Hardy was speaking too loud now, standing too close to the witness. In desperation, Freeman had given him a question that probably broke his own cardinal rule, but phrased in such a general way that there could be no wrong answer, and maybe, just maybe, a very good one. "Have you ever had occasion," Hardy asked, "to enter the evidence room in the basement of the Hall of Justice?"

The change of direction wiped the complacency from Visser's face. "Yes."

Hardy successfully kept the exultation out of his voice, although he thought he'd just hit the jackpot. "And when was the last time you did this?"

Visser tried to keep up the show of nonchalance, but it wasn't as convincing as it had been. "I don't know exactly."

"You don't know?" Hardy pressed. "We can find out in five minutes by calling downstairs, Mr. Visser. Would you like us to do that, or do you think you can remember? You have to sign in upon entering down there, don't you?"

"Yeah. I don't know," he repeated. "A couple of weeks ago, maybe. Maybe less."

"A couple of weeks ago," Hardy repeated. "Maybe less."

He caught a glimpse of Hill out of one eye. The judge had straightened up in his chair and was now leaning in toward the witness. A keen intensity had galvanized him.

"Now, Mr. Visser, it is my understanding that a private citizen cannot be admitted into the evidence locker unless they are accompanied by a lawyer or police officer. Isn't that correct?"

"I think so."

"Were you so accompanied the last time you were there? In the last couple of weeks," he couldn't help repeating.

"Yeah, I usually go with some lawyer I'm working with, something like that."

"And two weeks ago, who was that?"

For the first time, the facade weakened. Visser looked to the floor, then drew a nervous hand over his jawline. "I think . . . it probably must have been Dash Logan," he said.

"You think? Are you sure?"

Another pause. "Yeah. I'm sure. It was Dash Logan."

"Mr. Logan," Hardy began. "When you went to the evidence locker within the past couple of weeks with Mr. Visser, what was your purpose?"

Logan spread his hands, turned in the witness chair and faced the Cadaver. "This is ridiculous, your honor. What is this all about?"

"Just answer the question," Hill shot back.

Hardy had a sense that he was on to something. The current had finally begun to flow in his direction, and he was going to ride it as far as it could take him. "Mr. Logan," he said. "Would you like me to repeat the question?"

"No." Where Visser had used confidence to blunt Hardy's attack, Logan thought he'd go with arrogance. His eyes were shining with ill-concealed anger. His jaw was set. "I was there, in the locker, to review evidence in one of my cases. That's why you go there, Mr. Hardy, to review evidence."

But Hardy didn't rise to the bait. A cool detachment had settled over him. He even allowed himself a cragged grin. "Thank you for that information, Mr. Logan. I'll keep it in mind. Now, the specific case you were working on, how would you classify it?" This was another question for which Hardy didn't know the answer—except that by now the answer had become all but a certainty.

"I don't classify my cases. I work for my clients. I don't understand your question."

"Well, for example, was your client being charged with robbery? Murder? Rape?"

"No. None of those."

"How about traffic in narcotics?"

"That's privileged information," Logan said. "I don't have to discuss the nature of my cases with you or anybody else."

Hardy turned to the judge. "Your honor?"

Hovering almost over the edge of his podium, Hill had never looked more cadaver-like. "Your cases are public record, Mr. Logan. Tell the court what this one was."

Logan cast his eyes from side to side. Seeing no escape, he sat back in the chair, crossed one leg over another, adopted a wounded air. "Yes. It was a narcotics case."

"And you were there with Mr. Visser?"

"Yes."

"And afterwards, did you both go together to Jupiter?"

"All right, so what?"

Pratt, who'd been little more than a bystander for the past hour and a half, finally rose to her feet. A simmering anger scalded her voice slightly, but she managed to keep it under a lid. "Your honor, if the court please, there can really be no relevance here between Mr. Logan's and Mr. Visser's visit to the evidence locker less than two weeks ago and the death of Elaine Wager more than two weeks ago. She was already dead when these events that Mr. Hardy is so interested in transpired. I understand the latitude that you've given defense in this case, but none of this can possibly matter. He's *allowed* to go there. So is Mr. Visser. *So what* if he's got a drug dealer for a client? Almost every criminal defense attorney does. The whole thing is just a smoke screen, a desperate, un-ethical smoke screen."

Sharron Pratt half turned now, aware that she was also playing to the gallery, which had come to life behind her. Perhaps she took the judge's silence for forbearance. Whatever drove her, she took another deep breath and forged ahead, her voice becoming louder and more shrill as the volume behind her in the courtroom increased.

"This hearing is about the actions of Cole Burgess, your honor. Not Dash Logan and Gene Visser. They are not the criminals here. Let's not lose sight of that fundamental truth in our zeal for fairness here." And suddenly she was all but screaming, turning to the defense table, point-ing her whole hand. "That boy there is a cold-blooded killer. He killed Elaine Wager. There can be no doubt. Look at the facts, your honor. My God, this is insanity. Look at the facts."

She stood at the prosecution table—firm, proud of herself for having spoken out, for having put the judge on notice. She, not Hill, was con-trolling the agenda at this moment. The judge might have the power of the bench, but she had the power of righteousness. The people had elected her to do what she was doing now—driving the appeal to higher ground, toward justice and away from these lawyers' tricks. Enough was enough.

The Cadaver sat back in what Hardy took to be a state of disbelief, even awe. He held his gavel in his right hand, inches from the top of the bench, and did not lower it, but instead let the noise in the room sub-side for what seemed an eternity, although it probably wasn't more than forty seconds. Finally, when the silence was complete, Hill placed the gavel carefully in front of him and spoke in a moderate whisper.

"Because of your elected position, Ms. Pratt, I'm going to do you the courtesy of not throwing you into jail. I do, however, find you in con-tempt of court for that outburst and order you to pay the sum of one thousand dollars to the clerk of the court before noon tomorrow. In ac-cordance with the business and professions code, you will report this in-cident to the state bar."

The buzz began again, and this time Hill didn't hesitate a second, but slammed his gavel three times rapidly in succession, until once again he addressed a tomb. "Let there be no mistake that this is a court of law. It's not a soapbox upon which to make election speeches. Now," he continued to the courtroom at large, "Mr. Hardy will proceed with this witness until he is finished or for the next twenty-five minutes, whichever comes first. After which we'll adjourn for the day." He stopped speaking for an instant, then raised his head and started again. "And for the record, Ms. Pratt and Mr. Torrey, I am quite persuaded to this point that the testimony elicited from the past few witnesses, as well as the evidence presented to the court, will pass any relevance standard you'd like to propose. So I'd prefer to let this direct examination continue with a minimum of objection for a while. Am I making myself understood? Ms. Pratt?"

Hardy had been facing her through all this. Now, her eyes glistening with anger, she stared at the judge, mute. Was she daring Hill to make her respond? If so, it wasn't her best idea. But Torrey, sensing the same thing and hoping to avert further crisis, put a hand on her arm and stood up. "Of course the People reserve the right to object, your honor."

An evil apparition, the Cadaver glared down at the prosecutors, held his expression, then at last nodded crisply. "Of course," he said. Left unsaid, but clearly stated nonetheless, were the words "Make my day." The judge gave it a last beat, then handed the witness back to Hardy.

He turned back to Logan. If Sharron Pratt thought the last set of questions was irrelevant, she would go ballistic over what he intended to do next. But the judge had just given him free rein, and if he was ever going to get it in, now was the time. "Mr. Logan, last year were you yourself involved in a traffic incident at the corner of Fifth and Market?"

The witness shifted in his seat, nervously cleared his throat. "Yeah. Somebody cut the brakes in my car. I nearly got killed."

"You also nearly hit two pedestrians running a red light, did you not?"

"I couldn't stop. What would you expect?"

Hardy didn't reply to that. Instead, he asked, "When this incident occurred, were you under the influence of drugs or alcohol?"

Logan sat up self-righteously. "Absolutely not. And nobody charged me with anything."

But Hardy had an answer for that. "Isn't it true that after you were arrested and booked by the police, all charges related to this accident were dismissed by the district attorney?"

"Well, yes, that's . . ."

"And you're aware that Mr. Torrey personally made that decision?"

"There weren't any . . ."

Hardy raised his voice. "Yes or no, Mr. Logan?" Notching it up again. "Yes or no?"

"Okay, but . . ."

Hardy jumped in again. "That's a 'yes,' for the record, is that right?"

Logan hated it, but was afraid of what Hardy knew or might be able to prove. "Yes." He spit it out like a bitter seed.

"Thank you," Hardy said. Having now tied Visser to Logan to Torrey on the record, Hardy was at last ready to bring it all back home. He glanced at Hill and thought he imagined an almost conspiratorial nod from the judge—surely, he thought, he must be getting tired. "Mr. Logan, did you know the victim in the case, Elaine Wager?"

"Yes, I did. Professionally, not personally."

"In other words, you knew her as another lawyer here in town?"

"Excuse me. Mr. Hardy?" The judge, interrupting. "I'm gratified to see the beginning of a line of questioning that relates to one of the principals in this case, and this might be a good time, if the People don't object," he added pointedly, "to call it a day and resume tomorrow. It's been a long session and I'm sure we could all use the time to reflect on the day's events. Are there any objections?" There were not. "All right, then. Court's adjourned."

37

Glitsky didn't wait around for Logan's testimony. As soon as Gene Visser was excused, after he heard him say on the stand that Ridley Banks had been to his office on Pier 38 on the night of his disappearance, he hightailed it out into the hallway and up to the homicide detail.

Half of his troops were in the room and looked up. They greeted him warmly as he entered. It came to him with a sense of satisfaction that his people here weren't really the most respectful-of-authority group in the known universe. They were a lot like him, in fact, trying to do their very dangerous jobs the right way in spite of the barriers erected by the media, the politicians, the brass. And suddenly he didn't care any longer if he was supposed to be there or not—let them try to fire him, just so long as *right now* nobody tried to get in his way. There was police work to be done, Elaine's murderer at last to be found. It was a sacred and very private debt, and he was going to pay it off.

"What are we looking for?" Paul Thieu asked him as he filled out the search warrants on both Visser's and Logan's offices. Hardy, who had delivered Elaine's letter to Judge Thomasino that morning, along with Jeff Elliot's *Examiner* article and an earful of what he surmised, had told him that he thought the judge might sign off on the warrants. They were trying to discover what had happened to Ridley Banks. If a homicide inspector now needed to take a good look at any of these offices and connect the dots to three murders, he was sure Thomasino would want to cooperate. And since Logan was now a suspect, not an innocent custodian of records, no special master was required.

"Basically," Glitsky said, "everything. Guns, drugs, canceled checks, evidence of struggle. Take the damn places apart. Visser may have shot Ridley where he sat, and if he did there's splatter."

Thieu looked up in a state of high excitement. From another desk in the detail, Marcel Lanier came over to join them. Glitsky nodded at him. Here was Jorge Batavia, too. Sarah Evans, listening in. Until now the unit hadn't been particularly aware of all the ramifications of Glitsky's clandestine investigation. Now it was beginning to dawn all around that this was a cop killing. Their colleague Ridley was part of this. "We're talking the full drill here then?"

"Everybody you can round up," Glitsky said, bringing them all in. "And as soon as you can. The two of them will be moving as soon as court's out. Bet on it."

"Are you coming along, Abe?" Jorge asked.

If Vincent Hardy had been there, his father definitely would have had to let him shave his head. "I'm not here at all," Glitsky said. "This isn't happening."

What was happening was that Glitsky was going to go on an errand of his own, armed with the picture of Elaine that he'd kept in his desk.

The musketeers had already accumulated notes on sixty-seven eating or resting establishments around Maiden Lane, and Glitsky either had to assume that his theory was mistaken or that they had been asking the wrong questions.

He chose the latter.

Elaine had left Treya at Rand & Jackman at five-thirty to meet someone she knew for an appointment. She was walking back to her place of business when she got shot. And she wasn't walking alone. Maiden Lane was a walking street, and she was far enough down it for Glitsky, even without taking into account the condition of the body, to preclude the possibility that someone had dumped her out of a car. He stood by the side of his desk and studied the city map that he had put up as wallpaper when he first made lieutenant. The red-tipped pin was still stuck in the wall at the site of Elaine's death.

He felt like an idiot, as though he'd wasted a lot of unnecessary time sending the kids out with his clever ideas about the area surrounding where she'd gotten shot. Because now, reading the map, it was obvious that it hadn't been a circle at all. She hadn't been out taking a leisurely stroll. It was after midnight, and she had been coming back by the most direct route from a specific location that probably, he now realized, was more or less in a straight line defined by two coordinates: Rand & Jackman's offices on Montgomery and Bush, and the corner of Maiden Lane and Grant Avenue.

Further, if he traced what he thought were the logical streets—the ones *he* would have taken—he thought he could eliminate any route north of his imaginary line, and east of Grant. If Elaine had begun walking on any of the streets in those areas, it would have meant backtracking to get to Maiden and Grant, and she knew the city well. She wouldn't have done that.

It was by now well past six on a Thursday night. The lights were on dim outside his door in the detail. Every inspector on duty had gone out with Thieu for the two searches. Glitsky had studied his coordinates. He knew, generally, where he was going. Now he turned out his own lights, closed his door and sat. He'd said it before to Treya, about how weird it sounded. But he was going to give Elaine a few more minutes, see if his daughter wanted to talk to him, to tell him something.

Sitting at his desk in the dark, unaware of any conscious thought, his mind went to a story he'd heard or read somewhere about a woman who'd been adopted at birth and had never known her mother. Over the course of her life, if something made her so emotionally upset that she couldn't sleep, she'd developed the habit of getting up, boiling water, and cooking up a plate of plain pasta. After she ate it, she could go back to sleep.

When she was thirty-five, she decided to try and locate her birth mother, and after a difficult search, was eventually successful. She wrote to the woman, introducing herself and asking if they could meet. Her mother had agreed—she could come to her house for a weekend, and they could get to know one another.

The meeting went well, but when it was time for bed, the emotional upheaval of it all kept the daughter awake well into the night. After tossing and turning for half the night in her mother's guest bedroom, she finally gave up and went downstairs to the kitchen.

Where her mother was fixing a bowl of plain spaghetti for herself! She said she always did that to help her get back to sleep. Would her daughter like some, too?

Glitsky snapped back to where he was. Why had he thought of that?

His damn heart was beating a strong tattoo against his rib cage, but there was no pain as he stood up and turned on the light in his room again. He thought he knew exactly where he was going now, but he wanted to check to make sure.

Yes, there it was. Dead smack in the middle of the parameters he'd just established, and probably half a block outside the circle he'd drawn for the musketeers.

Hardy ate at home, but was back downtown by eight o'clock, in his office. At the Solarium table, all the attorneys—Freeman, Roake, Wu, Ingalls and Rhodin—had gathered and were sharing their information and opinions.

Of the musketeers, the most successful during the day had been Amy Wu. She'd been working on the Abby Oberlin matter, and had discovered that Gene Visser had interviewed several staff members at the Pacific Gardens Senior Health Center in Visitation Valley, where Abby's mother had been in residence. Though he'd been more subtle than he had with Rich McNeil, he had still managed to intimidate two part-time nurses, as well as the owner of the facility, into believing that their license was in jeopardy if they did not disassociate themselves immediately from the first sign of this particular patient mistreatment lawsuit.

Wu had done well, Hardy told her, but he didn't think they needed what she'd found anymore. "We've got enough tying Visser to Logan at this stage," he said. "The Cadaver has gotten the message—I'm sure of that. What we need now, it seems to me, is some strong connection to Elaine that will bring Torrey into the picture. Lieutenant Glitsky and Treya might have found a little something for us this morning, but before we discuss that, I'd be happy to entertain any other suggestions anyone might have."

Wrapped in cigar smoke, huddled down behind his glass of red wine, David Freeman was a contemplative gnome, alone at the far end of the large table. He'd been uncharacteristically quiet during the initial discussions, and now he cleared his throat and sat forward. "We ought not to forget that we are deep, deep in the trees here, people. They're pretty trees, I admit. They form nice patterns on the forest floor and their leaves are a wonder to behold."

The younger attorneys caught each other's eyes, glad that they didn't sully their evening minds with alcohol. Hardy and Gina Roake shared their own look, but they knew David better, and their expressions didn't convey the same message. Here came a profound, and probably unwelcome, insight.

His forest-for-the-trees metaphor, subsumed by the legal issue, was forgotten. Freeman took in the faces around the table, focused on Hardy and continued gravely. "You can tie your three boys into the neatest knot you've ever seen and drop the whole package at Hill's bench and you still don't have nearly enough."

Ingalls and Rhodin both started to respond, but didn't get far as Freeman shook his head, summoning silence again to the table. "Ask yourselves this simple question. From the evidence presented in this hearing, disregarding all the hoopla about Torrey, Visser and Logan, did Cole Burgess happen upon a lone woman walking in an alley and kill her for her money and jewelry? Yes or no." More silence. "Let's take a straw vote. Gina?"

She considered for a beat, not liking her answer. "Probably."

"Amy?"

"I don't want to admit this, but yes, I do think so."

It went around the table, ending with Hardy, who made it unanimous.

"But why, then," Ingalls demanded, "is the judge letting all this in? He's got to see it as connected to the crime, right?"

Hardy, converted, took the answer. "Maybe not even, Jon. He's giving us rope, that's all. This is a death penalty case. All the issues have to be on the record. Hill's going to hold Cole to answer and he's willing to let us thrash around for a while before he does it. He might also enjoy watching Pratt and Torrey sweat."

"It's more than that, I'm afraid, Diz," Freeman said. "He's letting you develop an alternate explanation of events so completely that there won't be any room left for appeal if you lose. He's letting us lock ourselves in and throw away the key."

"But these guys," Rhodin began. "I mean, this whole thing with Cullen's death. It's got to mean something."

Freeman nodded, acknowledging the point. "Sure, it means something. It means that these three guys are all slightly to very dishonest allies and may have tried to cheat to win this case, which in turn is politically important to Torrey's boss. Okay, so they overstepped their bounds. Does that mean that they purposely gave Cullen pure heroin so that he could inadvertently kill himself? What happened to Ridley Banks? I mean, what are we trying to get at here? And, most importantly, does any of it mean that Cole didn't probably kill Elaine? I don't think so. The judge is going to want to let a jury decide and a trial court won't allow hearsay, which means we've got nothing at all."

And to this simple truth, there was no rebuttal. Hardy rose to his feet and began pacing. "So what are you saying, David? Are you suggesting we stop trying to make the connections?"

"No. We still need those."

Gina Roake asked, "Then what?"

Freeman removed his dead cigar long enough to take an appreciative sip of his wine. "We must be crystal clear in our minds that this is not some clever and ultimately empty legal strategy. Let's clearly acknowledge what we're doing here, and make no mistake about the gravity of it."

Amy Wu spoke up. "We had better be accusing somebody else of murdering Elaine, is that what you're saying?"

Freeman nodded. "Otherwise it's just what Pratt called it. A smoke screen."

Hardy stopped walking and fixed his gaze on the old man. Gina was bobbing her head in agreement. Jon Ingalls flashed a look around the table, then said what he obviously believed they all were thinking. "Visser."

"We don't know that. Not yet," Freeman corrected him gently. "It might just as well have been Logan. Or even Torrey."

"No offense, Mr. Freeman, but I can't see that," Curtis Rhodin offered. "Either one of them would have used Visser if they had wet work, don't you think?"

He shrugged. "If Logan was coked up, if Torrey was cornered. Who knows? And again, it might have been none of them." They were waiting to hear more. "The point is that even if Dismas succeeds brilliantly in tying up our connections between these three men—and I have no doubt he'll do just that—all it gives us, at best, is a possible motive."

"It gives us means, too, David, doesn't it?" Gina put in. "Any of them could have gotten their hands on the gun, couldn't they? After all, they're all in the criminal business one way or another. They're going to have access to guns."

"Okay," Freeman conceded, "maybe. But if they were playing cards together—or if they say they were—until two o'clock on that night, we lose. If they see where Dismas is going with this and talk together tonight, for example . . ." He let his voice trail off.

Jon Ingalls pushed his chair back from the table. "You're saying we need to know if they had alibis."

"I'm saying," Freeman amplified, "that we'd be damn negligent if we got this far and lost sight of what we're really trying to do, which is provide an alternative to our client as Elaine's killer. Not a theory, a person. Nothing less is going to do it."

"How are we going to do that"—Curtis Rhodin checked his watch—"in three or four hours?"

"I don't know," Freeman conceded. "I admit there's precious little time and it's really police work that they probably haven't done. But if we don't have that information, we're looking at ugly surprises just about when we think we've won."

After a moment, Amy Wu shook herself and sat up straight, smiling. "Okay," she said. "How do we do this? Where do we go?"

After the musketeers had broken off and left on their various assignments, Freeman, Gina Roake and Hardy had stayed on for over an hour to discuss the possible meaning of the blank entries in Logan's check register. Hardy thought it completely in keeping with Logan's character that his office still seemed to use a low-tech, one-write system approach to its check-writing and bookkeeping. Before computers had come into his life, Hardy had used the same kind of system himself, so he was familiar with it. You wrote your check and tore it off. Under it, a light blue NCR-paper copy of the check, was your receipt. And finally, under the copy, the check was automatically entered in the ledger. The blank lines could have been anything really—voided checks, a ditzy secretary inserting a piece of paper between the ledger and the checks, a purposeful hiding of records. The last was Hardy's favorite notion, but there was simply no way to tell.

The musketeer assignments were desperate and dangerous, but necessary. The very cute Amy Wu was going with Jon Ingalls as her invisible chaperon to spend some time at Jupiter, where, according to the bartender when they'd phoned, Dash Logan was currently having a few drinks. He looked to be in for the long haul tonight.

From the Solarium, Curtis Rhodin had called the home of his friend at the A.G.'s office—they'd been unsuccessful getting a judge to issue any kind of warrant on Logan's office that morning, and both had been frustrated, aching for another chance. This was it. They would take an investigator—three of them together would ensure their safety, they hoped—and call on Visser first at his office and then at his home address. When they found him, they would ask him what he had to say about his movements on the night of Elaine's murder.

The same drill would not work on Torrey, not that Freeman, Roake or Hardy really considered that the chief A.D.A. could have pulled the trigger on Elaine. They all agreed that he would have used Visser. But why would Torrey even see them? Certainly, he would blow off Curtis, his friend and their investigator. And even if they did get in and pushed him for his alibi, he'd tell them to get lost—he wouldn't miss the message. His guard would be raised even higher.

Freeman, though, wanted to be thorough, and he had an idea. He believed he'd be able to bait Torrey into giving something away the next morning before court went into session.

It was closing in on ten-thirty and Hardy sat alone in the glass room.

The ledger sheets from Dash Logan's office lay fanned in front of him. They had been important enough for Elaine Wager to have copied them separately and carried them away with her—illegally. Her special master mandate was specific about her duties in searching a lawyer's office. She had two and only two options on how to treat documents such as these that she reviewed in a search. She determined whether they fell into the categories specifically described in the affidavit. If they did, she gave it to the cops or, if the lawyer claimed a privilege, she took it to a judge. If they did not, she left them alone. And never, ever discussed them with anyone, not even a judge. It was that simple.

And yet she had risked her license and quite possibly her life to copy and remove what Hardy had in front of him.

Why? Why?

Freeman had left a few inches of wine in his bottle. Hardy got up, thinking he'd go see what tonight's choice had been. He went and sat in the chair David had been using. But he didn't reach for the wine right away. Just to his right, on the seat next to him, was the cardboard box full of Elaine's personal items.

On the top of it, facedown, was a framed something. He lifted it up. It was the picture of her mother, Loretta, that Treya had put up on the table when they'd first brought all the stuff down here. The other morning, Abe had asked the gang at the table if anybody minded if he put it back in the box. He didn't want to look at her face all day while he worked, and Hardy thought he understood pretty well why that was.

Still holding the frame, his fingers absently moving up and down the cardboard backing that held the photograph in place, he stared at the familiar visage of the senator, well-known public figure. Like her daughter, a beauty; and like her daughter, dead.

Hardy sighed wearily. Maybe his daughter was right after all to be frightened of everything. Maybe there was no security. A snatch from Matthew Arnold's "Dover Beach" flitted across his mind. ". . . neither joy, nor love, nor light,/Nor certitude, nor peace, nor help for pain . . ."

He placed the photograph carefully on the table and reached for the wine bottle. Groth Reserve Cabernet Sauvignon, 1990. He swirled and sniffed, then tipped the bottle up to his lips and tasted it, thinking it was no wonder David could keep up *his* good attitude most of the time.

Abruptly, he stood. Carrying the bottle out with him, he crossed the lobby and walked down the hallway to the coffee room, where he turned on the light and took a wineglass from the cabinet. This stuff was too outrageously good to swill. He poured, put the bottle down, and suddenly the wine had vanished from his mind, driven away by a cascade of realizations.

He checked his watch.

It was too late now to call Judge Thomasino, but he could stop by his chambers first thing in the morning. The evidence locker, on the other hand, would be open all night. If he busted his hump, he could get down there, verify what he realized he had to know, and still—maybe—make it home to get the five hours' sleep he needed to survive another day.

Stopping back at the Solarium to turn off the lights, he saw that he'd left Loretta's picture on the table. Abe would see it first thing when he came by for the morning briefing, but Hardy didn't even have the energy to walk around the table and put it back into the box. Abe was a big boy. He'd be able to handle it.

38

"Mr. Torrey, excuse me."

An hour before court would be called into session, Torrey sat in his office behind the Desk, reading the second part of Jeff Elliot's article on Abby Oberlin in yesterday afternoon's *Examiner*. David Freeman had pulled his forty years of familiarity and rank on the clerk who controlled access to the D.A.'s offices, and so achieved the element of surprise, which showed all over Torrey's face. Jerking the paper down when he saw who was interrupting him, he made an effort at quick recovery, but it wasn't fast enough. He inclined his head, his manner curt. "Mr. Freeman." A pause. "Did we have an appointment?"

"No, sir. This is a courtesy call."

Torrey coughed up a dry, humorless chuckle. "I could use a little of that." He indicated the newspaper. "Have you read this latest scurrilous slander? Well, who am I talking to? Of course you have, if you didn't help write it."

Freeman lifted his shoulders theatrically. He moved a step further into the room and waited.

Torrey set the newspaper down on the Desk. "But I guess appealing to your sense of fair play is whistling in the wind, isn't it?" Then, suddenly: "How did you get in here?"

"I had an appointment on another matter with one of your staff. Since I was here . . ." Another noncommittal shrug. "And for the record, I did not write a word of that article, nor did I contribute to it, although of course I'm aware of its contents. Mr. Hardy shares office space in my building, after all." Freeman waved the topic away. "But that's not why I'm here. Mr. Hardy's not my problem, though our mutual client is." He clarified it. "I'm talking about Cole Burgess."

"What about him?"

The old man closed the distance between him and the Desk, though he remained standing. "Look, it's not rocket science to see the direction that Mr. Hardy is going with this hearing. The whole proceeding has become a personal and professional attack on you. If I'm reading Judge Hill correctly, and I am, he's inclined to let it continue. What happens to you isn't my concern, either."

"All right. What's your point?"

"My point is this: Mr. Hardy's going to continue in the same vein over the course of today's testimony. He's going to be probing the relationships you have with Mr. Visser and Mr. Logan."

"From which you are trying to protect me, I suppose. You'll forgive me if I'm skeptical of your altruistic motives."

But Freeman didn't rise to the barb. Instead, he shook his head and spoke mildly. "There's nothing altruistic about it, Mr. Torrey. I apologize if I gave you that impression. As I've said, my only concern is my client. Mr. Hardy and I have had a few words of disagreement as to strategy. I believe he's become obsessed with this vendetta against you, to the detriment of Cole Burgess."

"It's just more rope, Mr. Freeman. He's hanging himself."

"Let me make myself clear," Freeman said. "The direction he's going now, the way he gets Burgess off is by accusing you three men of complicity in Elaine's killing, and I'm thinking the judge is going to let him do it."

Torrey pulled himself up to his full height in his chair. "That's the most ridiculous—"

"It may be, but Hill's going to let it happen. Unless all of you have solid alibis for the time of the murder . . ."

"Oh, please . . ."

"You think I'm joking? You think it won't get to there? Do you know what you were doing that night, for example?"

Torrey shook his head with disgust. "As a matter of fact, it so happens that because of Elaine's murder, I remember that night specifically. I had dinner with Sharron Pratt. Until very late." He met Freeman's gaze, challenging. "But even if I hadn't—"

Freeman interrupted. "If you hadn't, there's still Visser and Logan, or even some third party, to say nothing of all this"—he pointed down at the newspaper—"all this hatchet work. What I'm suggesting is that you can end it all this morning. Drop the charges, at least the specials, against my client, and Mr. Hardy pleads it out. The whole thing goes away."

Torrey stared across the Desk in disbelief. "You're suggesting that I let a murderer go to save myself some personal aggravation? Do you really think that's what this office is all about?"

"Let's not open that can of worms," Freeman snapped. "I said when I got here that this was a courtesy call. I've extended the courtesy."

Torrey's tone was ice. "A blackmailer's courtesy, counselor. There is no connection between me and the death of Elaine Wager. None at all. And this thinly veiled threat about what you or your partner might accuse me of isn't going to fly around here. Because that's what it is," Torrey fumed. "Blackmail."

"I'm sorry you see it that way." A modest disappointment. "It's your funeral."

On the way out to the courtroom, Freeman enjoyed a private chuckle. Of course the offer he'd made was stupid on the face of it. No matter what, at this point Torrey couldn't risk lowering the charges on Cole, but Freeman thought it was beautiful to wave the temptation in front of his face.

And Torrey for his part probably was thinking that Freeman's senility was by now well advanced. He possibly wasn't even aware that he'd given the old man his alibi, which had been the whole point of the exercise.

Contrary to expectations, Hardy did not begin the day with Dash Logan, but first asked the Cadaver's permission to call on Elaine Wager's paralegal for a couple of questions to establish the provenance of some documents, labeled Defense G, which would prove critical in his examination of Mr. Logan.

So when Dash Logan took the stand, he looked quite a bit the worse for wear. He'd been out partying until late, in the course of the night finally revealing to this knockout—Amy something—that he'd been in L.A. on the night of Elaine's murder. All that talking and spending, pretty sure he was going to get over with her, and then she'd excused herself to go to the bathroom and never come back. After that, he'd had to deal with this morning's news that the police had been and were still searching his office, this time in overt connection to Elaine. They were going through everything file by file. Patsy, God forbid, was there. He was sure that after last time, after the long weekend he and Visser had put in sterilizing the place, they would find nothing, but it was still nerve-racking.

He hadn't slept worth a damn, and the coffee hadn't done nearly enough, so he'd decided he needed a few lines to calm his nerves, but it had been so early—he didn't dare snort up in the Hall of Justice—that now he was just about back to straight.

On the witness stand. And here came that son of a bitch Hardy again, a pit bull with a mouthful of his leg.

"Mr. Logan, yesterday you told the court that you were professionally acquainted with Elaine Wager, isn't that so?"

"Yes. I was."

"Do you recall the last time you saw her?"

"Yes. I saw her in my office sometime in the middle or late January." He went on answering questions that explained a bit about her special master duties, his lack of cooperation with the police and his purported reason for it.

When he'd finished, Hardy went to his table and retrieved a thin stack of paper, bringing it forward to the witness box. "You have heard the previous witness, Ms. Ghent, identify these pages, Defense Exhibit G, as being included in a folder given to her by Elaine Wager after she'd come from your office a few hours before she was killed. Can you identify these pages for the court?"

He stared at them for a long moment, flipping through the pages, the sight of which cramped up his stomach.

"Mr. Logan?"

"They look like photocopies of my business ledger."

"They *look like* them, Mr. Logan? Take your time and go through them carefully. Surely you are familiar with the checks you write?"

He stared at the pages for October and November, but he didn't understand how he could be looking at what he was seeing. There had only been that short period of time when, okay, he'd made a few errors. He'd let the partying get a little out of hand and wasn't following the business details as closely as he should have. Patsy had made some checks out to Gabe personally instead of writing them to the usual account, and he'd signed them and mailed them off.

Patsy, the idiot, had remembered to block the carbon that went all the way through to the ledger on the bottom, but she'd filed the duplicate checks—the NCR copies—in the physical files under Gironde.

He and Visser eventually found them and removed these check receipts from the file, then voided some bogus lines in the ledger. He specifically remembered doing it.

Now he answered the question. "It's a copy of my business ledger, all right, but somebody's erased some of the entries. It's not right."

"It's not right?"

"No."

Hardy nodded as though he expected this answer. He moved back to the defense table and took another folder forward. "All right, then, how about these pages, Mr. Logan? Do these look any better?"

Rattled enough to begin with, Logan was so happy to see the pages he'd doctored that he didn't think to ask where Hardy had gotten them—which was through Glitsky after the police search of Logan's office last night. The ledgers had been the first thing they had copied. Logan studied the pages for a while, then said that yes, this looked more like his ledger.

"Looks more like it? Is it or isn't it?"

"Yes, it is."

Hardy had it entered as Defense H, then came back to him. "Mr. Logan, looking again at these business ledgers, Defense Exhibits G and H, you'll notice that there are six entries in the latter that were originally made out to various business payees and then voided. Can you explain these entries?"

"My secretary screwed up. I don't know."

"In Defense H, these same entries are blank, as you noticed. How do you explain that?"

A shrug. "I don't know that either. Somebody could have whited out the entry, then copied it. So it would look blank."

"Or the record of the original checks was purposely kept out of the ledger. Isn't that really why they were left blank, Mr. Logan? Isn't it true that the voided entries are fallacious, intended to camouflage the real payee on these checks after the fact?"

"No. What are you talking about? Give me a break, would you?"

Pratt had been forebearing with her objections for quite a while and finally she decided she had to get back on the boards. "Your honor? If this line of questioning is even tangentially related to the death of Elaine Wager, I fail to see it. Do you?"

Judge Hill scowled. "I'm taking that as another relevance objection, counsel. Mr. Hardy, I'm inclined to sustain this one unless you can bring me some closure. Where is this going?"

"This is going to the original payee on these six checks, your honor. We have gone to great lengths in this hearing to draw the inescapable conclusion that Mr. Logan and Mr. Visser have colluded in illegal activities together, possibly even the delivery of uncut heroin to Cullen Alsop, which caused his death. Ms. Wager's discovery of these illegal activities—"

"Your honor," Pratt interrupted, "not only is the conclusion far from inescapable, it's demonstrably false. Elaine Wager couldn't have discovered anything about Cullen Alsop's death. He died a week after she did."

"And she was killed"—Hardy raised his voice—"because she discovered something Mr. Logan was trying to keep covered up." The gallery came to life behind Hardy, but he spoke loudly through it. "Something she found in his office while she was working there in her court-appointed role as a special master—"

"Your honor!" Torrey was on his feet, interrupting even more loudly. "This is inexcusable. We've seen no evidence for any of these outrageous accusations. Now Mr. Hardy is simply arguing, creating some grand conspiracy out of whole cloth when he hasn't been able to produce one document or any other shred of evidence. These are monstrous charges against Mr. Logan and who knows who else. We have to see some evidence, some actual proof of all this illegal activity, this conspiracy to cover up and commit murder. If he doesn't have it, it's time to call this to a halt."

The gallery's volume swelled and Hill gaveled it quiet, then glowered down over the edge of the bench. "Mr. Hardy, Mr. Torrey's right. If you've got some proof of any of these accusations, the court needs to see it now."

Hardy stood alone in the center of the courtroom, in the now-dead stillness. "Of course, your honor," he said, turning back to David and Cole at his table. He grabbed the folder David held out for him and walked back before the bench. His footfalls echoed.

As expected, Glitsky had come into the Solarium first thing in the morning. He had, in fact, noticed the picture of Loretta Wager that Hardy had left out on the table. And seeing it had jogged his memory—it was the one item in the box that he hadn't had the heart to really look at. Which is what he did then, taking the cardboard backing out of the frame, discovering the NCR copies of checks that Elaine had hidden there after she'd removed them from Logan's office.

Hardy was now presenting them to the court. "Your honor, I submit for the court's inspection Xerox copies of Mr. Logan's supposedly voided checks, numbers 314, 322, 337, 343, 351 and 374, all referenced to various subcontractors with Gironde Industries, with which I'm sure the court is familiar. And all of these checks are made out to the same payee." He turned and faced the prosecution's table. "Gabriel Torrey."

After the uproar in the courtroom passed, Pratt, especially, wanted to retire to discuss this startling evidence in the judge's chambers. If she thought this was going to somehow play to her advantage, Judge Hill, his ire now truly aroused, disabused her of that notion.

Hardy was glad to see that he didn't have to draw a map for the judge. Just inside the door to his chambers, the Cadaver didn't even bother shucking himself out of his robes, but spun on the assemblage with a hail of invective as the court reporter struggled to set up and record what he was saying. The chief assistant district attorney's involvement in any scheme like this was unconscionable and probably criminal. The judge opined that it might be a good idea for Torrey to get himself a good attorney of his own.

"Your honor, there is a simple explanation. I—"

Hill cut him off. "I'm not interested. Whether or not you have done anything unethical or even criminal is beside the point, and I'm predicting you're going to get all the chance you need to explain everything you've done." He whirled now on the district attorney herself. "And in any case, Ms. Pratt, the appearance of impropriety is so strong, I'm surprised that you let your deputy proceed at all in this matter. No, I'm more than surprised. I'm appalled. Can it be you had no knowledge of your chief assistant's involvement in any of this?"

Pratt's face had gone from crimson to pale, from rage to a tight-lipped, controlled panic. She seemed unable to respond at all, but it didn't matter as the judge turned again. "Now Mr. Hardy."

Reluctant to throw any water on the judge's blaze, the defense team had been doing a fair imitation of a couple of statues over by the window, and now at the summons, Hardy came forward a step or two and assumed an at-ease position. "Yes, your honor."

"It appears that you've produced your smoking gun linking Mr. Torrey here to his friends outside in the gallery. I'm willing to buy that there was something to hide at Mr. Logan's office, and that Ms. Wager found it. For the sake of argument I'll even concede the possibility of criminal collusion—destroying the checks, the copies, cooking the ledger entries. But here I must caution you—we are engaged in a hearing on a charge of murder—"

"Your honor, excuse me." Hardy found it difficult to believe that Torrey had the brass to speak up and interrupt at this juncture, but the man's arrogance apparently knew no bounds. He didn't wait for the judge's acknowledgment, either, but went straight to his point. "The court ought to know that I talked to Elaine about this problem several weeks ago, just after her first time at Logan's, when, in fact, she did run across the check receipts by mistake. She knew she had no legal reason to have seen them. She came to me because we used to be friends."

"More than friends," Freeman corrected mildly.

Torrey shrugged that away, although Pratt once again seemed to take it almost as a blow. "The point is I've got the notes of that meeting in my minute file. You're welcome to send somebody up and check right now. So there wasn't anything to cover up. And just for the record, your honor, I'm aware of what it looks like, but Dash isn't the world's best bookkeeper and his secretary . . . in any event, the money was payment for personal gambling debts—"

Hardy couldn't restrain himself. "Oh, for the love of God . . ."

But Hill held up a hand, spoke up. "This is eighteen thousand dollars we're talking about, Mr. Torrey."

"Yes, your honor." He hung his head briefly in a show of embarrassment or contrition. "I've spoken to Ms. Pratt about it. We've decided I ought to seek some counseling—"

Hill's expression curdled in distaste, but he wasn't going to pursue this line any further. "Well, as I've said, Mr. Torrey, you'll have ample opportunity to bare your soul and transgressions over the coming weeks. But, Mr. Hardy, this does bring me back to my topic." He inhaled deeply. "The fact is that we're here to determine if the evidence says that your client ought to go to trial for Ms. Wager's murder. The *evidence*," he repeated solemnly. "And I must tell you that to this point the evidence remains overwhelming, simply overwhelming, against Mr. Burgess. I trust you haven't lost sight of that."

"No, your honor."

"So you wish to continue with your case in chief? If you want to make a motion to relieve the D.A. and substitute the A.G., I'll hear it. But I still haven't heard anything casting doubt on Mr. Burgess's guilt."

"We have a few more witnesses, your honor, yes."

The Cadaver wasn't even sure that he'd heard right. Certainly, he conveyed to everyone in the room his belief that no one Hardy could call would make any difference to the evidence already arrayed against Cole. But it was still a capital case and the prosecution had proven itself inept and possibly—hell, probably—venal if not pathetic. If Pratt lost a slam dunk of a case like this after making it a political barn burner, it would serve her right. Maybe she'd learn something, although Hill doubted that very strongly. "All right," he said to Hardy at last. "But they'd better be talking about evidence in the Wager murder case. Keep them on point or I'll dismiss them out of hand. Am I making myself clear?"

"Yes, your honor," Hardy said.

As he answered questions about his rank and professional duties, Paul Thieu sat upright in the witness chair—confident, alert, professional, cooperative. Hardy knew that he had not slept a wink in more than twenty-four hours, yet his eyes were clear, his face shaved, his coat and slacks crisply pressed. The man was a marvel.

And now it was time to get to the meat of it. "Sergeant Thieu, as a homicide inspector, can you explain how you are involved in this case before the court today?"

"Sure. Another inspector in the detail, Ridley Banks, has been missing now for over ten days. The presumption is that he has met with foul play. One of the witnesses in this case, Gene Visser, admitted on the stand here that he'd talked to Inspector Banks, apparently on the night he disappeared. We believed that meeting concerned the murder of Elaine Wager, but we didn't know exactly why Inspector Banks had asked for it. Based on that, and since Mr. Visser was the last person to see him, I requested a search warrant on Mr. Visser's place of business."

"And what were you looking for?"

"I guess the best answer is anything we could find that might relate to this meeting, including documentary evidence to verify whether it actually took place and how long it lasted."

"Inspector Thieu, when did you conduct this search?"

"Well, we began this morning at around seven o'clock, and I believe it's still going on."

"Thank you." Hardy turned and walked back to the defense table, under which he'd placed the cardboard box from the Solarium. Reaching down, he pulled out a large Ziploc bag which contained a gun and brought it forward.

The gallery, seeing what it was, began its buzzing again, and kept it up as Hardy got to the stand. He raised his voice slightly. "Now Sergeant Thieu, do you recognize this gun?"

Thieu took it, looked at the evidence tag, checked inside and nodded. "Yes, sir, I do."

"Would you please tell the court about it?"

"This is a Glock .38 automatic that we found in the course of our search of Mr. Visser's office in the lower left-hand drawer of his desk."

Hardy was aware of an increase in the noise behind him, but it abruptly ceased when Pratt's voice cut through it, objecting. "The murder weapon in this case has already been entered in evidence. What's the significance of introducing this new gun?"

Hill looked the question at Hardy, who responded, "Your honor, the provenance of the murder weapon in this case has been a critical issue from the beginning."

"But this new gun is not the murder weapon."

"No, that's true. But as your honor will see with my next witness, it bears on it."

"All right, I'll allow it. Go ahead."

Hardy took a breath, blew it out in a rush of relief, and had the Glock entered into evidence as Defense J and excused the witness. Pratt chose not to cross-examine.

Hardy stole a glance back out over the bar rail. The tension in the gallery was, he thought, palpable. Logan and Visser were sitting next to one another in the first row on the prosecution side. There wasn't a soul in the courtroom who wasn't aware of their earlier testimonies yesterday and today; Glitsky had whispered to him at the break that he had had them both reminded by the door bailiff as they attempted to leave earlier today that they were still under subpoena. If they needed so much as to go to the bathroom, another bailiff would be happy to accompany them.

Jonas Walsh sulked in an aisle chair on the prosecution side, three rows from the back and another four behind Muhammed Adek and some of his friends.

On Hardy's side, Clarence Jackman and the Three Musketeers sat midway back, along with Treya and Glitsky, Gina Roake, a few other R&J associates. As Logan had left the stand at the beginning of the first recess, Hardy had seen that he obviously recognized Amy Wu from last night. He had charged back with a clear notion at least to verbally abuse her until Jackman stood up, intimidating and unmoving, and blocked his way. Similarly, before court had been called into session, Torrey had all but attacked Jeff Elliot for his *Examiner* article as his wife Dorothy, who'd finally relented about supporting her brother, had wheeled him up the aisle. Now a phalanx of Jeff's fellow reporters surrounded both of them—a deal of the background white noise originated in this area. And finally, up close, front row center, sat Cole's mother, who'd been in the same seat every day, who'd kept her son's spirits alive with her jail visits and her unfailing hope.

Now Hardy looked down at his client, gave him a small confident nod and called his next witness. "The defense calls Officer Gary Bellew."

Like Thieu, Bellew was a policeman, but the similarity between the gung-ho, brilliant Vietnamese homicide inspector and the young, surly custodian of the gun room of the evidence locker ended there. Bellew's uniform hadn't been cleaned or pressed in days and he needed a haircut, but then before this morning, he had had no warning that he would be appearing as a witness. More instructive was Bellew's obvious resentment at his presence in court today. He seemed to project a defensive attitude, that somehow whatever he was made to disclose would turn out to be his fault. And, Hardy knew, in this he wasn't all wrong.

"Officer Bellew, can you tell the court your assignment at the present time?" Hardy kept the questions simple, nonthreatening. One following the other, falling like dominoes. "Is this assignment a rotating one?" "How long have you been in charge of the gun room down there?" "And what is its basic function?" "Who's allowed down there?" "Is all evidence assigned to a specific case?" "Are there other guns kept there?" "How does that work?"

Hardy got Bellew talking until the overt resentment began to settle out. Now the young officer was sitting back, answering matter-of-factly. "How does what work? Oh, the other guns? Usually some uniform comes in with a piece . . . a gun . . . that he picked up off the street, you know. If it's not registered, he keeps it and brings it on down, no case assigned, so it's not evidence really. It's just a gun nobody should have."

"So what happens then?"

"Then we log the registration number into this big book and throw the gun in a box."

"You throw the gun in a box?"

"Yeah. We call it the piece box."

"The piece box. I see. How many guns are typically in this piece box?"

"I don't know for sure. When it's full, maybe a hundred, something like that."

"A hundred guns. And this box is just sitting out where anyone can see it, or get their hands on the guns?"

"Yeah, well, yeah." Bellew sensed a criticism, but couldn't draw a bead on it precisely. "But it's not like anybody can get in there in the first place. You've got to sign in and then somebody's with you every minute."

"So a person couldn't come in, for example, and sneak an unregistered gun out in their pocket?"

"No." Shaking his head. "No way."

"You'd say that it would be difficult?"

"Impossible."

"All right, then. Now these guns. What happens to them eventually, after they've sat in this piece box for however long?"

"It's usually a month, maybe a little more. Then they come and empty the box, we put the serial numbers into the computer, and crush the guns and melt 'em down. Then we start over."

Hardy had established a nice rhythm, and kept it casual as he strolled back to Freeman and Cole, lifted the ancient heavy book from the cardboard box and brought it to the stand. "Officer Bellew, at my request this morning, did you bring some documents with you to the courtroom?"

"Sure. First, that's the log-in book I was talking about."

Hardy wanted to get it completely straight. "The log-in book for firearms that are turned in by the police department and wind up in the piece box in the guarded evidence lockup downstairs here in the Hall of Justice, is that correct?"

"Yes."

"And these entries are handwritten when the gun gets turned in, do I have that right?"

Bellew turned a few more pages, closed it back up. "Yes, sir. That's right."

"Excellent," Hardy enthused. He had the book entered into evidence as Defense I and, still at the evidence table in front of the bench, he found an entry in the log and pointed to it. "What happened to that gun, Officer?"

Bellew leaned over the entry, then back up to Hardy. "It was entered into the piece book on—"

"No, I'm sorry," Hardy interrupted. "I mean what happened to it after that. Eventually."

"It was crushed and destroyed."

"When?"

"That would have been the end of last month. January."

"January," Hardy repeated. "Officer Bellew, would you please describe the weapon we're talking about here and read the serial number to the court?"

"Sure. It was a Glock .38, serial WGA-15443889."

"Thank you." Picking up the pace. "And just before this gun was crushed, at the end of January, you entered the serial number into the computer, did you not?"

"Yes."

"Did you, at my request, bring a printout of the computer log of all the guns crushed at the end of January?"

"Yes, sir, I did."

"All right, then. Would you please find then, on the list, the Glock .38?"

Bellew went down the list. The courtroom hung in a thick silence. It was obvious when he began looking for the second time. His face had begun to flush. "It's not here."

"So this particular Glock .38 was not crushed, is that right?"

Bellew was seeing his career flash before his eyes. "Oh, it was crushed all right. There's no way this firearm was not crushed."

"All right," Hardy said ambiguously. "Let's leave that for the moment. Let me ask you this—to your knowledge, has Mr. Visser been in the gun room in the past month?"

Bellew's eyes went to the gallery. "Yes."

"To your personal knowledge, did he handle any of the guns in the piece box?"

"Yes, but he put them back."

"He didn't take a gun away with him? That would have been impossible? Is that what you're saying? Did you personally see him replace every gun that he picked up?"

"No, but he couldn't . . ." Bellew stopped speaking.

Hardy had crossed to the evidence table, and now was back in front of the witness. He had picked up the tiny North American Arms .25 caliber derringer. "I show you now People's Four, Officer Bellew. This gun has been identified as the murder weapon in this case. Would you be so good as to read the registration number of this gun—under the barrel there—to the court?" Hardy handed it to the officer, who turned the gun over, squinting. Hardy moved back toward the evidence table, and Bellew read aloud. "NA-773422-25."

"Thank you." Hardy held out one hand, and Bellew passed him the gun. Hardy then gave him the handwritten log-in book again. "Now, Officer Bellew, would you please read the entry from November fourteenth of last year, line four. The type of gun and its serial number."

Bellew got to the page, hesitated, looked up. Hardy nodded. "North American Arms, .25 caliber derringer, serial NA-773422-25."

The courtroom had been uncharacteristically silent as Hardy had led Bellew on this path, and now that silence ended with a restrained explosion of sound. And this time, Judge Hill acted to quell it promptly, gaveling the gallery down to a rumbling silence. He also gave a signal to the bailiffs, who moved out through the sides of the gallery to the back door. At long last, here was evidence that was both material and relevant. The Cadaver wanted to see where it was leading.

And Hardy was ready to show him. "Officer Bellew, while you've got that book in your hands, would you please read the second line entry from January twenty-ninth, three weeks ago."

Bellew found it and was reading as Hardy walked again back to the evidence table, picked up yet another gun. "Glock .38 caliber automatic, serial number WGA-15443889."

Hardy stood in front of the bench holding the Glock in his hand. "Your honor, let the record show that Officer Bellew has read the serial number of the gun marked Defense Exhibit J. This was the weapon retrieved this morning from Eugene Visser's office." The gallery was buzzing again.

Hill startled everyone with a sharp gavel. "Bailiffs!" He called out. "No one is to leave the courtroom!"

Hardy turned to see Visser on his feet, stopped in his tracks a couple of steps up the center aisle. He turned back toward the bench, looked to Torrey and Pratt, to Hardy. One of the bailiffs from the back door came forward, but hadn't gone more than a couple of steps when Visser took his seat and began whispering furiously to Dash Logan.

39

He didn't get to whisper long, though, because Hardy called him back to the witness stand, and things got louder in a hurry. Dash Logan stood up next to him and announced that he was representing Mr. Visser and, seeing the way the defense was orchestrating this case, his client was taking the Fifth Amendment. Visser told Logan, loudly enough for everyone to hear, that he should shut up. He wasn't pleading any Fifth. Nevertheless, Logan accompanied Visser to the stand.

It was a tricky moment. Leaving aside Logan's ethics and chemical problems, the man was an experienced trial attorney who would at least be effective in blunting or flanking Hardy's attack. On the other hand, Hardy thought he might be able to back them both into a corner. He already had the murder weapon in Visser's hands.

The clerk reminded Visser that he was still under oath. Did he understand that? He grunted something like an acknowledgment which Hill made him repeat until it was a recognizable "yes."

"Mr. Visser," Hardy began. "Can you explain how Defense Exhibit J, the Glock automatic weapon, got into your desk drawer?"

"I have no idea," Visser replied coolly. "I assume one of your cop friends planted it there."

"Really? You did not remove it yourself from the evidence lockup downstairs?"

"No."

"You never touched the gun?"

"No. Not once."

"So you did not treat the barrel and the grip with Armor All?"

Finally, a slight reaction. Visser threw a quick glance at Logan, then came back front. "No."

Pacing a few steps to one side, Hardy appeared to be deep in thought. "Mr. Visser, you used to be a homicide inspector, did you not?"

"Yeah. So what?"

"So in that capacity, were you familiar with the use of Armor All as an agent to prevent fingerprints from adhering to surfaces such as the metal or grips of a gun?"

"Yeah, sure. It's everyday."

"So you never touched the gun, Defense Exhibit J?"

"Your honor," Logan interrupted. "Mr. Visser has already answered this question. He never touched the gun."

Hardy spoke up. "I just wanted to give Mr. Visser a chance to consider that answer, your honor. So he'd be absolutely sure."

Logan gave Visser an almost imperceptible nod, and the witness answered. "I'm sure."

"I wonder, then." Hardy adopted an exaggerated calm. He was about to take a calculated risk, a pure bluff, but it seemed necessary. The two guys were slick enough not to give anything away. He had to get one of them running, startled into a false first step. "I wonder how you explain the presence of your fingerprints on the bullets in the weapon."

Visser swallowed visibly, answering too quickly, grabbing at a police trick he did know. "I'm sure they transferred the print from the tape on the heroin bag. It's the easiest thing in the world."

"Really?" Hardy smiled coldly and kept pushing. "How do they make a thumb turn into an index finger?"

"I don't know. They . . ." A flush was creeping up Visser's face. His panicked eyes flicked again to Logan, who suddenly had nothing to say. "All right, but I . . ."

"All right?" Hardy almost jumped at him. "All right you took the gun from the evidence locker? Is that what you're saying now, Mr. Visser?"

"Big deal," Visser snapped.

Finally Logan, a step too late, seemed to realize that Visser had been tricked. "Don't say any more, Gene." Then to the judge: "Your honor, my client will refuse to answer."

Hardy stepped quickly up to the stand, his voice urgent now.

"Mr. Visser, let's go to the murder weapon in this case. Did you get it the same way?"

The witness didn't answer. Hardy followed his desperate stare and turned to see Torrey with his head lowered, looking down at the prosecution table. Logan stood tongue-tied next to him. His allies were all abandoning him. "I never—" he began to blurt out.

"Gene!" Logan warned him.

"After you stole it, Mr. Visser, did you treat that weapon with Armor All as well so it wouldn't hold your prints? Is that your standard practice?"

Visser's jaw was working under his jowls. It was far from warm in the courtroom, and yet sweat had broken on his high forehead. "I didn't take that gun. You can't prove that I did."

"I can't? I think I just did," Hardy replied evenly. He really didn't care. He'd gotten what he wanted. Visser could deny until he was blue in the face, but he knew that the Cadaver was with him on the murder weapon. Now all that was left was to get that gun to Maiden Lane on February 1. "Your honor, I may need to recall this witness once again, but for now I'm through with him."

Hill gave Hardy a surprised look, then asked Pratt if she had any questions in cross-examination. She did not.

Visser and Logan hadn't even gotten to their seats when Hardy turned back to the bench. "The defense would call Estelle Gold."

The sprightly Mrs. Gold was pushing sixty. She dyed her hair bright red to match her lipstick and nail polish. She combed it back, held by large clips, to show off the gaudy costume jewelry earrings she favored. Wearing a simple cotton housecoat under a down overcoat and no-nonsense walking shoes, she got up from her chair in Glitsky's row and marched in a slightly bowlegged fashion past the last witnesses and up into the bull pen, while the gallery hummed with conjecture. Who the hell was she?

Hardy wasn't going to keep them waiting long to find out. "Mrs. Gold, can you tell us your profession, please."

"I'm a waitress, honey, and proud of it. Been a waitress for forty years and hope to go another twenty if my legs hold up, and I don't see why they wouldn't."

"I'm sure they will, Mrs. Gold. Can you tell the court where you are working now?"

"David's Deli."

"On Geary Street?"

"That's right, honey. Same location for about a hundred years. David's on Geary." She nodded, adding, "Across from the ACT." The American Conservatory Theater.

"Yes, ma'am. That pretty well nails it down. And were you working there on Sunday night, January thirty-first, of this year?"

"Yes, I was. I always work Sundays. Better tips than you'd think." She played a bit with the back of her hair, shifted for comfort in the witness chair.

"Mrs. Gold, did you personally know Elaine Wager, the deceased in this case?"

Her face clouded over. "I certainly did."

"How was that? Was she a regular customer?"

"Yes, sir. Never went more than a couple of weeks without she'd stop by for something. And always asked for me," she added with pride.

"And did she come to David's on Sunday, January thirty-first?"

Mrs. Gold nodded. "She was there most of the night in the very back booth."

"Most of the night?" Hardy repeated. "Was she eating alone?"

"No, sir. I don't think she even ate much at all. Just drank a lot of tea. She was having some serious talk. Real serious, it seemed to me." She frowned at a memory. "She even told me to stop coming by. She'd come get me if she needed something. She was never like that usually."

"So you'd say she acted upset?"

"Yep. Impatient, like. Frustrated."

"But she stayed there most of the night, is that right?"

"Right."

"Until what time, would you estimate?"

"Well, we'd already closed up the rest of the back room, so it was after midnight. Say twelve-thirty?"

"Twelve-thirty on the night she was killed," Hardy repeated, glancing up at Hill. "And was she there with another person the whole time?"

"Yes, sir. They met at the front door and came back together."

Hardy stepped away to the side of the witness box. "Now, Mrs. Gold, I'd like to ask you to take your time and look carefully and tell me if you recognize that person—the person who sat arguing with Elaine Wager on the last night of her life. Is that person in this courtroom?"

"Yes, sir," Mrs. Gold said with no hesitation, raising a hand and pointing. "Right there, at that table. The woman, not the man."

"Mrs. Gold, are you pointing to Sharron Pratt, the district attorney of San Francisco?"

"Is that her name? Yeah, whatever, that was her."

40

Stunned by Estelle Gold's testimony, the courtroom collectively seemed to suck in its breath. Pratt herself opened and closed her mouth several times, until she finally got to her feet and managed to speak. "I did not kill her," she whispered. Then repeated, more strongly: "I did not kill her."

From his spot in the middle of the courtroom, Hardy spoke gently. "No, I don't think you did, Ms. Pratt."

"But then . . ." Hill all but stammered up on the bench. "Mr. Hardy?"

"The defense calls Gabriel Torrey."

In spite of everything, the chief assistant gave no sign that he was beaten yet. He sat straight-backed in the witness chair, his face set but by no means fearful. If anything, he appeared ready for a fight.

Hardy stood squared off five feet in front of him. "Mr. Torrey, did you meet with Elaine Wager on the night she was killed?"

"No, of course not."

"No? Was that because you were, in fact, out with Ms. Pratt the entire evening?"

"No. I wasn't out with Ms. Pratt."

"That's right, you weren't. If you had been, Estelle Gold would have seen you at David's Deli, isn't that right?"

"I guess she would have, if she saw Sharron, as she said."

"But just this morning, didn't you tell my associate David Freeman that you specifically remembered that you had spent the entire evening of Elaine Wager's murder with Sharron Pratt?"

For the first time, there was the slightest hesitation. "So what if I told him that?"

"So it's not true?"

"No."

"It was another lie, you mean?"

A sardonic snort. "When did I stop beating my wife, is that it? The answer is that I wanted to get rid of him. He's a pest. I told him whatever would serve that purpose."

"All right." Hardy cast a glance at Judge Hill, then came back to Torrey. "Will you then please tell the court, and truthfully, what you were doing on the night of Elaine Wager's murder?"

"I was at my apartment, alone."

"And what is the address of your apartment?"

"564 Bush Street."

Hardy repeated the number. "And how many blocks is that from Maiden Lane?"

Torrey shrugged. "I don't know. I've never counted them."

"Interesting," Hardy said. "I'd have thought you would have. I did this morning. It's three blocks."

Puffed up in his arrogance, Torrey turned to the bench, queried the judge. "Your honor? Was that a question? This is ridiculous. I'd like to be excused."

But Hill wasn't buying that. "I don't think so, Mr. Torrey. Mr. Hardy, continue."

"Thank you, your honor." He came back to his witness. "So you spent the entire night at your apartment three blocks from Maiden Lane, is that correct?"

"Yes."

"You never left your apartment, not even once?"

"No."

Stymied, fighting his frustration, Hardy took another tack. "Isn't it true, Mr. Torrey, that Mr. Visser supplied you with a firearm?"

This brought an actual laugh. "Absolutely not. I don't own any firearms. Never have."

"You did not get any weapon from Mr. Visser, is that so?"

"That's right."

"You realize that your friend Mr. Visser is going to give you up for immunity, don't you?"

This wasn't any kind of reasonable question, but no one objected, and Hardy had had enough. He wanted to bring this all home to Torrey.

And, in fact, the reality of Hardy's point did slow him. down. It showed on his face.

Hardy didn't let up. "Visser was in on the Gironde scam, too, wasn't he? And Logan? Once they're charged with conspiracy to kill Ms. Wager . . ."

"Get a grip. They were both in L.A. that night."

Hardy turned and faced the D.A. "Well, that would only leave Ms. Pratt, then, wouldn't it? She was with Ms. Wager . . ."

Torrey considered a beat, then he shrugged. "I don't know about that. I doubt it."

Hardy's eyes stayed on Pratt as the truth hit her—if he had to, and it looked as though it had come to that, her chief assistant, lover and political mentor was prepared to give *her* up.

And this, finally, was more than she could bear. She came to her feet. *"You doubt it!"* she all but screamed. "No, you *know* about that, Gabe. You know it wasn't me."

Torrey looked straight ahead with all the expression of a dead man. As Hardy watched, Pratt's face first broke, then hardened as she finally came to accept what she'd obviously feared and denied for all this time. In ten seconds, before Hardy's eyes, she aged a decade.

He spoke to her. "You telephoned Mr. Torrey sometime during the night, didn't you, Ms. Pratt, while you were arguing with Elaine at David's Deli? After it became clear that things weren't going well? You weren't going to be able to convince her to let it go, were you?"

"It was Gironde." Pratt hung her head and now she raised it. "The minority contracts. That part was sacred to her. That's what she couldn't forgive Gabe for manipulating."

Torrey snapped at her. "Shut up, Sharron. For God's sake"—he was coming up off the witness chair—"don't be a fool."

A brief bitter laugh before she reassembled her face. Now she faced her betrayer calmly. "Were you going to let them pin it on me, Gabe? Do you think I'd sit here and let you do that?"

She came back to Hardy, to the judge. "He lied. It wasn't gambling debts with Logan—it was kickbacks from Gironde's competitors. When Elaine came to him the first time—because she'd once liked him—and called him on it, he told her he'd call off the harassments, which turned out to be another lie. That's when she came to me."

"Sharron, you can't . . ."

She ignored him, dead eyes on the judge. Nothing could stop her now. "He wasn't at his place when I got there that night. He told me that when I called him he'd gotten upset and gone out for a walk to clear his head . . ."

"Sharron!" Torrey not giving up. "Stop. Don't you understand? There's still no proof. There's nothing tying me to the gun . . ."

Withering him with a long stare, she finally spoke without any inflection. "Visser gave you the gun, Gabe, and everybody in this courtroom knows it."

"There's nothing—"

She cut him off. "You know how it works." She shook her head miserably. "They'll find all the proof they need now. They'll go through your clothes, match fibers to something on Elaine. There'll be blood on your shoes."

Pratt looked to the bench, stopped talking.

In the stillness, Hardy walked solemnly back to the defense table, behind his client, and rested his hands on the young man's shoulders. "Your honor," he intoned, "the defense rests."

41

He must have dreamed it, but so often the left hand didn't know what the right was doing that it had the force of epiphany.

Glitsky, alone, woke up completely alert in his bed on Saturday morning. Before his eyes were really open, he reached for the telephone. Sergeant Ridley Banks hadn't signed out on a city-issued vehicle on the night he drove out to see Eugene Visser in his office on one of the piers. He'd taken his own car. Glitsky's dream, or whatever it was, had Ridley pulling into an open spot a block off the Embarcadero. On his first call, Glitsky got the license plate number of Ridley's personal vehicle, then he called the city tow lot.

Yep, they told him, they had the car. Cost him a hundred and twenty-five bucks if he wanted to get it out.

Glitsky, Hardy, Thieu, a crime scene investigation team, the dragline dredge unit and half a dozen uniformed officers made it a substantial party, but nobody was happy. Contributing to the gloom, a cold storm had blown in overnight, bringing with it a steady rain driven by winds gusting to twenty-five.

Thieu was down by the dredge, wanting to see how it all worked. Glitsky had satisfied himself on that score years before on a body they'd pulled out of Lake Merced. Now he stood silently by the railing along the walkway above the bay, his hands in his pockets, the collar of his raincoat up around his ears. Hardy the Boy Scout had thought to bring an umbrella, but it had already blown itself inside out once and now wasn't working as its manufacturer had intended. He, too, was watching the dredge line, the water, silently waiting to see what they might pull up.

The quiet was in itself unnerving. But the increased noise by the dredge—they'd hooked up with something—didn't lighten anyone's mood.

Glitsky threw a look at Hardy. It was the type of assignment where you mostly wished you would fail, and they both started moving forward, but slowly. Ridley Banks had a favorite black leather jacket, and that's what Abe saw first as it came clear of the murky green water. The scar tightened through his lips.

By the time they got to where Thieu stood, the body was hung up on the line at about the water level. They stood a moment, heads hung, sick in their hearts.

"How did you know?" Hardy asked.

Rain was dripping down Glitsky's face, although he paid it no mind. He motioned behind him. "He left the car he used parked back over there. We knew he'd been to Visser's, but nobody knew where he'd gone from there when he left. Once I found where the car had been towed from, I realized he hadn't gone anywhere." A look down over the railing. "Except there."

Hardy had a hard time taking his eyes off the body. "I don't get it," he said after a while. "Visser didn't need to kill him."

Thieu shrugged. "So? He didn't need to kill Cullen Alsop either. Maybe he found out he liked it. Maybe Ridley told him more than he had to and he felt threatened."

"Easy, Paul," Glitsky said. The sight of his colleague's body had put the young sergeant on edge. "I've got a theory," Glitsky added. "Anybody want to hear it?" He didn't wait. "These three guys—Torrey, Logan, Visser—they're splitting up some good money working together, more or less as equals. Everybody's got their own part in the various scams. Torrey's using his office. Logan's scouting up the business. Visser's the muscle."

"All right so far," Thieu said.

Glitsky nodded. "When Elaine came to Torrey the first time, he thought he'd convinced her to forget about blowing the whistle on him, on them all. Maybe even bragged about it to the other two. I'd bet he did." Glitsky stopped, his eyes following the activity at the water. The crew down below was working to untangle the body from the dragline. From this distance, he couldn't make out what damage had been done by the sea and its creatures, but the body was now recognizably, undoubtedly, Ridley's. He pulled his gaze back up, tried to gather his thoughts.

"Torrey bragged to the other guys," Hardy said, helping him out. Although he, too, was captured by the drama unfolding on the dredge.

"Yeah," Glitsky said, "okay. So they all knew Elaine was on to their scene. But mostly she was a threat to Torrey, on all kinds of levels. If he got exposed, they were all screwed, but he had the farthest to fall. In any event, when she turned up killed, Visser's no dummy, he knew it was Torrey."

"How did he know that?" Thieu asked.

Glitsky blew rainwater away from his mouth. "At the very least, because he'd given him the gun. But then they already had this perfect suspect—I'd given him to them—and Torrey had a history of working the system to all of their advantages, so Visser decided he'd wait and see what happened. Maybe it would all work out. But the other thing that really changed everything was that Visser knowing about Elaine gave him heavy leverage on Torrey."

Thieu didn't know the players as well as his lieutenant did, and wanted to get it straight. "Wouldn't Logan have it, too?"

Glitsky shook his head. "I doubt if Logan knew."

Hardy added to that. "All he would have cared about was that Elaine was out of their lives. They could keep partying. That's who he is."

"Anyway," Glitsky continued. "Visser's got this leverage and Torrey makes a mistake. He brokers the deal with Cullen Alsop."

"Why's that a mistake?" Thieu again.

"Because from Visser's point of view, Torrey got an unreliable junkie involved who's got a better than good chance to screw up an already locked-up case. Maybe Visser even knew Cullen, knew he'd renege, break on cross, something. So anyway, now the new Visser is thinking he's smarter than Torrey, who before has always been the brains. He decides he knows the best way to save them all from Torrey's stupid mistake . . ."

Hardy picked it up. ". . . is to make sure Cullen doesn't testify."

"So he gives him a bag of China White." Thieu nodded in appreciation. "I can see that."

"I bet we'll know for sure soon enough." Visser and Torrey had both been arrested just outside the courtroom yesterday. Now, with the appearance of Ridley's body and whatever forensic evidence it might still have on it, both would be available for questioning for at least the near future. "These rats will fall over themselves trying to save their own sorry asses by giving the other one up, you watch."

"So Ridley spooked him?" Hardy asked.

"Total blindside, is my opinion," Abe said. "Caught him completely off guard. Here's Visser, he just supplied Cullen with the pure smack, and it kills him. Everything had worked perfectly, and now suddenly Ridley's at his door out of the blue, working without a partner, and he puts Visser on the griddle. Visser's an ex-cop. He knows he's made. Ridley pretends things are cool, but he's not going to go away. There's nothing else to do, so Visser does him."

"With the Glock, you think?" Thieu asked.

Glitsky looked down over the railing again. He wiped his whole hand over his eyes. "With something."

EPILOGUE

In the aftermath of the Cole Burgess hearing, it became apparent that the upheaval from the Elaine Wager case was going to play a critical role in rearranging the city's political landscape for some time to come. When Judge Timothy Hill ordered both Gabe Torrey and Gene Visser remanded into custody as they sat in Department 20, it signaled the beginning of a new era of judicial activism in San Francisco as well as the end of Sharron Pratt's career.

The district attorney, humiliated in both the public sector and her private life, did herself even more damage proving that, as Malraux declared long ago, character is fate. She spent nearly two weeks formulating reasons that feebly tried to explain away her own unconscionable behavior on the night of Elaine's death. Even in San Francisco, these excuses did not play. In early March, abandoned even by her closest advisers and under assault from every imaginable quarter, Sharron Pratt resigned her office and within another week had moved out of the city, reportedly to Albuquerque, where she had family. On the day she resigned, the grand jury formally indicted Gabe Torrey for the murder of Elaine Wager.

The mayor appointed Clarence Jackman—notorious workaholic hard-ass—to fill the position of district attorney until the election in November, which suddenly loomed wide open. Jackman was of course no one's idea of a liberal, but as usual the mayor had his finger on the pulse of the city, and the appointment was greeted with near universal praise. For his own part, Jackman was persuaded to take the job at least partially because he had a falling out with his partner, Aaron Rand, over the latter's sexual involvement with Elaine Wager soon after his firm had hired her.

One of Jackman's first acts as D.A. was to initiate an investigation of his own office's prior handling of Gironde's subcontractors regarding their minority hiring practices. Although he found that most were not in strict compliance with the city's guidelines, none were so egregiously noncompliant as to trigger the claims of fraud that his predecessor had so vigorously pursued. He dismissed the pending cases, then signed and sent out a couple of dozen warning notices. Within two months, the long-delayed airport construction project was at last ready to go forward. Jackman had answered his critics in his usual, no-nonsense style: "Gironde may not be a charitable organization, but it was the lowest bidder for the project and it won the job fair and square. Now let's let 'em go to work."

He hired Treya Ghent as his personal assistant—full-time city position with full benefits. Her new employment package gave her seven years' seniority for the time she'd previously worked at the Hall. Her starting pay was nearly twice what she'd been making as a paralegal with Rand & Jackman.

Dear Mom,

It's four months today, exactly 120 days. I know you wanted to come down over Memorial Day, but I think it's better if you don't visit at all. In person, I'm still not who I want to be. In writing, I'm closer. But having you see me during the process, trying to survive, day to day, it wasn't working. I'm sorry, but I'm more comfortable with this. I hope you are.

Anyway, I'm letting myself believe that it isn't going to be too long. Mr. Hardy tells me that with the chronic overcrowding here, the average yearlong only lasts 184 days. They need the cell space. I shouldn't get my hopes up, except they are. If I've only got sixty-four more days, that will be August 2.

Thanks for the offer, but whenever it is when I get out, I'll be finding my own place. There are programs here—Mr. Hardy laughs at the word, but they're not all bad—that will help get me work someplace when I get out. A lot of it's physical, but that's all right with me. Maybe a gym, something like that.

The point is, I'm clean now. I'm going to stay that way. Start over. Maybe take a class in something. It's a day at a time, just like they say, but I don't think having you there to lean on is going to be any help.

Jeff and Dorothy sent me a birthday card. The kids signed it, too. Maybe you know that. I owe them big-time. If it comes up, tell them how sorry I am for how I treated them. Still am.

I'm at 174 pounds. Today I broke two hundred push-ups.

They just rang for lockdown. Got to go.

Glitsky had gone through the whole administrative fandango and had finally been reinstated in his old job. He worked one floor above Treya in the same building, but they hadn't seen each other in eleven days.

Their last discussion—about whether they should consider having a baby and starting a new family of their own together—had been a little tense. It ended with her walking out of his place well after midnight with no apparent plans to return.

Now, at just after seven on the first day of summer, he stood in the alcove stoop of her apartment house and rang the outside bell and waited. He pushed the button again, waited some more. No response.

"Perfect," he said.

He turned and went back out onto the sidewalk, looked up and then back down the street. It was a glorious evening, the sky clear blue overhead, the sun casting long shadows—Glitsky was standing in the shade from the apartment buildings across the street. On the warm breeze, he picked up a scent of something delectable from one of the restaurants a few blocks down on Clement—garlic and ginger, pork.

He turned all the way round once, undecided. He could come back. Call. Make an appointment for later.

But no. He knew he had to stay here and wait. It was too important.

He went back and sat on the edge of the stoop. A half dozen physical-fitness types jogged or biked or power-walked by him in various stages of comfort or pain. A couple of guys in a serious discussion walked by with their dog. Four kids appeared from one of the doorways halfway down the block and—shades of Glitsky's own childhood—started a game of stickball in the middle of the street. It wasn't the season, but he caught a whiff of crab.

Finally, he stood up again and walked to the curb. The evening sky had perceptibly darkened—the high clouds shone in purples and pinks.

Treya's building was completely in shadow now, and over the rooftops across from him, Venus appeared.

He knew it was her before he could have truly recognized her. Still nearly two full blocks away, she was walking with someone—her daughter?—an arm around her shoulder. Drawing in a breath, Glitsky checked his resolve one last time.

All right. He was going to do this.

He began to walk toward them.

When she saw him, she stopped. Glitsky did, too. Half a block still yawned between them. She turned to Raney and said something. Her daughter responded briefly, reached out a hand and touched her shoulder, then started to move toward Glitsky.

When she came abreast of him, she slowed, met his gaze with a somber one of her own, nodded. "Please be sure," she said, and then had passed before he could think of anything appropriate to say.

They both came forward. When they'd closed to a couple of yards, they stopped.

He found himself incredibly taken with her physical presence—her hair pulled back severely from the strong, angular face. She was wearing stonewashed jeans and a sleeveless T-shirt with a New York Yankees logo over the left breast. The shirt seemed to shimmer with her breathing, perhaps her heartbeat.

"I used to hate the Yankees," he began, "until Derek Jeter."

Her mouth was tight, but she nodded. "Me, too. But I like them now. Raney bought this for my last birthday. I don't get to wear it too often."

"No," Glitsky said. "I don't imagine so." San Francisco was a sweater town—sleeveless wouldn't be in unless goose bumps became all the rage. He stood impotently before her for another eternity. Finally, he said, "Orel's moving out in two years. He's the last one. I'm done. I've done this."

"You've only done it with boys. It might be a girl. You haven't done a girl."

If things had been different. The reference to Elaine hit him powerfully, brought him up short. "I'm fifty-two years old," he said at last.

"I know that."

"I'll be seventy-three, minimum, by the time any child we have is twenty. You realize that?"

"Of course. I'll be fifty-four. So what?"

"So a lot of things . . ."

She stared at him expectantly, angrily. "We've already done this part, Abe."

"I know, I know . . ."

"So if it's the same answer, we don't need to do it again."

He nodded. Time had completely ceased to exist. He forced his voice to work. "I didn't come here because I had the same answer."

She waited.

"I came here to say yes if you still . . ." He stopped, tripped up in the words, in wanting to get them perfectly right. "Yes," was all he could come out with.

Her eyes began to fill and they moved toward each other. His arms closed around her.

"It might be unbelievably hard," he whispered. "I might not live that long. We might . . ."

She pulled back far enough to put a finger against the scar on his lips. Her eyes bored into his face and a smile tickled the corners of her mouth. "What's your point?" she asked, and shut him up with a kiss.